Bess

a woman's life
in the early 1900s

carol crawford mcmanus

WESTERN REFLECTIONS PUBLISHING COMPANY®

Preface

In *Bess*, I've tried to characterize the emotions and attitudes of a typical Western Colorado ranch wife of the early 1900s. Although women had begun to enjoy a new social freedom, they were still living the same rural lifestyle of their mothers and grandmothers.

The ranch wife's workload wasn't made easier by the modern conveniences available to women in the cities. There was no electricity in parts of rural Western Colorado until after World War II. Many phone lines were available only to private subscribers. Some rural wives didn't even have the benefit of mail service.

The strong independent streak of the Western Colorado woman often created a conflict between her wants and needs. Women had, historically, viewed their subservient status with resignation, if not acceptance. After 1900 they began to analyze the reality of their lives, and some yearned for more. Divorce was still a forbidden option, except for the few who dared to buck the establishment and risk public censure. However, that did not stop some women from dreaming of, or engaging in, extramarital affairs. Anecdotal information shows that infidelity happened more often than you might think.

Although the story is fictional, it is based on real people and real events. I have not used actual names except in the context of newspaper stories or documented facts. One exception is Dr. Fred Miller. I have presented the doctor's medical practice as reflected in personal stories and my own recollections. The Hart and Stuart families are fictional, but members of the Herwick family are real.

Actual news stories have been sprinkled throughout to give the reader a sense of the headlines of that day. The new century was an awakening time in Western Colorado, but it was still a hard life for the second generation pioneers.

Acknowledgments

I need to acknowledge the people who helped me bring *Bess* to the moment of birth. I'm grateful to family members Dave Crawford, Jay Montoya, and Zelda Montoya who supplied many bits of historical information and pictures.

Virgil Parkhurst helped to refresh my memory about sheep ranching. Jody Lindauer spent many hours, including a trip to Wallace Creek, to share her recollections about her life there as a child. Evelyn McKay supplied the Grand Valley school roster for 1908-09. Iris Huber and I have spent time talking about Grand Valley and its people.

Credit is also due to the people who acted as critics and unofficial editors. Thanks to Deb Roberts, Alice Allan, Vivian Habliston, Ann Seaney, and Jimm Seaney. I couldn't have done it without your superb support. I appreciate the thorough work of my official editors, Debbie and Karen, who helped to create a tighter story.

I have great admiration and appreciation to librarians throughout the Western Slope, who are the nicest people on the planet. Special thanks to my friend Judy-Prosser Armstrong, curator of the Loyd Files Research Library at the Museum of Western Colorado.

Last, but not least, I am grateful to Western Reflections Publishing for helping me to produce another glimpse into Western Colorado's past.

Prologue

Clickety, clack, clickety, clack—the rhythmic sound of steel wheels making contact with the rails annoyed the young girl. She tried to find a more comfortable position on the hard train seat. A little boy lay curled up in her lap, sleeping soundly despite all the noise and commotion, and her arm felt like it might fall off from cradling the child's head. Shifting her slight body, she turned to look at the swiftly changing scenery outside the window. She wanted to resume her fitful sleep but anxious thoughts kept pushing against her rest. She could hardly believe that they would soon be at their new home. What would the future hold for them?

Bess Kelly thought about the past three months, and a muffled cry escaped from her compressed lips. Life had taken on a surreal existence. She would have given in to the sorrow if not for the child in her lap. Her last promise to her ailing mother was that she'd take care of her brother, Lin, and make sure they got to Colorado. Never mind that she was only twelve years old.

Her rise to early adulthood had begun for Bess a year earlier when she could see her mother getting sicker. Annie Kelly, never a strong and hardy person, bravely struggled to provide for herself and her two children after her husband, William, died of consumption in 1894. Annie did sewing and washing in order to care for her baby and six-year-old Bess. There were no family members in St. Louis to help her out. Myra, Annie's older sister, had moved to Colorado ten years before.

William Kelly's family was far away in New York City. He'd severed ties with them at the end of the Civil War when he decided his future was in St. Louis not the slums of New York, where a poor Irish longshoreman had little hope of a better life. He'd been a happy-go-lucky fellow who remained positive even while the consumption ate away at his lungs.

Bess had been only six years old when William died, but she could remember her mother's grief. Annie Kelly had held her six-month-old son in her arms while William's body was lowered into the pauper's grave. Bess, standing at her mother's side, felt the desolation of saying good-bye to her papa.

While still very young, Bess learned to watch over her brother while Annie washed, mended, and delivered the heavy loads of laundry. After Bess started school, she took care of her brother when she arrived home in the afternoon. She often worked alongside her mother late into the night to complete all the mending jobs. Money was scarce and there were days when everyone went to bed a little hungry, but they managed. Although it was a hardship, Annie Kelly insisted that Bess attend the parochial school in their parish. Annie's Catholic faith never wavered in spite of her advancing illness. She had her heart set on Bess becoming a teacher, and she was sure Bess would get a better education through her church.

At first Bess refused to accept her mother's obvious decline. She pretended each health setback of Annie's was temporary, but it was no longer possible to pretend when her mother started to spit up blood daily. She, like her husband, had developed the dreaded consumption. Annie gently explained it to Bess one night when they were sharing some stale pieces of bread with a cup of weak tea. That night Bess became a partner in the moments of indecision and worry. What to do, what to do? How would they survive if Annie couldn't work? There were nights of fear for both until Annie told Bess about a plan she had devised.

Shifting her brother's weight, Bess reached into her pocket to retrieve the copy of a letter her mother sent to Annie's sister in Colorado. Holding up the first sheet, Bess was able to read the words.

March 1900

St. Louis, Missouri

My Dearest Sister:

It has been such a long time since I last wrote and I extend my apologies for this lapse in manners. I can only plead that long hours at work, plus care of the children, keep me from being the kind of sister I should like to be. Since the death of my husband in '94, I have been finding it more difficult to provide for my family.

I regret to tell you that I'm in poor health. In fact, the doctor tells me I have consumption and it is doubtful that I will fully recover. I am forced to rely on the generosity of friends and neighbors to provide for Bess and Lin when I'm too sick to do the laundry and ironing. It is frightening to think of what will happen to them if I'm not able to work again. I suspect they will be sent to the orphanage. I hope I am dead by then because to see that happen would be more than I could stand.

Is there some way you could find it in your heart to take my son and daughter if I cannot get well? It has been so long since we shared sisterly confidences, and I'm not sure whether you are set up to handle two children. I barely remember Mr. Carpenter but do recall that everyone thought he would be a good husband. I'm praying he will find it in his heart to reach out and give a home to another man's children. I do believe you would be willing. You were always the little mother to me when we were young.

Bess and Lin are such good children. I think you'd find them strong, obedient, and a real help to you on your ranch. Bess has taken over most of the household chores, and I think you would not find her lacking. They haven't been raised on a farm but I know they will quickly learn those new chores if given a chance.

Bess will be twelve years old in July and is a very good student. She takes good care of her little brother. We have talked about her studying to be a teacher, and I grieve to think I may not live to see that happen. Do you have public schools in Colorado? It would be wonderful if the children could get some schooling, but it is under-standable if that isn't possible.

I am growing weary in body and spirit so will close for now with my prayers for your well-being. I will also pray for God to kindly dispose you to my plight. Please don't make my children go to an orphanage.

Your loving sister,
Annie Kelly

Bess tucked the first sheet of paper into her jumper pocket and reached for the second one. She could almost recite it by memory:

April 4, 1900
Parachute, Colorado
Dearest Sister Annie:

How sad to hear of your illness. I have been saying many prayers for your full recovery. Modern medicine may yet come up with the very thing to heal your body. I will continue to hold that prayer on my lips in the coming months.

I can understand how terrified you must be for your children's future. My being barren has spared me knowing of such a situation, but I can imagine the fear. I have had many long talks with my husband. At first he was very opposed to taking on the care of two young children. He reminded me we are not young people. He will be 45 years old this year and I will turn 40. He believes that we are destined to have a childless marriage and has become resigned to

*that fact. But I have yearned for children every day of my life and I
cannot say no to my sister in her time of trouble.*

*I have been successful in convincing my husband to accept the
children if, God forbid, your health is such that you are not able to
care for them. But he wants me to tell you we are not rich folks, and
he will expect them to work for their keep. There is a public school
near here, and they may be enrolled. He will, however, expect them
to do all their chores before and after school hours. He is a stern
man but a just one, and the children will be given good care.*

*Please let me know how you fare. Is there someone to help with
the transportation costs if that should become necessary? I will pray
unceasingly for your recovery.*

Love from your older sister,
Myra Carpenter

As the railroad miles sped by, Bess remembered how rapidly her mother
declined once she knew her children would have a new home. Bess resisted
leaving until she realized her mother wanted her and Lin to be situated in their
new home before she took her final breath. Childhood died in Bess at that
point, and determination was born. It was up to her to assume the role of parent
for her little brother. She could not afford the luxury of being a child anymore.
Her mother was depending on her, and Bess wouldn't let her down.
Swallowing her own grief, she set about getting them ready to leave.

Looking sorrowful beyond description, Annie enlisted the help of an
orphan relocation society who would pay the railroad fare for Bess and Lin as
well as give them a small amount of cash for the food they would need on the
four-day trip. She packed their meager belongings and tried to prepare them
for whatever the new life might bring. She would soon be going to the "pest
hospital," run by the Catholic Church, from which there was little hope she'd
ever return.

The night before she left, Bess crept into her mother's bed and wrapped her
arms around Annie's thin, hot body. Lin was too young to understand, but
mother and daughter knew they would likely never meet again this side of
Heaven. Their few moments of sleep were washed with the tears of the other.

Eastman Kodak introduces the $1.00 Brownie box camera, making photography
accessible to the average household.

August 1900

Bess would have enjoyed the adventure of her first train ride, if not for the sad circumstance of the trip. Frequent stops allowed her to experience the sights, sounds, and smells of each railway depot. Bess was tempted to buy an assortment of unfamiliar food from various vendors. Instead, she used the dwindling number of coins in her pocket to make thrifty purchases of meat and bread for herself and Lin, turning a deaf ear to his pleas for pies and cookies.

The rolling farms, seen from the train window, held little fascination for her; Bess was accustomed to that in St. Louis. The first glimpse of the Rocky Mountains, however, caused Bess to catch her breath in amazement. Could any sight be grander—more intimidating? As the train approached the foothills, her fascination turned to dread. How could the train stay on the rails? Surely they'd fall off the side of the mountains! The conductor, perhaps sensing her fear, talked to Bess, telling her how safe train travel was for folks who would not be able to get over the mountains otherwise. He set her mind at ease, and by the time they approached Glenwood Canyon, Bess felt less frightened of the hills looming either below or above her. What a rugged new land!

Now, the trip was almost over. They'd soon be pulling into Parachute where their aunt and uncle would be waiting. Many emotions were going through Bess's young body—grief, fear, apprehension. What would their new home be like? What kind of people were her aunt and uncle? Would they all grow to love each other?

"Wake up, Lin Boy. We're almost there." Bess gently shook her little brother's shoulder, trying to rouse the sleeping child who whimpered as he resisted leaving the warm, comfortable world of sleep. "I've got to wash your face and comb your hair. We want to look good for our new family."

"Hurry, Elmer, here they are, hurry. I think I've found them!"

Peering out the door of the coach, Bess saw a plump little woman trotting along the side of the slow-moving train. Tiny wisps of hair stuck out from under her severe black hat on which an ornamental bird bobbed up and down as if it were trying to fly away. A rusty black dress strained at its seams. The wearer had probably gained a few pounds since the dress was new. Could this be Aunt Myra? Bess assumed it was.

The train finally came to a complete stop in front of the yellow painted depot where a few people milled about on the platform. The baggage man hauled his cart out and awaited any potential baggage. As far as Bess could see, the people here looked much like the folks from her neighborhood. Several teams of horses with wagons waited for their drivers to return. A few horses were tied to the hitching post.

At last, the woman caught up to the door of Bess's car. Willing her shaking hands to be still, Bess took Lin's hand and stepped down to a pair of open arms.

"Are you Bess and Lin Kelly? Oh my goodness, I'm glad to see you both," Myra Carpenter exclaimed. "Lands sake, Bess, I didn't know you'd be so tall. Why, you're almost as big as I am. Of course, I guess you wouldn't have to be too tall to beat me. You dear children, I'll bet you're tired after that long, long trip. We'll get you both home and feed you a good supper then tuck you in bed. You must hungry, aren't you, little fellow? Elmer, come here and meet your niece and nephew."

A tall, angular man with a severe set to his mouth stepped forward. He was dressed in the common blue shirt, overalls, and high-topped boots of a farmer. He took off his short-brimmed hat to wipe the sweat from a head that contained a few wisps of brownish-gray hair. His eyes were a shade of slate gray peering out from under bushy eyebrows. He gazed at the pair for a long moment before speaking.

"Welcome to Parachute, children. You're a good-sized young lady, but we'll have to put some meat on your bones, young man. Let's stow your luggage and get home. It's comin' on to milkin' time." Elmer Carpenter gripped the two small valises and started for a team hitched to a wagon on the other side of the train depot.

"Come along, my dears," Myra said. "Your Uncle Elmer is anxious to get home and get the chicken feed stored away. I doubt you've ever seen a cow milked before, have you? There'll be all sorts of things to learn at your new home."

Bess and Lin were hurried away to the wagon. Bess had the feeling that Aunt Myra tried very hard to please Uncle Elmer. She made a silent vow to try to do the same. Her memory of her loving father had dimmed over five years. She intuitively knew that Uncle Elmer would be far different from her own happy-go-lucky papa.

September 1900

Five weeks had passed since the children stepped from the train. Aunt Myra entered their bedroom at dawn to wake them. "Good morning, my darlings. Time to get up and get ready for your first day of school." Aunt Myra bustled around the little bedroom making sure the school clothes were laid out for Bess and Lin. "Your Uncle Elmer expects you to do some of the morning chores, so you'd better get moving. I want you to have a good breakfast before you leave for school. There's oatmeal simmering, and I've cut up some of that good bacon to fry. Bess, I also need to braid your hair. I've got a little surprise for you—a pretty new ribbon for your first day at school."

The morning was glorious. The birds were singing in the tall cottonwoods surrounding the house. Bess could also hear the strident sound of the rooster heralding the day. She saw the sky colored in brilliant shades of reds and oranges, when she arose and moved to the window

Red sky at morning,
Sailor take warning.

Bess had learned the little ditty while almost a babe in her mother's arms, and she knew a storm was likely brewing. She hoped that she and Lin would make it home from school this afternoon before it hit.

Bess nudged Lin, who had gone back to sleep. "Hurry up," she whispered to her little brother. "We want to show Uncle Elmer we can do the chores and still get to school."

Lin grumbled, but he moved his head, turtle-like, from under the covers and climbed out of bed. "Golly, Sister, do we have to get up this early?"

Lin didn't know how important school was. This would be the six-year-old's first day in class. Even though his big sister had been coaching him for some time, she was sure he really didn't know what to expect. Nevertheless, he hurried as much as his sleep-fogged body would allow. Bess was determined to carry out her mother's wishes of education for her brother as well as herself.

"You feed the chickens, and I'll slop the hogs," Bess said, "then I'll come gather the eggs. You can help me do that. Maybe we can wait to pick the tomatoes and corn when we come home this afternoon. Aren't you excited about your first day of school?" The sleepy look on Lin's face suggested that he would rather stay in his warm cozy bed.

As Bess lugged the heavy slop bucket out to the pigpen she thought about her new life with her aunt and uncle. Their farm was proof of what hard work and frugality could produce. Elmer Carpenter had been smart to buy land on the fertile banks of the Colorado River. The property was located several miles east of Parachute, and provided for almost all of the family's needs. Elmer had a small herd of cattle, which grazed upon the acres of pasture. In recent years he had started a truck garden, transporting the produce to the high country, where the growing season was much shorter. His tight barn, corrals, equipment, and livestock all reflected the industry of the hard-working man.

The little clapboard house was equally neat and tidy. Aunt Myra worked as hard as Uncle Elmer in her domain. The house contained three bedrooms, a parlor, and a large kitchen with an attached storeroom. The cellar had been dug right into the foundation of the house, and opened directly into the storeroom. This was a godsend when the cream and milk buckets had to be hauled down to the cool storage.

The house was furnished sparsely with sturdy but plain furniture guaranteed to last for years. Uncle Elmer would not spend hard-earned money on junk. Aunt Myra had softened the austere interior with lovely crocheted doilies upon all the surface tops.

The kitchen reflected Aunt Myra's personality. The slight clutter was only a sign of a busy farm wife, who had many tasks to perform each day. Delicious smells wafted forth, inviting one and all to accept her hospitality. Infrequent visitors were always offered something to eat, if only a slice of Aunt Myra's freshly baked bread with homemade jam and butter. She loved having company.

Aunt Myra, a loving, somewhat overwhelmed, woman tried hard to please. She did her best to make Bess and Lin feel loved and wanted. Bess's first impressions of her reserved uncle had been accurate. Elmer barely noticed them unless he issued orders for chores to be done. He expected everyone else to work as hard as he did. It was apparent that he resented losing the children to school each day. He could have found plenty of chores to keep them busy. Aunt Myra insisted until Elmer, begrudgingly, said the children could attend school if their chores were done both before and after school. Bess was determined to keep up even if she also had to do Lin's chores. Her mother had set a great store in an education, and Bess would not disappoint her if she could help it.

The walk from the river ranch area passed quickly on that sultry September morn, and they were soon in sight of the Parachute School. It was an imposing brick structure, built in 1890 to educate the children from Parachute and the ranching communities surrounding it. There was one large room on the ground floor, which housed the first four grades. The second floor room accommodated grades five through eight. There was no high school between Glenwood Springs and Grand Junction, a distance of fifty miles in either direction. Aunt Myra said there was some talk about forming a high school district.

Bess thought it would be exciting to actually get a high school education. She'd be the first person in her family to do so. Girls with a twelfth-grade education could almost guarantee their future as rural school teachers.

When Bess and Lin arrived at school the boys were playing stick ball while many of the girls were walking around in small groups, their arms linked together. All stopped to look over the new arrivals, but no one stepped forward to say hello. Bess understood that most of these children had known each other their entire lives and she was the outsider, but their indifference made her feel sad. Bess had been isolated from normal childhood friendships because of her mother's illness, and she'd hoped she would find some chums in her new school. Holding her head high Bess nudged Lin toward a bench.

Well, you aren't here to make friends, Bess, you are here to get an education like Mother wants. You can learn to live with it and make the best of the situation.

Nine o'clock arrived and one of the two teachers rang the bell, calling all the children in from the schoolyard. Bess took Lin's hand and led him inside to his downstairs class room. She could feel his hand tremble, and she squeezed his shoulder. "I promise, your first day of school will go quickly. I'll see you at noon. You can tell me all about what you did this morning while we eat our lunch. It will be great fun, Lin."

If I can only make myself believe it will be fine.

With a fluttery heart Bess climbed the steep stairs to her class.

When school let out that afternoon Bess hurried Lin home. His afternoon session had gone as well as the morning one.

"You should see how well I did my numbers, Bessie. I could spell my name and the others couldn't."

Bess was pleased that he had taken to school easily. Her own day at the Parachute School had been pleasant enough. Bess was grateful that she was further ahead of the other classmates in the sixth grade. Five years of parochial school had helped her to excel. It would be just terrible to be behind the rest of the class. There was also a library in the school, which she planned to use.

She'd wondered how in the world she would survive without escape into her beloved books. Bess and Lin walked in the door, and saw Aunt Myra had been crying. Her pug nose was red and she had a tremor in her voice. "Oh children, I heard from St. Louis today. I'm afraid the news isn't good."

Bess snatched the letter from her aunt's hand. With trembling hands she read the page.

27 August 1900

My Dear Mrs. Carpenter:

It is with regret that I write to tell you of your sister Annie's passing. Friends kept her company to the end, and Father O'Reilly administered last rites. She wished me to tell her children how much she loved them and how thankful she was that they have such a wonderful family to care for them. She cherished the few letters which she received since the children left for Colorado and was so grateful to you and your husband for this opportunity. She asked that you gently break the news to the children because they have had so much grief in their young lives. There was little left of her possessions, but I will see to the sending of a small parcel of personal items which the children may want. We have said several masses for her. My prayers are with you in your time of sorrow.

Sister Mary Francis

Bess thought her knees might buckle.

Oh, Mother, I can still feel your arms around me. I can't believe you are really gone. Why, oh why, did God take you from us? Lin and I are now truly alone. What will happen to us? I'm so afraid!

Aunt Myra gathered Lin into her arms. She looked ready to cry. The confused boy said, "What does the letter say, Bessie? Is Mama gonna get better and come to Colorado to live with us?"

Lin's all I have left, and I must be strong for both of us. We can't be separated. I'll need to make sure we do everything we're told. I have to prove we can pull our weight. Then maybe Aunt Myra and Uncle Elmer will keep us. This is no time for me to show my tears.

Bess took a deep breath, "Later, Lin Boy. Let's do our chores first, and then I'll tell you all about it." She pulled him from the arms of his aunt and marched to the door, her shoulders squared and head held high.

When Bess and Lin came in the house at suppertime their eyes were puffy from crying. but neither mentioned their mother's death. Uncle Elmer looked up from the day-old paper and cleared his throat as if he was preparing to say something. The expression on Bess's face, however, squelched any condolence he'd planned to offer.

Bess was certain that he'd not tolerate much outward grieving, so she pushed the tears down deep inside. Aunt Myra looked as shaken by the attitude of her charges as by the sad news of her sister's death. Somehow it just didn't seem quite normal for children to keep their grief so private.

Later that night, after Aunt Myra and Uncle Elmer were in bed, Lin crept into Bess's bed and wrapped his arms around her neck. They could feel the other's tears upon their cheeks as they quietly wept.

"We've got to work really hard, Lin Boy, to make sure Uncle Elmer keeps us here at the ranch. If he doesn't, we'll be headed to the orphanage, and we might get split up. You're all I have, little brother. I couldn't bear to be separated from you."

"I promise, Bessie. I'll work as hard as I can. I'll be a good boy and mind Uncle Elmer. I won't sass, and I'll do all my chores without bein' told."

"That's my good boy. We'll both try to do our very best. We'd better get to sleep because tomorrow is another school day."

> Marijuana, heroin, and morphine were available at drug stores in Western Colorado. According to one pharmacist, "Heroin clears the complexion, gives buoyancy to the mind, regulates the stomach and the bowels, and is, in fact, a perfect guardian of health."

Life on the Carpenter ranch was hard with the daily labor. Aunt Myra remained a buffer between the children and their uncle. She made sure the children got rest and good food even though they did almost a grown person's job on the fertile river-bottom ranch. In spite of the labor Bess and Lin survived and flourished.

Elmer Carpenter worked hard in his alfalfa fields and with the small herd of dairy cattle. When Bess and Lin grew big enough to help with the twice-daily milking he increased the herd. Every other day Elmer drove to the rail station, taking the cream cans to be shipped to the creamery. The excess milk, mixed with other slops, went to the squealing, fighting hogs, which they butchered each fall for family use, as well as selling to town folks. The rich sandy soil was ideal for growing almost any kind of fruit or vegetable in the large truck garden. Elmer continued hauling the produce to Glenwood Springs to sell during the summer growing season. People in the higher elevations clamored for the fresh foodstuff that matured much faster down-valley. He was gone overnight, leaving Myra and the children to assume his duties as well as their own.

Bess learned to accept that she would not have chums because of her work at home. Most of the young ladies were pleasant enough, but they had an after-school friendship circle of which Bess could never hope to be a member. The ranch chores came first and there was little time to cultivate friendships, even if she'd known how.

1902

A majority of Rifle, Colorado, businesses were destroyed by fire on June 9, 1902. The J .W. Hugus store, a drug store, jewelry store, barbershop, Wiseman's Livery, Clarkson's Livery, a meat market, and millinery shop all fell victim to the inferno. One residence, owned by R.C. Brenton, was also burned.

There were nights when Bess and Lin could barely make it to bed before falling asleep.

Their life could be described in shades of gray, no physical abuse but also little enjoyment. Their only escape was school. Uncle Elmer remained doubtful that they should be wasting all that time, but Aunt Myra stood firm about their attendance. In 1902 Bess turned fourteen and completed the eighth grade, the highest offered at the Parachute school. A high school was still just a dream for the more progressive citizens of the town.

Bess longed to take her high school test, which couldn't be done until she became eighteen years old. After that she wanted to study for her teacher's certificate, but she couldn't imagine how she'd reach that goal. Uncle Elmer would never pay for her go to another town that offered the required classes.

Miss Hubbard was Bess's teacher. She knew her pupil wanted to continue with her studies. The kind lady admired Bess for her intelligence and supported her goal of getting a rural teaching certificate. On the last day of class she took Bess aside to discuss the requirements for a high school diploma. "Bess, I know how much you want to get your teaching certificate. I may be intruding into a family matter, but I'm guessing that it will be impossible for you to go to an out-of-town high school. Is that correct?"

"Yes, ma'am, there's no way that Uncle Elmer will pay for me to go to Glenwood Springs or Grand Junction. I guess I'll just have to forget about it." Bess bowed her head.

"What would you say if I told you there might be a way for you to still do it?"

"What do you mean, Miss Hubbard? How in the world could I do that?"

"It's simple, Bess. I would tutor you in your studies. We could write the school superintendent for a list of the required subjects, and then I would give you assignments to do at home. You could come in once a week for me to grade your work, and I'd give you the next assignment. If you need books I can check them out of the school library. Would you be interested in doing that, Bess?"

"Oh, Miss Hubbard!" Bess resisted the temptation to hug the woman.

It wouldn't be seemly to hug my teacher.

"Would you really do that for me? It would be a dream come true! Thank you so very much."

When Uncle Elmer found out about the offer, he loudly complained. "Young lady, I think you're just a slacker who wants to continue your studies so you can get out of your farm chores.

"Why do you need a high school diploma? You'll soon find some young buck and get married. How much good will that piece of paper do you then?"

Bess stood, her blue eyes trained upon him, refusing to argue. She was so different from Aunt Myra, with her incessant chattering, that Uncle Elmer, for all his bluster, didn't quite know how to deal with Bess's silent determination. This time, he gave in after a great deal of grumbling and fussing.

Sugar cost 4 cents a pound. Eggs were 14 cents a dozen. Coffee cost 15 cents a pound. More than half of the population lived on farms and ranches where they raised most of their food. Many wives traded eggs, butter, and poultry for the goods they couldn't produce.

1906

> Jake Borah, renowned guide and hunter from Eagle County, was organizing a
> ten-day hunt in the De Beque area on February 1, 1906. The hunters would be
> stalking coyotes, bobcats, wolves, and mountain lions. He reported there would
> be seventy-five dogs available to track the wild prey.

Bess worked full time on the ranch for the next four years, then spent several hours each evening practicing proper English, working on math problems, and poring over history books. At noon each Saturday she walked into Parachute to spend the afternoon with Miss Hubbard—her generous friend and mentor. Aunt Myra usually sent some tasty treat with Bess in addition to the butter and eggs that paid for the teacher's time.

The trips into town gave Bess an opportunity to see a part of the world outside of school and ranch work. Interesting events took place that barely touched the Carpenter family. A train robbery west of town, and a name change from Parachute to Grand Valley both occurred in 1904. Great excitement arose when President Theodore Roosevelt arrived for a hunt on Divide Creek in 1905. Bess heard all the news on Saturday afternoons. She was grateful to Miss Hubbard for giving her a break from the ranch for a few hours.

Aside from the Saturday afternoon sessions, Bess escaped into the fantasy of books borrowed from Miss Hubbard. Her apron pocket frequently contained a small book of poems or other essays. It could be pulled out for a few precious moments of reading while she herded the cows in the evening or did other chores. The tales of romance filled her young heart with thoughts of a handsome prince who'd sweep her off her feet. A practical girl in all other things Bess fantasized about the most impossible romantic situations in which she was the heroine. When she retreated into her literary world there wasn't loneliness or longing. She became Guinivere to King Arthur or Queen Victoria to Prince Albert. Bess's all time favorite, however, was *Jane Eyre*, the story of a poor orphan girl who finds her own true love after many challenges.

"Come and bid me good-morning," said he. I gladly advanced; and it was not merely a cold word now, or even a shake of the hand that I received, but an embrace and a kiss. It seemed natural: it seemed genial to be so well loved, so caressed by him."

It would be wonderful to have someone love me like that. Then I wouldn't feel so alone. I wouldn't have to be afraid for Lin and me. How would it feel to be kissed as Mr. Rochester kissed Jane?

Bess loved and was beholden to Aunt Myra for their home, but her aunt didn't offer much in the way of mental stimulation. Aunt Myra was a steady talker who tended to soothe herself by the sound of her own voice. It didn't matter whether you answered her, nor did it really matter what she was saying. Bess suspected that this habit came from years of living with a silent husband who never talked if a hand signal or grunt would work as well. Bess felt guilty for her private thoughts about Aunt Myra's eccentricity, and she worked extra hard to help with her aunt's many daily chores.

Lin unconditionally accepted Aunt Myra as his new mama, having been so young when his own mother died. The woman and boy enjoyed a special bond, which fulfilled the parent-child needs in each other. Bess was occasionally envious that she didn't feel the same special attachment to anyone.

Bess's eighteenth birthday arrived on April 6, 1906, and Aunt Myra fussed over her. "Close your eyes, Bess, I have a surprise for you." She proudly brought out a beautiful white organdy dress which she'd secretly ordered some weeks before.

"You can open your eyes now! I thought this dress would look lovely on you, Bess. Maybe you'd like to wear it when you go to Glenwood Springs to take the high school exam. Try it on, my dear girl."

Bess had never owned such a lovely dress. The sailor collar was edged with a deep ruffle of lace and the bodice was pin-tucked down from the shoulder. A wide blue satin sash nipped in the tiny waist, which made Bess seem even more willowy than usual. The skirt of the dress flared out with the hem stopping at the tops of her leather boots. She whirled around her bedroom feeling the weight of the skirt as it swished around her legs.

"Oh Aunt Myra, thank you! It's the nicest present I've ever received."

Is that really me in the mirror? I feel beautiful for the first time in my life. I don't look like a ranch hand or a frightened orphan girl. I didn't know a dress could make such a difference!

She surprised Aunt Myra by hugging her soundly. "You are so good to me. I love the dress, and I love you!" Bess seldom showed that kind of affection. For once the kind woman seemed to be at a loss for words.

In September Bess boarded the train and traveled to Glenwood Springs for the high school exam, which she passed with a very respectable score. She joyously returned to the praise and congratulations of Aunt Myra, Lin, and Miss Hubbard. Uncle Elmer's response had been typical of him. "What's the big deal to getting a high school diploma? Most folks do fine without gettin' all uppity."

Bess held her tongue but she was hurt and angry.

I wonder if I'll ever please him? Well, no matter, I don't care what he thinks. I know what I can do with hard work and a little luck. I'm a high school graduate—imagine that! I'm going to make something of myself!

Miss Hubbard was thrilled about Bess's successful exam and started to discuss what her student would have to complete for the rural teaching certificate. Bess knew she was on dangerous ground with this kind of thinking. Uncle Elmer would surely put his foot down to further studies. Since Bess and Lin had come to the ranch in 1900, Uncle Elmer's operation had expanded every year, with more milk cows and a bigger truck garden. He now depended on the dawn-to-dark chores of his wife, niece, and nephew, especially during the growing season. She might be able to convince him that she'd be self-sufficient if she were able to obtain a teaching position, but she was pretty sure he wouldn't let her go. She was cheap labor.

1907

A phone system was installed on Battlement Mesa during February 1907.

At Miss Hubbard's insistence, Bess resumed studies with her. She'd confront the problem of obtaining Uncle Elmer's permission for the teacher's exam when the time came. If nothing else, Bess could look forward to a bright spot in her week. She enjoyed discussing the assignments with Miss Hubbard. The teacher wrote to the Garfield County superintendent of schools and obtained a list of the requirements that Bess would have to complete before asking permission to sit for the teacher's test. The spinster was enjoying the challenge as much as her pupil. Her personal goal would be achieved if she could successfully assist Bess to get her certificate. The day finally came when Miss Hubbard heaved a sigh of satisfaction as she looked over Bess's assignments.

"You're ready, my dear," she declared. "I can't think of another thing that you need to complete. I'll send the assignment packet up to the school superintendent, and although I'm not a betting woman, I'd be willing to wager that she will schedule you for the exams."

"Are you sure, Miss Hubbard?" Bess said. A tingle ran down her spine. "Now all I have to do is convince Uncle Elmer to let me go."

In the end she could think of no other way except to approach him and tell her uncle what she wanted to do. The slender young woman stood straight before him, her blue eyes staring into his. "Uncle Elmer, I'd like your permission to take the teacher's exam. Miss Hubbard has been giving me special instruction, and she thinks I can easily pass."

Uncle Elmer's face turned red. "Why in the hell would you want to do that? I thought you'd be satisfied with a high school diploma, but now you've got bigger ideas. What are you planning, girl? Looks to me like you're getting pretty high and mighty. If you ask me, that teacher has been filling your head with nonsense."

Bess considered how to respond to her uncle. "I guess you are the reason I'm doing it. It isn't fair to expect you to take care of Lin and me for the rest of our lives. If I can pass the exam and get a rural teaching job then I can also bring some money into the household. Of course, that might be a few years from now, but it doesn't hurt to be able to make a living, does it?"

A spark of understanding came to Uncle Elmer's eyes at the mention of money. "I think it's damned foolishness, but I suppose you're right. It can't hurt to have a job to fall back on. Of course, you're needed here, you know. Don't get any ideas about taking off as soon as you get all educated. That's the least you can do after all we've done for you and your brother. I suppose you'll be needing the money for the ticket, but that's the last time, you hear?"

Bess silently nodded her head, afraid to open her mouth for fear she would say something that would cause Uncle Elmer to cancel his permission.

Oh, yes, Lin and I owe you, but how much do you owe us? What would it cost you to hire someone to work on this place?

> Alvin Potter was arraigned for trial on June 25, 1907, in Glenwood Springs, Colorado. Mr. Potter, one of the alleged men in the 1904 train robbery west of Grand Valley, was arrested in Grand Junction by the famous railway detective Doc Shores. Mr. Potter reportedly hid out in the 'dobe hills around the base of Grand Mesa for one year before opening up a repair shop in Grand Junction. He was arrested at his shop in March 1907 and taken to the Garfield County jail.

"I can hear the train whistle, Aunt Myra," said Lin as he hurried to remove Bess's small suitcase from the buggy.

"It will be coming around the curve any minute. I guess I'd better put the flag up so they'll know they've got a passenger," said Uncle Elmer, in a cranky voice. Bess wondered why he even bothered to come see her off. They certainly didn't need his help. Why did he have to ruin her day?

The train pulled into the station, and Aunt Myra started fussing with Bess. "Now be careful, dear. Make sure you ask to help Mrs. White with the chores, although I doubt she'll let you. I never saw anyone with as much energy as that woman. No sir, never saw anyone so all fired up as my friend. I packed the eggs and butter well, and they should hold up on the trip. It will be a treat for her to have them fresh, what with having to buy at the store. Tell her I am grateful to her for boarding you a few days, and tell her…"

"All aboard!"

Elmer grabbed his wife by the elbow. "For God's sake, woman, hush it up, and let the girl board before the train pulls out."

"I promise, Aunt Myra. Thank you. Bye, Lin. Bye, Uncle Elmer." After a final hug from Aunt Myra it was a relief for Bess to climb the train steps and escape her aunt's affectionate clutch. She was tense and anxious, making conversation difficult. Almost as soon as she was settled in her coach seat, the train, issuing its shrill whistle, started pulling out from the railroad depot. She watched the landscape whiz by the window. She hadn't been on the train since going to Glenwood Springs the previous year. Leaning her head back against the seat, Bess thought about the past seven years leading up to this day. At last, her long-sought goal was in sight. A breath caught in her throat as she considered what might be waiting for her at the exams. Bess thought she was prepared while under Miss Hubbard's tutelage, but now felt wholly inadequate for the task.

What can I be thinking? I'll be taking the exam with men and women who have a lot more formal schooling—people who are surely much better educated. How could I have been so brash to think I'd be able to pass?

Perhaps because of Bess's apprehension, the ninety minutes to Glenwood Springs passed by too quickly. The passenger train was soon pulling into the railway station.

The die is cast, and I'll just have to do my best. Even if I don't pass, I hope I don't bring shame upon myself or my teacher. I feel alone and frightened. I wish Miss Hubbard was here with me.

● ● ● ● ● ● ● ● ●

Bess was about to pop from excitement. She'd passed the rural teacher exam! It was more difficult than the high school exam but, from the talk among the other students, she thought she had done as well as most. She willed the train to hurry so she could get home to share the good news.

Did I really pass? I can hardly believe it! Mama, I wish you could see me now. You'd be so proud of me. Your daughter—the teacher!

Miss Hubbard was standing with Aunt Myra and Lin on the platform when the train came to a stop. They all gathered around Bess to get the news.

"I did it!" Bess exclaimed. I passed the test, and I have my teacher's certificate."

Aunt Myra let out a whoop and grabbed Bess in a bear hug while Lin patted her on the back. Even proper Miss Hubbard was laughing and twirling around in joy. She had tears in her eyes, which she dabbed at with her lace hanky.

"Oh my, this calls for a celebration," declared Aunt Myra. Let's go up to the drugstore and have a nice ice cream sundae. Would you like to do that, Bess? Of course, we want you to come, too, Miss Hubbard."

"That would be wonderful, Aunt Myra, but don't we need to go home and get supper cooked?"

"Oh, fiddlesticks, supper can wait for a little while. Besides it's early, we have plenty of time."

The foursome walked the block to the drugstore, all talking at once. Each ordered a favorite sundae and savored every bite of the hand-cranked dessert. Bess tried to recount every detail of the test. Before they knew it, an hour had gone by and even Aunt Myra realized they needed to start home.

"Thank you for including me in your graduation celebration, Mrs. Carpenter," said Miss Hubbard. "I'm pleased to have been a part of Bess's success. I have never felt more proud of a student's accomplishments."

The teacher continued, "Bess, I insist that you come to see me next Saturday. I will finish reading *Jane Cable* this week, and you can take it home to read." Miss Hubbard knew that George Barr McCutcheon was one of Bess's favorite authors, and she was sure that Bess would pay her a visit, come rain or shine

During that summer of 1907 Bess continued her Saturday afternoon visits. At her teacher's urging, Bess sent out several letters of applications to rural schools in the immediate area. Each school board president wrote back with his regrets, suggesting that she apply again in 1908. Bess was secretly relieved because she could delay the inevitable upheaval that her leaving would cause. The last thing she wanted was an angry confrontation with Uncle Elmer.

A smallpox epidemic in late 1907 caused several months of panic for the citizens of Grand Valley. Uncle Elmer finally allowed Dr. Miller to vaccinate the family, even though he doubted its effectiveness. Aunt Myra and Bess prepared food for the sick folks in town. Uncle Elmer, not trusting the vaccination, forbade them from going into the infected homes to help with the nursing. They left their bundles on the doorstep for one of the occupants to pick up. Folks in the community heaved a sigh of relief when the epidemic finally abated. There were no direct fatalities, although several children may have died from later complications.

Bill Duplice came home to Battlement Mesa from Shoshone Falls in the Canyon of the Grand River, east of Glenwood Springs. Mr. Duplice reported that work on the new hydroelectric plant was very dangerous, and only fifty out of two hundred and seventy-five men were still working on it. Many of the jobs involved the men hanging from lines high above the canyon wall.

On August 2, 1907, the Keystone Mine, west of New Castle, exploded following a cave-in. Five miners were killed and another five injured.

1908-1909 Grand Valley School All-Grade Roster

Seventy-four girls: Alice Aplin, Fay Armstrong, Iva Bailey, Olive Bailey, Wilma Bainter, Alice Baughman, Mamie Baughman, Nettie Baughman, Annie Brennan, Ella Brennan, Mary Brennan, Margaret Brennan, Bessie Chapin, Esther Chapin, Mamie Chapin, Ellen Clayton, Velma Clayton, Anna Connell, Mary Connell, Bertha Craven, Estella Cravens, Pearl Davison, Florence Daviss, Katy Dere, May Franklin, Nora Franklin, Zelta Gardner, Josephine Goodwin, Jetta Helm, Leona Helm, Daisy Hurlburt, Jessie Hurlburt, Winnie Hurlburt, Alice Hailey, Ruth Hinman, Esther Hinman, May Hyde, Florence Martin, Mary McGuirk, Margaret Miller, Anna Murray, Lila Murray, Bessie Popple, Gladys Patterson, Alda Pratt, Thelma Pratt, Della Robertson, Ada Rivers, Marge Rivers, Rose Rivers, May Simpson, Katie Shehorn, Clara Sherwood, Eloise Sherwood, Estella Sherwood, Lotte Sherwood, Alice Smith, Annie Smith, Grace Smith, Annette Sibley, Fannie Sibley, Anna Starr, May Starr, N. Stroud, Edna Talbott, May Thompson, Francis Trimmer, Olive Trimmer, Minnie Wells, Beryl Wilson, Beulah Wilson, Bertha Withrow, Sadie Withrow, Susie Withrow.

Sixty-six boys: Paul Armstrong, Bivian Bailey, Earl Bailey, George Bailey, Guy Bainter, Glen Bainter, Walter Bainter, Clarence Baughman, J.C. Baughman, James Brennan, Jeremiah Brennan, Patrick Brennan, Edward Brennan, Code Cline, John Cline, John Connell, Daniel Connell, Charles Davidson, Robert Dawson, Frank Dere, Charles Dere, Fred Dere, Forest Drake, Norman Franklin, Arthur Galloway, Leo Goodwin, Clifford Helm, Herbert Helm, Ray Helm, Ashley Hunter, Fred Hurlburt, William Lutkiewicz, Robert Lutkiewicz, Clarence Martin, William Martin, Richard McGuirk, Otis Murray, Ross Murray, Scott Murray, John Osburn, John O'Toole, Hugh O'Toole, Granville Robertson, Ralph Robertson, Harry Scoggin, Elliott Sibley, Willard Sibley, _____ Simpson, Joe Shehorn, Oscar Shehorn, John Starr, Everett Tracy, James Trimmer, John Trimmer, Lyman Van Horn, Frank Wallis, Fred Wallis, Robert Wallis, Arthur Wells, Charles Wells, Joseph Wells, William Wilson, Adolph Withrow, Everett Withrow, Samuel Withrow.

1908

Bess arrived for her weekly visit with Miss Hubbard in June 1908 and could see the lady was very excited. "Come in, my dear Bess. I have the most marvelous news, but first our tea and cookies." The teacher bustled about boiling the tea water, and laying out lemon-flavored tea cookies upon a dainty plate.

"Miss Hubbard, don't keep me in suspense! Is it something about your job? Has something happened at school? It must be special to make you so excited."

"I think it's just wonderful, Bess. Let's sit down and I'll pour the tea." She filled the tea cups before continuing. "Now mind you, we can't be sure of anything at this point, but what would you say if I told you there is a teaching job with a ranching family?"

Bess was speechless.

How do I feel about the possibility of getting a teaching job? I never thought it would happen so soon! Look at Miss Hubbard, she's very happy about this. What should I say?

"Wh-what is this all about, Miss Hubbard? How do you know about this position?"

"I happened to be in Doll Brothers last Tuesday when Mrs. Stuart came in for supplies from the Horse Mountain Ranch. It must have been an act of Divine Providence because she asked me if I knew of any young teacher who was looking for a fall teaching position. The oldest Stuart children boarded in DeBeque this past winter, but it was difficult when the weather became too bad to travel back to the ranch each weekend. This year, Mr. and Mrs. Stuart thought they'd consider bringing a teacher to the ranch, and let her teach the six children right at home. The children range from the first to the sixth grade. It will be a challenge for you, but I believe you can do a very nice job. The family members are quality folks from the South, and I think you will fit in well with them. These are people who value education. In addition, I'm told they have an outstanding library. What do you think? Should we write Mrs. Stuart today?"

Bess, with some hesitation, nodded. "I suppose so, Miss Hubbard, but are you sure I could do a good job with these children? It sounds to me like the Stuarts are society folks. I don't know anything about that kind of life."

"My dear, you sell yourself short. Mr. and Mrs. Stuart are just like any other ranch family. They have a bit more money, and a bit more culture, but I think you'll find them down-to-earth folk."

Miss Hubbard brought out her best writing paper and a pen with a new nub. "Come over here to the writing desk where there's better light." The teacher peered over Bess's shoulder, making occasional suggestions about what she should say in the letter.

12 June 1908
Mrs. Wade Stuart
Horse Mountain Ranch
Dear Mrs. Stuart:

My name is Miss Bess Kelly. My former teacher, Miss Hubbard, told me you are seeking to hire a teacher for this coming fall school year. I would like to be considered for this position.

There will be such an explosion from Uncle Elmer when he hears the news! I know he wants me to buckle down and become a free hired hand on the ranch. I'm sure he thought I'd soon get the school plans out of my system. I'll feel guilty knowing that Lin and Aunt Myra will have to take over my duties. Uncle Elmer won't part with any of his hard-earned money for an extra hired hand.

I can't believe I'm sitting here writing this letter!

I have been living with my aunt and uncle on their ranch. My brother will continue to help them, so I am free to take advantage of this position...

What am I doing, writing to these people of quality? I'll never fit in there. You're a silly goose, Bess Kelly!

Miss Hubbard knew nothing of Bess's internal struggle as she prompted her. The teacher's enthusiasm was contagious, and Bess became almost convinced she really was qualified. They soon signed and sealed the letter, as well as Bess's fate.

"Let's put a stamp on it and walk over to the post office," said Miss Hubbard. "The first time someone from the ranch comes into town they'll take it back. Hard to say when that will be, so we must be patient. Mrs. Stuart will reply to my address, and I'll get in touch with you if a letter arrives."

Bess doubted that Mrs. Stuart would send a reply. She said her good-byes to Miss Hubbard and started the walk home determined to make the best of her life on the ranch. The afternoon had been frightening, but exciting.

It's wonderful being with someone as optimistic as Miss Hubbard, even though I don't have as much confidence in myself as she does. I don't think there is any reason to tell Aunt Myra or Lin about the letter. I'm sure I'll never hear from Mrs. Stuart.

• • • • • • • • •

Bess reached the end of the sweet corn row that hot, sultry day in July. She straightened up to wipe the moisture from her forehead when she saw a buggy coming through the railroad underpass which intersected the ranch road. Peering through squinted eyes, Bess could make out the figure of a slight woman holding the reins. Who could it be?

As the buggy drew closer Bess saw it was Miss Hubbard. The teacher brought the horse to a halt in front of the ranch house and stepped down from the buggy.

Bess hurried forward. "Miss Hubbard! It's good to see you." Bess felt herself tremble. She knew why the teacher was here. "It's too hot to be outside in this sun. Come in, and I'll pour us a cool drink. Aunt Myra, look who's here." Bess's voice quivered with tension. She braced herself for what might be coming.

At the sound of voices Bess's aunt came to the door, wiping her hands on her apron. "Miss Hubbard! Come in. It's enough to cook your brain out there. Bess, take Miss Hubbard into the parlor where it's cooler, and I'll get some lemonade and fresh sugar cookies."

Bess had barely gotten Miss Hubbard settled on the stiff sofa, when Aunt Myra came trotting in from the kitchen. "I'm afraid you've caught me at a bad time. I've been canning peas and beans all day, and this house is a mess. Mercy, I'll bet I look a sight!"

Miss Hubbard waved away Aunt Myra's concern. "No, I should be the one to apologize for barging in unannounced, but I just couldn't contain myself. I received a letter this morning, and I believe you and Bess will be most interested in what it says. I'm sure Bess has told you about the letter we sent out last month about a possible teaching job. I've heard from Mrs. Stuart, and she's interested in interviewing Bess for this position. Isn't that wonderful?"

Aunt Myra's face was a study in puzzlement. "Well, I-I guess that is good news," she finally stammered. "It's just that it's such a surprise. Bess hasn't said anything to us about this." She turned to look at her niece's bowed head before continuing. "Her Uncle Elmer and I hoped that Bess would be with us for a while. We knew she'd find a teacher's job some day, but I certainly didn't think it would be this soon."

"That's what's perfect about this teaching position. Bess will be with cultured people who make sure she is protected during her first year away from home. She'll live with the family, and her schoolroom will be one of the ranch buildings. I believe it is the original cabin. I'm sure that will cause you less worry. When the weather permits, she'll be able to visit and you can write all the news. After you have had time to think about it, I hope you'll agree this is a wonderful opportunity for Bess."

"Bess, does the cat have your tongue?" asked Aunt Myra. "You haven't said a word. What do you think about this? Why haven't you said something?"

Bess stirred herself as if dazed. "To be honest, Aunt Myra, I never thought Mrs. Stuart would write. She can afford anyone, and I'm still baffled why she would want me."

"My dear girl, how typical of you to be so modest," exclaimed Miss Hubbard. "I think Mrs. Stuart is looking for someone exactly like you. You have many assets. You are strong, you understand ranch life, and you won't be intimidated with either the children or the remote location of the ranch. I can see this is a bit overwhelming for you and your aunt, but please talk it over tonight. Mrs. Stuart will be coming into town next Tuesday, and she's asked me to arrange a meeting. We will be glad to drive out here that day, if it's convenient for you."

Bess, rather than remain with Aunt Myra, escaped to the corn patch as soon as Miss Hubbard left the yard. She wanted to avoid the hurt in her aunt's eyes as long as possible.

As horrible as I feel now, this is nothing compared to what I will face tonight. Uncle Elmer will be in a rage! I don't know which is worse, facing Aunt Myra's hurt or his anger. And the worst part of all will be to tell Lin that I might be leaving. I feel that I'm abandoning everyone in my family. Why did I let Miss Hubbard talk me into writing that letter? I'm not ready to leave!

When they gathered for supper that evening, Bess could tell a conversation had already taken place between the members of her family. Everyone wore a different expression. Aunt Myra looked hurt, Lin perplexed, and Uncle Elmer, true to form, looked like a thundercloud. The meal was a silent one. Bess cleared and washed the dishes before drying her hands and taking a deep breath.

May as well get it over with.

Her aunt, uncle and brother were sitting in the parlor as dusk came on. They all turned to watch Bess as she took her place in the family circle.

"I know you must all be very surprised by the news that Miss Hubbard brought today. I didn't say anything to you because I really didn't think I had the slightest chance of getting this job. It just seemed like a lark for us to write the letter. If I had any idea Mrs. Stuart would reply, believe me, I would have told you."

Uncle Elmer's face was redder than usual. "Then it's true, you're planning on desertin' your family and run off to this god-forsaken ranch to be somebody's servant? Is this what you're telling us?"

Bess was desperate to deflect the coming temper tantrum. She had seen far too many of these episodes in the past. She took a deep breath. "I should think you'd be happy to get rid of me, Uncle Elmer. You keep telling me how much money you've had to spend on Lin and me over the years. I thought you'd be glad that I'm finally able to make a modest living for myself. Miss Hubbard says I could be making as much as fifty dollars a month plus my room and board. I'll have to keep a little for myself, but I plan to pay you the lion's share for Lin so he won't continue to be a burden."

Returning Uncle Elmer's words to him was a good strategy. He couldn't seem to find any comeback that would put him in a good light. He finally harrumped and said, "You know I've never asked either one of you for anything beyond helping with the farm chores. I've heard of these Stuarts, and I suppose they are alright, if a little high and mighty for my taste. I don't want to talk about it anymore, until we see whether Mrs. Stuart is really interested in hiring you."

Bess let out a sigh of relief, and imagined Aunt Myra and Lin were also grateful that the outburst had been averted. Conversation resumed, although they still avoided looking at Bess. She knew that it was only the first obstacle to leaving home.

Bess and Aunt Myra were both in a tizzy before the next week's interview for very different reasons. Aunt Myra expressed concern about the appearance of her humble little house, while Bess wavered between hoping she'd be hired and wanting to stay home. Aunt Myra embarked on a cleaning frenzy that caused Lin to tease her about a king and queen coming to visit. Uncle Elmer stayed clear of the house as much as he could.

Bess stood in the yard the following Tuesday. She'd been watching for the buggy to come through the underpass, and she stepped forward as the horses came to a halt. "Good afternoon, Miss Hubbard, let me help you down."

"Thank you, dear. Mrs. Stuart, please meet Bess Kelly and her aunt, Mrs. Carpenter."

The woman had already alighted from the buggy and came around the back to greet Bess and her aunt. She and Bess stood for brief second, sizing each other up. Isabella Stuart was one of the most beautiful women Bess had ever seen. Rose-colored cheeks and lips were perfect compliments to her dark cream complexion. Tall for a woman, the dark hair piled high on her head made her seem even taller. A leghorn hat put much of her upper face in shadow but penetrating brown eyes peered out, seeming to probe into Bess's very soul. Her afternoon dress was of fine material but plainly tailored. Mrs. Stuart was the picture of severe good taste. A bare smile and slight nod acknowledged the introductions.

"It's good to meet you, Mrs. Stuart. Please come in." Bess opened the screen door for the women.

Aunt Myra followed them inside, "Please come into the parlor. I hope it isn't too warm in there because it gets the afternoon sun. I try to keep the curtains pulled, but it doesn't help much. Now you make yourselves at home, and I'll bring in some lemonade. We've still got a bit of ice left in the icehouse, and it should cool it nicely." Aunt Myra scurried off to the kitchen, leaving a tongue-tied Bess to entertain the ladies.

"Bess, you certainly have an admirer in Miss Hubbard. She tells me you are her star pupil. Have you always wanted to be a teacher?"

"Yes, I suppose I have, ma'am. My mother and I had a dream that I would be a teacher someday, and when she died it became even more important. But, if not for Miss Hubbard, I would never have realized that goal."

"Yes, she tells me that you have studied with her for five years. That's admirable, for both of you. How do you feel about children, Bess?"

Aunt Myra trotted into the room in time to hear the last question. "Mercy, this girl has about raised her brother. My poor sister was sick for a long time, and Bess has taken care of Lin since he was a tiny baby."

Many topics were discussed that afternoon. Mrs. Stuart appeared to be impressed with Bess's demeanor and abilities although she was not the type of woman to be overly chatty. "Bess, you appear to be the type of young lady we've been looking for. Would you be willing to teach my children at the Horse Mountain Ranch?"

Bess, surprised that she'd been asked, turned to her aunt. "Aunt Myra, I don't know what to do. I'd like to accept the position, but I don't want to leave you and Lin to take over my chores, too. Help me to make the decision."

Aunt Myra squared her shoulders before speaking. "I don't think there is anything to do but accept Mrs. Stuart's offer, Bess. You've worked a long time to become a teacher, and this is a good opportunity for you. I'll certainly feel better knowing that you are safe and sound with a good family. If the ranch work gets to be too much, we'll just have to hire some help. Now go on, tell Mrs. Stuart you'll take the job."

* * * * * * * * *

Bess's lingering doubts were put aside in the haste to pack for her new job and decide what to take. Miss Hubbard helped her with a list of supplies and books that she might need until she again came to town. Her personal effects were few, but simple and sturdy. After all she was going to be teaching at a ranch not going to a social event.

"Lin, let's take a walk," Bess said the evening before she left for the Horse Mountain Ranch. "I'd like to go down by the river, if that's okay with you."

A cool breeze was coming off the water as they strolled along the bank, watching fish jumping for bugs in the shallow parts. "Lin, I know that you probably wonder why I'm taking this job when I could stay right here and be with my family."

"No, I don't, Sis. I know you've wanted to be a teacher all of your life, and I guess there's no other way to do it except leave home. Aunt Myra and I will do just fine. Don't worry about us."

"That's one of the things I wanted to talk to you about. I do worry about leaving you, and I'll miss you so much. But, you are a big strapping fourteen-year-old and you'll do just fine. It's Aunt Myra that I really worry about. She has too many chores to do all by herself, and I want you to promise me that you'll help her out every night, even if Uncle Elmer says it's woman's work. Please carry the canned fruit and vegetables down the steep cellar stairs. And you can haul the milk and cream down there, too. It wouldn't hurt for you to do the dishes for her, once in a while…"

Lin interrupted in a high falsetto, "Gee whiz, Sis, you want me to end up with hands like a girl's?" Lin grinned as he whacked her backside with a willow branch. "Don't you worry about us. We'll take care of each other. You go do your teaching thing."

Mrs. Stuart sent a man from the ranch to get Bess. Uncle Elmer was on his overnight trip to Glenwood Springs, sparing Bess the need to say good-bye. Aunt Myra and Lin stood waving as the buggy passed under the railroad bridge, and they were lost to her sight. Bess shivered.

Well, my girl, there is no going back now. You may as well enjoy this adventure.

● ● ● ● ● ● ● ● ●

Bess had never been far from her home, and she looked forward to the scenery as the ranch hand transported her to Horse Mountain Ranch.

Bess's driver, Tom, explained that when he brought a wagon or single horse to town he used the more direct route of the river ford at Una. For Bess's comfort he'd brought the buggy, but it wasn't made to ford a river. That meant they'd have to go the long way around from Grand Valley to Battlement Mesa via the bridge over the Grand River. Bess didn't mind—she'd see more sights.

Bess had never visited Battlement Mesa. Tom was familiar with some of the places which they passed. "Off to the left is the Gunn place. Alex and Vi have worked hard to make it real nice. Beyond them are the Browns."

After a long climb the buggy topped out on the main mesa. "See all those cherry trees? In the spring they're sure purty. Mr. Vaughan owns them. And that big house on the other side is the McGuirk place. Right around this corner is the Battlement Cemetery, and just across the road is Jess Kerlee's. See the big stone building? That's the school. They just got through buildin' an addition. They have some fine dances there."

Everywhere Bess looked there were green fields surrounding each farm house. "I never knew it was so pretty up here. I wouldn't mind living on one of these places. The scenery is wonderful."

"Well, ma'am, if you think this is purty, just wait 'til you get to the Horse Mountain Ranch."

As they made their way across the mesa, Tom pointed out other places: The Clark and Jenny property, the Spencer place, which looked like it had been built by the same person who built the schoolhouse. Having reached the end of the mesa, they descended to the Wallace Creek road where they passed the ranches of the Lathams, Ellithorpes, and Haywards.

Turning south from the main road the buggy started its climb up the various mesas to the ranch. They'd now traveled nine miles, and it would be another five miles to the ranch. Sagebrush scenery ended and was replaced by cedar and pinon trees. As the travelers reached the top of the mesa, hay fields offered a green vista to what might otherwise have been a rather drab landscape. There were few trees on the plateau, no doubt having been cut down to provide wood for cabins and fuel. Lush fields of hay replaced the previous timber. Bess thought it was a grand sight. The mountains were ablaze with quaking aspen trees decked out in their fall finery of shimmering gold. They made a perfect backdrop for the green fields.

"Would you show me where the ranch is located?" Bess asked,

"Wal, Miss Kelly, you cain't see it from here." Tom pointed. "It lays right under that mountain. See there? It's a long way off, yet. Actually, the Horse Mountain Ranch isn't on Horse Mountain, which lays a little southeast. It's actually due north of Housetop Mountain, but I guess Mr. Stuart thought Horse Mountain sounded better."

They passed several ranch houses as they climbed higher up the mesa. Tom said, "That's the Murphy place. They've been here quite a while. And, you'll soon see the Egbert place to your left. Mrs. Egbert was on the train the night those fellas blew up the baggage car on Streit's Flats. Gol-durn, that was four years ago! Where's the time gone?"

The road continued to climb up the mesa, and Bess could see that they were getting closer to the mountain. The air was invigorating, and the sun no longer felt so warm. Tom veered off to the right, taking a road that looked more traveled than the other which, he said, continued on to the head of Wallace Creek. Bess was finally able to see the ranch, and her breath caught from the imposing sight.

The Horse Mountain Ranch sat on a wide mesa, the highest one before climbing up the side of the mountain. Green fields surrounded the log ranch house and outbuildings. The breeze was now more chilly. Bess shivered in her cotton dress.

"You gettin' cold, Ma'am? It starts to get nippy this time of day. We're at about sixty-five-hundred feet, so it's quite a bit higher than town."

The scent of the last cutting of hay wafted in on the breeze. Bess sniffed deeply. She loved the smell of new-mown hay. Off to the side of the road was a huge truck garden, which she assumed was used to feed the large group of family, staff, and hired hands.

Tom continued, "The ranch has a thousand acres plus the government grazin' land which butts up to the place. The cattle will be brought down from the mountain next month, and they'll be turned in to graze on the fields for a few more months before we have to start feedin' them."

A two-story log house rose out of the center of many trees and outbuildings. The massive logs must have been cut and hauled for a long distance because Bess had never seen any with such diameter. There was a wide porch across the front of the house which faced the northwest. Bess thought it would be wonderful to sit there in the evening. A path led through a gate to the front door, but Tom drove Bess to the left and stopped in front of the back door, which led into the kitchen. The Stuart family might be wealthy, but they owned a ranch, and ranch folks always used the back door. The front door was only used for ladies who came calling or visiting dignitaries.

After greeting Bess, Mrs. Stuart escorted her to her second-story bedroom. "There will be time for you to take a tour and meet the children later. I'll let you rest for a while and freshen up before dinner," said Mrs. Stuart. She laid out clean, thick towels on the washstand before turning to leave the room. "We eat dinner at five o'clock, which I know is quite early. I hope that will be satisfactory." She said the latter more like a statement than a question.

Bess nodded her head in agreement while she silently made a note to call the evening meal dinner. Her family always referred to it as supper. She supposed that was the difference between the two social circles. The Stuart family, relative newcomers to Western Colorado, clearly came from a much different

COLORADO RIVER BRIDGE AT GRAND VALLEY, CIRCA 1911

world of breeding and culture. Bess wondered how they happened to be on a ranch next to nowhere.

Bess poured cool water into the basin and dabbed at the thin veil of dust that had settled on her face during the buggy ride. She recalled the many decisions and events that had led up to this moment. She stood in the Stuart home, trembling from both excitement and fear. She looked at her image in the mirror.

My goodness, can I really do this? Well, whatever else you are, Bess Kelly, you're no quitter. I guess you'll never know until you try.

● ● ● ● ● ● ● ● ●

Bess soon found out that culture and breeding don't, necessarily, extend to children in the classroom, even when that classroom was a few hundred feet from mother and father. Her charges were as different from one another as humanly possible. She went back and forth between feeling competent and being completely overwhelmed. She was grateful that they weren't older. She wasn't sure she could handle any more challenges. At the end of the first week Bess took stock of what she now knew about the children. She wrote to Aunt Myra.

…Twelve-year-old Josephine is definitely the leader. I think it's because she has many of her mother's qualities, not because she's the oldest. It's too bad that she's missed most of her mother's striking good looks. I think, though, that she'll grow out of the awkward stage, with her mousy-brown hair and slightly protruding front teeth. She does have lovely brown eyes with emerald green flecks. I wish she would use that charming smile more often. She has an air of superiority to me as well as her brothers and sisters. Josephine will be the biggest challenge because she's older. It's lucky I discovered she likes romance novels. This young girl is a hopeless romantic at heart in spite of her mother's contempt for the popular books. When she found out I had a copy of Beverly of Graustark, she changed her attitude toward me. Maybe this will be the key to a growing relationship with Josephine.

Wade Jr. will be an equal challenge because he really doesn't want to be in school. The ten-year-old's best times of the day are when he's out with the ranch hands. Wade Jr. is a bright boy, but he doesn't apply himself. Thank heavens I've had a lot of experience with a boy who is used to getting into some form of devilment. If he thinks I'm afraid of snakes and dead rats, he should think again!

The cabin, the oldest on the ranch, was built by the first known person to squat on the land. Its roof was constructed of cedar posts over which a layer of wood shingles was laid. It leaks water in heavy rains, but in dry weather it dries out and the cedar bark becomes crumbly. On the first day Wade Jr. stomped around on the cabin's roof causing debris to fall down on us. I, of course, made him clean up the mess. I hope that will break the young fellow of his naughtiness. There is always the threat of telling Mrs. Stuart! The children dread having their mother told about any pranks.

With Katherine and Scott my challenge will be to find some way of entering their private world. The greatest strength and defense of the eight-year-old twins is their own special bond. Mrs. Stuart told me they adopted a special language known only to each other, when they were just babes. I'm glad they've given that up. How would you penetrate that kind of relationship?

I have so much fun watching John David. The round little fellow reminds me of Lin when he was six years old. He looks like him too, with brown hair that falls over the forehead and into his eyes. Unlike Lin, however, he's proven to be an eager learner. When he completes another reading or a math lesson, it's a good day for him. Not that he doesn't have his naughty moments. I have a hard time correcting him, especially when he uses the same wide-eyed look of innocence that Lin always uses on me. I love watching his green eyes sparkle with fun.

Elizabeth Ann—-our Bibby—-is the darling. One look at her melts even the most hardened heart. Light brown curls bounce around her head like a halo, and her smile is full of sunshine. I seldom have to correct or punish her. Bibby is rarely naughty, except when she wades in puddles to make mud pies for her dollies. What a rewarding task to teach this little charmer the alphabet and her numbers. I wonder if there will be more children after her...

Bess was permitted full use of the Stuart library. What delight to have that many books within her reach! The assortment offered a wide variety from Edgar Alan Poe and Sir Walter Scott to the Greek classics. For a few moments before sleep each night Bess could escape the confines of her world and revel in the romantic adventures of *Ivanhoe* and the like. This was worth the many tasks of the day.

In contrast to his wife's aloof nature, Wade Stuart was one of the least pretentious men Bess had ever known. He was a southern gentleman, who never failed to compliment the ladies, but he was also a man's man. Wade's advice was often sought on a variety of issues from water rights to other legal matters. Bess wondered if he had studied for the law.

She still didn't know just why cultured folk would decide to pull up stakes and move to such an uninhabited part of the country. Her imagination could have run wild with her, but she was too busy for idle guessing. Western Colorado had been settled by folks who had come to the area looking for a better life. It was better to live and let live.

Area ranchers often met at the ranch. At times Bess would pass by the door to Mr. Stuart's office where they were discussing the government grazing fee, implemented in 1906. There were occasional dinner guests, who would also complain about having to pay twenty-five cents for each head of cattle that grazed on the public range lands. They all agreed to back any politician who proposed getting the fee abolished. Congressman Ed Taylor seemed to be that man.

Bess's front window afforded a wonderful view of the Roan Cliffs to the north. The stark, barren slopes sharply contrasted with the green north slopes of the mountain where the ranch was located. Bess conceded, however, that the play of morning and evening light created interesting shadows. She often smelled a whiff of cedar or sagebrush in the evening breeze. Bess tried to imagine how this land must have looked twenty years ago before all the irrigation ditches were dug and the land cleared. She much preferred it in this state.

During the first part of November Bess asked to ride into town with one of the ranch hands to see her family. She knew she would likely be stuck at the ranch when the storms hit. Arriving in Grand Valley, she walked to the Carpenter place where she found Aunt Myra and Lin lovingly pleasant, but a little distant. Bess wondered if they would ever understand why she needed to get out on her own. She was thankful to have missed Uncle Elmer, who had taken the last load of winter squash to the high country.

"Are you catching up on all the summer work? Lin, are you helping Aunt Myra with some of the household chores? I still feel guilty that I've left you to pick up all my jobs."

"Don't worry, Sis," said Lin. "We're managin' just fine, ain't we Aunt Myra? I'll be out of school next summer and able to take on more chores. After this last frost there won't be any garden to harvest, and things will slow down for the winter. Uncle Elmer has hired old Gus White to come out and help with the mornin' milkin' and some of the other chores. Then I do the evenin' ones."

"How's school going, Lin?" Bess asked. "What kind of grades are you getting? Is your teacher good to you?"

Lin ducked his head, his hair hanging down over his eyes. "Aw Sis, you know I'm not too bright—at least not smart like you. It's hard for me, and I don't even think I should stay in school. I know all I need to know right now."

"That's not true!" Bess cried. "You're as smart as the next boy. You just don't apply yourself. And you do need to be educated. I'll quit my job and come home if it means you'll do better in school. Do you want me to do that?"

"No, 'course not! You seem to be satisfied down there, and we really are doin' okay. Tell her, Aunt Myra." Lin didn't seem anxious to have a nagging sister back in the home.

"Yes, darling, we are," agreed Aunt Myra. "You're a delight to your old aunt and uncle. I know I can count on you." Bess caught a trace of sarcasm, which was so unlike her aunt.

"Promise me you'll complete the eighth grade, Lin. Then we'll talk about what to do next. You've only got the rest of this school year…promise? And I want to see your grades improve!"

"Yeah, yeah, I promise, but I'm telling you, Bessie, I'm not gonna study any more after that."

Bess walked into town to catch her ride back to Horse Mountain, troubled in spirit. Her decision to leave home had caused her to choose between the desires of her loved ones and her own personal wants.

Why do these struggles have to be so painful?

● ● ● ● ● ● ● ● ●

The Christmas season was approaching. The first of the storms rolled through, leaving over twelve inches of fresh snow on the ground. The thermometer hovered just above zero. Bess allowed the children some time during the warmest part of the day to build snow forts and ride down the slope on their sleds. She occasionally joined them and laughed uproariously when she and Bibby went into a snow bank. Bess hadn't been able to play as a child, and she enjoyed the children's activities.

As she and the children were making little gifts for their parents, Bess wondered what she could give each child as a present. There hadn't been an opportunity to purchase anything in town, and she didn't have the material to sew anything.

I know what I'll do. I'll write a private story for each child, and incorporate all the things I know about him or her.

Bess found it surprisingly easy once she got started. She discovered some nice paper in the library, copied each story in her best penmanship, and tied them with small bands of ribbon.

Christmas Day dawned bright and cloudless. Bess broke the ice in the pitcher, and poured water into the basin to wash her face. She hurriedly dressed in the frigid room then rushed downstairs to the warmth of the kitchen and dining room.

"Merry Christmas," Bess said, as she entered the large kitchen. Cook and her helper were preparing platters of bacon, eggs, and pancakes for the family. The huge cookstove radiated welcome warmth. Bess moved forward to pour a cup of coffee from the large granite coffeepot. "Is there anything I can do to help?"

"Good morning, Bess," Cook said. "Yes, you can fill the children's glasses with milk and set the table. It's always a rush to eat breakfast on Christmas morning, with the children being so anxious to get to the presents."

Mr. and Mrs. Stuart came down the stairs with their young family in tow. "Good morning!" Mr. Stuart boomed as he entered the kitchen. "The children tell me this is a special day. Can anyone tell me why it's special?"

"Presents, Papa. Santa Claus left us presents!"

"Children!" Mrs. Stuart reprimanded them. "You know that's not the real reason for Christmas. Elizabeth Ann, please tell me why we celebrate Christmas."

Little Bibby, looking much like an angel, answered in a rote voice, "Mary and Joseph went to Bethlehem and had the baby Jesus."

"That's right. Now let's sit down so Cook can bring in the food."

After a quick breakfast everyone assembled in the huge parlor. Wade and Isabella Stuart, being very democratic folks, invited the whole of the ranch in for gift-giving. There was something under the tree for every person. Of course, the children got many more.

When Bess opened her package, she was stunned to see a beautiful shirtwaist and skirt made of a hunter-green, silk broadcloth. It had delicate ruffles down the front of the bodice. The fabric glistened in the light. Bess sat silently admiring it.

"Do you like it, Miss Kelly?" Katherine asked.

"Oh I do, indeed, Katherine. Thank you, thank you all so much. It's just lovely."

"Will you wear it for dinner today?" said Bibby.

"I promise you I shall wear it for Christmas dinner," Bess replied.

The day flew by with everyone pitching in to help Cook prepare the meal of gargantuan proportions. Just before dinner Bess slipped away to try on the lovely new dress. It slid onto her slim body as if it had been made to order. Looking in the mirror Bess could scarcely believe the image.

I haven't felt so pretty since Aunt Myra gave me the dress on my eighteenth birthday.

Bess's rose complexion was heightened by the dark green color of the fabric. It made her blue eyes bright. She unpinned the severe bun and allowed her long auburn hair to fall in waves about her shoulders. Picking up the hairbrush she ran it through her silky hair until it shone. Bess looked in the mirror one last time, then raced down the stairs to join the family.

Everyone was preparing to sit down to dinner. The younger children ran to embrace her.

"Miss Kelly, you are so boo-ti-ful!" Bibby clasped Bess around her legs while Katherine and John David encircled her waist.

"Yes, children, I agree," said Mr. Stuart "Bess, that dress certainly becomes you, doesn't it, my dear?"

"Yes, it does," said Mrs. Stuart. "I guess I made the right choice. Come children let's get you seated at the table. Cook will soon be bringing in the turkey."

During the holiday week folks arrived from the various ranches in their sleighs or on horseback. The house teemed with visitors. Bess soon gave up keeping any semblance of order in the children's lives. There was talk of a New Year's party with musicians and dancing.

I don't know how to dance. I hope they'll let me stay in my room so my own ignorance won't embarrass me. I'd feel so awkward and out of place with all the folks who are good at that sort of thing.

Bess's plans were soon sabotaged. The children received permission from their mother to stay up for a few hours at the party, and they expected Bess to be there. That evening she donned her Christmas dress, and with butterflies in her stomach, descended the staircase. She'd never seen so many people in one room. Bess looked for a quiet corner where she could hide away and watch all the activities.

The ranch hands had already moved the furniture along the walls of the parlor or taken it completely out. Mrs. Stuart's prized carpet had been rolled up and moved to the barn for the night with many instructions from her about its care. The musicians arrived early in the day and would be staying the night. They came by buggy over Battlement Mesa. The ranch hands met them at the bottom of the mesa with the sleigh and transported them up to the ranch. There was a fiddler and several guitar players. Mrs. Stuart, an accomplished pianist, would round out the group for a while, and then let other ladies share their musical talents while she danced.

Bess had thought the room almost cavernous until tonight. People crowded in to take their place on the patch of the floor assigned for dancing. Grandmas and grandpas, too old for dancing, sat on the sideline tapping their feet to the music. Some of the women bounced a baby on their knees.

Other women were in the kitchen helping to put mounds of food on the dining room table. Bess's eyes took in the heaping platters of fried chicken, roast beef, and thick slices of ham. Bowls of potato salad, baked beans, cabbage slaw, and other various side dishes vied with baskets of fresh breads and rolls.

The food table was impressive, but the desert table held top honors. It looked like each woman had outdone herself in making a favorite delicacy to share. Apple, mince, and pumpkin pies shared table space with cream pies, piled high with meringue. Cakes of every color and flavor were cut and waiting to be eaten by hungry dancers.

Mr. Stuart led young Josephine to the floor. The twins shuffled their feet around in imitation of the adults. Wade Jr. leaned against one wall with the young hired hands. Some were searching the crowd for a likely partner, others were too shy to ask anyone to dance. Bibby and John David were more interested in sampling all the treats. Bess worried they would stuff themselves and end up sick. She herded them away only to discover them sneaking back. As she returned from one of these rescue trips, Bess looked up into a smiling pair of brown eyes.

"Would you like to dance, Miss Kelly?" The man was tall and thin—too thin. Brown hair fell over his forehead much like her brother Lin's. She thought his eyes were the kindest she'd ever seen. There was an air about him that felt safe. He had a smile that lit up his face.

"I'm sorry, but I don't dance," replied Bess, ducking her head in embarrassment.

"Is that because you just don't want to?"

Bess wanted to run away. "Uh, I never learned," she said in a barely audible voice. "I don't think I'd be a very good dancer."

"Nonsense," said the man. "There's no such thing as a bad dancer. This is a waltz, and you'll be able to figure it out quick enough. Come on, put your hand on my shoulder. Now just relax. One-two-three, one-two-three. You're doin' fine—relax. Just listen to the music."

As she and her partner moved around the floor Bess could feel a little of the tension leave her ramrod-stiff body, but she was still very anxious. She had never been held in a man's arms, and it created strange, new feelings. She would have escaped if not for his firm grip and that it would be terribly impolite to walk off the floor. The music finally stopped, and her partner led her back to the sidelines.

"See, that wasn't so bad, now was it? By the way, I forgot to introduce myself. My name is Jim Hart. Would you like to go again?"

"No, thank you," Bess whispered. "I think I'd better get something to drink. I'm terribly thirsty."

"Well, so am I," replied Jim. "Let's go get somethin'." He took her elbow, and steered Bess to the punch bowl. She tried to think of a way to politely distance herself from the friendly man. Bess longed for an excuse so she could escape with the children to their respective bedrooms.

The dancers, men and women alike, were having a grand time. The men were aided, no doubt, by some of Wade Stuart's private liquor cache. Many escorted even the oldest grannies, with creaky legs, out to the floor for a slow waltz. The children, having eaten enough for several days, were put to bed on pallets along the wall in the dining room or wherever they would be out of the way of dancing feet. It looked like the party might go on for hours.

Bess excused herself from Jim Hart to help the Stuart children get into bed. "It's been a pleasure meeting you, Mr. Hart," she said. "I really must get the children upstairs. Happy New Year."

"But, you're comin' back down once you get them tucked in, aren't you? The party's just gettin' good."

"No, I'm afraid not. I'm very tired, and the children will be awake early no matter how late others are up. So I think I'd better say good night." Bess marched off to gather the children without looking back.

As Bess closed her bedroom door she could hear the strains of music and laughter floating up the stairs. She hurriedly undressed in the chilly bedroom, and snuggled down in the heavy bed covers. Though tired, she found it impossible to sleep. Jim Hart's face floated around in her brain.

So that's what it's like to be held in a man's arms. I've read about it, but I didn't realize it would be so unsettling. I wonder why I reacted that way? I don't even know this man. Bess, you are a ninny!

I wonder how Lin and Aunt Myra are. Maybe I should have stayed in that quiet life. Then I wouldn't be learning new things like dancing.

Bess fell into an exhausted sleep sometime in the early hours of 1909 to dream of things she'd never dreamt before.

1909

Twenty-one thousand sheep, with a pack train of more than thirty burros, passed through Grand Junction on January 3, 1909. The herd, owned by E.L. Ryan of Montrose, Colorado, was trailed from Montrose County to Cisco, Utah, for the remainder of the winter months. Residents became concerned when parts of the huge herd were driven through residential neighborhoods of the city. One herder's death from a fall at the foot of the Fifth Street bridge was declared accidental. Almost two hundred herders were armed, and one pulled a gun on some young men who wouldn't get out of the way. A group of cattlemen followed the herd as it reached the Utah state line. Another herder disappeared and was later found with a bullet through his head. Armed sentinels guarded the sheep day and night.

The winter, while not a drought, could have been better. Horse Mountain Ranch saw a fair amount of snow, but the lower ranches frequently had bare ground during the early months of 1909. Bess got the children back into their normal school routine following the holidays. It was the quiet time on a ranch except for tending to the stock. Ranch hands spent long winter nights playing cards, reading, and making halters and lariats. Children at the big house whiled away the long evenings by reading good books in front of a blazing fire or playing games. They'd occasionally have a songfest while their mother accompanied them on the piano. Mrs. Stuart decided it was time for Josephine to learn the piano, which the young lady suffered through. She much preferred to curl up with a good book. Bess understood. She often escaped to her cold bedroom where she wore gloves to turn the pages of a book she couldn't put down.

The New Year's party had all but left her mind when Bess stood up one morning to peer out the small school window. A familiar figure was riding into the barnyard.

Why is Jim Hart here?

Bess shrugged her shoulders and decided he had come to talk about the grazing fee, which had all the ranchers up in arms. She turned back to her charges, who were bent over their lessons.

When lunch time arrived Bess and the children walked over to the main house for their meal. To her surprise Jim Hart had joined the other ranch hands at their big table at one end of the kitchen. She hurried the children into the dining room, hoping that he hadn't seen her.

I don't want to be rude, but I'm not interested in chatting with him. I think he's a little too friendly, sort of like a puppy dog!

After lunch she marshaled her charges out the door for a short play period in the chill air before they resumed their studies. Rounding the corner of the house, she ran smack-dab into Jim Hart.

"Why, Miss Kelly, what a surprise!" The laughing man steadied her by her arms. "I wondered if I'd be seeing you today. How've you been?"

"Fine, Mr. Hart. I'm fine, and I hope you also are well," Bess said, trying to be polite but impersonal. "If you'll excuse me, I must supervise the children."

"It looks like they ain't havin' any problems," Jim replied. He pointed to the young people playing ball on the least muddy part of the yard. "I'll walk over there with you."

Bess's good manners prevented her from being impolite to the bold man. *Quick, think of something to say! I don't know how to visit with a man!*

"What brings you up this way, Mr. Hart?"

"I've been talkin' to Wade about hiring on for the calving season in exchange for some bummer calves to start my herd. I just took up a homestead, which was turned back to the government because the guy didn't prove up on it. It's located down on the sagebrush flats next to my parents' place, and I don't have the ready cash to buy stock. I thought maybe Wade would work out a deal with me, and it looks like he's gonna think about it. You never can have too many hands during the calving season."

"Perhaps not," replied Bess struggling to make polite conversation until she could take the children into class. "Where did you say your parcel of land is?" She pulled her heavy knit scarf closer to her head and neck.

"It's pretty close to the mouth of Pete and Bill. The water rights sure ain't much for the upper part, but I get an inch or two of river water for the bottom land. It's right next to a quarter section that my folks bought close to ten years ago. The old guy that filed on this piece decided farming was way too much work, and he left for greener pastures. It'll take me a few years to prove up on it, but it may eventually make a livin'. Dad and I can work the two pieces together and that'll help."

"My family has a river bottom ranch up by Para...er... Grand Valley. Uncle Elmer grows produce for the high country and runs some dairy cattle."

Jim chuckled. "I see you have as much trouble with Parachute's name change as I do. Seems like they could've left well enough alone. Say, is your uncle Elmer Carpenter?"

"That's right, but actually he's not my uncle. He's married to my mother's sister. My brother and I came out to live with them when our mother died. We've been there ever since…well, I guess I should say Lin's still there. He's a good help for Uncle Elmer and Aunt Myra."

"I'll bet that's welcome to Elmer. I've met him a time or two, and he ain't a young man. That's why I want to stay close to my folks. I'm all they have since my sister died, and they ain't gettin' any younger."

Bess looked at a little watch hanging on a chain around her neck. Recess was over, and she needed to get the children inside for their afternoon lessons. "If you'll excuse me, I really must go. It was nice talking to you."

"You may be seeing more of me if Wade takes me up on my offer. Calving should start in a month or six weeks so I may be back sooner than you think."

Wade Stuart was a generous man who liked to help his neighbors. One day Bess saw Jim Hart ride into the yard and move his stuff into the Horse Mountain Ranch bunkhouse. She supposed that he had been able to make a satisfactory arrangement with her employer.

Calving started almost immediately. For the next five weeks the ranch hands slept in shifts so that someone was patrolling the herd around the clock. Bess saw them coming and going in the kitchen dining room, gray-faced from fatigue. She hadn't known there would be so much activity during a calving season, and she was fascinated.

The weather remained warm and dry through the end of March, which proved a boon for stock owners. The calf crop was good, and Bess wondered if Jim Hart would get enough calves to give him a start. She'd only talked to him in passing while going by the barnyard. The men managed to keep going on gallons of coffee and a few hours of sleep. There were still several weeks to go.

A late storm in mid-April dumped almost a foot of snow on the ranch, and the cowboys were kept busy making sure the calves survived. There were always a few cantankerous old cows who wouldn't care for their calves or didn't have enough milk to feed twins. The potbellied stove in the bunkhouse often had a calf or two stretched out on horse blankets within the circle of its heat. Ranch hands rubbed their bodies to get the circulation going and then started the little animals sucking warm milk from a bottle. The calves had to be fed by hand until they were old enough to join the other calves in the orphan herd. They were kept in a separate pen by the big barn. Hands took turns feeding the calves two or three times a day. Jim Hart would get his starter herd from these calves.

The end of April saw the last of the calving. Bess and the children visited the calf pens almost every day to play with the frisky animals. The younger children loved to feed them from the bottle until they learned to drink from a bucket. Katherine and Scott especially loved this time away from their studies.

On one of their visits Bess saw Jim Hart saddling up his horse and tying his belongings behind the saddle seat.

"Well, Mr. Hart, I hope this was a successful time for you."

"It was more than I'd planned on," replied Jim. "Wade Stuart said he'd had a good year and gave me a few more animals than we'd agreed upon. I'll leave them here for a few weeks until I can drive them down the road. Right now I've got to get home to do the plowing and try to get water on the top part of the place. Unless I get those fields soaked up soon, there won't be any runoff water to put on it. Sorry we didn't get to do any more visiting. Maybe I'll see you when I come to get the calves."

"I don't know whether I'll be here, Mr. Hart. I'll also be leaving in a few weeks. I'm needed at home to help with the garden work. Uncle Elmer is on the road most of the summer. Aunt Myra and Lin will need as many hands as they can get."

"I don't get into town too often. If I do, maybe I'll drive out to see you and your folks. Would that be all right with you?"

"I-I suppose it would be all right," Bess replied.

What in the world would I tell the family if he does show up? I certainly wouldn't want to give them any false ideas about a friendship with Mr. Hart. How would Uncle Elmer react to a male visitor, no matter how casual? Maybe Jim really didn't mean it—maybe I'm worrying over nothing.

"Good luck with all your ranch work this summer."

Before Bess left for home Mrs. Stuart extracted a promise from her to come back for another year. Bess was glad. She admired the Stuarts and was flattered they thought she'd done a good job of teaching their children. It would be Josephine's last year in grade school. A decision would have to be made next year where to send her for further education. Bess knew that she lacked the training to take the children beyond eighth grade studies, but she looked forward to one more year.

On June 22,1909, several hundred passengers were stranded because east-west trains were being held at Grand Junction. A railroad bridge had caught fire, and been destroyed, four miles west of DeBeque. It was believed the fire had been caused by sparks from an engine or hot ashes that were dumped out. The bridge was about forty feet high and ninety feet long.

There were rumors that the tunnel in DeBeque Canyon was flooded due to heavy spring runoff water from the Grand River. It was proven untrue but some water had overflowed onto the railroad tracks at Webster Hill, west of Rifle. It had not, however, impeded travel from Glenwood Springs to the bridge fire. For the next few days, passengers and baggage were transported to the area of the fire, unloaded and taken to a train waiting on the other side of the bridge. This type of shuttle continued until the bridge was restored by a huge work force.

Bess arrived home to find her family working to get the first crops planted and the hay field irrigated. The early summer was cooler with less rain. Elmer fussed that the truck garden wouldn't start producing early enough for the hungry consumers in the higher country.

Bess thought the temperature couldn't be too cool after she'd spent a day of weeding the corn and tomato fields. She rolled up the long sleeves on her dress to bare her arms. They were growing more brown by the day. Bess would get done with one field only to start all over. Most evenings she came into supper wrung out from the long day, but she never complained because the others were working just as hard. Despite Uncle Elmer's dire predictions, the first produce came on in mid-July, and he started his weekly treks upcountry.

Elmer conceded they needed to hire someone to help with the milking. The rest of the farm animals still needed tending in the morning and evening. While Lin did the evening chores, Bess helped Aunt Myra with supper and took care of the milk and cream. With a stab of guilt she realized that her aunt, who would soon be forty-nine, was looking very tired these days. She worked too hard and never complained. Bess felt like such an ungrateful niece. By being gone in the winter she placed an additional burden upon her aunt. Although Lin had helped her, Aunt Myra still did most of the inside work. Bess again vowed to work harder to help the older woman while she could.

One morning Bess took the team and wagon into town with the latest shipment of cream. Aunt Myra was busy preserving all the extra fruit and vegetables which weren't fit for Uncle Elmer to haul to the high country. She needed more supplies, and Bess said she'd do both errands. She arrived at the station and was trying to wrestle the heavy cream cans from the back of the wagon when she felt a pair of arms reach around her to grab the handles of the can.

"It looks like you could use some help, Miss. Step aside, and I'll put your cans over on the platform."

Bess, surprised, stepped back while Jim Hart lugged both cans to the loading dock. Then he turned to her.

"My God! Miss Kelly—Bess—is it you? Your back was turned, and I didn't get a good look at your face. I should have known it was you. No one in this country has such beautiful auburn hair. You look thinner. Have you been under the weather?"

Bess shook her head. "No, I'm fine. It's been so hot, and I haven't had much appetite. I've been out in the fields most of the summer. The weeds are growing faster than the garden, and it's a never-ending chore. Thank you for helping me. My brother usually does this, but Uncle Elmer's gone upcountry, and Lin had to get the water on the east fields now that the hay's cut. How's your ranch coming along?"

"I guess things are goin' pretty well. Most of my calves are doin' okay. I ended up with about twenty of 'em. Wade did right by me. I got one good cuttin' on my upper place before the water ran out. We could use a good gentle soaker, but with this heat it'll probably be a gully washer when it does come."

"Are you in town just for the day?"

"Yeah," replied Jim. "Our supplies were low so I thought I'd better come to town between watering and cuttings. Ma's busy preservin' all of her garden, and she needs more supplies."

Bess chuckled. "That's my next job. Aunt Myra's doing the same thing. I'm going to drive across the street to Doll Brothers. Is that where you're heading?"

Jim swung his long leg over the side of the wagon and settled himself in the seat. "Well, let's go!"

They both laughed when it took the horses less than one minute to change direction and pull the wagon in front of the store, located kitty-corner from the railroad station. Jim jumped down and held out a hand to help Bess over the wheel. It was rather nice being with him. He reminded her of happy times on the Horse Mountain Ranch. Bess missed being up there above the heat of the valley floor. They purchased their supplies, and Jim packed Bess's groceries to her wagon then stowed them in the back.

"I don't know whether I'll see you again before you come back to Wallace Creek. You are comin' back this fall, aren't you?"

"Yes, although I admit I'm concerned about my Aunt's well-being. I feel it's terribly selfish of me to leave home when she could use my help so much."

"Won't your uncle try to find someone to help her?"

Bess scoffed. "Not that man. He'd sooner die than part with a cent of his money. Uncle Elmer is not an easy man."

"Look on the bright side, Bess. The winter work is never as hard. You're helping your aunt when she needs it the most. That's what counts. Well, I guess I'd better get down the road, or I won't get home before time to milk. I'll look forward to seeing you this fall. Maybe we can take a ride, and I'll show you my place."

"Perhaps, Jim. We'll see when I get down there. Who knows what the weather will be like. Have a good trip home."

Bess was halfway to the ranch before she realized that she and Jim Hart had graduated to first names.

Glenwood Springs, Colorado, July 29, 1909:

A three-hour standoff occurred between the Garfield County Sheriff, his deputies, the Glenwood Springs police and Patrick O'Neill, owner of the Silver Club saloon. Arthur Stacey Gray, member of a wealthy St. Louis family, lost $6,500 on a roulette wheel in the saloon. A friend, who was presumably knowledgeable, offered to check the machine to see if it was rigged. When the friend arrived to inspect the machine, O'Neill knocked him down. Law enforcement was called and met by a very angry O'Neill with pistols in each hand. He stood on the stairs, refusing admission to the officers until they, in disgust, finally left.

"For pity sakes, Aunt Myra, let me help you with that kettle! You look completely done in. Why don't you sit and take a breather while I pour the jelly into the glasses? I need to be in here helping you instead of outside doing hired hand work." Bess knew her tone was too sharp, and Aunt Myra would feel obliged to defend Uncle Elmer. She was right.

"I'm all right, truly I am," said Aunt Myra. "This is the last batch of jelly. Once I get some food on the table I can rest. I must say, though, I'm glad that the season's coming to an end. I don't think the cellar will hold much more. It seems that's all I've done this summer."

"You probably have enough to feed half of Grand Valley," teased Bess. "I won't have to worry about you going hungry this winter, will I?"

"I wish you were going to be here to eat it with us, Bess. Are you sure you want to go back to the Stuarts for another year?"

Bess hesitated before she spoke. "I'd like nothing better than to stay here with you and Lin. But, honestly, you know Uncle Elmer and I would bicker all winter long. I can't seem to do anything to satisfy him. And you'd feel in the middle. I just think it's best for me to leave when he's at home. He'll be on the road next summer, and I'll be back to help you. Maybe by then the old tightwad will hire a man for the garden so I can help you inside. You just sit yourself down in your rocker and rest your feet. I'll fry up some of the potatoes from noon with bacon, slice some tomatoes and put out the cottage cheese. The men won't starve."

"Bess, I know he isn't the easiest man to live with, but you're also stubborn. Elmer works pretty hard for all of us, and I wish you'd try to find a way of getting along with him."

"If there is, I guess I haven't thought of it, Aunt Myra. Lin says it's because we're too much alike. If I had charge of the purse strings I wouldn't make you work like a dog. You should have some help. He hires men for the outside work and never thinks of you. I think, however, it would be worse if I stayed to help you. You'd be upset over our wrangling all winter."

"You worry too much about me, Bess, but I suppose you're right. I just wish it could be different. I miss you when you are gone."

● ● ● ● ● ● ● ● ●

It was mid-September 1909, and everybody on Wallace Creek came together for a fall picnic at the Horse Mountain Ranch. Jim Hart and his father, Big Jim, had ridden in with some other families a short while before. The elder man sat tall in the saddle astride a very large gelding. A smaller mount would have been unable to carry Big Jim who easily exceeded six feet by several inches and was heavily built. Young Jim had inherited his father's height but not his girth.

The men laid boards across sawhorses to make tables on the lawn and then went down by the corral while the women set out the food. Bess was watching the youngest children while helping to carry out the food.

"Bess, take this platter of chicken. Josephine, grab that basket of bread and rolls. John David, run down to the corral. Tell those men to stop what they're doing and get to the table while the food is still hot." Mrs. Stuart was issuing orders like the general she believed herself to be. "Bibby, get out from under the table and make sure that dog is outside, or we won't have any food left in the kitchen."

When the men trooped into the yard for the meal, Bess wrinkled her nose at the strong smell of liquor. Mr. Stuart had apparently passed around some of his whiskey.

Bess had the children settled at the benches around the table when Jim Hart made his way to her side. "Mind if I sit with you? We haven't had a chance to talk since you've come back. Dad is with some of his old cronies, and I don't have anyone to eat with."

Bess looked up at the tall man. "Hello, Jim," she replied while looking around to see if anyone was frowning about their socializing. She wasn't sure how Mrs. Stuart would feel about her teacher sitting with a man. "I guess it will be all right."

She scooted over on the bench. No one seemed to be paying any attention to them. The giggling children interrupted their conversation with funny antics, until Bess sternly warned them to mind their manners. The youngsters

DOLL BROS. & SMITH STORE IN GRAND VALLEY, CIRCA 1905

then hurriedly ate so they could go play with other children. At last Bess and Jim were alone.

"Did you get the crops in before you left?" Jim asked. "You're as brown as a nut from all the weeding."

"Yes we did. Or at least we got most of it in. Uncle Elmer will take a load of winter squash up to Glenwood Springs and Aspen before it gets too cold, and then that will be all for the year. Aunt Myra and Lin will get some rest for a little while, not that a rancher ever really gets to rest. How did your crops fare?"

Bess and Jim sat and visited until they were interrupted by the women gathering up the food and transporting it back to the kitchen. Bess reluctantly took her leave from Jim to help them. When she returned, he had gone back to the corrals with the other men. Bess could see several of the hands working with some broncos amid hoots and cheers from the onlookers.

The women bedded down babies on blankets under the big trees in the yard while they did needlework and visited. Bess, becoming bored, took a small book of poems and retreated a distance to read. Before she knew it, the shadows had grown longer. People were packing the wagons and buggies so they could get home in time for the evening milking.

Bess was standing in the yard watching the visitors leave when Jim Hart rode up beside her.

"This was a nice day. Maybe I could come up again in a few weeks, and we could go for a ride?"

Bess hesitated, "I'm not sure, Jim. I think I should ask Mr. and Mrs. Stuart for permission."

"Well, if that's all that's holding us back, why don't I just go ask right now?" Jim reined his horse around and headed off toward Mr. and Mrs. Stuart. A brief conversation produced a grin on Jim's face as he rode back to Bess.

"It's all set. I'll be up Sunday after next if the weather's decent. It should still be warm enough to go on a little picnic. Would that be okay?" At Bess's silent nod he whirled his horse and trotted out of the yard.

• • • • • • • • •

"Put your little foot, put your little foot, put your little foot right here…" The laughing dancers followed the caller's instructions to the *Varsouvianna*. It was New Year's Eve, and most of the Wallace Creek folks had once again come to the Horse Mountain Ranch for an all-night party. Bess and Jim Hart were vying for a few inches of dance floor, while he led her through the simple, rhythmic steps. She was finally getting familiar with dancing and enjoyed it now that she didn't feel so awkward.

Bess and Jim developed an easy friendship during the fall months and into December. When it became too cold for a buggy ride, he joined the Stuart family on Sunday afternoons to play cards or sing along to the popular music of the day. Mrs. Stuart received a new song by a composer named Irving Berlin, and the whole family enjoyed singing the words of *Alexander's Ragtime Band*. Bess discovered that Jim had a fine tenor voice, which blended well with her own alto range. They would occasionally find themselves in perfect harmony, and Bess marveled they sounded so pleasant together.

The Stuart family Christmas holiday had been very much like the previous one. This year Bess picked up gifts and supplies when she'd made a late fall visit to her aunt, uncle, and brother. She was able to give a few well-chosen gifts of her own. Her gift from her employers was another lovely gown of a dark-blue, silk broadcloth. The skirt was cut in the slimmer style, which had become the current fashion.

I wonder if I'll be able to dance in this skinny skirt?

The children clamored for her to try it on. They said it was more lovely than the one from the previous year. Bess stroked the fabric.

It's kind of Mrs. Stuart to understand I can't spend money on frivolous things like fancy dresses.

Most of her wages were still given to Uncle Elmer, who never refused the payment. Bess didn't care. It eased some of her guilt at being gone.

Jim hadn't been up on Christmas Day. His absence left a void because Bess had grown accustomed to his weekly visits. However, Jim promised that he would be at the New Year's dance. He arrived early that evening, just in time to help carry out the rugs and bring in more chairs. At the first note of music they joined other whirling couples, who dodged youngsters playing on the sidelines.

"You look pretty tonight, Bess. Is that a new dress? I like that color on you. It makes your cheeks almost as rosy as your hair."

"Thank you kindly. Yes, it was my Christmas present. You look quite handsome, yourself."

Bess's heart had skipped a beat when he arrived. Jim Hart was a nice-looking man with his hair slicked back, clean-shaven, and exuding a heavy scent of bay rum. His tall, lanky frame was made for a pair of tight-fitting riding pants. A wool plaid shirt and freshly polished boots completed his wardrobe.

Bess glanced at his large hand encircling her own and was struck by its wiry strength. Most engaging, however, were his laughing brown eyes and an infectious grin. Jim managed to see the best in everything, whatever the subject. Bess felt a little guilty that she wasn't as patient or charitable as he.

After the third dance Bess pulled away from Jim's arms. "I think I'd better go check on the children," she said. "You remember how Bibby and John David stuffed themselves last year? Their mother won't be happy if they're sick all night."

"I'll tag along," said Jim. "I could use something to drink, and maybe I'll step outside and have a smoke."

"Just so that's the only thing you have outside, Jim Hart," laughed Bess. "Don't think I don't know about the jug that's being passed around."

"Ah, Bess, you wouldn't deprive a man a sip or two. I dance much better after a couple of snorts."

Shaking her head, Bess headed in the direction of the dining room. She found John David and Bibby in the dining room. The food-stuffed children were sitting under the table with a new puppy and Bibby's kitten. Pieces of chocolate cake were smeared on their faces and the floor. It looked like the animals had been sharing the children's feast. The puppy was chewing on a chicken bone, which Bess hurriedly retrieved. The cat busily removed remnants of food from her whiskers.

"Come along, you two. It's time you went to bed. I swear, if you eat another bite you'll explode! Where are the twins? They should come, as well."

Having found Katherine and Scott in a corner of the living room, Bess pushed all four of the children up the stairs to their bedrooms. Once she made sure they were settled, and not in danger of being sick, Bess went downstairs to continue the dance. She compared her present confidence to that of last year and was pleased. Two years with the Stuart family had helped to increase her social ease. Bess smiled as she saw Jim crossing the floor to claim her for the next dance.

1910

On February 23, 1910, a Colorado Midland passenger train was stranded in deep snow drifts on Hagerman Pass between Leadville and Basalt. A rotary snowplow, sent to cut through the deep drifts, also became hopelessly stuck. One hundred men were dispatched to hand-shovel through the packed snow but were hampered by the continuing storm. Railroad traffic was at a standstill due to the other trains piling up on the tracks behind the snowbound train.

The March wind cut through the couple, causing them to huddle deeper into their heavy coats. "Do you want to turn back, Bess? I thought the wind would let up by now." Jim tucked the blanket in around Bess.

"No, let's go on. I think it will get warmer when we get down off the mesa. It's always so much colder and snowier up here. I look forward to patches of bare ground. It's been a long winter."

The couple were on their way down to Jim's place for a Sunday outing. Bess had asked him so many questions about his little spread, he finally decided it would be easier to let her see it for herself. They'd waited until the worst of the weather was over and the sun shone in spite of the wind. The crisp, cold air invigorated the horse who trotted down the road at a good pace. They were soon at the bottom of the mesa and turned east onto the main road to Battlement Mesa.

"There's my folks' place," said Jim as they rumbled by. "They have a better spread, but mine will be okay someday. The two places will do well together. I wish the water rights were better, but I can't be too choosy. Most of the good land's already taken."

A brown landscape greeted Bess's eyes no matter where she looked. Several good-sized fields had been cleared, but the rest of the land still contained sage and rabbitbrush. The roadbed snaked across the flat land between the Grand River and the sloping hills. The elder Hart's house was a snug-looking building made of cottonwood trees cut from the groves along the river. It squatted low on the north side of the road. Numerous barns and corrals were scattered between the river and the house. A barren bush or two suggested that someone had, at one time, tried to plant flowers in the unkempt yard.

A short distance beyond the elder Hart place, Jim pulled the buggy into his yard. Bess took in every aspect of the view. A square-built clapboard building made of weathered, unpainted boards stood in front of her. She estimated it contained two or three rooms. The ground was bare around the house, but sagebrush grew in wild abundance just a few yards beyond the dwelling. Cedar trees lined the hill behind the small house. Except for the trees and brush, the brown landscape lay unbroken. A short distance from the little house stood a cluster of weathered sheds and a barn. Jim's place was very different from the Horse Mountain Ranch.

Bess struggled to say something positive about the bleak piece of property. "It looks like you have a tight little house, Jim. Do you suppose we could go in and warm up a little bit?"

"Why sure Bess…sure we can. You must be nearly frozen. I'm afraid the house isn't too clean. I don't have much time to do women's work. Maybe I need a wife to take care of it, ehhh?" Jim gave her a lopsided smile as he led Bess into the kitchen.

The room was still warm from the banked fire in the big cook stove. Jim stoked up the fire and added more wood. He slid a battered coffeepot to the front lid. Bess could feel a cold draft blowing up her skirt from the cracks in the wide board floor. She held her hands out to the feeble warmth of the fire while glancing around at the bare little room. Jim hadn't been joking about its condition. A mismatched table and two chairs squatted in the middle of the room. Along one of the bare wood walls stood an old painted cupboard which held a few dishes and a dirty-looking wash pan. Large nails on the other wall held an odd assortment of old coats, hats, and lariats. Several wash towels, which probably hadn't been clean for some time, also hung there. Through an open door Bess caught a glimpse of a painted iron bedstead covered with a heavy wool quilt.

Jim's voice was apologetic. "I guess I should have cleaned up a little bit. I didn't think about us stopping here. Figured we'd stop off by my folks on the way back so we could warm up."

"I'd like to meet your folks," said Bess. "I saw your dad at the picnic, but I didn't get to meet him. Was your mother ill that day? I wondered why she wasn't there."

"Ma doesn't visit much anymore. We lost my older sister, Mary, to smallpox a few years ago, and she can't quit grieving. It's like the life also went out of Ma. Dad and I have given up on trying to get her to go visit the way she once did. We keep hoping she'll come out of it one of these days."

"Well, if we wouldn't be intruding, I'd like to meet her," Bess replied. "I understand what it's like to lose someone you love."

"Just so you know, sometimes she's a little testy with people. I don't want your feelings to be hurt. We never know if she's having a good day."

Bess was glad she'd been forewarned. When Jim escorted her through the door of his parents' house she was confronted by a short, rotund woman in a dingy gray dress, which matched her straggly hair.

"Ma, I want you to meet Bess Kelly. She's the teacher up at Horse Mountain. Remember me telling you about her?"

"Yes, I remember. Well, come on in. Don't stand there lettin' the cold air in. You missed dinner, but I suppose I could scare something up to eat." The woman's irritable voice almost stopped the polite greeting that Bess was about to offer.

"Please don't put yourself out Mrs. Hart. I'm truly not hungry, but I did want to meet you because I haven't had the chance."

Jim's mother didn't respond as she led them to the kitchen. It was slightly better equipped than her son's, but only a notch cleaner. Bess excused the lack of housecleaning. Just like Aunt Myra, she probably had too much to do for a woman her age.

Nellie sliced big chunks of fresh-baked bread which did smell delicious, and Bess realized she was hungry. The woman set a tub of churned butter and some apricot preserves on the oilcloth-covered table. Two thick china mugs full of steaming coffee completed the fare.

"I guess that'll hold you until you get up the hill and back, Son," Nellie said. She ignored Bess who tried hard not to feel offended by the woman's bad manners.

A burst of cold air whooshed through the kitchen as the back door opened, and Big Jim Hart walked in. "Well, well, who do we have here, Mother? I see we have company." Big Jim's cheerfulness was gladly received. Bess smiled at him.

"It's Miss Kelly, isn't it? I saw you at the picnic, but I didn't get a chance to meet you. I was havin' too much fun watchin' those bronc busters fall on their backsides."

Bess warmed to the large jovial man. Nellie Hart simply harrumped and continued to pour hot water into a battered dish pan. She started to wash the noontime dishes.

While Bess listened to the men's conversation, she stole glances at Nellie, who looked to be oblivious to the others. Bess had never met anyone who was so deliberately rude. Although Jim had warned her, Bess was not prepared for this reception. It was a relief when she and Jim finished their snack so they could leave. Jim helped her into the buggy and tucked the blanket tight before climbing up and snapping the reins.

"Now that we're all warmed up, we should make it to the ranch before we get too cold. It's a little bit warmer. I'm glad we decided to stop so you and Ma could get acquainted. She was doin' better today."

Bess turned to look at him in disbelief, thinking he was joking. The look on his face clearly told her he wasn't. If Nellie Hart was having a good day, Bess decided she never wanted to see her have a bad one!

> On July 16, 1910, an article in *The Daily Sentinel* reported on a promotional auto trip that was made from Grand Junction to Glenwood Springs. The vehicle was an E.M.F. 30. The party of four persons left Grand Junction at 8:30 in the morning and arrived in Glenwood Springs at 8:00 P.M. that night. They were stopped for two hours to eat and to escape a storm at Rifle. The driver reported that the worst piece of road was near DeBeque.

Bess returned home for the summer work. The normally hot weather turned rainy and cool in July. Uncle Elmer complained that the produce was not getting ripe, but Bess was privately glad for the respite from the garden work. The sun, however, broke through the clouds on that Sunday morning. Bess left for the corn patch to prepare for another day of hard work. She was almost in the middle of the field when Aunt Myra came loping toward her.

"Bess, come to the house! Your friend, Mr. Hart, is there, and he's asking for you." The middle-aged woman was struggling to speak as she tried to catch her breath. It wasn't every day that Bess had a gentleman caller, and it certainly wasn't every day Myra Carpenter ran so fast.

As Bess returned to the house with her aunt she was full of conflict. As much as she looked forward to seeing Jim, she was reluctant to bring him into any friction with her uncle. It was hard to say how Uncle Elmer would react to a male visitor. As Bess hurried to the house she hoped he wasn't being as rude to Jim as Mrs. Hart had been to her.

Jim stood when Bess came in the door, the admiration in his eyes clearly visible to all. "Good to see you, Bess. I can't get into the field to cut the hay, and I thought this might be a good time to come see you. Once the hay is down it's hard telling when I'll get to town. I thought maybe you'd like to take a ride up Parachute Creek. You said you've never seen the falls on East Fork."

Bess stammered, "I really shouldn't. The corn needs to be hoed, and I should help Aunt Myra with the strawberry jam…"

Aunt Myra interrupted, "Well isn't that nice! I think it would be lovely for you to visit the falls. It should be so pretty after all the rainy weather."

Bess carefully avoided looking at her uncle. She knew he must be fuming that she might take a day off from her chores. "I don't know whether I should."

"Nonsense," Aunt Myra said. "You go get yourself ready, and I'll throw a few things in a basket for a picnic. It will do you good to take a day off."

When there was no protest from Uncle Elmer, Bess finally agreed. She went to get ready for the ride. Through the bedroom door she could hear Jim chatting with her family. He and Uncle Elmer were talking about stock prices, and Bess breathed a sigh of relief. She was sure her uncle wasn't pleased with Jim's appearance, but at least he wasn't being impolite. Lin, who'd come in to check out the company, seemed to have no reservation about her friend. She could hear him and Aunt Myra chiming in on the conversation from time to time.

Aunt Myra fixed them each a ham sandwich and poured some cool lemonade into a stoneware jug. She tucked a handful of cookies into the basket. The couple was soon on the way, with the horses going at a brisk trot. The road was still muddy after the hard rain, but it would be dry by afternoon. Bess had heard about the beauty of the East Fork Falls, and she was excited that she'd finally see it. It was a favorite spot for local picnickers. The warm July day promised to be hot by midday. The cool comfort of the canyon would be welcome by the time they arrived.

Bess and Jim happily visited about many things as they traveled the Parachute Creek road, periodically waving to other Sunday travelers on the twelve-mile trip. Bess wanted to know how the Wallace Creek families were faring, and whether Jim had seen Halley's Comet.

Both expressed disbelief about the federal government's plans for a transcontinental highway. "I'll tell you, Bess, I can't imagine how that newfangled automobile will ever replace a good reliable horse," Jim said. "What will the drivers do when they have to ford a creek or river? And, how will they get around in the wintertime when the snow's four foot deep?"

The couple talked about the oil drilling rig on Streit Flats across the Grand River from Jim's ranch. The lights on the derrick were visible from his house at night. Oil shale prospecting was also taking the rural area by storm.

Nevertheless, the biggest debate in Grand Valley those days was the matter of allowing hard liquor in the town limits. Opposing sides were adamant in their beliefs, and it had divided the town in two. Bess and Jim grinned at each other knowing they'd be on opposing sides if it ever came to a vote.

The couple was comfortable with each other. Bess cast sidelong glances at Jim as he handled the reins.

He really is a nice-looking man, and I've missed seeing him. Except for Miss Hubbard I've never had a close friend. I think I could tell him anything and he'd understand. Well, maybe I couldn't talk to him about his mother's rudeness. I think he and his father are blind to her behavior. Otherwise, I wouldn't be reluctant to say what is in my heart.

By noon they had pulled into the green canyon a short distance from the falls. Jim unhooked the horses and gave them grain and water before hobbling. Taking the small picnic basket in his left hand, he offered his right arm to Bess.

"It looks like it's rough walking, Bess. Why don't you take my arm, and we can both fall down?" Jim chuckled at they started up the path.

The crashing water beckoned to them. It cascaded over a shale cliff at least one hundred feet high. The cool spray caressed their faces as they picked their way among the huge boulders, some which were as large as a house. Finding a shady spot by the side of a huge rock, they spread the buggy blanket and leaned back to enjoy the refreshing coolness.

Bess sighed, "This is lovely! No wonder it's a favorite place to visit. Wouldn't it be nice to have a cabin up here?"

"Yeah, but it would get mighty cold in the wintertime. The sun would shine down here only a few hours a day."

They ate their meal and reclined on the blanket, dozing in the afternoon warmth. Bess was lost in her own thoughts when she felt her hand being taken into Jim's larger one.

"I've missed you, Bess." His voice was husky with emotion. "I didn't realize how much I'd miss you when we said good-bye this spring. Every time I go to Horse Mountain I remember all the times we spent up there. I'm really gonna miss you this winter when it gets too cold to come to town. Are you sure you won't reconsider comin' back to teach?"

"No, Jim, I'm going to stick it out for Aunt Myra's sake unless Uncle Elmer makes it impossible. I've felt so guilty for leaving her these past two winters. Every time I come home she seems to have more to do. Just making the butter and cheese is almost a full-time job. It's typical of Uncle Elmer that he got a man to haul his produce, but he'd never consider getting help for her. No, I've got to make the best of it as long as I can. Besides, I really want to spend more time with Lin. He turned fifteen this spring, and he won't be around for much longer. I'm a little concerned about his cock-sure attitude. I think it would be best if I was living at home."

Jim's hand tightened around hers. "I guess I understand how you feel, Bess, but you need to also consider that maybe others need you as much as your aunt and brother." His head came close to her. His lips touched hers in a long sweet gentle caress.

Bess's eyes flew open in surprise.

I haven't planned on this!

Jim backed away and looked into her face. "Don't you know how I feel about you, Bess?"

"Truthfully, I had no idea," she shakily replied. "You're a good friend, Jim, and I cherish our friendship but I…" Another kiss silenced her. A tingling spread through her body. Jim's lips pressed urgently against her own, while his arms enfolded her into an embrace. When his lips finally left hers, their breaths were ragged with emotion. Bess's lips quivered from the kisses. She'd never felt that way before, but she liked it.

"Well, I guess you know now," Jim replied as he tucked her head into the hollow of his shoulder. "I don't want to rush you, but will you marry me, Bess? I understand you think you should stay home this winter. But, I'm hoping you'll get things situated so you and I can have a life together. What do you say?"

Bess was struck dumb by his marriage proposal. "I don't know what to say, Jim. It-it's all happened so fast. I need time to think about this. I'm very fond of you but…" She sighed and could not continue.

"That's okay Bess. I don't need an answer today. I just want you to consider bein' Mrs. Jim Hart, and I'm willing to wait a little while."

● ● ● ● ● ● ● ● ●

Bess stopped to wipe the sweat from her forehead. The sun beat down, ripening the produce at an alarming rate. She longed for the coolness of the falls and that magic afternoon with Jim. Bess wondered how much more she could take. Since her day with Jim, Uncle Elmer had picked at her from dawn to dark. It seemed she couldn't do anything to satisfy the old man. She had no idea why he had suddenly intensified his attacks, except they coincided with Jim Hart's visit.

Bess had done little but think about Jim's marriage proposal. She felt torn in two.

Part of me longs to accept. He's a good man who'll provide for me as best he can. Another part tells me to say no. I care for Jim, but I'm pretty sure I'm not in love with him. I think there should be more to love, but maybe not. Maybe that's all there is. I do know I like his strong arms around me. I love his kisses, and I love the way they make me feel!

That's not all there is to life. I'm concerned that Jim doesn't share many of my values about life. I've planned on marrying someone who is educated, maybe another teacher. Jim's education ended at the sixth grade when he left school to help his father with the ranch. He's not one to scoff, but I know Jim sets less value on education than I do. He tells me he already knows everything he needs in order to make a living. That disturbs me. A week-old newspaper is the extent of his regular reading, and only then to read the farm and livestock reports. Bess, listen to yourself—you sound like such a snob!

There's also the matter of his mother. I wonder if I could ever gain Nellie Hart's approval. The woman has lost one child, and she may not be willing to let go of the other. Would she approve of our marriage? Surely Jim wouldn't let his mother interfere. Perhaps Big Jim Hart would be an ally if we did decide to marry.

Jim never said he loved me, but I'm sure he does. It's very flattering to know someone cares that much for me. I've wanted that all my life—I need to feel secure. I'd enjoy having my own home. Jim's ramshackle house doesn't bother me. I could make it presentable in no time at all. The question is, do I love him enough to spend the rest of my life as Mrs. Jim Hart? Could I make him happy—would I be happy?

Her daydream was violently interrupted by Uncle Elmer's harsh voice.

"For God's sake, Girl, can't you move any faster? You should have been done with that field at noon. Here I am, waitin' to get the water on it, and you're just pokin' along."

"If you're in such an all-fired hurry, sir, why don't you pick up a hoe and help me out? I don't recall seeing you out here in this patch."

"You'd like that, wouldn't, you, Young Lady? Well, let me tell you something. I work mighty hard on all the rest of the ranch. I don't think it's too much to ask you to help out…"

"Helping out and being your slave are two different things," Bess interrupted. "While we're talking about that, when are you going to get some help for Aunt Myra? She takes care of the milk and cream, makes the cheese and butter for the store, plus doing the regular housework and meals. Then, in the summer, she adds the canning to her workload. I'd help her more if you didn't have me in these fields from dawn to dark."

"You never mind tending to our business!" Elmer's voice boomed. "If your aunt needs help, we'll decide on it, not you."

Their harsh voices could be heard clear up to the farmhouse, one yelling and the other responding. When Bess and Elmer came in for supper both looked very angry, and conversation was sparse. Aunt Myra and Lin stayed out of the way. Later that evening Bess approached her aunt. "Aunt Myra, what am I to do? I know my being here makes it uncomfortable for you and Lin. Yet, if I leave what will you do? You can't continue to work so hard, and I seriously doubt that Uncle Elmer will ever hire someone to help you."

Her aunt took Bess's hand. "Oh, my dear, don't worry about me. I'm stronger than you think. Besides I can still handle your uncle if I have a mind to. If I was to stay in bed for a few days, and he had to take care of the milk and cream, I imagine he'd find someone pretty quick. Let's talk about you. If you left, where would you go?"

"To be honest, I'm not sure. I suppose I could always hire out as a housekeeper if I can't find a teaching job. Quite a few women my age are working up in Aspen or Glenwood Springs. I do, however, have another possibility. Jim Hart has asked me to marry him, but I'm not sure how I feel."

"Oh, I really like that young man! He has the kindest eyes, and he's got his own little ranch, and..."

"I know all that Aunt Myra," Bess interrupted. "But how can I tell if this is the right thing to do? His land is not the best, and the water rights are terrible. It's going to be hard to make a living on it, even combined with his father's place. And I have a greater concern. Remember how rude Mrs. Hart was when Jim took me to meet her? I'm not sure she'd ever accept me or anyone else, for that matter, as Jim's wife."

"Of course she will, Bess. You're so good, she's bound to come around. Once she gets to know you better, you'll be friends—you'll see. I want you to be happy, my dear. You need to be settled with a kind man who will provide a good home for you. You're twenty-two years old, and it's time you were having a family. I want you to have some babies to love. Don't worry about me and your brother. We'll be just fine. I have a few ideas up my sleeve."

"Well, there's Lin to consider, too, Aunt Myra. He's growing up so fast, and I feel I should be here for him, as well as you. I can hardly believe he'll be fifteen this year."

"Bess, please don't take this wrong, but Lin isn't your child. He shouldn't be a reason for you to give up a life of your own. Despite the conflict between you and your uncle, Lin and Elmer get along just fine. I know that Elmer is very fond of him. He's the son we never had, and he'll be fine and dandy. Besides, he can always visit you whenever he wants."

Bess later talked to Lin about Jim's proposal, and Aunt Myra's words rang sadly true. He really was more Elmer's son than her brother. Although he still had a semblance of boyish innocence, Bess could detect faint signs of Uncle Elmer's influence. Occasionally he would display the same demanding attitude, and Bess longed to shake him for his impolite behavior. Still, Aunt Myra was right. The moment for her influence was long gone. She had to let him go.

Bess's news had not surprised Lin. "Uncle Elmer said you'd soon be leavin' home. He figured Jim Hart'd be poppin' the question before long."

Bess resisted the urge to reach out and grab her brother. "Of course he won't admit the reason I might be leaving is because he's so nasty to me. I don't feel that I have many other choices, Lin. What do you think I should do?"

"Gee-willikers, Bess, don't ask me! I guess if you like him you should maybe marry him. It's not like you're gettin' any younger. He seems like a decent guy. As far as Uncle Elmer and you are concerned, you're both too stubborn. I don't let him bother me, and we get along just fine. Uncle Elmer says this will be mine someday, and I reckon I need to stay here to help out."

It had been almost four weeks since she and Jim went to the falls. She didn't know when he'd be coming to town. He was probably getting the last cutting of hay mowed, raked, and stacked. Bess was sure Jim couldn't go any place until the fall work was done. She wished there was an RFD mail route to Wallace Creek like there was for Morrisania and Battlement Mesa. She'd have to rely on someone picking up the mail when they were in town.

Bess wanted to make the commitment before she could change her mind. She'd considered talking to her mentor, Miss Hubbard. But, what would a spinster know about marriage? The teacher had devoted her life to teaching, and Bess feared she would be disappointed because Bess had chosen to teach only two years. In the end Bess had made the decision herself. Late on a September afternoon she walked into Grand Valley to post a letter. The envelope crinkled under her fingers. Bess had memorized every written word. This was a decision which would affect her for the rest of her life.

I hope it's the right one.

The answer to her letter arrived from Wallace Creek a few weeks later. She could tell that Jim was happy about her acceptance of his marriage proposal:

… I'm sorry I can't get away right now because the last cutting of hay still has to be stacked. I'll be up as soon as I can, I promise. We'll have to go to Glenwood Springs for the license, and I guess we could just get married there unless you want to come back to Grand Valley. Let me know what you want to do and I'll write again to tell you when I can get away…

Well, that was that. Bess felt some relief at the answer. Now she knew what path her life would be taking, good or bad. She stuffed the nagging doubts to the back of her mind. Jim Hart would be a good husband, and she'd work hard to be the best wife for him. She reminded herself that many people married for reasons other than passionate, romantic love. She'd just have to put her girlish notions aside. At least she'd have her own home, and she'd work hard to help Jim become as successful as Uncle Elmer.

Jim and Bess had exchanged a few letters by the middle of October when he wrote to say he would come for her on November 1. He planned to board the train at the Una station and meet Bess in Grand Valley. They'd go to Glenwood Springs for the marriage license.

Bess replied that the plan met with her approval. She thought they should get married there rather than coming back home, although she would have liked to have Aunt Myra and Lin at the wedding. The train schedule would make it difficult to get up there and back in the same day.

That meant there would be the extra expense of another room if they'd didn't get married there.

As usual, Bess was a realist.

On the morning of November 1, 1910, the No. 6 Denver & Rio Grande train pulled into the Grand Valley station promptly at 9:10 A.M. Jim jumped from the railroad coach almost before it stopped and ran over to where Bess, Aunt Myra, and Lin were standing. He grabbed her in his arms, but seeming to become bashful at his public display of affection, he ended with a swift kiss on her cheek.

"Welcome to our family, young man," Aunt Myra said in an trembling voice. "I know I don't have to tell you this, but we expect you to take care of our Bess. We love her a lot, don't we Lin?"

Lin ducked his head and murmured his agreement, while he shifted his weight from one foot to the other. He acted anxious to get the good-byes over with. Bess could see that he was eager to get on home.

"Yes, ma'am, I promise to take good care of her," Jim said. "The train will be through here about 11:35 A.M. tomorrow morning. However, we'll go on to Una, and then come back in a few days for Bess's stuff, so we'll visit with you then. Are you ready to get on board, Bess?"

Bess and Aunt Myra exchanged a long hug, and Bess felt her aunt press something into the palm of her hand. "Have yourself a nice wedding dinner tonight," Aunt Myra whispered in her ear. Bess could feel the crackle of paper and closed her fingers around the gift.

Lin reached over to give her a one-armed hug before taking his aunt's arm and propelling her toward their wagon. "We'll see you in a few days, Bessie," he called over his shoulder. "Bye Jim."

The train pulled from the station, and Bess sat down by Jim's side. She unfolded her hand to see a wad of bills. She counted out ten dollars and wiped away the tears from her cheeks. "Aunt Myra wants us to have a nice wedding supper tonight," she said with a trembling voice, "but that should also pay the hotel bill. She probably snuck this out of Uncle Elmer's stash of money that he has hidden somewhere. He'll be so mad if he finds out. Don't say anything to her in front of him or Lin. I'll have to find a time to thank her when she's alone."

Jim promised he wouldn't and held her hand while she grew quiet. They passed by the ranch, several miles outside of town, and she roused herself to smile at him. "Well, I guess this will be a great adventure, won't it? I promise I'll be the best wife I can possibly be."

Jim looked at Bess. "That goes for me, too. I know it won't be the easiest life for you. I don't have a lot of comforts like you've been used to at Horse Mountain or your uncle's. But, I'll work hard to make you happy. What kind of wedding do you want? Should we find a church?"

"No," Bess quickly responded. "Let's get our license and then find a justice of the peace. Maybe they can recommend someone at the clerk and recorder's office."

By midafternoon Jim and Bess left the Garfield County courthouse. They'd received the marriage license and been directed to a justice of peace a short distance away. Bess shivered as they walked to his office.

"You cold, Bess?"

"No, I guess I'm just a little nervous."

"Well, that's natural, wouldn't you say? I'd be nervous, too, if I wasn't so sure that you're the right lady for me."

I wish I could be so confident.

The ceremony was brief and impersonal. The justice of peace summoned his wife and sister-in-law to be the witnesses.

"Do you take this man to be your lawful husband?"

It's not too late to back out, Bess. Make up your mind!

"I do," Bess replied.

"Do you take this woman to be your lawful wife?"

"Yessir, I do," Jim said with a strong voice.

"I now pronounce you husband and wife. You may kiss the bride."

Jim gently planted a chaste kiss on Bess's lips. His look of adoration let her know she was loved. Jim paid the two dollar fee, and the newlyweds walked out.

"Where would you like to spend the night, Bess? The Hotel Glenwood is just a block away. I hear they have real good food. If your heart's set on it, we could go to the Hotel Colorado but it's pretty expensive."

"No, let's go to the Hotel Glenwood. We might be able to save some of Aunt Myra's money after we pay for the room and meals. We can use the rest to get groceries."

That night Bess laid in Jim's arms. Whatever doubts or concerns she had about her marriage, the intimate side of it wasn't one of them. Jim was a gentle lover, who patiently taught Bess the secrets of the marriage bed. She'd surprised herself, and likely her new husband, with her body's passionate

PASSENGERS FROM THE WALLACE CREEK AREA BOARDED THE TRAIN AT
UNA (PHOTO COURTESY OF JODY LINDAUER)

response. Bess didn't know this part of marriage could be so good. Aunt Myra, being too embarrassed, hadn't explained marital intimacy to Bess. Romance novels of the day rarely spoke about the sexual side of love, and then only in the most vague terms.

So this is what it's all about—wonderful!

Bess rolled over and was fast asleep.

> The Wallace Creek community rejoiced when the bridge over the Colorado River was completed in late 1910. It was 271 feet long, constructed of metal girders at a cost of $24,000. The joy, however, was short-lived. High water seriously damaged the center pier in the spring run-off of 1911, causing the bridge to settle so much that it was declared unfit for travel. The pier had to be reconstructed later in 1911.

Bess and Jim settled into their married life in the Wallace Creek community. The only real thorn was his mother. When Jim Hart brought his new wife home, Nellie Hart still treated Bess as if she didn't exist. On the few occasions when Bess accompanied Jim to the elder Hart's home, Nellie spoke in generalities or addressed her husband or son. Bess couldn't recall the woman ever speaking directly to her in those first months. The only acknowledgment Jim's mother made regarding his marriage was to stock a few household items before the couple arrived home from their wedding.

Bess was grateful for a clean change of linens and scrub rags because she immediately launched into a frenzy, cleaning what she called the "bear's den." Jim grinned as his new wife worked her way from the back to the front. Before he knew what hit him, he was outside in the chill air trying to build a clothesline. Bess next instructed him to find some wash tubs and bring in plenty of water. She stripped the bed, towels, and anything else that was washable. She was sure the dirty fabric could stand by itself. When he found a plausible reason to escape, Jim departed for the barn and corrals, leaving Bess in the kitchen scrubbing her knuckles raw on the washboard. After several days of hard work Bess was reasonably satisfied with the cleanliness of her honeymoon house.

When they picked up Bess's belongings in Grand Valley, they also picked up some supplies. Jim had eaten his big noontime meal with the elder Harts. He hadn't stocked food in the house aside from stale crackers, sardines, and other sundry stuff which, Bess determined, should be thrown out. She was dismayed at how much it cost to feed a household and planned to plant a huge garden next summer. Bess purchased only the essential things and was grateful for the charge account at Doll Brothers and Smith. When she unpacked her clothes, she was touched to find that Aunt Myra has tucked numerous jars of fruit, vegetables, and jelly into the folds of the cloth. That dear sweet woman likely knew provisions would be scant those first months.

"Thank you, Aunt Myra," Bess whispered under her breath.

1911

West Slope water users up in arms over a decision rendered by Grand County District Court Judge McCall in early 1911. The ruling said that no matter where Colorado residents lived they might divert water from streams flowing through Western Colorado if they possessed water rights to the river. The Henrylyn Company diverted water from the Williams Fork of the Grand River and sent it through a tunnel under the Continental Divide. This diversion may have been one of the first occurrences of East Slope interests taking West Slope water.

Bess and Jim were formally introduced as husband and wife to the Wallace Creek community at a New Year's dance, which was held at the Wallace Creek schoolhouse. Of course, no one was surprised. The news made its sweep of the area shortly after they arrived home. Several women had waved to Bess as they rumbled by on the road to Battlement Mesa. The ladies reported to their friends that you could actually see how the Hart windows gleamed in the sunlight. Many ladies privately thought Bess brave to marry into the Hart family with Nellie being such a bad-tempered sort of person.

When they arrived at the dance Bess and Jim heard the musicians tuning up. People nearest the door greeted them. Bess exchanged pleasantries with a few of the women whom she'd met while at Horse Mountain Ranch.

"Congratulations, Bess," Aggie Strong said. "I guess you'll now be with us permanently. Have you seen Isabelle Stuart yet?"

"No, I haven't spoken to her, but I did send her a note when Jim and I set the date. I plan to go see her this coming week."

The men pumped Jim's hand.

"It's a good thing the weather's been so cold," drawled one man. "Otherwise you'd be given a proper welcome with a good old-fashioned shivy-ree. Doesn't mean we still cain't do it, eh Mother?" The woman shook her head and winked at Bess while steering her husband toward the dance floor.

Bess questioned Jim as he led her out for the first dance. "What was he talking about?"

"Don't you know what a newlywed shivaree is? That's where they wait until you turn the lights out and go to bed. Then they start bangin' on pots and pans until you're forced to get up and let them in. Usually you can't get rid of them until they're fed. It's all in fun, and I've participated in a few myself. I guess it would be payback for me."

Whatever the reason, the community apparently decided it was far too cold to brave a wintry night just for the sake of some cake and coffee. Jim and Bess were spared the indignities of such an event and left alone to settle in as any other married couple on the creek.

Bess eagerly looked forward to their nighttime lovemaking. She could forget all her daytime struggles while being carried away by on a wave of desire. She knew that Jim was delighted by her response. It was the only time she felt totally unreserved and able to meet Jim's love with a personal part of herself.

Jim and Bess worked hard to make a good home and ranch those first months of 1911. The winter weather was warm and dry. Jim hoped for a wet spring to make up for the lack of moisture, so their puny water share for the upper fields might stretch into the summer.

That spring she learned to mend fences and repair an old broken-down shed for a chicken coop. Still, that paled in contrast to the first time she helped pull a calf. Jim was having trouble getting his big hands in to turn the little critter who was coming out with one foot back and one foot forward. He ran up the field yelling for Bess to come help him. She followed him with her heart pounding. She'd never done anything with Uncle Elmer's cattle, so she didn't have a clue what was expected.

"You can do this, Bess. Your hands are so much smaller than mine. Just slip your hand into her and gently push the calf back a bit."

"I can't make it move, Jim," said Bess, her body shaking. "I don't know how to move it," she wailed.

"Listen to me, and I'll tell you what to do. Just pay attention. You'll have to wait until the contraction is over and then move the leg back so you can get it straightened out. Just give it a good shove. You're strong, and you can do it."

Jim walked her through each step. She felt the wall of the cow's uterus closing in on her arm. As the cow relaxed, Bess finally felt the little body shifting and she could touch the other leg. "I can feel it!" she squealed. "I think I can move it out now." Bess gently folded the leg under the calf until it could pass through the opening and be pulled out along with the other one.

"Good work, Bess. Move aside so I can help this old cow. She's about played out. Run up to the house and get some gunny sacks from the barn. We'll need to help get the little fellow dried and on its feet."

She felt so happy at being able to save a new life. She was even happier that she could be an active ranch wife for her husband.

Bess planted a big garden and hoped there would be enough water to irrigate. In the spring they would fill an underground cistern from a ditch carrying water from Pete and Bill Creek. That would have to last them for the summer unless they wanted to haul water from the dirty Grand River. Not one ounce of water could be wasted. Bess's dish, bath, and wash water went around the young spring plants popping up from the ground. She was bound they'd survive so the small cellar would be filled with good produce by the time fall came.

A rancher had a sow who couldn't feed all her litter, and he gave Bess a starving piglet. Jim begged skim milk from his mother until the animal could eat on his own. Bess intended to feed him all summer until he was a good-sized pig who'd be big enough to butcher in the fall. She also paid several dollars to a neighbor lady for some hens and an old rooster, who admirably performed their duties. The eggs hatched out in due time, and Bess had a start on a little flock of chickens.

> The Balzac Bridge was completed over the Grand River west of Webster Hill in 1910 and taken out by high water in the spring of 1911. The ensuing litigation lasted some years while the residents of that community were without a bridge. Members of the Seventh Day Adventist Church formed a colony to the south of the river. The settlement, which was called Rulison in honor of an early settler, boasted a store, a schoolhouse, and a railroad siding. Farmers shipped out twenty-five cars of beets, twenty-two cars of potatoes, and fifteen cars of apples.

1912

"Please Jim, I really want to go to the New Year's party at Cecil and Ila Smith's. I'm dying to see their new log home. I don't think it will hurt me to go. I'll be careful."

Jim was concerned about Bess riding the few miles in her advanced pregnancy, but he finally gave in to her plea. He was also hankering to attend the biggest party of the year. He put some hay in the wagon and hitched up the team for the ride. The crunch of the wheels on the snow-packed road created a rhythmic sound as the horses trotted west toward the Smith place. When they arrived Bess hurried into the house while Jim unharnessed the horses, put saddle blankets on, and tied them to the wagon bed. The horses could munch on the hay through the anticipated long night. A line of similar wagons were already parked in the Smith barnyard.

The fiddler, having started his celebrating early, was in no condition to carry out his duties. Other musicians came from Grand Valley in a spring wagon, which delayed the dancing for an hour or so. Everyone enjoyed visiting, so the time passed quickly before the music started. The women toured the snug, two-story house, admiring all the tight windows which kept out the cold drafts. Aunt Ila beamed with the compliments. She'd lived in a variety of dwellings while in Aspen. This house was just what she wanted. Children raced up and down the stairs, which was a novelty to some. They finally wore themselves out and were bedded down in the upstairs bedrooms.

Bess and Jim danced a slow waltz or two but sat out the more lively square dancing because of Bess's condition. It was pleasant simply being with other people. There were few social opportunities in their otherwise drab ranch life.

Once the frigid winter morning dawned, the women accompanied Ila Smith to her kitchen to prepare a hearty breakfast before everyone left for their homes and the morning chores. Bess and Jim hurried home and hastened to do the chores so they could nap for a while. She remembered thinking they'd not be able to do that once there was a baby to care for.

● ● ● ● ● ● ● ● ●

The storm finally struck, and the view outside was a scene of solid white. No telling when they'd again see the bare ground, although it was the last of April 1912. Bess sat rocking the tiny baby close by the kitchen stove, the only heat source in the small house. If they continuously fed the fire, a little heat escaped to the bedroom. Bess, however, kept the baby's small basket near the stove where she could be sure her baby girl would be warm.

This was the coldest winter in many a year, and Bess felt she'd been chilled for months. The wintry blasts came through the bare board walls in spite of the old newspapers that Bess tacked up between the studs. Before next year she hoped to find better insulation, even if it was mud or straw plaster.

The baby, Kitty, had been born fussy. Bess tried to keep up the household and comfort the crying child since her birth in late February. Bess, a new mother, struggled with frequent bouts of feeling incompetent. She knew it must be her imagination, but she often felt the baby was struggling against her. Kitty complained even while nursing, and Bess would have suspected she wasn't getting enough to eat if not for the child's weight gain. She was a healthy baby, albeit a cranky one. The fact that Nellie Hart was able to soothe the baby better than anyone else heightened Bess's sense of inadequacy and resentment.

"Damn! That storm is a wooly-bugger!" Jim loudly exclaimed as he came in the door on a blast of frigid air. "I'm sure glad I got the stock tended to 'fore it hit."

The baby jumped from the unexpected noise and started howling again. "See what you've done," Bess angrily replied. "I finally got her to sleep, and now I'll have to start all over."

"Sorry, Bess. Let me get my coat off and warm up a little then I'll spell you for a while. Ma was comin' over today, but it's too cold to be out even for her favorite granddaughter."

"Well, I can be thankful for small favors," Bess muttered under her breath.

"What's that?"

"Oh nothing, I was just grumbling about the storm."

Bess's mother-in-law had become a regular visitor after the baby's birth. To Bess's surprise Nellie Hart arrived the day after the baby was born, and she'd been coming over several times a week or more. Nellie had even thawed toward Bess, although she was still far from affectionate. She saved her wholehearted love and attention for the baby. Kitty responded in kind to her grandmother.

When Nellie walked in and picked Kitty up, she soon grew quiet, no matter how fussy. As much as Bess appreciated the few moments of peace and quiet, she deeply resented that her mother-in-law could do for the child what she was unable to do.

"Some fellows were by the folks' today. They've been examining the ice on the river and said it's frozen a solid two feet, even in the swifter parts. I don't believe I can remember a time when that's happened."

"I can hardly wait for the spring thaw," replied Bess, shivering. "I've never been so cold in my entire life. I wasn't this miserable when I was walking three miles to school. It's snowed every day this past month, and it looks like it will dump another batch tonight."

Jim folded Bess and the baby into his arms. "I know it's been hard on you with the baby and all. We should start seeing some signs of spring in another few weeks. May is sure to bring some warmer weather. Just try to be patient."

Standing in the circle of her husband's arms Bess felt guilty about her constant complaints when he was the one suffering most from the frigid weather. Every day he and his father had to be out in it to tend and feed the stock. They spent hours clearing ice off the water holes on the slough, which froze over as soon as the old ice was cleared. The hay that had looked to be so abundant last fall was getting dangerously close to the end. Bess knew Jim was worried about running out of feed. He didn't have the ready cash to buy additional hay if the snow and cold lasted for another month. The cattle would have to fend for themselves, and probably die of starvation, or Jim would have to find someone who was willing to trade livestock for hay. The problem was finding another rancher who had an abundance of feed. Everyone was running short.

Jim took the baby from Bess, while she punched down the bread, which was threatening to rise over the bowl. As she went about her work, she kept glancing at Jim and their small daughter. He was a good father as well as a kind and loving husband. Being his wife was easy. Jim made no demands upon her and was generally even tempered. Bess was mostly happy and contented except for the occasional middle-of-the night nagging doubts. Her feelings toward him and their marriage remained loving, if not excited. She had looked forward to her child, thinking it would help to cement her life with Jim. Now, she wasn't so sure.

Bess stoked up the stove and thought how glad she was they'd gone to the New Year's party. It now seemed so long ago. As she looked out the window at the solid wall of white, she wondered if spring would ever come.

One of the premier events in Garfield County was a Glenwood Springs to Basalt bicycle race sponsored by the Colorado Midland Railroad. The fifteenth annual race, held August 4, 1912, featured seventeen riders from throughout the area. Fred Halbouer of Grand Junction won with the best time of one hour, fourteen minutes.

A special excursion train followed the racers for part of the race. Other special events included bands from Grand Junction and Marble with special soloists, a tightrope walker who crossed on a wire strung over the Grand River, and a high-dive artist who plunged into the river. Onlookers held their breaths while waiting for him to surface from the treacherous water and swim to the shore.

The baseball game between Glenwood Springs and Palisade was won by the latter. A young man from Aspen won the pushmobile race that day. His name was Lawrence Elisha, and he would later become one of the most prominent owners of the famous Jerome Hotel in Aspen.

1913

> Western Slope wet and dry factions bickered back and forth in 1913 about whether towns should allow the sale of alcoholic beverages. Newspaper editors, capitalizing on the controversy, wrote scathing editorials about liquor establishments within their city limits. Town elections had been previously held, and the measure went down in defeat for another year. However, the town of Grand Valley eventually had two voting precincts. The one that encompassed most of the town was pro-prohibition, and all the surrounding area was generally pro-liquor.

"Look at your cake, Sweet Baby. Do you know you're one year old, today?" Nellie Hart cuddled the red-haired child in her arms while she called her attention to the angel food cake sitting on the kitchen table. She'd asked Jim and Bess to bring Kitty over for her first birthday, declaring they had to have a birthday party for her. The cold and snow had abated for the day, so Bess bundled Kitty up and they quickly walked less than a mile to the elder Hart place.

Kitty, while less fussy, was still a temperamental child who tested Bess on a daily basis. To see Kitty with her grandmother, however, one would swear she was the most angelic child in the world. Why did she have to have such a strong affinity for Nellie Hart, of all people? Bess loved her child and yearned for the same connection. The more she tried, however, the less Kitty seemed to draw close.

What's the matter with me that my little girl would rather have her grandmother than me? The only thing Kitty shares with me is her looks. She really is a beautiful child with her peaches and cream complexion and red hair. The only thing of Jim's are her brown eyes. The Kelly blood lives on through her.

"Come darling, there are some presents on the table for you. Let Grammy help you with the wrapping. See the little puppy dog I made you? You'll look so sweet in your new dress. Here, Grammy's going to put it on so we can see what a pretty girl you are."

"Don't you think you should wait until she eats her cake, Mother Hart? She'll get it all dirty." Bess looked at the pair with envy.

"Oh tish, what's a few cake crumbs? Her Grammy will wash and iron it again if you don't want to."

Bess started to protest but bit her tongue, as she often did when around her mother-in-law. Both her husband and father-in-law had learned to defer to Nellie Hart. They seemed oblivious to her rude behavior toward Bess, which had gone from outright silence to the more recent sarcasm.

Be still, Bess. You know Jim wants peace at any price.

"A small herd of deer came through the place this morning," said Big Jim. "They didn't look too poor. We should take the rifle and go see if we can get one. Some fresh meat would taste mighty good right now."

"I thought the deer season was closed until 1918,"said Bess. "I read that they need to preserve the few deer herds until they can again build up their numbers."

"Well, a blamed law shouldn't keep a man from gettin' food for his family's table," chuckled Big Jim with a sidelong look at his son. "What does the state know about our needs? A lot of people would starve if they couldn't hunt. Besides, they're comin' down to eat in our hay fields. Why do you think we put up fences around the hay stacks? It's tough enough feeding our cattle without feeding all the deer on the creek. I guess if they eat our hay, we've got a right to eat 'em."

Bess kept quiet. She knew that her father-in-law was expressing the same viewpoint as every other rancher in Western Colorado. Nevertheless, she was troubled that he would break the law without a thought. What if the game warden caught them? How would they pay the fines? Jim sensed her distress and attempted to soothe her.

"Well, I reckon we could go out in a day or two just to see if the herd's staying down in the river fields. Don't worry Bess, we'll be careful. Unless there's a snitch on the creek, no one would think of turning in their neighbor for doing what they're also doing. We stick together."

A few days later a fresh hindquarter of venison appeared on the Hart tables. Bess admitted that it was a welcome change, and she knew that many poor ranchers would go hungry if not for poaching. But it did seem strange that Aspen folks were importing elk from Wyoming to multiply the local herds, while farmers and ranchers continued to hunt the game whenever they chose.

> In May 1913 the DeBeque Bank vault was blown up, but the robbers were scared away before they could carry off the strongbox containing ten thousand dollars.

It was a hot July day. Jim and Big Jim had just gotten the first cutting of hay raked. They were leaving the house after lunch when they saw a number of vehicles going back and forth on the newly built road on the north side of the river. The last time Jim was in Grand Valley he'd heard the Indiana Automobile Manufacturers' Association was driving nineteen cars through their area to the Pacific Coast, but didn't know what date it was going to be.

Jim stood in the front yard and looked across the river. "I wonder if they're gettin' ready for those cars to come through? Do you want to go see what's up?"

"Just a minute," Bess replied. "Let me put the dishpan on the back of the stove." Taking off her apron, she climbed up on the wagon to which Big Jim had hitched the horses. Jim lifted Kitty up to Bess and then squatted on the rim of the wagon bed as they lumbered over to the elder Hart's place.

"Ma, you want to ride over and see the autos go through? I think they must be arriving soon from the look of the traffic on the road."

"Give me a minute, Son. I need to wash off the apricot jam, and I'll be right with you."

Bess and the baby moved to the back of the wagon with Jim while Big Jim helped Nellie onto the high seat.

There were a number of vehicles already parked along the road when they arrived. Some had hurried from town in advance of the auto caravan so they could observe the vehicles again. Others were folks from around Wallace Creek who'd had advance warning.

"Hey there, folks, if your horses are skittish, you might want to park back from the road. We try to warn people ahead of time because some have gotten hurt by runaways." The speaker was an advance-man for the caravan.

"I doubt that my team will much care," replied Jim. "They're accustomed to the noise of the trains. Will the cars be louder than that?"

"I doubt it, but I thought you should be warned, just in case."

They didn't have long to wait. The first of the vehicles was seen coming over a rise, followed by one after the other. When the caravan drivers spotted the observers, their squawky horns blared. Soon all were honking nonstop, which produced a commotion unlike any Bess had ever heard. Kitty set up a howl of terror and refused to be comforted, even by Nellie.

Jim had his hands full with the team of horses, who may have been accustomed to trains but this blaring noise was altogether different. Other teams were also acting up, some more than others. Kitty, meanwhile, was rivaling the horns with her screams.

The caravan was only halfway through the intersection when Jim turned the team around and headed for home. The horses, grateful to be going away from the terrifying noise, needed no encouragement to trot home at a fast clip. By the time the family arrived at the elder Hart's, Kitty was still sniffling but had stopped her screaming. As Jim and Bess continued on to their house, they agreed that was enough excitement for one day!

● ● ● ● ● ● ● ● ●

Bess traveled over the new road when she went to see Aunt Myra one late August day and discovered it significantly cut her travel time. Her aunt loved seeing Kitty, even though the temperamental child was cranky. Bess was happy to find her aunt and brother about the same as when she'd seen them in late spring. Aunt Myra surprised her by taking her through the kitchen where Gus White's wife, Emmy, was preparing batches of green beans for canning. Aunt Myra giggled when questioned but couldn't be coaxed to share her secret of getting Uncle Elmer's permission to hire some kitchen help.

However she did it, I'm grateful for one less thing to worry about.

Bess and Jim went up to the Horse Mountain Ranch several times during the summer. They took Kitty with them for the annual fall get-together, and the little girl was charmed by the Stuart children. Seventeen-year-old Josephine supervised the baby's care while the grown-ups visited. She had finally grown into a pretty young woman who showed promise of rivaling her mother's beauty. She confided to Bess that she hoped to pass the state boards and become a teacher. Bess was greatly pleased by the news and grew nostalgic as she remembered back five years when she'd first met the family. The children were growing so fast, even nine-year-old Bibby. The little girl, still enchanting, was beginning to find her own independence.

When Bess looked around the prosperous ranch, she compared her own home with that of Isabella Stuart's. Next to the affluence of the Horse Mountain house, her place looked very shabby. While pangs of guilt stung Bess for her silent criticism of their home, she still felt resentment.

Jim and I work harder than any two people on the Horse Mountain Ranch. It doesn't seem quite fair that some people have so much and some so little, no matter how hard they try. I thought it would be easy to get ahead, but even though I'm doing everything I can, it still isn't happening. Three years later and we're still no further ahead. It's very discouraging.

The DeBeque and Grand Valley areas crawled with petroleum and oil shale promoters who believed the up-and-coming auto industry would soon require vast amounts of oil and gas. Everyone was in the hills staking out placer claims or wheeling-dealing with other promoters. If Jim wasn't so busy on the two ranches, Bess thought he might have been tempted to traipse off with the others. Men found that sort of exploration exciting. Bess supposed it was akin to striking a rich gold claim.

Unlike the previous year, there was little rain from March through November 1913. The riverfront fields fared better, but Jim's upper fields, dependent on the few shares of water, had done poorly. They'd be lucky to have enough feed to last the winter, especially if it was another bad one.

In October Jim sold off the steers and a few older cows, which provided them a little ready cash to pay off the grocery bill at Doll Brothers Store. He'd saved back fourteen dollars to prove up on the homestead claim that he'd filed in 1908. It had taken five years, but his land would soon be free and clear. Jim was proud of his accomplishments, and Bess gave him verbal support. Privately she wished there were enough money to improve their home. That, however, would have to wait for a better financial year.

"Ya know, Bess, maybe we should have you file an eighty-acre desert claim on the land that lays east of us. I understand a lot of the women on Battlement Mesa are doing that. It doesn't have any water rights, but we might be able to use it for winter or spring graze. I've taken all my one hundred sixty acres so I can't file on any more homestead land, but you haven't used your entitlement."

Bess, never one to turn down a possible land acquisition, agreed. Early on a November morning she and Jim left Kitty with her grandma. Big Jim hitched up the team to drive them over the river to the Una Crossing. The couple boarded the eastbound train for Glenwood Springs. There was some talk, mostly from Si Herwick, about getting a land office established in Grand Valley, but it hadn't happened yet. When they emerged from the land office that day Jim looked pleased as punch about their land addition.

"By damn, Bess, I never thought I'd actually own land and now look at us—we both own some! It's a mighty good feeling, let me tell ya. No one can take it away from us as long as we scrape together the property tax payment every year. We can even borrow against it…"

"Over my dead body!" Bess snapped. "That's the best way in the world for a person to lose their place. What happens if we have a really bad year and can't make the mortgage payment? That banker will be at our place quicker than you can spit. No, we'll just have to either save up for what we need or do without."

Jim looked at his wife with amazement, but he couldn't keep the pride out of his voice. "You're right as usual, Bess. We can't risk losing what we've worked so hard to get."

The Hart family's needs were relatively few that fall because Bess's garden provided much of the yearly food supply. Another pig and the flock of chickens helped to round out their diets. The best present was a milk cow, which Bess had yearned for. A family on Spring Creek moved into Grand Valley and didn't have a place to keep it, so Jim had been able to make a good deal. The fresh milk, cream, butter, and cheese added greatly to the family table.

On the last day of 1913 Bess tossed away the old calendar and decided the year had been partly bad, partly good. A blast of cold December air reminded her that she hadn't been able to cover up all the holes in the drafty house. There simply wasn't enough money to buy lumber for the inside walls. Bess had tried to seal all the cracks with grass and adobe mud. Many were too small to chink, yet let in large gusts of cold air. She bundled Kitty up day and night, afraid that she might catch pneumonia. Thankfully the little girl was very healthy.

Bess sighed as she thought longingly back to previous New Year's festivities. There was a dance in Grand Valley but she and Jim had decided to stay home. *I wonder if we made the right decision? It might have been fun to get out and see others, although it doesn't seem worth the effort.*

> R. J. Reynolds introduced Camel cigarettes in 1913. Experts agree that it was probably the first of the various ready-made commercial cigarettes to be extensively advertised. However, it wasn't until 1921 that the famous slogan "I'd walk a mile for a Camel" was created.

1914

Headlines from Grand Junction *The Daily Sentinel,* April 14, 1914:

"NEWCASTLE SECTION MAN KILLED IN FREIGHT WRECK ON "NIGGER" HILL EARLY YESTERDAY MORNING. FINN CRUSHED BY MACHINERY; SCION OF RICH FAMILY."

The article reported that six cars went off the track while approaching the dangerous, sharp curve a few miles east of DeBeque, and rolled down the thirty-foot embankment. Charles Makt was riding under a boiler on a flat car and was crushed when the car derailed. His companion stated that he was the son of a wealthy family in Finland and had been in the United States only a few years.

It was Saturday night, and that meant it was bath night. The galvanized wash tub had been brought in earlier from the porch, so the metal would have time to get warm. Although it was mid-April the temperature was cool enough to make the warmth of the kitchen stove welcome.

Big kettles of water boiled on the stove. Bess and Jim filled the good-size tub, and then it was Kitty's turn.

"Come, Kitty, get in before it cools off."

"Ow, ow, ow!" The toddler yelped and danced around. "Mama, hot!"

"Oh nonsense, I tested it with my elbow. It's just fine."

Jim called from the parlor, "Your mother doesn't think you can get clean unless you scald off the first layer of skin."

Kitty was finally persuaded to sit in the water, and Bess sudsed the wash cloth with a bar of homemade soap. Every crease and dimple of the little girl's body was scrubbed by her mother.

"Step out and I'll wrap you in the towel. Then we'll put on your clean nighty. Mmmm, you smell so good. Go give your daddy a kiss." Bess tucked Kitty into bed. "Do you need anything? You'd better speak up because I don't want you running out to the kitchen in five minutes. Daddy and I are going to bathe."

Jim was next. He completed his bath while Bess kept busy in the bedroom. It was one thing to explore your spouse's body under cover of darkness, it was another to view the human body folded into the small confines of the wash tub!

Finally, it was Bess's turn. She would have preferred to completely empty the tub and start fresh, but that was a waste of good water. She compromised by dipping out several small pails, setting them aside to scrub the floor. Two pails of new hot water made the tub almost fresh.

Bess draped several towels over the kitchen chairs, making a cozy space in which she could enjoy the momentary satisfaction of soaking her tired body. She thought she knew why she'd been feeling so worn out.

Later, Jim laid in bed, and watched Bess brush her hair before she plaited it into one thick braid. "You do that every night, don't you? I've seen you brush your hair when you were too tired to move. How come you do it?"

Bess had been thinking of another subject, and it took her a little time to focus her thoughts on Jim's question. "It's very simple, the more you brush your hair, the shinier it is."

"Well, it's working! Your hair is beautiful, Bess."

"Thank you," she said in an absentminded way.

Bess slipped under the covers, welcoming the blessed feel of lying flat. "I have something to tell you."

"Oh?" Jim replied. "Okay, tell me…or do I have to guess?"

"What would you say if I told you we might have a baby around Christmastime?"

"Bess, honey, are you serious? Why that's great news! At least I think it is. How do you feel about it?"

"I'm happy about it. Kitty's two years old, and I think this is a good time to have another baby. Maybe I'll be able to give you a son. I've been very tired lately. That's what tipped me off."

"Well, you'll just have to take it easy."

"If you can tell me how to take care of a two-year-old, tend a garden, and do my housework, I'll be glad to take it easy. We'd better get some sleep."

Maybe I'll have a baby who's mine this time. A baby that will love me the most.

●　●　●　●　●　●　●　●　●

The warm May sun helped to reduce the chill from the breeze blowing off the edge of the mesa. The hay fields looked brilliant green as Bess started the team down the road from the Horse Mountain Ranch. She and Kitty were returning from a visit with Isabella Stuart. Mrs. Stuart had given Bess an open invitation to come borrow books any time, and she gratefully accepted the offer. Her own few books had been read so many times she believed she could actually recite them from memory. The basket at her feet contained not only enough books for a month or so but many recent newspapers, which Bess and Jim couldn't afford to buy. Bess wasn't sure she'd have much time to read with all the summer work, but at least she'd be able to read a few pages each night.

A sack behind the seat contained some of Bibby's outgrown clothes, which Mrs. Stuart thought Bess might want to put back for Kitty. Bess took them although Nellie usually kept the child well supplied with everything she needed. It was hard to imagine a little girl more indulged than Kitty. Every time Bess mentioned this fact to Jim he reminded her that his mother had been given a new lease on life with the birth of the child.

I know Jim's mother believes Kitty was sent to make up for her daughter Mary's death. I also know I'm fighting a losing battle, and I need to keep silent. It wouldn't be fair to deny the child something that we aren't able to afford. I wonder, though, what will happen when Kitty asks for something I don't think she should have—when I have to say no? Will I be able to battle both her and her grandmother?

Another sack contained some discarded adult clothing, which Bess was most grateful for. She was reluctant to spend their few precious dollars on clothing for herself and Jim. His old mackinaw coat had been mended so many times it was barely more than patches upon patches. A new one cost up to fifteen dollars, a vast sum of money, so she'd continued to add fabric. Mrs. Stuart hesitated to make the offer, but Bess assured her she would welcome anything from which she could either convert into other clothing or make rag rugs and quilts. One way of keeping some of the drafts out would be to put down as many rugs as possible. This would be even more important because she calculated the baby would be due in December.

Mrs. Stuart promised to save all the newspapers for Bess so she could add more layers to the inside walls after she'd also read them. She wanted to move Kitty into the other bedroom before winter, and the walls needed all the insulation she could find.

Bess was very grateful for Mrs. Stuart's friendship and generosity. Bess knew the older woman cared for her and was sincerely interested in helping her out. Some people might have been offended by the so-called charity donations. Bess knew she couldn't be choosy about that sort of thing, so gratefully took them.

Mrs. Stuart never made her feel inferior for accepting the used items. Jim didn't question where things came from. He was far too preoccupied with his own problems of eking out a living on their hardscrabble ranch.

The lengthening spring sun allowed Bess and Jim to sit outside that evening and read some of the area newspapers. Curious two-year-old Kitty toddled around the yard, filling a small pail with dirt. Jim, as usual, read just the farm and market reports or news of the latest government grazing fees, which had been raised to twenty-seven cents per head for cattle. Bess started at the front and read every word on the page, articles and ads alike. She wanted the experience to last as long as possible.

Each paper contained articles about the bootlegging, prostitution, and gambling in Western Slope towns that had voted to go dry. The battle raged about the pros and cons of the issue. Another article reported how a Palisade minister was missing and believed to be a ringleader in a diamond theft gang operating out of Texas.

A travelogue on the Panama Canal fascinated Bess. She imagined herself being one of the wealthy passengers who rode the luxury ships through the canal, while viewing the lush fauna and flora of the area. Bess sighed as she acknowledged she would never be that person.

Spared a late freeze, fruit growers were looking forward to a bumper crop in the Grand Junction area. Bess thought that it was fine for the folks with good irrigation projects, but the Hart's crop success depended on snowpack in the mountains. This spring there was still plenty of snow on the Battlement Reserve. Each year they raced the edge between too much and not enough water. Most of Western Colorado's agriculture went through the same challenge.

"Hey, Bess, the paper says that honey is selling at twelve pounds for a dollar. That's not bad. Dad and I were talkin' the other day about gettin' a few hives. Maybe we could get some extra use out of our alfalfa. The bees should do good down on the lower fields."

"Just as long as you don't expect me to handle them," Bess laughed. "I'm scared to death of bees. I got stung by a swarm when I was young, and I swelled up something terrible. I wouldn't want Kitty to be close to them, either."

"I could always put them on the eastern edge of the lower field. I doubt they'd get up this way. There's not enough vegetation here. I think Nels Good has quite a few hives. Maybe I'll ride over to his place one of these days and see if I can buy or trade for some."

"You know what I'd love to have? A few fruit trees would be nice, especially an apple tree. I miss not having good canned or dried apples to use over the winter."

"Well, why don't you just get some from Ma? She's always got more than she needs."

"Because I thought she'd offer if she wanted me to have them, and she never has."

"I don't think she's thought of it. Why don't I ask her?"

Yes, you do that! You can't see what that woman is really like or else you choose not to see. The only person she's generous with is your daughter. If you were to tell her that it's for Kitty she'd give us a ton.

Assertive about all other issues regarding their life, Bess held her tongue and failed to say the things that she felt about her mother-in-law.

I'd like to tell Jim how I feel, but I'm not sure how to explain so he'd understand. Some of the things she says to me she also says to Jim or his dad, and they don't even pay attention. Maybe I'm too thin-skinned, but it hurts when she makes me feel so inferior. I thought she'd grow to like me—Aunt Myra said she would. After four years I've given up hope that she will. At first I was sad she wouldn't give me a chance, but now it just makes me mad. The answer is to stay away from her as much as possible.

That fall the Wallace Creek and Una families all came together for a big potluck picnic at the newly built Wallace Creek School, which replaced the older, smaller one. The largest room contained a stage at one end. On one side was a cloak room, on the other side a library. A smaller room could be used for another classroom or a kitchen. The women thought they should have a kitchen. There would be many dances or other entertainments which would require them to serve food. Teachers could also use it for extra heat during the winter months or to supplement the children's meals.

The September day was sunny and bright, growing warm by mid-afternoon. Some of the men sawed up cords of wood for the coming winter. Others painted and repaired the first school, now used as a barn, and the outhouses. The women sat inside and discussed what items they could contribute to the kitchen. One of the first things they'd need was a big boiler or coffeepot to boil the coffee. Everyone knew you couldn't have a dance without gallons of coffee. Others pledged tea towels, coffee, sugar, and cooking utensils. If they could get everything gathered, they'd be all set up by the first dance, which was to be held in several weeks.

Bess rubbed the small of her back which ached from the day's activities. Her pregnancy was obvious to everyone.

"I can see that you won't be dancing too much longer, Bess," said Ila Smith. "When are you due?"

"I think around Christmas time," replied Bess. "I've felt pretty well with this one. I haven't been as sick as I was with Kitty. I do hate having a winter baby, though. It's so hard keeping them well. I guess we don't get to pick when the children come, do we?"

The conversation shifted to having and taking care of children—things common to each woman. Danger was never very far from young children, either by accident or illness. Mothers knew that having babies was a gamble at best. The cemeteries were full of little graves. Although either Dr. Staley or Dr. Miller would come out from Grand Valley to help in the delivery, someone would have to go get them. The travel time usually resulted in the baby being born before the doctor arrived. Each woman learned to cherish her female friends who could be available to assist or even deliver the child in the doctor's absence.

"Have you asked anyone to help you out, Bess?"

"I think Minerva Jones will be there. She lives pretty close to us, and Jim could stop at her place on the way into town, if he goes by way of Battlement Mesa. She helped me with Kitty, and I didn't have a bit of trouble. I guess she helped her husband deliver a lot of babies when she was married to the doctor."

The conversation stopped abruptly as it always did when a divorced couple was mentioned. It was 1914 but it was still unacceptable to divorce one's spouse for any reason. Bess privately wondered about Minerva's divorce and subsequent second marriage, but if anyone knew the reason it was never discussed. It didn't matter to Bess. She just needed assurance that someone, whom she could trust, would be with her.

The harvest was productive. Sufficient hay was stacked in the fields, the little rock cellar brimmed with the bounty from Bess's garden, and several hams hung in the elder Hart's smokehouse. A few steers were sold, and the cash went to pay the grocery bill. It would be run up again during the coming year. Although she didn't know when, Bess could count on the fact that some fresh venison would appear one of these days.

One day Bess was surprised by Jim driving the wagon into the yard with a load of used lumber. "Jim," she exclaimed as she flew out the door, "Dear Man! Where did you find the wood?" She'd been talking to him about the need to put something on the inside walls of the second bedroom which was the furthest from the stove. It was time for Kitty to move out of their room and into her own bed. The new baby would be taking Kitty's place in Bess and Jim's room.

"You know that old house on the road up to Battlement Mesa? No one's lived there in a long time. I think the homestead has been turned back to the government. The wood ain't very good looking, but I guess it'll keep the drafts out for Kitty. Ma's been having a fit about us moving her into that cold room without some lining on the walls."

Bess felt like she'd been dipped in ice water. She hadn't been able to persuade Jim, but his mother snapped her fingers and Jim hurried to obey. Bess tried to be happy about the wood. She'd wanted it for so long, but her victory now felt bitter. She turned and walked away.

How does Mother Hart get Jim to do things, when he won't do them for me? His mother still controls him, and I end up feeling frustrated. It makes me so blamed mad!

• • • • • • • • •

Christmas was approaching. Jim cut a little pinon tree up on Dry Mesa and brought it home. Bess popped corn and made some paper chains to decorate it, but there were no candles or holders. She searched around for other things to put on the bare little tree. Alas, her assortment of decorative items was sadly sparse. Looking out the kitchen window, she spied a barrel where they stored the few tobacco tins and other cans until Jim found time to take them to a dump site up in the gulch.

"Jim, you have some tin snips, don't you?"

He looked at Bess blankly. "Well, yeah, I've got tin snips. Why do you ask?"

"Never you mind. Just go get them and a pair of your heavy gloves. On your way back grab a few of those Prince Albert cans."

That evening was spent making a shiny ornament out of each metal can. Bess drew simple designs on the tin and Jim followed the lines, cutting out hearts, stars, and various other shapes. They hung them on the tree and stood back to admire how the metal picked up a gleam from the lamplight. It suddenly became quite a charming Christmas tree. Bess went to bed feeling good from their shared moment.

Christmas Day dawned cold and bright. Four inches of new snow gleamed in the early morning light. Bess could hear Jim in the kitchen getting the fire started in the cook stove. With luck there were still coals left from the night before, so it wouldn't take too long for the house to warm up. She stretched under the heavy woolen quilt, feeling her huge belly rise above the level of her body. Bess had grown so big in the last month she had trouble walking.

Thank goodness I don't need to bend over a garden patch.

Nellie Hart had insisted on preparing the Christmas dinner. She'd used the excuse Bess wouldn't feel up to cooking, but Bess thought it was because Nellie could have her granddaughter close to her all day. That was okay with Bess. It would be good to have someone else to do the cooking for a change, even if it was her mother-in-law!

The house was getting warmer, and Bess smelled the coffee boiling. Kitty would soon be up to unwrap the few gifts under the little Christmas tree. The toddler really didn't understand the meaning of the day, but she loved opening presents. Bess thought she'd like the shiny tree ornaments, although the sharp-edged tin would have to be kept out of her reach.

Just as Bess's legs hit the cold floor a wave of pain washed over her distended belly. She paused and let the contraction pass before standing on her feet. The pains had been happening for the past several weeks but soon subsided.

Jim slammed the door on his way to the barn to do the milking. Waddling to the kitchen Bess put the iron skillet on the fire and prepared some fresh side meat coated in flour. The odor of frying pork filled the kitchen.

Maybe I'll make a batch of biscuits to go with the meat and fried eggs.

Less than ten minutes later another spasm hit, causing Bess to hold her breath. This time it lasted a little longer. She looked up to see Jim coming in the door with the milk pail. He was watching her quizzically.

"What's the matter, Bess?"

"I'm not sure, but it could be getting close to my time. Maybe you should get Kitty up. I'll dress her, and you can take her over to your mother's. I've got a feeling you might need to go get the doctor before long."

By noon Jim returned with Dr. Miller just in time for the physician to deliver a baby boy. Minerva Jones had things well in hand, and it was a simple matter for the doctor to do the final honors. A loud squall came from deep inside a pair of newly inflated lungs.

"It looks like you have a fine baby boy, Mrs. Hart."

Bess looked wearily at the baby tucked in the crook of her arm. Jim stood by the bedside beaming with pride. A man's first son was a special event. He put one finger in the palm of the infant's tiny hand, and the fingers curled around it. "He's a strong little mite," said Jim happily. The baby had a shock of light brown hair, and Bess thought he had his father's nose. A pair of dark brown eyes tried to focus. Hard telling what color they'd be in a few months.

"If you're done in here, Doctor, I'll make sure Mrs. Hart is settled so she and the baby can have a little nap," said Minerva Jones. "They've had a hard day."

Bess smiled down at her son. You're a regular little Christmas boy, aren't you? I think you look like your daddy." Her eyes closed, and she was sound asleep.

1915

"Kitty, don't you wander away! You stay right here on the blanket with your brother." Bess straightened up to wipe at the sweat running down her face and neck. She'd thought she would be done by the time it got hot, but there were too many weeds and too many distractions.

If I could have just a couple of days where I didn't have to stop to nurse and change a baby, distract a three-year-old, or prepare a meal, maybe I'd get caught up.

The sun beat down without the hint of a cloud in the sky. It had been two months since the last rainfall and everything was baked in the powder dry soil. Bess had saved every drop of wastewater from the house for her vegetable garden. She could be found long after dark pouring the precious trickles onto each plant so that the night air would consume less of the moisture. Once she made Jim haul a couple of barrels from the river, which she carefully portioned out. If all the other crops failed, they must have the produce from her garden for the winter.

Bess had reached the end of the bean row when she heard a buggy coming down the road from Battlement Mesa. She shielded her eyes and saw tiny Ila Smith, whom everyone lovingly called Aunt Ila, hauling on the reins. In answer to Bess's wave, Ila steered the horse into the yard.

"Aunt Ila, good to see you. Get down and come inside for a minute. Where have you been? Would you like to have something to drink?"

"No, my dear, I can't stay long. I'd better get on home and put some supper on the table for Mr. Smith. I just took a notion to go calling this morning, so I went over to see Mrs. Underhill."

"What kind of news did you hear? We haven't been to town for so long, I don't know how everyone is doing. Aunt Myra does write me once a week, but she doesn't get out much, either."

"Well, of course everyone is still talking about the Ulrey shooting," Aunt Ila said. "Just think, being married only a week when your husband is killed. I suppose poor Sadie has gone back up Parachute Creek to her folks. I can only imagine what she must be going through right now.

"Mrs. Underhill says that the Kerlee family is very upset about Harrison being arrested. Of course they haven't had his trial yet, but everybody knows how taken he was with Sadie, and they did find a gun in his tent. I feel sorry for the Kerlee children, even though they are only half-sisters and brothers to Harrison. Mrs. Underhill says some of their schoolmates have been saying awful things, and she threatened her children with their lives if they participate."

"People can truly be cruel at times," said Bess while she tied seven-month-old Bob to the chair with a tea towel and made sure Kitty was playing with her dolly in the next room. "How's everyone faring with the drought?"

"Pretty much like us. Some ranches, like the Clark and Jenny place, are doing fairly well because they have such a good water right out of the Huntley Ditch. But many of the places that only have high water rights are burning up."

"Just like we are on the upper fields. Jim only got one watering this year. He took one small cutting off, but I doubt there'll be any more. Thankfully, we have the fields along the river. We get enough irrigation water to keep them pretty green. It's going to be a slim year, Aunt Ila."

"I know, my dear, but we've weathered it before and we'll do it again. It's not easy, but it's so much better where it doesn't get so cold and snowy in the wintertime. When Carl and I lived in Aspen there were only three months of good weather, if we were lucky. I couldn't grow much of anything but root crops and cabbage."

Jim came riding in as Aunt Ila was preparing to leave. "Howdy there, how's everything over your way? Will Cecil have a decent crop?"

"Just like you folks, Jim, some good, some bad." She climbed aboard the buggy, looking so small behind the big team of horses. Bess could scarcely believe she could handle them so easily. Tiny Aunt Ila was one of the most intrepid pioneers of the Wallace Creek area.

"Oh, I almost forgot Bess. Ida Herwick and some of the other women are thinking about starting a Sunday School at the Battlement Schoolhouse. Neil Goad has agreed to do some preaching if there's enough interest. Would you like to go?"

Bess stammered a little over her reply. "I-I really don't know at this point, Aunt Ila. The children and the house keep me very busy. I doubt I'd have time right now. Maybe I can go this winter when I don't have to tend the garden."

"Well, keep it in mind. Good to see you folks."

Later that evening, while Bess parceled out the meager drinks of water to the plants, she pondered why the invitation to Sunday School had created such a response within her. Religious activities were familiar to her. As a child she'd been involved in the parochial school and was studying for her first communion. It wasn't even the dread many Catholics felt about going to a Protestant church. No, it was something else, but she couldn't quite put her finger on it. Whatever the reason, she couldn't solve it then and there. All of a sudden Bess felt so fatigued she wondered if she could make it to bed. Turning to the house she plodded to bed and blessed rest.

The summer drought raged on and caused forest fires in the higher mountains. A particularly bad one occurred on Holmes Mesa. Bess lived in fear, as did most ranch women, of chimney fires or lightning strikes that would burn their homes to the ground. A fire was devastating to a family who struggled to just stay afloat. Bess tried to keep the water in the pails filled at night to be thrown on the roof in case of fire. In all honesty she knew that two pails of water wouldn't do much good, but it gave her some small comfort. With everything extremely dry, any kind of wood would go up in a flash. Several small children had burned to death across the mountain in the Mesa area, which made Bess shudder. That was too awful to even think about.

> Western Colorado was in the grip of religious fervor during 1915, perhaps brought on by the pros and cons of prohibition. Newspapers made frequent announcements of revivals being held in the region, especially the Grand Junction area. Twenty-five-hundred people gathered at a big shed or tent, called The Tabernacle, on September 28, 1915.

The skimpy harvest was all in by a sunny afternoon in October. Jim returned from town where he'd gone to pay a few dollars on their account and pick up more supplies to get them through the winter. Bess cut the list to the bone because she knew the grocery bill would still be large. Flour, tea, coffee, and Jim's tobacco were about all they could afford. Instead of sugar they'd have to make do with the honey Jim had taken from his hives and saved for their own use. Bess had hoped to buy material to make the children some nice clothes for their Christmas. She consoled herself there was plenty of good material in Isabella Stuart's hand-me-down box. Not that she needed to mind about clothes for the children. Grandma Nellie would make sure they received something nice.

Jim stomped his feet at the doorstep, shaking off the road dust from his pants and boots. "You'll never guess what has happened! Harrison Kerlee and five other prisoners sawed their way out of the Rifle jail yesterday, and they're still on the loose. Someone smuggled in a file, and they made saws out of their table knives. No one will say it to his face, but everyone's bettin' it was his brother George. He's taken care of Harrison and gotten him out of more than one scrape. One thing's for sure, Harrison knows these mountains like the back of his hand. If he got a head start it's doubtful they'll ever catch him. They're talkin' about forming a posse. They asked me if I wanted to go, but I begged off. I don't want to get mixed up in that mess."

"I'd hope not!" Bess exclaimed. "You've got enough to do without running all over the country playing lawman. That cellar needs to be dug out. I can't get any more stuff down there, and I don't have room in this small house. I thought maybe you could work on it before the first snow hits. What do you say?"

"What do I say? Well, darn it all, Bess, I was thinking about goin' out with some of the other fellows to see if we can bag that bear that's roaming around east of Horse Mountain. We've all agreed to share the meat. They say he's pretty fat."

"Well, that just makes a lot of sense, doesn't it? I've worked my fingers to the bone putting up enough food to get us through the winter, and now you're telling me you don't have time to make a place to store it? At the same time you're going to go gallivanting off to get more food! What would you like me to do? Maybe I should throw it in the middle of the road. When people ask why, I'll tell them my husband would rather go off on a bear hunt than take care of his family. If you don't care about us then you can just get your own supper!"

Bess stomped out of the house and headed up the gulch to cool off. She'd never talked to Jim like that before, and she realized she was being unfair. She was very tired from all her summer's work. The thought of him being able to escape, while she was stuck at home, made her see red!

The sun had set and the evening growing chill when Bess returned from the upper fields. She'd spied some coyotes crouched down, watching a herd of does and their fawns. Before leaving she scared the deer away. As she headed for home, she heard the mournful wail of the coyote, seemingly in reproach for denying him his meal. Bess's anger had abated by the time she arrived at home. She saw a small pile of dirt and rocks near the front of the root cellar. She laughed to herself.

It seems my husband has decided to dig the cellar out, after all.

On November 23, 1915, the body of a prominent Yampa stockman, Ira Chivis, was found along the road six miles west of Rifle, in the Webster Hill area. He'd spent several days in Rifle and was on his way to Grand Junction. Only a small amount of cash was found on the body, and robbery was suspected by his friends although the Garfield County coroner ruled that heart failure caused his death, not foul play.

The snows kept coming, piling up against the small frame house, covering the country in a four-foot blanket of white. It started snowing on Christmas Day of 1915 and would continue every day throughout January. The Hart family, along with everyone else on Wallace Creek, was engaged in a day-to-day struggle to keep stock fed and watered. The fire was stoked around the clock to keep the children warm, while Bess tried to find activities that would amuse and entertain them.

Jim and his father made trips twice daily to the fields to check on the cattle. Jim came home half frozen and ready for a bowl of the vegetable soup left simmering on the back of the stove top. It was a time for drawing in. Infrequent visitors stopped by for a hot cup of coffee on their way to or from Battlement Mesa. They'd bring bits and pieces of news about their neighbors. Occasionally some brave soul would to go to town and bring back everyone's mail from the post office. The roads were nearly impassable, but a single horseman could stay on the railroad grade and make pretty good time. Aside from that there was little contact with their friends and neighbors.

Bess lived for occasional newspapers. The national news reported on the conflict with the Mexican rebel leader Pancho Villa as well as the war raging in Europe. Closer to home boosters of highway and oil shale development raved enthusiastically about the prospects of both. And the battle continued over the pros and cons of prohibition laws. None of this mattered much to Bess who preferred to lose herself in the serialized fictional stories, even if she wasn't sure of getting the next installment.

The first of many oil shale development companies, Colorado Carbon Company, was incorporated on November 18, 1915. It was located on Kimball Creek, north of DeBeque. Despite speculation no retort was ever built or a tram erected. The corporation would close its operations by 1924.

1916

Records for snowfall were broken in January 1916 when over sixteen inches fell in the city of Grand Junction. There were only seven clear days for the entire month. More than twenty-five inches were reported on Glade Park. A period of extreme cold followed. The temperature fell to minus sixteen degrees on the last morning of January.

Sometime during that winter of 1916 Bess began to realize that another surprise was in the offing for the Hart family. She broke the news to Jim one night as they nestled under the heavy quilts. "It looks like you may have another farm hand one of these days," she said, drawing his hand over her rounded belly.

"Well I'll be...are you sure, Bess? How can that be? I thought we'd been pretty careful."

"I can't be sure, but it may have been when we made up over digging the cellar," Bess said with a laugh. "It'd be about the right time. Remind me never to get mad at you again."

"Are you okay about this? I know you sure don't need the extra work of another baby. What can I do to make things easier for you?"

"Let me think about that," she laughingly said. "I'm sure I'll come up with something. The best part of being pregnant is that we don't have to be careful any longer." She pulled him to her in an embrace.

Later, as Bess lay in the curve of Jim's arm, she thought about this child growing in her belly. The last thing she needed was another baby to care for, but she also acknowledged she was to blame. Her mother always said that you had to buy a ticket in order to take a ride. A high price for a moment of passion she grimly decided. A high price, indeed, but they'd make do.

● ● ● ● ● ● ● ● ●

Bess struggled to her feet in the garden patch. She felt large and ungainly, and she thought she'd never get her footing. She kept at her work because the garden needed to be planted whether or not she was big as a barrel. It was the first week of May, and the storms had finally stopped pounding the area, but the weather was still cool. The lettuce and peas would do well, but the other seeds needed hotter weather.

Kitty was riding a stick horse around the bare yard while Bob toddled after a butterfly flitting from one weed to another. Bess rubbed her large belly, trying to still a nagging worry. The baby wasn't moving. She couldn't remember when she'd last felt the timid stirring within her womb. This child had never been as vigorous as the first two, but Bess hadn't been concerned. Now there was nothing.

She made up her mind to see Dr. Miller, if she didn't feel movement by the time she got the garden planted. It would also be a good excuse to see Aunt Myra and Lin before her time came sometime in July. If Bess failed to go before the summer work started, she'd not get to town until fall.

Two days later, Bess roused the children early and got them ready for the trip.

"Are you sure you want to go by yourself, Bess? I could take the day off and go with you if you want me to. The irrigating can wait another day if there's a need."

"Absolutely not," said Bess. "For once you've got a good head of water, and you need to get that upper field irrigated. The children and I will be fine. Kitty will help me take care of her brother, won't you, Missy?"

Bess preferred going over the Battlement Mesa road in case she'd meet a friend or acquaintance, but the Una road into Grand Valley was quicker, if not as scenic. The air was still chill, and the early May morning sparkled from the sun shining on dewy plants. Even the sagebrush sported a lovely bluish-green hue in the early light. It was a good day for travel. Bess temporarily forgot her primary purpose for going to town in the pleasure of the moment. She savored the rare times when she could break free of household chores.

The team trotted along at a brisk pace, and the wagon pulled into Grand Valley in an hour. Bess was pleased to see the graveled road was being maintained now that automobiles were using it more often. She thought she'd rather have the horse. Those machines were smelly and noisy.

Her first stop was Dr. Miller's office. She was relieved to see he was available. He ushered her in while his wife, Margaret, took charge of the children.

"Are you feeling better, Dr. Miller? I heard that you were sick with blood poisoning this past winter. I hope I'm not imposing on you?"

"Nonsense, nonsense—I'm fine. That was way back in February, and Dr. LeRossignol fixed me up. What can I do for you, Bess? It looks like you'll be needing some assistance in a few months. When do you think you are due?"

All of a sudden Bess felt foolish. Maybe she'd blown her concern out of proportion.

What should I say to the Doctor?

"Well, speak up Bess, there must be a problem, or you wouldn't have come all this way to see me. Do you want me to examine you?"

"Well…yes, Dr. Miller. I'm sure it's just my imagination, but the baby doesn't seem to be moving. I don't know when I last felt it kicking. It may have been a week ago. It's probably just a lazy, big boy." Bess nervously laughed.

"Well, we'll soon see if there's a problem," said the doctor whose gruffness masked a heart of gold. "You can remove your outer clothes behind the screen. Take off that blamed corset and leave it off! Pregnant women shouldn't be wearing such things. Let me know when you're ready." Bess flinched as the cold metal of Dr. Miller's stethoscope probed the warmth of her belly. Her anxiety rose as the doctor went back and forth over every inch, listening then moving to the next section. Finally he raised his head to look into her eyes.

"I can see why you are concerned, Bess. The baby isn't moving much, and its pulse is a little hard to find. But, that doesn't always mean something bad. You're right, sometimes you just have a big, lazy baby who doesn't want to do anything but eat and get fatter. Tell you what, I'll ride out in a week or so to see if anything has changed. If not, we'll talk more about what needs to be done. Try not to worry. You may awake tomorrow morning with the little dickens kicking you to pieces. You go visit your Aunt Myra. She'll love seeing the children. Tell her I said hello."

The rest of the day was a blur of activity. Aunt Myra was delighted to see Bess and the children. Kitty, as usual, wanted to run around instead of being hugged, but little Bob crawled into Myra's arms and promptly went to sleep. The look on the elderly woman's face was sheer contentment, and Bess was sad they couldn't see each other more often.

Lin came in for lunch, and Bess was struck by the fact that her younger brother was now a man. He'd turned twenty-one in March and looked to be a self-confident, slightly arrogant young fellow.

"Bessie, what do you think about all the fightin' we're into these days? It looks like that Mexican bandit is pretty well done for, but the Kaiser's another thing. You mark my words, we're gonna be in the war before long." Lin's eyes shone with excitement, and Bess shuddered.

"John Lin Kelly, don't you even think such a thing! You actually sound excited about all this. We have enough to do to keep body and soul together without taking on someone else's fights."

"Oh, Bessie, don't be so serious. I was only teasin' you." Lin grinned at her with his crooked smile. His eyes peeked out from beneath his shock of brown hair. "I get all the fightin' I want at the Saturday night dances... lovin' too, for that matter." He left the room, and his laughter trailed after him.

"Aunt Myra, is Lin really thinking about joining the army? Has he said anything to you?"

"I think he's pulling your leg, Bess," Aunt Myra laughed. "He's certainly never mentioned it to your uncle or me. Lin's become quite popular with the ladies at the dances, and I can't say I blame them. Hasn't he grown into a handsome young man?"

"You may be right, Aunt Myra, but that young man thrives on excitement. I'd feel a lot better if he'd find some nice girl and settle down."

Bess had plenty to occupy her thoughts as she rode back to Wallace Creek. Despite Dr. Miller's calm attitude about the baby, she wasn't able to quiet the nagging doubt deep within her. Added to that was a nagging worry about Lin. He was entirely too taken with this military thing to suit her. Why would anyone be so willing to go to war?

Bess didn't have long to wait for one of her answers. Two nights later she was roused from a deep sleep by a jolting pain coursing through her. Her moans woke Jim, who groggily rolled over.

"What's the matter Bess? Do you have a cramp? Can I help?"

"I don't know, Jim, I think it's the baby. I have several months to go but I don't know what else it could be. Ooooh, there it goes again. Take the children to your mother's. Go get Dr. Miller...hurry, Jim, hurry."

By the time Jim returned from his parent's place, Bess knew he wouldn't be able to get Dr. Miller in time.

"Jim, stay with me. The baby's coming fast. You'll have to help me."

"Of course I'll help you, Bess. Tell me what I need to do." Jim held her hand tightly while she swam through the next contraction. In between the pain Bess hurriedly told him where the baby supplies were. He laid everything out then stoked up the fire, so he could bring some water to boil. When done, he hurried back to the bedside to look anxiously at Bess.

"Don't worry, Jim." Bess tried to joke. "Just think of me as one of your heifers. Hopefully I won't cause as many problems. Owwww, here it comes. Help me, Jim! Catch the baby!" Bess panted between pushing.

"I can see it, Bess! The head is comin'out." Jim put two fingers under the tiny shoulders to ease them out. The little baby slid into his hands.

Bess relaxed for a brief moment, then looked at Jim who was working with the baby. No sound came from the child. Jim's expression confirmed the fear Bess had felt.

"What is it Jim? Tell me what's the matter with the baby?" Her voice was raised with fear. Tears welled up in her husband's eyes. "No, Jim, let me see! Bring my baby to me!"

Jim quietly wrapped the baby and laid it beside Bess. "I'm sorry. It's a little girl, Bess," he said, his voice cracking. "It was a little girl."

Bess rolled over to take the tiny bundle into her arms. A low-pitched keen started deep within and erupted from her mouth. Jim sat silently in the early morning light, while his wife crooned and rocked.

The summer passed in grieving numbness. They'd named the baby Nina and buried her in the Battlement Mesa cemetery. Bess soon took up her household chores but did it with little enthusiasm. The sense of loss was not the hardest thing to bear. She felt remorse she may have neglected to take care of herself properly.

Maybe it was because I didn't want the child and that somehow caused her death.

Dr. Miller assured her little Nina probably had a heart defect, but Bess was still torn with guilt. It was many months before she got through the day without thinking of her tiny baby.

● ● ● ● ● ● ● ● ●

The water was adequate, if not abundant, for the crops on Wallace Creek. The hot summer sun helped create a growth spurt in all the field crops and Bess's garden. It looked like this would be a better year for the Hart families.

"We'll have a few steers to ship this year, Bess," said Jim with satisfaction. "If the herd keeps growin' I'll have to start putting the cattle on the mountain during the summer. The bottom land won't handle many more than twenty or thirty head."

"What about running sheep, Jim? I'm told they can survive better than cattle, especially with the type of forage we have. And you get two cash crops— one from the meat and one from the wool."

"Are you out of your mind woman? No self-respecting cow man would ever have one of those damned stinkin' things on his ranch! I'd just as soon sell the place and move to town than be forced to become a sheepherder."

Although Bess was well aware of the still-raging controversy between sheep and cattle ranchers, she was a little taken back by her husband's vehemence. He was usually soft spoken about most things. "Don't get all excited, Jim, it was just a question. I've been reading some of the reports in the paper about running sheep and cattle together. Some of the experts say it can be done because the two animals eat different kinds of forage. Cattle are a lot more particular about what they eat."

"They sure as hell are picky, and they won't have a thing to do with any graze where a smelly bunch of sheep has been. I don't know about those experts, Bess. I doubt they've ever done any actual ranching."

"Sorry I brought it up, Jim. I just wondered if we could be doing better than we are."

The minute the words left her mouth Bess knew it was a thoughtless remark. Jim worked himself to exhaustion trying to make a success of the ranch, and she didn't want him to think it wasn't good enough.

"Well, I'm sorry that you're so dissatisfied with your lot, Bess."

"I'm sorry, Jim, I didn't mean for it to sound that way."

Jim turned and left the kitchen without answering. Bess deeply regretted voicing her feelings, even if they were true. It looked like they went backward instead of forward each year. Jim worked hard, but if a bad drought or another natural disaster hit, everything they'd struggled to obtain would be wiped out. She looked for any way they could make more money.

I do blame Jim for being so unwilling to do anything new. He wants to go along with the old tried and true ways. Why won't he look at other options?

Bess thought about her uncle's ranch. However she felt about Uncle Elmer as a person, she had to admit the old rascal had carved out a successful living on the Grand River with his small herd of cattle, truck garden, and milk cows. He relied on more than one source of revenue. Bess grudgingly admired her uncle's ingenuity and hard work.

She was actually a little envious. It would be nice to go into town and buy a pretty piece of fabric for her or the children. She couldn't remember her last new dress. Of course other women on Wallace Creek ranches were in the same boat. Their clothes were as dowdy as her own. Without question, life was hard for everyone.

> The Oil Shale Mining Company, created by Harry Flynn and his brothers, was incorporated on October 2, 1916. The company controlled over nine hundred acres on the Dry Fork of Roan Creek and erected the first oil shale retort in Colorado.

Nellie Hart made a special effort to be more friendly toward Bess that summer. Maybe it was because she felt compassion for the loss of the baby. Bess thought Nellie's increased presence was a mixed blessing. On one hand she was very helpful with the children and other tasks. On the other hand her bossy attitude was an irritant to Bess's frayed nerves. There were times that gritting her teeth was the only way Bess got through one of Nellie's visits.

Nellie did, however, suggest something that surprised the whole family. "I think we should go into town for the second annual Grand Valley Fair. It will be held the third weekend in October. I wonder if I should enter a few of my prize apples? And maybe a quilt or two that I've been working on? We could take a picnic lunch and spend the day visiting and looking at the other displays. There will probably be a baseball game in the afternoon for you men to enjoy. There might even be a boxing match between Art Johnson and someone from around the area."

Nellie hadn't been to town since her daughter Mary's death. She had resolutely turned down social invitations for four years until Kitty had been born. That brought her out of her grief-stricken state, and she started to do a little visiting with the neighbor women. This, however, was a big step and the Hart men were delighted. No one would say no to Nellie.

Preparations for the trip were started. Riding in an open wagon might be chilly, so everyone would have to dress warm. Early storms had been drenching the area. Snow was falling in Pitkin County, and the road from Rifle to Meeker was impassable. Bess hoped it would clear up before the middle of the month. She looked forward to a diversion from her mourning.

Early on a clear, nippy October morning the family loaded up their team and wagon and headed to town. Frost laid on the ground, as it had for the past several days. The women piled plenty of quilts in the wagon. Big Jim drove the large black team, and Nellie rode on the seat beside him. A quilt was wrapped tightly around her bow-legs. Jim, Bess, and the children, who were a little groggy from sleep, were snuggled into the old quilts in the back.

The air remained chilly even after the sun peeked over the mountain. Signs of fresh snow could be seen on the Battlement Reserve. A hazy fog hovered above the Grand River as they crossed the Una Bridge and started east toward Grand Valley. The sun would burn the haze away in an hour or so, which always disappointed Bess. She loved the white mist and could pretend she was back on the Mississippi River with her parents and brother.

After watering the horses down at the stockyard, Big Jim pulled alongside other wagons parked on Parachute Avenue in the vicinity of the Doll Brothers store. They'd be stocking up on some supplies later in the day, and this would be a handy place to load them.

Everyone climbed down and stretched their cramped muscles. They joined other folks who lined the sidewalks to watch the parade. It started to form on First Street. Darrell Saylor hurried by in his fancy uniform to catch up with all the other musicians who'd lead the march. Cowboys and lady riders sat on prancing horses. Assorted carriages, wagons, and automobiles were gaily decorated with harvest themes. Pretty girls perched upon the seats, flirting openly with the cowboys.

Kitty and Bob were wide-eyed with wonder at the unusual activity. They'd never seen so many people in one place, or heard so much noise. Both clung to their mother and grandmother's skirts, peeking out to survey the strange and somewhat scary scene. Their shyness disappeared when the band started down the street. They clapped their hands with the rest of the spectators.

Bess was delighted to see her old friend and teacher, Miss Hubbard, in the crowd. They waved to each other, and Bess planned to seek her out later. She hadn't seen her good friend for some time. Bess excused her long absence, telling herself it was frivolous to spend precious time visiting with anyone other than her aunt. Secretly, Bess admitted she hadn't wanted to face her mentor's questions about life on the Hart ranch. It would be easier for Bess if she had something positive to talk about.

Bess spied Lin on horseback looking spiffy in a blue shirt with a kerchief around his neck. His attention was on the young ladies riding on the floats. For the most part, that attention was returned twofold. Lin clearly enjoyed being the center of everything. It would do no good to try and get his attention right now, but she'd wave as he went by. Perhaps he'd see her.

"Kitty, Bob, do you see your Uncle Lin? Look, he's right over there, and he'll be riding this way in a few minutes. Be sure you wave to him."

Lin spotted the Hart family and reined in close to the sidewalk.

"Hey there, folks. And there's Miss Kitty and Mr. Bob." He touched the brim of his cowboy hat. "Young lady, how would you like to ride in the parade with your Uncle Lin?"

The little red-headed girl stood wide-eyed, hesitating. She looked at her mother who nodded. Kitty smiled and lifted her arms. Lin settled her in front of him on the saddle.

"You be careful with her," called Nellie Hart. "Don't you let that horse buck or anything."

Lin smiled his crooked grin and nodded his head in agreement. He wheeled his horse down the street after the other riders. Kitty looked at the crowd and showed her delight when people waved to her.

Later, while Nellie Hart showed off Kitty and Bob to some old acquaintances, and the Hart men congregated for a smoke, Bess sought out Miss Hubbard.

"Bess, it's good to see you," said her old teacher. "It's been too long. I read about the loss of your baby. I'm so sorry. That must have been dreadful for you and Jim. Are you feeling better now?"

"As well as expected, Miss Hubbard. You'll have to meet my children. Their grandmother Hart is showing them off right now. And you—are you well?" Bess searched her friend's face. It was thinner than Bess remembered, but her hazel eyes were still bright and alert.

"I've recently had a few health problems, but I'm fairly well. I haven't missed many school days. Tell me, do you still find time to read? My word, I never saw anyone that loved to read as much as you did! If you are ever in town and want to borrow some books, you may. I try to obtain a few good ones ever so often."

"That's a very kind offer. I'm afraid with all the ranch work, and tending to the children, I don't have as much time to read as I'd like. Mrs. Stuart is good about letting me borrow a book or two when I go to Horse Mountain. Maybe when winter sets in I'll have more time. The next time I'm in town I'll come by, and we can catch up on all the news, I promise. I need to check on the children. Will you walk over to those trees with me to meet them?"

When their wagon pulled out of town late that afternoon, the Hart family was tired and lost in their own thoughts. Nellie Hart was sulking because one of her quilts only got an honorable mention, and her apples took second place. The Hart men were content to relax, perhaps thinking of the chores to be done when they got home. Kitty and Bob were asleep before the team cleared the edge of town, and Bess was free to sit back and think about the day and her old teacher.

By the look of her, Miss Hubbard is ill. I hope it's temporary but, somehow, I really don't believe it is. Her color is so pale, almost with a bluish cast, and she seems to have difficulty breathing. If there is any possible way, I must go see her before winter sets in.

Something else was nagging at Bess. She wasn't terribly proud of the resentment, but it was there nonetheless.

When I saw Miss Hubbard, I had to face the reality of my life, my marriage. It's so different from what I thought it would be. I love Jim and the children, but I feel like I've lost myself in the process. When I was a young girl I thought it wasn't possible to work harder than I did for Uncle Elmer. Even then I had time to read and think about the finer things of life. I believed it would be different when I married Jim, but it's worse. Now everything's crowded into the day, demanding attention. I don't know myself anymore.

The year 1916 came to a close with news that President Wilson had created the Naval Oil Shale Reserves from more than forty-five thousand acres of land on the mountain between Rifle and Grand Valley. This further increased the prospecting frenzy around the area. Bess thought this latest craze was the only thing more risky than ranching. She was pleased that Jim didn't seem to be interested in joining the other men heading for the mountains to file on placer claims. They had enough problems without taking on any more.

Ranchers were pleased the 640-acre grazing law was passed at the end of December. This would allow them to apply for larger permits in most areas. In the Wallace Creek area only the biggest ranchers would benefit from the increase although there was talk of forming a pool for cattle owners with smaller herds. Jim and his father discussed the possibility of using it if their little herd kept increasing. They needed to keep all the fields in hay production for the winter months.

New Year's Eve 1916 was bitterly cold with the thermometer hovering at the zero mark or below. Nevertheless, most families braved the frigid night to gather for a dance at the Wallace Creek school. It took more than icy blasts to keep people from attending a long anticipated night of entertainment.

> After many years of strife, sheep ranching was finally able to get a toehold in Western Colorado. Cattlemen retaliated whenever they could but privately realized they were fighting a losing battle. Some, in fact, even sold off their cattle and invested in sheep. Trains pulled out from Montrose and Garfield counties on December 21, 1916, with a total of six thousand sheep headed for the market. They brought a record price of almost ten cents a pound, with an average weight of one hundred pounds per sheep. The gross sale was sixty thousand dollars, an unprecedented price.

1917

On January 20, 1917, a DeBeque man, William Robinson, and his son, Jake, were caught in a snowslide in Boldt Gulch thirteen miles northwest of the town. The two men were cutting mine timbers on a steep slope when the avalanche occurred. The father was able to summon help at neighboring ranches although his foot was badly crushed. The son was buried under twenty feet of snow. Two sleighs filled with men left DeBeque in an attempt to rescue the youth. It had been snowing heavily all week, and the temperatures dropped to as much as twenty degrees below zero. Unfortunately, the son was not found alive.

The war in Europe raged, and it was getting closer to home for the citizens of Grand Valley. President Woodrow Wilson, having declared the United States neutral in 1914, was finally forced to build up army and navy forces. He emphasized they would be used for peaceful purposes although many influential citizens, including Teddy Roosevelt, were clamoring for U.S. involvement in Europe. Wilson sought approval from Congress to arm American merchant vessels, which alarmed certain senators who wanted to remain neutral.

Battles went back and forth. There were promises of peace plans every week, only to have the war to increase in intensity. The news reported there would be U.S. intervention unless the Germans stopped their unrestricted submarine warfare. The interception of a secret note directing the German minister to Mexico to seek an alliance against the United States became the deciding factor.

Winter was mild in the lower elevations. Many people traveled back and forth to Grand Valley in the first months of 1917. Visitors regularly stopped by the Hart house on the Battlement Mesa road, each person contributing to the stream of war news that flooded the area. Bess worried about her brother Lin. She sincerely hoped he hadn't been serious about signing up for duty.

One noonday in mid-April Bess looked out the window to see her brother riding into her yard. Her heart skipped a beat. Why was Lin coming all this way to see her? She stepped to the door.

"Hey Sis, you look like you've seen a ghost. Has it been that long since you've talked to your brother?" Jumping to the ground, he grabbed her into a big bear hug, whirling her around.

"Oh, Lin Boy, what's the matter? You never come to the ranch! Is it Aunt Myra—Uncle Elmer? Don't just stand there, tell me what's wrong!"

"Do I have to have a reason for visiting my one and only sister? How 'bout a cup of coffee to warm me up? Where're those youngsters? Where's the pretty little girl who rode with her Uncle Lin in the parade?"

"Kitty's spending the day with her Grandma Hart, and I've just put Bob down for his nap. There's some soup on the stove. Do you want a bowl?"

"That'd be great, Sis. It's been a while since I ate breakfast." Lin removed his leather gloves, hat, and coat before sitting down at the kitchen table.

Bess sensed Lin wasn't about to talk about his real reason for visiting until he was ready. She tried to quiet her rising anxiety and sat down across from him.

"Are Aunt and Uncle well?" she probed.

"Yeah, they're doin' fine. The old man's hired another guy to help out, but I think it's just because he wants to take it a little easier. He's just as cantankerous as ever so he must be okay."

"And, Aunt Myra?"

"She's okay, too," replied Lin in an unconcerned voice. "You know Aunt Myra. She's just like a tiny sparrow hopping from place to place, chirping all the time."

"Lin Kelly, that's not a very kind thing to say about the woman who loves you so much!"

"Shucks, Sis, I didn't mean nothin' by it. You know I think the world of her. You've got to admit she does jump around like a little bird sometimes."

Lin caught Bess's suppressed smile. "I knew you'd agree. Say, this is good soup! Can I have some more?"

Bess and her brother chatted about the news from Grand Valley, and she heard about the young ladies who were interested in Lin, and vice versa. An hour passed quickly, while Bess relished being able to spend these precious moments with Lin. She almost forgot her initial fears.

"What do you think about the war news, Bessie? Do you know that President Wilson officially declared war yesterday? We're in the thick of it, now."

Alarm bells went off in Bess's head. She struggled to catch her breath. "What does that have to do with you, Lin?" His eyes told her the truth. "You can't, Lin Kelly, I won't let you enlist!"

"Now, don't go gettin' all upset, Sis. It won't do you any good. I went to Glenwood a few days ago, and I signed up. I figure it's just a matter of time until I have to go anyway, and I want to do it while there's some action. Everyone says it won't take long once we get over there and kick those krauts' behinds."

Bess sat like she was made of stone. Then a tremor shook her body, and she began to sob. Lin rushed to her side and enfolded her in his arms.

"Aw, Bessie, please don't. Doggone it, I didn't think you'd carry on like this. I'm gonna be fine, I promise. When this war is won I'll come back and take care of the ranch. I'll marry a pretty lady, and I'll have a flock of kids. Don't you see, this is my only chance to see what life is like outside of Grand Valley, Colorado."

Brother and sister looked at each other in silence. Bess remembered the little boy who used to look up at her underneath the shock of brown hair, much as he was doing now, and the tears came anew. "You're all I have left of my family, and I'll live in fear every day while you are away. Uncle Elmer needs you on the ranch—I need you. Please, please don't go."

She saw his mind was made up and pleading would do no good. Lin had obviously been planning this for some time. She dried her eyes and listened while Lin told her of his plans.

"I'll be leaving in two days for the training camp. I'm guaranteed of bein' sent overseas because I volunteered. I've also been promised my pick of aviation, artillery, or cavalry service. I'm not sure which one I'll choose. I'd like to join the air service, but I doubt I'll be accepted. There are hundreds of trained pilots who have already signed up."

After a final hug Lin mounted his horse and rode out of the yard. Bess's final view of him was when he turned to wave as he crested Kearny Hill. She shivered—would she ever see him again?

The declaration of war mobilized people throughout the United States, and Grand Valley was no exception. Local men, age twenty-one through thirty, were required to go to Glenwood Springs to sign up for military service. Jim Hart had turned thirty in January. When he received his notice, he made plans to go to the county seat for the day. Bess, still upset about Lin, was doubly concerned about her husband.

"For crying out loud, Bess," said Jim, "you've read the letter yourself. The chances of my bein' called for active duty are slim to none. In the first place I'm married with two children. In the second place I'm doing agricultural work. My number may be called, but I'm sure I'll be exempted if it does."

"I know, I know," she replied, "but I can't help worrying. I can't run this place all by myself, and it would be such a burden on your dad to take over both of the places. Whatever would we do?"

"If worse comes to worst, we'll have to figure something out. Let's not borrow trouble until it arrives, okay? I'll bet you there's nothing to worry about."

Every week there was a drawing to see who would be called up for active duty. The seventy-member Cavalry Troop M, made up of many local boys, would patrol along the Mexican border, a far cry from what some imagined their military service might be. Mothers, wives, and sweethearts wrung their hands in anguish while young men laughingly boarded trains, promising to return with an ear of the enemy. Emotions were heightened. Wallace Creek folk took turns going into town each week to get the mail and newspapers, which contained the latest war information. When Jim received no letter from the Selective Service Board, Bess sighed with relief. She wouldn't have two loved ones overseas.

> Each person who registered for Uncle Sam's army was given a number. The following is a partial listing for men from Grand Valley. A drawing was held on a weekly basis to determine who would be called to service.
>
> #535, Cassius Harrison Butler—#536, Fred Miller—#537, John Wm. Reeves—#543, Bernard Theo. McCormick—#546, Herber Thomas Evans—# 552, Dess LeRoy Hendricks—#553, Don Theodore Mead—# 557, Burl Nelson Kirkpatrick—#560, Harry Glen Gardner—# 664, Walter Joseph Kerlee—#665, Frederick Werhonig—#666, Frederick Moulton Simmon—#667, John Dothard Spencer, Jr.—#668, Ernest Allen Spencer—#669, Lloyd Jonah Blue—#670, Robert Jerome Gebhardt—# 671, Robert Ernest Green—#672, Harry Robert Hansen—#673, Elmer Isaac Wheeler—# 674, Clifford Yeoman—# 675, Christopher Henry Hinkey—#676, William Chester Cutshall—#677, James Alexander Trimmer—#678, Charles Raymond Hutton—#679, Harvey Clyde Gardner—#680, Benjamin Franklin Dere—#681, Charles Edward Pratt—#682, Claude Vernon Hayward—#683, Otis Murray—#684, Robert Leeman Helm—#685, Fred Green Hargis—#686, Louis Hargis—#687, Carl Willis Kitchings—#688, John Cox—#689, William Delbert Cox—#690, Arthur Charles Johnson—#691, James Thomas DeWitt—#692, Ross Conner—#693, John Gordon Crawford—#694, Truman Earl Milner—#695, Watson Dickerson—#696,

Robert Allen Baumgardner—#697, Andrew Harold Parkhurst—#698, Clarence Everett Tracy—#699, Jarvis Leslie Hayward—#700, Harlan Firman Harbey—#701, Nels Eaton Duplice—#702, Jacob Harrison Doby—#703, Glen Dale Waters—#704, Gustaf Reuben Nordstrom—#705, Frederick Fisher Hurburt—#706, Henry Christensen—#707, Walter Gordon Carter—#708, Clyde Maurice Morrow—#709, John Henry Cline—#710, Raymond Claude Eaken—#711, Jose Hernandez—#712, James Mistenz—#713, Joseph Clarence O'Toole—#714, John Harvey O'Toole—#715, Clarence Dell McKee—#716, Aaron Jones McKee—#717, Jonathan Curtis Baughman—#718, Oren Herwick—#719, Guy Herwick—#720, Albert Nelson Tomlin—#721, Clyde Samuel Tomlin—#722, Chester Arthur Cochran—#723, Claude F. Crouse—#724, John Thome—#804, John J. Connell—#805, Ollie E. Rhoades—#806, John R. Wheeler—#807, Clarence E. Ulrey—#808, David A. Benett—#809, Charles G. Wilkier—#810, Joe Aleck Shehorn—#811, Philip B. Hollingshead.

Isabella Stuart responded in her typical fashion by rallying the Wallace Creek ladies for Red Cross work. As the summer progressed, they met each week to roll bandages, make pajamas, or knit socks for the war effort. Bess much preferred to stay home and nurse her anxieties, but her friend wouldn't hear of it.

"Moping around home won't help bring Lin back one second sooner. Doing something worthwhile will help you to feel like you are helping him."

Bess didn't argue—she knew Mrs. Stuart was right. She drove to Horse Mountain every week whenever the weather permitted. Bess wondered if Mrs. Stuart had stripped every bed on the place. The mound of sheets was enormous. Many of them were probably better than half the sheets on Wallace Creek beds. This was typical of Mrs. Stuart's sense of charity and responsibility.

The women read the latest bulletins from the Red Cross and munched on cookies while rolling bandages. It was also a time to exchange news and gossip. Bess reluctantly admitted it did relieve the tedium and relentless worry for a little while.

"These are the funniest-looking socks I ever knitted," said Nan Sipley. "I wonder why the Red Cross wants us to make them without any heel. I can't imagine they'd be comfortable."

Isabella Stuart looked up from rolling the bandages. "According to the instructions it's because heelless stockings do double duty. When the soldier wears a hole in the bottom, the stocking can be turned around so he still has protection on his heel. Isn't that ingenious?"

"So, who's the latest to sign up?" asked Ollie Aker as she rapidly rolled a bandage.

Clara Jones spoke up, "I saw Mrs. Tracy in town the other day, and she said both her sons were going. Imagine that! Losing one son would be terrible but…"

"That's quite enough Clara," Isabella Stuart interjected. "We know that our young men will be coming home very soon, and everything will be fine. They are country lads, and they know how to take care of themselves."

Despite herself Bess shivered.

Please let that be true.

> Under Colorado law, Prohibition was enacted on April 30, 1917. From that date it was illegal not only to produce an alcoholic beverage but to also transport it across state lines in quantities. The limit was two quarts of whiskey, six quarts of wine, or twenty-four bottles of beer in one month. Permits, limited to one per month, were to be obtained from the county clerk's office, and the applicant had to swear the alcohol would be used for medicinal or other legal purposes. The alcohol could not be consumed in any public place.

A summer event happened that signaled emerging technology for homemakers. In late June the county extension agent paid visits to homes on Wallace Creek. He told the housewives there would be a demonstration of cold-pack canning at Grand Valley in early July. The Colorado Health Department was growing concerned about the high incidence of botulism and ptomaine poisoning from ill-prepared canned food, so they were bringing educational programs to the rural communities.

Bess's first thought was to decline the invitation, but the agent painted such horrible pictures of food poisoning cases he'd seen, she finally agreed to attend the day-long meeting. When she talked to her neighbors, Bess discovered they were also scared out of their wits. The women planned to fill up several wagons for the trip into town.

Nellie Hart flatly refused to go, but said she'd be glad to take care of the children if Bess thought she needed to learn how to do her work. Bess ignored the barbed comments.

I think my mother-in-law could use the education as much as anyone. I've seen how Mother Hart prepares some of her food. That's why I never eat any of her canned green beans.

The July morning dawned clear with no promise of rain. Almost six weeks had elapsed since the last rainfall, and any unirrigated crop was burned up. The upper fields at the Hart ranch would yield a small first cutting. That would likely be all, unless they got more moisture.

When the buggies pulled out from the Una Bridge, ten women were sitting proper-like under hats that shaded their faces. Isabella Stuart motioned Bess to sit next to her on the driver's seat. As soon as they hit the main road, a sense of freedom struck the occupants. It wasn't often one could escape daily chores under the guise of helping the family.

As the women relaxed, the conversation became more lively and, as people are want to do, the conversations became more titillating.

"They say that her first husband…"

"Well, I never! Did you know…?"

"That poor dear! I've heard her husband drinks too much. How does she manage with all those children?"

Bess and Mrs. Stuart heard all about the scandals of Grand Valley folk, but neither one joined in the conversations. Mrs. Stuart never stooped to that level of petty gossip, and Bess felt sorry for the victims of such talk. She sensed that, with one slip of propriety, she could be the next person they were talking about.

When the session began, the portly extension agent handed out some pamphlets from the Department of Agriculture. He introduced a tall thin lady, whose robust voice left little doubt of her commanding presence. She held the ladies' attention for the next few hours, overwhelming them with horrifying facts about the dangers of home canning unless they followed strict guidelines. Glancing at the watch pinned to her bodice, she finally dismissed her audience for the noon hour. As they filed out the door, she reminded them she would demonstrate the proper methods of home canning in the afternoon.

The women brought out their sack lunches and walked to the school lawn for their meal. July heat drove everyone to the sparse shade, so Wallace Creek women were joined by those from Parachute Creek, Battlement Mesa, and Morrisania Mesa. Old friends greeted each other.

"How's your youngest? I heard she was sick."

"I don't know why we bother coming to this when our gardens are burning up. If the dry weather continues, we might not have anything to can."

"I remember those dances we used to have at your place. Some of our best times."

"My dear, I was so sorry to hear about your husband. Who's helping you run the ranch? So many of the young hands have gone to war, it's hard to get help."

"If that lady thinks dirt is the enemy of canning, she obviously has never seen Corella's kitchen," one woman chortled.

Bess sat quietly among the bits and pieces of noisy conversation and contributed little. She was naturally quiet in groups—usually content to just listen. The ladies were all good neighbors, and she knew any one of them would be there to help in an emergency. There was, however, no one Bess felt particularly close to, with the possible exception of Isabella Stuart. These were ranch women, who were more concerned about exchanging recipes than the latest books they'd read.

The afternoon session started much too soon. Although they'd come to learn, it was pleasant to sit and visit with each other. The extension agent gathered them up, much as he might have done with school children. Everyone reluctantly filed downstairs to the stuffy kitchen in the Oil Shale Theatre to review what many of them thought they already knew.

The trip provided Bess with a short-term diversion from her worries about Lin. She'd heard from him a time or two while he was still at Fort Russell, Wyoming. The last letter, however, pierced her heart when she realized he was on his way overseas:

Fort Russell, Wyoming
1 September, 1917
Dear Sis:

It looks like we'll be leaving soon, but I won't be going as part of the cavalry. Out of 1,500 there will only be 300 men kept in the cavalry. The rest of us will be transferred to other duty. I might be transferred to the field artillery or infantry.

I was disappointed until I learned the 300 cavalrymen will be sent to the Mexican border instead of France. We went into quarantine last night. You know all troops have to be quarantined before they go overseas. I can't wait until I get there and see all that's going on. I'll write when I arrive.

Your loving brother,
Lin

Bess made an effort to get into town to see Aunt Myra more often because she knew the lady was lonesome without Lin. Bess remembered what poor company Uncle Elmer was, and she doubted he'd gotten any better. She also realized that Lin's presence felt stronger in the house where they'd grown up. It was comforting to be able to share those memories with her aunt.

Aunt Myra was always pleased to see the children. She even was able to win Kitty over, something no one else but Nellie Hart had been able to do.

"Lands sakes, child, you're such a big girl now. You grow another inch every month!"

"I'm five years old, and I'm going to school next week, Auntie Myra!"

"Oh my! That's exciting. You'll get to play with all the children and learn to read…"

"I already know my alphabet," the child interjected. "Do you want me to tell you?"

Three-year-old Bob, a silent little boy, climbed upon his great aunt's lap to pat her face. Bess thought she could see a tear run unbidden down Aunt Myra's face, and her heart went out to this generous woman. She was glad the children brought her aunt joy.

"I just got another letter from Lin, Aunt Myra. It looks like he'll be on his way overseas very soon."

"I know, my dear. I got a letter from him, too. We'll have to double our prayers for his well-being. God will take care of him, I just know it."

"I'm sure he will be protected, Aunt Myra." Bess wished she could truly convince herself of that fact. "Maybe the war will be over before Lin sees any fighting. Wouldn't that be wonderful?"

Despite concerns about the hometown boys in the military, life went on. The hayfields needed to be irrigated and mowed, the garden weeded, and the canning done. Bess found comfort in the everyday chores, which allowed her to momentarily forget her anxieties.

"Stand still, Kitty. How can I braid your hair with you wiggling so much?" Bess put the finishing touches on the last strand and smoothed Kitty's pinafore, which covered her dress.

"There, Missy, are you all ready for your first day at school? Let's not forget your lunch."

The little girl hopped on one foot and then the other in her excitement.

"Can we go, Mama? Is it time?"

"We still have a little while. Your father said he'd watch your brother, so we have to wait for him to come back from the barn. Bob would get tired before we got to school."

Mother and daughter were finally on their way. Bess opted to walk the two miles because she wanted Kitty to get acquainted with her route to and from school. Besides, it was a beautiful morning. The sun shone through a haze of autumn dust, bathing everything in a shimmer of golden light. The slight chill in the air would be gone by midmorning, but it was a preview of days to come.

Bess loved the fall months. The worst of the heat was over, much of her canning and preserving was done, and she enjoyed a small amount of time for herself on days when the children took their naps. She'd borrowed several books the last time she'd been to the Red Cross meeting at Isabella Stuart's and was hoping for a few moments today so she could start *The Prince of Graustark*. Books were still an escape from her humdrum life.

Nellie came out to meet her granddaughter and daughter-in-law when they reached her house. "Sweet little girl! I can't believe you are actually going to school. You look so pretty with your new pinafore. I'll see you this afternoon, and you can tell me all about your first day." Nellie reached down to hug and kiss Kitty.

Bess and Kitty reached the Wallace Creek schoolhouse about the same time as the other children. Most of them were former students, but there were several children Kitty's age. Kitty, so eager to get to school, suddenly became very quiet and lagged behind her mother.

"What's the matter, Missy? You've been so anxious to get here. You know most of these children. Look, there's Delphia. I think she'll be in the first grade with you, and there's Loran. See, you do know some of the children. Let's go meet your teacher." Bess grabbed Kitty's hand and walked into the schoolhouse.

When several old men had seen Miss Smith, they'd joked she could probably go bear hunting with a switch. The lady, recently come from Ohio, was quite large but with a very kind, pretty face and lovely glossy brown hair. Kitty had to crane her neck up to see her teacher's smile.

"Hello there. I'm Miss Smith. What's your name?"

As Bess left the school that morning, she thought Kitty's eyes resembled those of a roped calf being dragged toward the branding iron. Knowing her daughter, Bess was sure Kitty would adjust just fine, but she felt a brief moment of anxiety. For her it was also nostalgic. It seemed only yesterday she'd been calling other children to class at Horse Mountain.

• • • • • • • • •

The war in Europe raged back and forth. A spring offensive by both French and British troops was a failure, followed by rampant mutiny among the French troops. Summertime attacks by the British army failed to capture the German submarine bases from which there was tremendous damage to Allied navy ships.

Bess devoured old newspapers for word of the American Expeditionary Force, which landed in June 1917. There was no mention of where they were or what they were doing. At long last a letter arrived from Lin:

October 31, 1917

Dear Sis:

Well, here we are, finally in France. We landed in Brest after a 12-day voyage which was the next best thing to hell. Our food was rotten, causing more stomach distress than just the seasickness which afflicted many. I tried to stay on deck as much as possible because the smell down below was sure to make anyone sick. Finally the General in Command discovered how badly we were being fed and ordered better food prepared.

The threat of German submarines was present for much of the trip, but we were lucky not to have connected with any, although many soldiers swore they spotted some.

We were first housed in old stone buildings with high stone walls. Someone told us the compound used to be Napoleon's old barracks, but they smelled more like they'd been his stables. We were held there for a week playing cards and shooting craps before being moved out.

I can't tell you exactly where we are billeted, but we aren't on the front line yet. We are part of a construction detachment which is supporting the British lines. I can hear the big guns from here and smell smoke from the shell fire, which goes on twenty-four hours a day. I had trouble sleeping at first, but now barely hear the noise.

Don't worry about me, Sis, I'm doing fine. I'm ready to go into the trenches. I want to train my gun on some of these damned Boches.

I just realized that it is Halloween. If I was at home, I'd be help-ing some of my buddies tip over a few privies. Remember the year that we caught old man Smith in his, or did I ever tell you about that prank?

Be sure to write and tell me all that is happening there. This place is so different from back home. I think of you and the old folks often and want this to be over so I can see you soon.

Love always,
Your brother Lin

Almost two months passed without a drop of rain. Although there was less rainfall, the cooler weather compensated a little for the lack of moisture. In spite of the drought, the Harts had seen worse years. Jim sold off about a dozen steers, which paid the grocery bill with a little bit left over. He'd also sold about a hundred pounds of raw honey in a rail car shipment put together by Roll Gardner, Walt Carter, and Nels Goode. That added some money to the family coffers.

Bess was glad for their winter supply of honey because government rationing would go into effect by December. Folks were to be limited to three pounds of sugar per month for each person. The honey was a good substitute for most everything except for use in coffee. Both Jim and his dad needed the real stuff for that. While flour wasn't yet rationed, it was in short supply. People were asked to return any unused portions at the end of the month.

Area papers were full of the possibilities of the burgeoning oil shale industry in the area. *The Daily Sentinel* carried advertisements for the Mount Logan Oil Shale Mining & Refining Co. with capital stock of 800,000 shares. The officers, one of whom was a former Garfield County treasurer, were offering 250,000 shares of stocks to investors at ten cents each. Earlier in the year *The Daily Sentinel* printed a long article about Matt Callahan, one of the earliest oil shale promoters. A great deal of interest was generated from Denver investors. Many men were hired to help with assessment work on claims.

After the fall work was done, Jim brought up the subject of his joining one of the assessment gangs for several weeks, or at least until the weather made it impossible to work. Some of the placer claim owners were paying two dollars a day plus room and board. The catch was there wasn't a good trail coming down the face of Mount Logan, so he'd not be able to ride home every night.

"What do you think, Bess? Will you be able to milk the cow and feed the stock twice a day? I think that's really all you'd have to do right now. Dad can take a look at the cattle and make sure they're okay. As long as the weather holds there shouldn't be a problem. If it gets too bad, I'll be home anyway."

The thought of adding more to their meager wintertime supply of money tempted Bess, who always worried about being unprepared for emergencies.

"I've got about everything done I need to do, Jim. The carrots and potatoes are dug and the squash in. There isn't much more work for me in the garden. You say the bees are tucked away for the winter. I should be able to handle things all right, but promise you'll get off that mountain at the first sign of bad weather. It could get nasty up there."

Jim was able to work three weeks on the assessment gang, and the Hart household felt flush for the first time in their married life. On a trip into Grand Valley, Bess spent a dollar or two on some nice fabric to make Kitty a new dress and Jim and Bob new shirts. She looked longingly at a lovely piece of robin's egg blue material. It would make a beautiful new dress, and she ached to buy it, but knew she'd feel too guilty about the expense. They needed too many other necessities. She'd look through the hand-me-down box, to see if she could find something for herself.

• • • • • • • • •

The Wallace Creek community planned a dance after the children's Christmas play at the schoolhouse. Kitty was very excited to be one of the participants in the little play, which Miss Smith wrote and directed. Kitty was one of Santa's helpers, and she faithfully practiced her two lines every night. The Saturday night before Christmas the Hart family piled into the buggy to travel the few miles to the schoolhouse. Big Jim and Nellie were taking their own carriage so they could take Kitty and Bob home with them after the school program.

Bess prepared some food for the dance. She tucked some ground beef tongue and pickle sandwiches into the back of the buggy along with a sour cream apple pie, which was a favorite for many. All the ladies would spread out their food contributions for the midnight supper when the musicians took a break.

The night was crisp and cold, with just enough snow on the ground to make the steel rimmed wheels crunch as the horses briskly traveled along. Bess looked at her family in their new finery and was very pleased with their appearance.

She looked down at her homemade dress with satisfaction. The color looked nice with her auburn complexion. She'd rummaged through the Stuart hand-me-downs and found a dress that was similar in color to the material she'd coveted at the store. Late into several nights Bess altered the dress to create the newer, dropped waist fashion with pleats falling around her hips. The bodice was modestly cut, but showed more of her leg. Indeed, it showed off the lower portion of her calf.

She felt slightly scandalous and hoped other ladies would also be wearing their dresses a bit shorter. She'd pulled her hair back into a bun as befitted a wife and mother, but allowed the front to fall into a natural wave before confining it. The curling iron, used to curl Kitty's hair, did double duty on a pair of curls above Bess's ears. She knew she looked attractive that evening. Not even nagging fears about Lin's well-being could keep her from enjoying the festivities.

The skit about Santa Claus misplacing his list was well rehearsed, although some youngsters had to be prompted before they could recite their lines. The audience chuckled when Santa Claus's stomach kept shifting around to his back. Kitty made her family proud when she not only spoke her part clearly but added dramatic emphasis. She smiled at the applause her performance brought.

By nine o'clock Kitty and Bob were bundled into their grandparent's buggy. Bess and Jim went back inside to get the dance started. Bess helped the ladies start the wash boiler of water boiling for the coffee. A cotton bag of ground coffee would be floated in it until the liquid turned the right color. It had to be strong and hot to sustain the dancers. Other ladies were cutting cakes and pies while trying to keep children out of them until a little later. Some of the women gave up and fed the youngest, hoping they'd tire out and go to sleep on the chairs lined up on all sides of the large room.

Some folks from town were the evening's musicians. After helping the men tune their instruments, the pianist struck up *Alexander's Ragtime Band*, and everyone stepped out onto the dance floor.

Bess looked up at her husband and smiled. Jim looked particularly handsome that night. The angular planes of his face had filled out with maturity and her good cooking. His strong hands excited her as much as nine years ago when they first met. While still not a fancy dancer, Jim held his own on the dance floor, and Bess enjoyed being whirled around the room in his arms. These were the times that almost made up for the hardships of their lives.

After several fast dances and one square dance, the band took a break so everyone could catch their breath. Bess overheard the ripples of conversation around her as she nodded and greeted folks she'd not seen for a while. One conversation was particularly interesting.

"Hey there, neighbor, I guess you don't have a jug out in the wagon tonight, since the federal government saw fit to stop whiskey manufacturing."

"What the hell does that have to do with me? There ain't anyone alive that can stop a fella from making his own likker if he wants to."

"Well you'd better be careful about who you talk in front of. I hear they're raising hell with bootleggers in Mesa County. Old Abe's in jail more than he's out. You remember him, don't ya? He used to be in DeBeque."

"Yeah and I remember he wasn't too bright when it came to hiding his supply."

Bess, with a slight smile, glanced around the room. Above the crowd she looked into a pair of blue eyes that matched her own. She stood spellbound as they held her gaze, widening with interest. He was the most handsome man Bess thought she'd ever seen, looking much like the dashing heroes in her books. Embarrassed, she averted her eyes and turned toward the kitchen area to see if any help was needed.

Who is that man?

Bess imagined she could still feel his penetrating gaze. She wanted to turn around to check but resisted the temptation.

Bess took refuge in a circle of women, their idle chatter about home and family bringing her back to reality. She visited with a buxom, young bride who'd come to Spring Creek the previous spring.

"How do you like life down here, Annie? Have you gotten settled in?"

"I've been busy this summer getting the cabin fixed up and putting in a big garden. Men don't seem to care how their places look as long at they don't leak too much."

"I know what you mean," laughed Bess. "When I married Jim Hart there wasn't anything to keep the wind from blowing through, and hardly a thing to eat in the cupboards. No wonder he was so skinny."

The music started up again, and the two women sauntered into the big room. "Annie, do you see that man over there, the tall one? I don't believe I've ever seen him before. Do you know who he is?"

"I wondered myself and asked someone. They think he's taken the foreman's job up at Horse Mountain Ranch, but they didn't know what his name is. He's a handsome fella, isn't he?"

"Uh huh. I don't see any woman with him. Does he have a wife?"

"I doubt it. Those fellows are usually footloose and fancy free."

Bess avoided eye contact with the man for the rest of the evening, but she glanced his way whenever his back was turned. Taller than any other man in the room, he was dressed like the other men, but he wore his clothes with more style. His shirt was immaculately clean, boots polished until they gleamed, and his wavy blond hair combed to perfection. Some might look at him and say he was a dandy, but Bess intuitively knew this was a man who could hold his own with anyone. There was something about the stranger which was fascinating. He wasn't handsome in the classical sense. His face was too chiseled, his nose too sharp, his mouth too big, nevertheless he projected a handsome image. He danced with the younger, single women, including Miss Smith. Bess was touched he had asked the teacher, who'd been watching from the sideline. She'd meant to send Jim over to ask her. She decided this stranger was not only handsome, but he must be a gentleman.

The dance ended in the wee hours of the morning, and everyone started for home. It would soon be time to milk the cows and feed the stock. Bess snuggled close to Jim as the horses quickly trotted home sensing they'd soon be in their own corral. Stoking up the banked fire the Harts climbed into bed for a few hours sleep before starting the day.

"It was a nice evening, wasn't it?" asked Bess, as she snuggled up to Jim. "Everyone got along just dandy. There wasn't even a problem with ranch hands having too much to drink."

Jim pulled her close to him. "It sounds like you had a good time. Did I tell you how beautiful you looked?"

"No, but you can tell me now," she replied laughing. Bess moved closer to her husband and put her arms around him.

> The 1917 sales of Western Colorado sheep wool brought thirty-five cents to forty cents a pound. This was a record price, and it further stimulated the controversy of raising sheep versus cattle.

YOUNG BUCKS WITH THEIR MOONSHINE!

1918

The new year of 1918 blew in with a vengeance, blanketing the land with several feet of snow before it tapered off toward the end of January. Bess chafed because few people had gone to town to pick up mail or the newspapers. She was desperate for word from Lin. It would be wonderful if Wallace Creek folks could get a rural delivery route for their mail, but Bess heard there had to be a certain number of people before the postal service would consider it.

The weather abated by the first part of February, and Jim rode to town because he knew Bess was anxious for news. He returned with a bag stuffed with mail for all of Wallace Creek. In the sack was a letter from Lin.

15 January, 1918
Somewhere in France
Dear Sis:

Several of your letters were waiting for me when I returned from the front. Also, the Christmas packages which you and Aunt Myra sent. Thanks you for the cookies, candy, tobacco, and warm socks. I shared my food with the other Sammies in my outfit, but I saved the socks and tobacco for my own use. They are hard to come by.

Well, Sis, I've finally seen the enemy. I was gone for over a month, and now they've sent us back to a rest camp to dry out. The rain over here is nothing like you've ever seen in Colorado. The trenches are running full, and we have been wet for the entire time. This place is so different from back home. We are being deloused because the trenches are full of the little buggers. They are better, though, than the rats.

I think we are gaining some slow ground on the damned Huns, but each inch is hard won. Have you been following the battles in the newspaper? I guess you get that kind of news back there, don't you? If so, you can likely figure out where we were.

Keep up the letters and tell me how everyone is. Don't worry about me because I'm doing okay. I sure miss all of you, and hope we get this wrapped up so I can come home.

Love from your brother,
Lin

March 19, 1918
Wallace Creek
Dearest Lin:

I believe the worst of our winter is finally leaving. The last letters I've written have contained nothing but complaints about the snow depth and cold. But the past few days have been sunny. I know spring isn't here yet, but it's so wonderful to see patches of bare earth. I will go into town tomorrow to mail this letter and to see how Aunt Myra fares. She has done pretty well this winter except for her pesky rheumatism. Uncle Elmer has also been bothered a lot. It's hard to believe that old curmudgeon could be growing old, but he is.

You will be surprised by all the cars in town when you return. It seems somebody is buying a new one every week. I look at them and think it would be a convenience in some respects but a nuisance in others. The Stuarts bought a new Dodge touring car, but they were not able to use it most of the winter. When it was taken out, they had to make sure the radiator was drained every time the car was stopped for a long time. A horse doesn't have to be drained! You should have some army pay coming, and I bet you'll splurge on an auto of your own when you return. Even the cheapest ones are dear. A new Model T Ford costs about $900.

The farmers and ranchers are grumbling about the daylight savings which will go into effect at the end of the month. They complain their cows will not give milk an hour earlier. The government swears it will save on coal, gas, and electricity. That certainly won't bother those of us on Wallace Creek. I doubt the day will ever come when we have that type of convenience. Poor little Kitty will be going to school in the dark.

Are you getting your copies of the Grand Valley News? *If so, you will have read the sad news about George Bailey dying of pneumonia at Camp Funston. I feel sorry for his parents.*

Your letters seem to be more serious of late, and I'm sure you aren't telling me as much as you could about your situation. I read the papers and try to guess where you might be. Although the news tells us where the fighting is taking place, it does not tell us which companies are in the various regions.

Jim and the children are well and send their loving thoughts to you. Kitty is doing very well in school. She recites her daily lessons every night at supper. Bob is growing into a sturdy little fellow. He already loves to follow his father around so I suppose I have another rancher in the making.

I will be writing next week. Please take good care of yourself and come home safely.

Love always,
Bess

April 1, 1918
Somewhere in France
Dear Sis:

It has been sunny here today and all the farmers are working in their fields. It makes me a little homesick to see them plowing the soil. I'll bet you never thought you'd hear me say I miss plowing. By the way, the farmers are mostly very old people or small children and women. The men are all at the front lines.

We have plenty to eat, but the food gets monotonous. Bread is scarce around here and our mess sergeant threatens anyone who leaves scraps of it. You said flour and sugar rationing has started there so I guess we are all making sacrifices. A French woman came by today and offered to sell fresh eggs for ninety cents a dozen. The mess sergeant had to turn her down because he is supposed to use only official supplies. If we'd had any ready cash, we would have bought them ourselves. A nice fried egg would taste good right now.

I have seen some action again, and our regiment has been temporarily pulled back. I can't tell you why but it is nice to rest for a change. I did make it through Paris a while back but we weren't able to stop long enough to see much of the scenery. I hope I'll get that way again because I'd like to see the sights.

Several of the guys are keen on the French girls. I don't know how they communicate because the fellows don't speak French. You don't have to worry about me. The girls I've met eat so much garlic I don't even think about trying to steal a kiss.

I know you're worried about me, Bessie, but I'm taking good care of myself. Our outfit has been very lucky. We have suffered only one casualty and only minor injuries. I keep telling you that the Kellys all have guardian angels.

Write soon because I look forward to hearing about home.

Your loving brother,
Lin

May 11, 1918
Dearest Lin:

You'd think we were having winter again. There was ice in the chicken pan this morning. I fear the fruit trees may have gotten nipped. We might have a sparse fruit crop this year.

Until now we've enjoyed warm spring weather, which has brought all the oil shale folks to Grand Valley and DeBeque. The last time I was in town there were men everywhere, trying to hire workers for the claims, or owners stocking up on groceries before going to the hills. I hear the Herwick family has a small retort up in the ledge at Cottonwood and there is something being built up Parachute Creek. At least four companies are planning to build plants in the Roan Creek area. Did you know that the February National Geographic *even featured an article about oil shale production? I'll try to get my hands on a copy and send it to you so you can see our little area is having some national recognition. Maybe Jim can get some work again this fall like he did last year. Right now the ranch keeps him plenty busy.*

I have cans of bedding plants all over the kitchen. I hope to get them in the ground in the next week unless we get another cold snap. I've had to watch the setting hens to make sure they don't lay someplace out in the sagebrush. They can be so contrary. Remember how you used to hate them? I can't say I blame you, but fried chicken is certainly worth it. Wish I could send you some.

We had a Red Cross benefit at the school last week. It was a box social. You remember what they are, don't you? Every lady decorates her box, and she's supposed to keep it secret even from her hus-

band. Of course that's pretty difficult. I decorated my basket with bits of old silk bows which I cut from clothing in the Stuart hand-me-down box. All the men had to bid on the boxes or baskets and, of course, they had to pretend they didn't know which one their wife or sweetheart brought. There were a few mix-ups but for the most part husbands ended up with their wives. Jim got mine for 25¢. I don't think we brought in much money, but we did have a good time. It helps me to forget my worry over you for a little while.

The school year will be closing soon for Kitty. I think she is sorry to see it end because she's the teacher's pet. Bob now rides behind his father when Jim goes up to the headgate and is always begging to ride by himself. He's still too young to handle that big, old horse, but I'll bet he'll keep pleading until Jim gives in.

Speaking of children, you will have another niece or nephew about the middle of September. I hadn't said anything because I have been anxious due to little baby Nina's death. But, Dr. Miller says this baby seems to be healthy as a horse. He assures me there is very little chance of a problem. I hope you will be here to see the baby shortly after its birth.

I must bring this to a close so it can go to town tomorrow with Ray Maylong. Folks have been so good to make sure the mail gets picked up because they know how I worry when I don't hear from you. Please take good care of yourself.

Love always,
Bess

July 4, 1918
Somewhere in France
Dear Sis:

I'm sitting here in my newest home, which is a sheep barn. It has been raining for the past week and the ground is so soggy that I almost pull my boots off when slogging through the mud. But, the rain will let me take a few minutes to get a note off to you. I haven't had much time because we have been on the move a lot.

If it wasn't for the war, I would enjoy the countryside we are passing through. France has as many rocks as we do, and they have used them for every type of building and fence. It is very green here, which is different from our dry part of the country. It would be nice to see it when the war is finally over. Right now it looks pretty bad.

I expect I won't know the old town when I return. It sounds like *things are really buzzing there. I laughed when I heard about the dance hall fight a few months ago. Tell the rowdies to come over here, and we'll take the fight out of them. I'm surprised there are any men left in town.*

It has been a hard fight, but I think we are finally gaining some ground from the damned Huns. Captured prisoners, who have been released, are telling about the horrible conditions in Germany. Some have said the food supply is so short, people are turning into cannibals. It's about what you could expect from those people. War does terrible things to men.

As much as I hate these folks I felt sad that Mr. and Mrs. Ische were treated so badly they sold out their ranch and moved back to Pueblo. I'd met them a time or two, and they seemed like decent folks, even if they were Germans. I'm sure there are plenty of kind people in Germany, but they certainly aren't on the front line.

I think longingly of past July 4ths and look forward to when I can come home to enjoy more. It's hard not to get discouraged when you take and lose the same piece of ground several times. But I'm taking good care of myself. You can't keep a good Kelly down!

Your loving brother,
Lin

> A second military draft was held August 1918. This time they called up men from the ages of eighteen to forty-five. For the second draft the eligible age was increased by fifteen years.

Bess read the *Grand Valley News*. The front page contained a black-bordered headline proclaiming, "G.V. BOY SLAIN ON FRENCH FRONT." Ward Underwood was the first fatality from Grand Valley, and the news hit everyone hard. If it could happen to Adelia and Jimmy's son, it could happen to anyone. Bess's hands trembled as she prepared for the graveside services at Battlement Cemetery. The war had graphically and tragically come home to the citizens of her community.

Bess was not accustomed to praying, having decided a long time ago it was a useless waste of time. When had her prayers ever been answered? Now, she prayed almost unceasingly for Lin. Childlike litanies begged for his well-being. She remembered scraps of Catholic prayers she'd learned so many years ago.

Growing heavy with child, she slept fitfully at night, having nightmares of Lin. One night in mid-August she had a particularly vivid dream where Lin appeared, smiling his lopsided smile, a lock of hair hanging over one eye. He reached out to touch her and said, "It's okay Bessie, I'm doin' fine. Don't worry about me."

When Bess awakened, she felt oddly comforted by the dream. Maybe Lin was all right. Perhaps she was overly concerned for him. She went about her chores that week with a lighter heart. The kitchen was filled with jars of fruit and vegetables from her garden, which she would have Jim take down to the cellar. She didn't trust herself to do it because she could no longer see the steps. Her unborn child was kicking vigorously. She did not have to worry about this one being quiet. It was so active, it had to be a boy.

Kitty was spending the afternoon with her Grandma Hart, and Bob was in the fields with Jim. Bess was taking a short rest when she heard the sound of an automobile coming down Kearny Hill. Casually wondering who it might be, she struggled to her feet and walked to the kitchen door. A Ford Model T was chugging down the road. Bess could see two people in the little car but couldn't identify them. She didn't think it was anyone from Wallace Creek, but then folks were buying new cars every day. Curious now, Bess stood while the car drew nearer.

When the vehicle reached her house, it turned into the yard. Peering into the dust-covered windshield Bess finally identified her visitors.

"Dr. Miller! Aunt Myra! Wha-what's the matter? Is it Uncle Elmer?"

The Doctor and Aunt Myra, both silent and solemn, stepped down from the car. Aunt Myra, her face red and swollen, with tears in her eyes, came toward Bess with a piece of paper in her hand.

"Let's go sit down, dear girl. We have bad news."

Bess felt an icy chill wash over her body. She sat down and took the telegram from her aunt's hand.

WASHINGTON DC 558 PM AUG 30,1918
MR. AND MRS. ELMER CARPENTER
GRAND VALLEY, COLORADO
DEEPLY REGRET TO INFORM YOU THAT PRIVATE
JOHN LIN KELLY IS OFFICIALLY REPORTED AS KILLED
IN ACTION ON AUGUST FIFTEENTH. DETAILS TO
FOLLOW FROM COMMANDING OFFICER.
HOLMES, THE ADJT. GENERAL 6:00 PM

The telegram slipped from Bess's lifeless fingers. She stared as if in a trance, then a sound started. It grew in strength and intensity as she rocked her body back and forth. Her arms folded over her distended belly, as if finding comfort from their embrace.

"Bess, tell me where Jim is," said Dr. Miller. "I'll go find him. First, I'm going to give you something to drink." He put a glass to her mouth and she drank the liquid while still uttering the strange guttural noises. Aunt Myra patted Bess's back and caressed her shoulders. Tears ran down the older woman's face, unheeded, but Bess was oblivious. She didn't want anyone to breach the barrier of her solitary grief.

The day blurred into a series of disjointed events for Bess. People came and went in her small house, paying their respects, bringing food. Later, she couldn't say how she responded to their kindness. Jim, Aunt Myra, Uncle Elmer, Nellie, Big Jim, and the Stuart family gathered around Bess. They deflected the numerous visits from neighbors in the area.

Days merged into weeks, while Bess moved in a stupor. One September morning the sullen pain of her sorrow merged with another, familiar pain. Seeing Bess clutch her belly, Aunt Myra hurried to the garden patch where Jim was gathering the last of the crop and tearing out dead vines. He'd felt so helpless in easing Bess's grief that he searched for some task which he could do for her. The garden patch had seemed to be the right chore.

"Jim, dear, I think Bess's time has come. Go get Dr. Miller. He said he wanted to be here in case she has any problems."

"Oh God, I've been afraid of this, Aunt Myra. I figured the grieving would send her into labor. Thank God, the baby is almost due. It would kill Bess if she also lost this one. I'll saddle up and ride in to get Doc, but first I'll stop at Minerva Jones's. It's a good thing the kids are still with Ma."

Bess struggled through the waves of her pain, surfacing to recognize the doctor's face above her. "That's good, Bess. You're doing fine, and the baby is fine. It will be just a little bit longer. I think you're going to have a big baby boy."

Sometime in the late hours of the night a raucous, angry howl came from the bedroom. "That's a good little fella," said Dr. Miller. "You've got a great set of lungs. See Bess, I told you he'd be a healthy boy. And, it sounds like he's already complaining. Why don't you rest for a while? Minerva will get the baby cleaned up."

"No, I have to see him first. Put him up here so I can hold him." Bess looked at the little red face framed by the dark mane of wild hair. A distant memory caused the tears to come in Bess's eyes.

For a moment I thought I was holding my baby brother.

• • • • • • • • •

A month later Bess held the baby, Frederick Lin, at her breast. She heard the sound of Jim riding into the yard. He opened the door, and Bess caught a glimpse of a brisk autumn day. A puff of chill air caused Bess to cover the baby's face.

"Here's the mail, Bess. I went to see Aunt Myra and Uncle Elmer, and they'd received a letter from Lin's commanding officer. Do you want to read it?" He offered the paper with some hesitancy. Would Bess start her grieving all over?

"Yes," Bess tiredly replied. "I need to know what happened, and when Lin's body will be coming home to us."

September 10, 1918
Paris France
Dear Mr. and Mrs. Carpenter:

I deeply regret the loss of your nephew, Private John Lin Kelly. He was a good soldier, courageous to the last breath. He was killed, with many of his fellow soldiers, in a heavy artillery barrage. Unfortunately, we were not able to identify each body so they were all laid in a common grave on a grassy slope close to the Vesle River.

I am sincerely sorry we will not be able to ship his body back home to America, but I assure you our chaplain held a prayer service for these brave and true young men. May it comfort you to know death came very swiftly. I don't believe any of the soldiers did more than take a breath before they were gone. Their bravery enabled our army to push forward and clear the Vesle River area of all German troops. We captured 8,400 men and 133 heavy guns.

Your nephew signed up for the army life insurance, and I believe he has paid on some liberty bonds. The final accounting will be coming to you in the near future.

Let me again say I'm very sorry for your loss. You have my greatest sympathy. Please do not hesitate to contact me if I can be of further service.

Sincerest wishes,
Capt. John Wilkins
US Army Expeditionary Forces

"Well that's the end of it," said Bess in a flat voice. "I won't even have a grave to visit. It's as if my family never existed."

"I'm sorry, Bess. I wish I could do something to ease you. I know it's hard, but you've got me and the kids. And there's Aunt Myra and Uncle Elmer. I know how you feel about the old man, but I've got to say he's really aged. He cared about Lin—they both did. I'm worried about them."

FRED MILLER, M.D., PRACTICED MEDICINE IN GRAND VALLEY 1905-1949.
ALSO PICTURED IS MARGARET WERHONIG OF BATTLEMENT MESA.

Bess shook herself. "Yes, you're right Jim. This is the way life is, and I'd better accept it. I need to visit Aunt and Uncle before it gets much colder. I know they are suffering. Lin was one of the few people who really understood Uncle Elmer."

Her words were well-sounding, but Jim had a sense of uneasiness. He couldn't believe that Bess's grieving was over so soon. Likely the scars would last forever.

Oil Shale Incorporations for 1918:

Searchlight Oil Shale & Refining—1,120 acres on Clear Creek, north of DeBeque

Grand Valley Oil & Shale Co.—Starkey Gulch, Parachute Creek, north of Grand Valley

1919

"It says here we have to file an income tax return if we made more than two thousand dollars last year," chuckled Jim. "If I were making that much, I'd gladly pay my share, but the rich don't pay enough. I'll bet there are many millionaires out there who hire shysters to make sure they get out of it."

"I suppose you're right," replied Bess, absentmindedly rolling out pie dough. "The rich get richer and the poor get poorer. It would be nice to have enough money that we'd have to worry about dodging income tax. Kitty, see if you can amuse Freddie until I get this pie in the oven. He's probably hungry."

Bess popped the pie in and shut the oven door, before stepping over to her youngest child. Looking down to his basket, her heart swelled at the sight of him. Little Freddie was the perfect baby. Since his birth, five months before, he'd never been sick. A fat and happy baby, he was content to eat and sleep, while charming his mother with frequent toothless smiles. Bess snuggled him to her breast.

This child has a greater hold on me—not that I love him more than Kitty and Bob! It seems I have a deeper sense of connection with Freddie. In some mysterious way it's like he has been given to me because I lost Lin. He even has the same expressions as Lin had as a baby.

She kissed the soft wrinkles in her baby's neck, "Umm, you taste good enough to eat. Can you smile at your mama? That's my sweet boy!"

There were reports of numerous influenza cases in Grand Valley and all of Garfield County, but there had been no deaths. Bess was glad they were more isolated in the country. Even the school children had limited contact with those from town. The only people the Hart family had seen since Christmas were those returning from town with mail. Bess wanted to go into town to see how Aunt Myra and Uncle Elmer were faring. She hoped they hadn't gotten the flu. Lin's death had shaken Uncle Elmer. For the first time since coming to Colorado, Bess felt a sense of pity for the old man.

There was another reason she wanted to go to town. She and Jim, in a nighttime conversation, discussed the offer that Dr. Miller made to Bess some time ago. He said he'd be glad to discuss various methods of contraception with Jim and Bess if they ever felt their family was big enough. After Freddie's birth they both agreed three children were enough. Maybe it was time for them to see what the doctor could suggest. They'd ask the elder Harts to keep the children so they could spend the night with Aunt Myra and Uncle Elmer. Bess didn't want to expose her children to the influenza. Maybe they could even pick a Saturday night when there would be a dance at the Oil Shale Theatre. Several of their neighbors said the DeBeque Orchestra was very good.

As the calendar inched toward spring, the oil shale industry again geared up. The Mount Logan plant at DeBeque was supposed to be producing oil by the end of February. The company was a frequent advertiser in *The Daily Sentinel*, offering stock for ten cents a share. There were at least fifteen companies selling stocks, building plants, or both. There were so many newcomers to the area, they were having difficulty finding housing. More men would be needed during the summer months to do the assessment work and build the various plants. Parts of the county were booming, but life on Wallace Creek continued much the same.

> Area newspapers ran frequent ads for companies wanting to buy various wild animal furs. Coyote pelts sold from $2.00 to $28.00, depending on the condition of the pelt. Muskrat sold for up to $3.00. Trapping often provided the first money a young boy earned. They learned, while young, how to set the traps and how to skin the animal so the pelt would bring the best price.

It was almost to the end of March before the cold, snowy weather abated enough to make a trip into town. Bess sent a letter to Aunt Myra, telling her to expect them as soon as the weather cleared. According to their plan, they first stopped at Dr. Miller's office where, red-faced with embarrassment, they both listened as the doctor explained several forms of birth control. The year was 1919, and these things were not usually discussed outside the bedroom. The only thing worse would be to have ten more children.

After eating supper at her aunt and uncle's Bess prepared for the dance at the Oil Shale Theatre, while Jim visited with the old folks. Aside from their small Wallace Creek dances she'd never been to one with a real orchestra, and Bess was fumble-fingered with anticipation.

She donned a deep-green wool crepe dress that should be warm enough for the chilly evening. She'd dug through some of the Stuart hand-me-downs and was able, with little alteration, to make a very pretty and serviceable dress for herself. A lower neckline, long slim sleeves with lace edging, and a fashionably slim skirt complimented her trim, neat figure. Having four births hadn't harmed her shape, and her bust was considerably larger because she was still nursing Freddie. She felt a pang of remorse for leaving Freddie with pumped milk until tomorrow morning, but she shook off the feeling. Freddie was starting to eat from the table so he'd not go hungry.

Looking at her face in the bedroom mirror, Bess decided she liked what she saw. One fall day, perhaps in response to grief, she grew weary of her long hair. With three children and a ranch household to tend, it was too much trouble to wash, brush, and comb the heavy locks. While the baby slept, Bess took out her sewing scissors. By following an illustration in one of the more recent newspapers, she'd cut off her hair just below the chin line. To Bess's amazement, the natural curls and waves framed her face like a shiny auburn wreath. She thought she might have to revive Jim when he came in for supper. Being an easy-going fellow, however, he soon grew accustomed to it.

Bess took another look in Aunt Myra's mirror and thought she was as ready as she'd ever be. Her blue eyes sparkling with anticipation, she stepped into the living room.

Jim trotted the team down Front Street and reined them onto Parachute Avenue. Wagons and teams shared street space with automobiles for several blocks. It looked like there would be a good-sized crowd at the dance. Bess and Jim joined other couples entering the double doors to the hall. They stopped at the box office on the left where they saw Si Herwick selling tickets. He looked sad and lonely, having lost his wife, Ida, to cancer the first part of March. Bess thought it must be hard to lose one's mate after so many years. She felt sorry for the disheveled old man. The couple offered condolences, which were silently acknowledged by a nod of the large man's head.

Jim paid their dollar ticket, helped her off with her coat, and carefully guided Bess around the perimeter of the dance floor. "Careful, this floor is blamed slippery from the corn meal. I think they've used too much."

Bess saw the orchestra setting up their instruments on the stage at the end of the hall. Meanwhile, Jack Morton was pumping the player piano, recently bought for the weekly silent films. A small group clustered around him, singing with the music. Bess hankered to see one of the films. She decided the whole family should come in some Saturday night during the summer. Kitty and Bob would enjoy seeing a moving picture.

After tuning up the instruments, the orchestra began to play. Drums, piano, fiddles, guitars, and a horn were harmoniously rendering a popular tune:

Days are long since you've been away, my buddy...

Jim easily guided Bess around the dance floor. They had learned well from each other. Bess looked up at Jim.

If only the rest of our lives could be as much fun. Jim is such a nice man, a good husband, but life with him is more like living with a best friend...except at night, that is! He'd never think of sweeping me off my feet with a hug and a kiss. Maybe I'm yearning for something that doesn't exist outside my books. I wonder if other women think about this? I can't help it—I feel something is missing.

At the break they greeted people they knew and were introduced to others. Many of the dancers were young, unmarried men, who either came with a girl or were looking for one. She smiled to see the covert flirting going on. She sat down to rest her feet when Paul, a friend of Jim's, grabbed him by the arm and propelled him toward the door.

"I'll have him right back, Bess," he said to her. "I have something outside Jim really needs to see!"

Bess laughed and said to Paul's wife, Nancy, "Where are they getting the liquor now? I thought they weren't supposed to have any within the city limits of Grand Valley."

Nancy giggled. "Men will always find a way to get their supply. These hills are full of stills. I'm told Walt Wooley will sell anything out the back door of his saloon. If temperance comes to all the country, like some politicians are proposing, the fellows won't do without. My husband says he couldn't dance if he didn't have a few belts. It doesn't hurt in other areas, too, if you know what I mean."

Bess, embarrassed, nodded her head and changed the subject. The band was striking up another tune as the jolly men crowded back into the hall, smelling of tobacco and alcohol. As Bess searched for Jim, her eyes were drawn to another tall figure.

My word, if it isn't that man from Horse Mountain! He's as handsome as I remember. I can't believe that he's been on my mind from time to time. It isn't right for a married woman to think about another man. What is it that draws you to him, Bess? It isn't just his looks. No, it's something else, but I'm at a lost to define it.

Bess suspected she wasn't the only woman attracted to him. Looking to where the single young women sat, she could see them preening like colorful birds coyly trying to get his attention. Which one would he pick?

Jim took her hand from behind, "Where was your mind? You looked liked you were a hundred miles away." He swung her onto the floor to the tune of the *Black Hawk Waltz,* one of their favorite songs.

"Jim," Bess said casually, "who is that tall, blond man over there by the wall? I saw him down at Wallace Creek some months ago. Annie said he'd hired out to Mr. Stuart."

Jim whirled her around so he could see the man. "Oh, you mean the one with the tan shirt? Yeah, that's Alan Taylor. He's Wade's foreman. Seems like a good enough fellow but real quiet. Doesn't have much to say."

"Well, that apparently doesn't stop the ladies from hanging on him. Those girls are practically lining up to dance with him." Bess decided he was probably just another dance hall romeo who didn't want to settle down. But she couldn't help glancing his way every chance she got.

When the music ended, the Harts were close to Alan Taylor as he led his partner back to the side.

"Hey, Al," called Jim, "come meet my wife. Bess meet Alan Taylor."

The tall man sauntered over, his blue eyes smiling down at Bess. "Pleased to meet you, Mrs. Hart. Maybe your husband will let me borrow you for a dance?"

Jim stepped back as the music started, and Alan led Bess out to the floor. She was silenced by the suddenness of the introduction. What should she say to this handsome stranger? His large hand on her back pulled her close as they moved to the rhythm of the music. He expertly guided her around the floor, and Bess was able to follow the motion of his body. They danced very well together, but her mind was a mass of confusion.

Can he read my thoughts? Is his smile mocking me? Merciful Heaven, did he see me staring at him? Oh my word, what will I say?

Bess tried to keep her eyes averted. Surely the man could feel her heart pounding against his solid chest. Her resolve failing, she looked up to see him gazing back, a half-smile curving his lips.

"I think I saw you at a Wallace Creek dance some months ago, didn't I?" His eyes seemed to probe. "If I recall correctly you were wearing a blue-green dress—am I right? And I think you've cut your hair since then. It suits you."

"Well—yes, I think I was wearing a teal dress, and I did cut my hair. You must have a good memory, Mr. Taylor, to remember what a woman looked like so many months ago."

"It's simple, Mrs. Hart. You were the most beautiful woman in the room." He twirled Bess through a series of fancy steps, which successfully ended their conversation. Bess was content to let it drop. How would she have responded to such a statement? It was enough she was being held in this man's arms while gliding around the room. She wanted the moment to last, but the magic ended with the music. Alan led her back to Jim, thanked her politely, and walked away. As far as she could tell, he didn't even look in her direction for the remainder of the dance. Bess was relieved. She felt like a tongue-tied ninny.

Bess and Jim got in a short night's sleep before rising early the next morning. They needed to get home before Freddie ran out of his milk and set up a howl. Aunt Myra and Uncle Elmer were already up. Aunt Myra bustled around the kitchen putting thick slabs of ham into the big cast-iron skillet. Bess hurried to help her and they were all soon sitting down to eat.

"Ahem, Bess—Jim," said Uncle Elmer in his gravely voice. "Your aunt and I have something to tell you. Do you have it, wife?"

"Right here, Elmer," said Aunt Myra, reaching to take Bess's hand. "Your dear brother took out some insurance when he went into the army. A lot of the young men were doing it, I guess. The officer mentioned it in his letter, but we didn't think anything about it until this came a few days ago. We were listed as his beneficiaries. With the insurance and back pay the total came to $1,200. We want you to have half of it." Aunt Myra slid an envelope into Bess's hand.

Both Bess and Jim started to protest. "Aunt Myra, we can't take this from you. It's yours—Lin wanted you to have it. This is small pay for all the years you took care of him…"

"That boy didn't owe us a thing," interrupted Uncle Elmer with a tremor in his voice. "Nor do you. You both earned everything you got here. We're old folks and we've done okay. There's nothing we need, but I know that you could use some extra money with your family and all. Take it, and let's have an end to this talk." His voice was husky with emotion.

With tears running down her face, Bess moved over to embrace her aunt while Jim shook Uncle Elmer's hand. Then Bess moved to her uncle and embraced him for the very first time. She could feel his arms trembling.

I can hardly believe that Uncle Elmer is making this generous gift. I guess grief affects each of us differently. It seems that the sorrow has erased his sharpness. He certainly doesn't act like the cranky man I once knew.

On the way home both Bess and Jim sat in a daze. Six-hundred dollars! What all that could buy for them! Then Bess remembered where the money came from, and a sob escaped her lips. "Oh Jim, it just doesn't seem right to benefit from Lin's death. I can't imagine I'd ever be comfortable spending the money."

Switching the reins, Jim silently reached for her hand. "We'll do whatever you think is right, Bess. Don't trouble yourself right now." He knew she would likely come around once she got used to it.

Jim was right. Once the grief of the inheritance was dealt with, Bess soon started to think of ways to spend their windfall. "Jim," she exclaimed, "the first thing I'm going to buy is one of those Singer sewing machines. I'm so tired of trying to sew everything by hand for this family. And it will last longer, too. The children tear up their clothes so fast. And…"

"Whoa there! You don't have to justify anything to me, Bess. It's your money and you can spend it any way you like."

"No, that's not true. It's *our* money, and we need to think about what will benefit our family the most. I've thought about getting an automobile, but I'm sure they would be far too expensive. And I've thought about building on another room now that there's five of us. We could fix up the place a little bit with some calcimine and linoleum. But, Jim, we have to be practical. Should we use the money for more stock? How about new machinery?"

"We've been having some good calf crops, and we're handling about as many as possible, even if we decide to run them on the mountain. Would you really like a car, Bess? I thought you'd be the last person in the world who'd want one."

"I still think they might be more trouble than they are worth, but they do get places a lot quicker, and they're warmer in bad weather. I don't know whether I'd ever be able to learn to drive one of those things. You'd have to take me every place."

"Of course you could learn to drive one. There's no reason why you can't. As it happens a guy on Battlement Mesa is trying to sell a Model T for a couple of hundred. I think it's a little beat up 'cause he ran it into a barrow ditch. But he says it runs okay. So, maybe you can have everything you want, including a bigger house."

By the time school was out in May the sewing machine was ordered, the Model T touring car bought, and the foundation for two new rooms being laid. Jim spent his little bit of free time tinkering with the automobile, much like a boy with a new toy. He announced he'd have to build a little lean-to on the barn so they could keep the auto in there during the winter. But, he was now busy getting the fields irrigated, especially a new piece he'd cleared last year. If all went well, they'd take one cutting off it this year, although the water was drying up fast. After the first three stormy months of the year, Mother Nature had turned off the rain.

• • • • • • • • •

At night Jim came in from the fields and hauled a few rocks for the foundation. Lava rocks were all over so that was not a problem, but he was dead tired and the last thing he wanted to do was lay rocks. However, Bess had been promised. He'd thought Oren Herwick might be available to build the addition, but Oren's father, Si, said his son went back to Lusk, Wyoming, right after his mother, Ida's, funeral. The old man said Oren was building houses for all the people flocking to Wyoming with the oil boom. Si thought the biggest reason might be a young lady who had caught Oren's eye. Jim found several other gents who were willing to do the actual construction when he got the foundation laid.

By the time winter came Bess would have a nicely improved home, and she was a happy woman. The only thing left undone was for her to try driving the new car. Bess protested she was far too busy planting her garden, hatching chicks, and doing all the other spring household work to spend time on this challenge. She promised Jim she'd try driving it when she got caught up, but she never managed to catch up. Jim suspected Bess was a little frightened and would eventually need a hard nudge.

The Grand Valley and surrounding community was shocked when the ever-faithful Dr. Miller announced he was retiring and moving east. Eleven years of dedicated healing had taken their toll, especially after the latest flu epidemic. Area residents wondered what they would do without this man who was so much a part of virtually every household in the area. Folks would have to make do. Bess hoped the Hart family would stay healthy until another doctor came to take Fred Miller's place.

The doctor's absence became acute one evening when Minerva Jones stopped to say she was on her way to help deliver a baby from a young woman who lived across the river. The poor woman's husband was still soldiering in France, and there was no one on the small farm except her elderly father. Bess made Minerva promise to send the old gent back to her place if she needed any additional help. Thank God someone was able to help in these situations.

The fears of the community were short-lived. After a trip to the eastern slope of Colorado, Doctor and Margaret Miller returned to Grand Valley. They were quoted as saying they were happy to be home, but the doctor wasn't certain he would resume his practice. Many citizens said fervent prayers that he would change his mind. A few months later grateful thanks were offered that Fred Miller was once again practicing medicine. The community wondered what

Ford Model T Fore-Door Town Car
(*Fore-doors are detachable*)

6-Passenger—4-Cylinder—20 Horsepower Car. Price $900 includes speedometer, two 6-inch gas lamps, generator, three oil lamps, horn and tools—f. o. b. Detroit. No Ford Cars sold unequipped

1913 FORD TOURING CAR

precipitated both the leaving and returning, but their curiosity was never satisfied. Dr. Miller was a very private individual, who seldom confided his personal affairs.

Jim, after talking to Wade Stuart and other ranchers, decided to turn more of his summer pasture into hay fields and send his cattle out with the pool herd. He'd have to pay the grazing fee plus his share of the pool rider's salary. Bess hoped he was making the right decision. It was a gamble to spend the extra money when they weren't sure they'd recoup their investment. The cattle market had been steadily declining since the end of the war, when the demand for beef lessened. It was difficult to predict what the prices would be by autumn, when they shipped the cattle.

The bottom land possessed plenty of water rights to grow more hay for the winter feed of the larger herd. Jim would have to help trail their cattle up to the mountain and then work hard all summer to get the new fields cleared so he could do the fall plowing. He was sure the hard labor was well worth it.

All the farmers and ranchers throughout the country rejoiced when the Daylight Savings Act was repealed in August 1919. The agricultural industry could now get their milk cows back on schedule and not have to go to bed before sundown in the summer time. Part of the hardship had been that farmers couldn't adjust their cream pick-up schedules to the changed railroad arrival and departures. It wasn't a concern for the Hart family, but they thought it was silly to take an hour off the morning and put it on the evening. No doubt some city fellow was responsible for that.

A lull between jobs gave Jim a chance to spring a surprise on Bess. He'd casually mentioned the possibility a week in advance. He hoped to get Bess primed. On the following Sunday he told everyone to get up and dressed because the children were going to stay with Grandpa and Grammy Hart for a few hours while Daddy and Mama went for a drive. This announcement, though unusual, caused no major questions from any of his family, though Bess thought he was being rather secretive. Maybe he just wanted to show her something. Soon the three children were stashed at their grandparents while Jim and Bess headed down the road leading to the Grand River bridge.

Crossing the bridge Jim drove the car a short distance and rounded a curve where he stopped the car. He pulled on the emergency brake.

"Slide over in the driver's seat, Bess," he commanded. He came around the car to the passenger seat.

"What in heaven's name are you talking about? Jim, I can't drive this car!"

"Well, by damn, you're gonna try. Now, let me explain all the instruments."

Her heart was pounding so hard that Bess could scarcely make any sense of what Jim was saying.

I can't possibly learn to handle this machine!

"See these three pedals on the floor? The left one is the brake, the middle is for reverse and the right one is for low gear. You take the emergency brake off, put your foot on the right pedal and it'll start movin'. That lever on the wheel will let you accelerate. Then when you want to stop just put your foot on the left pedal. Okay, now put your foot on the brake and release the emergency brake. Let's see you try it."

Bess trembled so hard her legs felt like they were rubber. "I'm not sure I can do this Jim. Let's wait a while."

"No, you've got to learn. You just go slow, and I'm here to help. Take off the emergency brake right now!"

Obeying the sharpness of Jim's command, Bess did as she was told. The car started slowly moving forward.

"You're doin' fine. Pull back the lever just a little bit and turn the wheel to the right."

Bess's did as she was directed. The car spurted forward and headed straight for the barrow pit. "Oh my God, it's going too fast! I can't steer it! Where's the brake? I want to stop!"

"Turn the wheel, turn the wheel!" Jim reached over and grabbed the wheel to straighten it out. "Now just steer with your left hand and use your right hand to work the lever."

The car slowly wobbled up the road with Bess over-steering it all the way. Her heart gradually stopped pounding, and she was finally able to concentrate on Jim's instructions. She gave it a little gas as the car bumped over the railroad tracks. Bess managed to turn east onto the main road going toward Grand Valley. Her confidence increased and she pulled back on the lever. The car careened wildly, dust swirling around the back wheels.

"Slow down, Bess! You're goin' too fast!"

"I'm doing fine," replied Bess as she whipped the wheel right and left. "This is easier than I thought it would be."

An hour later the car came to an abrupt halt in front of the elder Harts' place. Kitty and Bob came running out the door. "Mama, Mama, you're driving the car! Is it fun?"

Bess stepped down, her hands feeling numb from all the wheel vibration. "Yes," she replied, "It is fun, and it's really very easy."

Jim climbed out, looking pale. He consoled himself with the fact that Bess hadn't wrecked the car. He remembered what Susan Herwick had done to her father's brand new Saxon roadster. He only hoped that more practice would improve Bess's driving. Otherwise, he feared a new menace would be on the roads of Wallace Creek.

> Area newspapers were advertising a two-day event in DeBeque on July 4, 1919, which would celebrate the myriad oil shale activity taking place there. It was expected many people would be staying overnight for the various events and the evening dance. Lobbying efforts were planned to get the town designated the site of the proposed $150,000 oil shale testing plant.

No one would forget August 16, 1919. Bess and Nellie Hart had been busy all morning preparing a fried chicken dinner for the hay crew, who were raking and stacking the Hart families' hay. The hay crew was a cooperative venture made up of many area men who took turns helping each other. The last man to host the hay crew usually held his breath in anticipation. If it rained before the crew arrived, they wouldn't be able to cut the hay. Even worse would be to have the hay mown and laying in the fields when the storm came. Wet hay became moldy hay.

Each wife was responsible for setting out the best meal possible for the hungry men. A personal goal, however, was to be the one who got the most compliments for her cooking. Woe to the woman whose cooking was so bad the hay crew refused to eat at her house. The wives tried to outshine each other, and they slaved for days, preparing pies, cakes, and other delicacies. Planks were laid across sawhorses in the yard to accommodate the diners. Big pitchers of lemonade, cooled with the last of the precious ice from the ice house, accompanied big pots of coffee. Huge bowls of mashed potatoes and gravy shared table space with the crisp chicken and various fresh vegetables. Fresh baked bread and baking powder biscuits with jelly rounded out the fare.

The dust-encrusted men trooped in from the field and took turns with the soap and water in the wash pan. Bess and Nellie bustled around, placing bowls and platters at both ends of the table. The women stood back to see what they had forgotten to bring from the kitchen. The men were nosily filling their plates when a strange noise could be heard.

"What the hell is that?"

"Damned if I know. Sounds like it's comin' from the west."

"Sounds like some kind of machine."

Three airplanes, later identified as *De Havillands*, roared into view from the west, flying in formation. Their powerful 400 horsepower engines vibrated the earth as they roared overhead at speeds of 132 miles per hour. The awestruck men forgot their hunger while watching the extraordinary sight. Folks were accustomed to seeing an occasional plane fly overhead from time to time, but this was different. This was the machine that helped win the Great War.

The next edition of *The Daily Sentinel* newspaper carried an article about the three lieutenants and their crew, who started their flight in Salt Lake City then stopped in Grand Junction before flying on to Glenwood Springs and Denver. The pilots appeared at rallies for the U.S. Airmail Service, which began its service in May 1918. Thousands of men were trained as World War I aviators, and the government wanted to recruit them for the mail service. Far-sighted persons felt this was important to America's future. Government authorities and private companies hailed the advent of the airplane as something akin to the invention of the automobile. More pilots would be needed every month, and it was a daunting task to fulfill the quotas.

Before the Hart family could blink twice, autumn was upon them. Kitty was anxious to get back to school—Bob was glad he wasn't old enough. He was a quiet little boy so unlike his sister. Bob was happiest when he trailed after his daddy.

Bess and Jim looked forward to a lessening of the work load. During the summer Jim and his dad had been able to get more of the fields cleared. It wasn't an easy task, sandwiched between cutting the hay and numerous other ranch chores. Somehow Jim also found time to lay the rock foundation, and the carpenters from town arrived to work on the addition.

By late October Bess looked about her new rooms and sighed with appreciation. The parlor looked quite bare, but she'd buy a piece or two of furniture as she could. The sewing machine, her pride and joy, was sitting in front of the southeast window. Once the winter came she'd have to move it into the kitchen, but right now it was good to have a place where she could spread out the mending and sewing. She reminded herself they should also look for a wood heater to put in the parlor.

Bess walked into Jim's and her bedroom, next to the parlor. She looked with approval at the whitewashed walls.

It would have been nice to put up wallpaper, but that will have to wait for another time. Right now it's enough that I have smooth plaster on the walls—that was more important than the wallpaper. They look so nice! The plaster and linoleum should stop the cold winter drafts. And my rag rugs look so nice on top of the floral pattern. I finally feel respectable. When people stop by to visit, I won't be ashamed.

Of equal satisfaction, to Bess, was the screened-in porch at the front of the house. It had been created from the cutback between the two end sections. Maybe she'd would now be able to control the swarms of flies that invaded her kitchen during the canning season. She hated the filthy things and would never accept their inevitability as Mother Hart did. Bess thought that she'd need to teach the children to keep the screen door shut. More than once she'd angrily yelled at them for holding it open while they daydreamed.

In the midst of Bess's happiness she remembered what had made this all possible, and she burst into tears.

Oh, Lin Boy, I'd gladly do without all of it if you could be here with me. It's been over a year since we got the word of your death. I still imagine you'll come riding down the road, then I'll discover it was all a bad dream. I sometimes fancy that I can hear your voice at night. You were such a bright, handsome young man, and I will grieve your passing until I die.

• • • • • • • • •

Jim shipped his honey crop with the Battlement Mesa beekeepers and planned to get some extra cash for it. A Rifle man had shipped twelve thousand pounds, and he'd received ten thousand dollars. Jim believed he got a fair price for no more time than he spent on the bees. It was a crop that fed and watered itself, while adding a few more dollars to the family coffers.

Bess canned huge amounts of produce from her garden. Jim helped to bring the cattle off the mountain and cut out the ones to ship. The pool herder was a good worker, and there was little loss during the summer. The fellow cautioned he'd need some help getting rid of the larkspur next year. It was rapidly spreading to all parts of the range, and he'd barely kept up with it this year. That meant Jim and his dad would have to spend a week or so on the mountain next summer. Jim tiredly pondered how he'd get it done. He seldom caught up on all the work.

The calf crop had done well. Jim planned to sell forty steers and twenty cows—the most he'd ever shipped. Stock prices weren't at the level they'd been during the war, but they were reasonable. Even after settling up for the grazing fee and pool rider's salary, the Harts would realize a reasonable amount for the shipment.

The crops were in and the ranchers relaxed as some of their hardest work ended for the season. They'd have a little respite before starting on the fall and winter chores. It was time to have some fun.

Jim and Bess took the children for an overnight visit with Aunt Myra and Uncle Elmer, and to show off their car. There was to be a dance at the Oil Shale Theatre, and the couple looked forward to the occasion. Myra and Elmer were delighted they would have the children overnight, and the children were happy to explore the nooks and crannies of the household and farm.

Every area was represented at the dance: Battlement Mesa, Wallace Creek, Parachute Creek, and even a few folks from Rifle and DeBeque. Everyone was ready for a good time. The pungent smell of liquor drifted through the night air. The bootleggers had arrived early to sell their illegal refreshment.

Bess could overhear a group of men hoorawing as she and Jim entered the hall. The biggest topic of conversation was why Congress had enacted the Volstead Act over President Wilson's veto. Liquor prohibition would begin January 16, 1920.

"Hot damn! There's gonna be so many bootleggers they'll have to sell to each other."

"No do-gooder government is gonna tell us what we kin do!"

"They'll have a helluva time trying to find stills in this country. There's a lot of hills and gulches to hide one in!"

"Yeah, ol' Jake's got the right idea. After he moves his still, he runs his sheep over the top of it. Not a damned thing they can find."

"It's the church people's fault. We oughta teach them to keep their long noses out of our business. Who the hell do we hurt?"

The federal government's involvement on the West Slope had been a hard-won victory. First, their former hero, Teddy Roosevelt, made national forests out of their grazing land. Then, the government started charging grazing fees for livestock and made sure the timber cutting was kept to only designated areas. Next, it let the damned filthy sheep on lands that, heretofore, had been used only for cattle. The farmers and ranchers could go on and on about their woes with the federal government. Now, it was committing the ultimate insult by messing around with one of man's favorite pastimes. The local fellows, however, still had a few tricks of their own. They intended to stay one step ahead of the sheriff.

Bess could think of a few men who would benefit from taking the temperance pledge. Several families in town were victimized by drunken husbands and fathers. Bess was grateful that her husband wasn't a drunkard.

The midnight supper hour was over, and the musicians began tuning up again. They'd eaten a sandwich and drunk several cups of strong coffee, or something stronger if they were lucky. Men were drifting back into the hall after having visited with others over a liquor bottle and a roll-your-own. The women visited the outhouse and combed their hair. They waited for their dance partners to claim them when gunshots were heard. As if by magic, the hall cleared of men as they dashed out the entrance. Young boys followed, wanting to see who was fighting. This was rare good fun!

Wives and girlfriends sat big-eyed, waiting for someone to return with news. It might be good fun for the young and overgrown boys, but it was a fearful incident for women. Gunshots meant killing, and they weren't that far from frontier days when the loss of a spouse was linked to a life of impoverishment.

At last the men returned, laughing as if it was a big joke. "Aw hell, wasn't nothing to it. Old Ed and Pete had a few bad words over last week's card game. Marshall Ulrey broke them up, and they'll spend a couple hours in jail until they sober up—no harm done."

The men's eyes gleamed with excitement from the fight. Whirling their partners onto the floor they danced right up until 2:00 A.M. Someone suggested taking up a collection so the orchestra would play a while longer, but most folks were thinking of how early they'd have to rise to get the cows milked. Soon everyone straggled out the door and fired up their cars or hitched up their teams.

On the way back to her aunt and uncle's, Bess snuggled down into her heavy coat and blanket. The only advantage to the Model T was it got them home a bit quicker. It had been a nice evening even if there was no tall blond-haired man there. She yawned as she remembered she'd felt disappointed when she didn't see Alan Taylor at the dance.

What woman doesn't enjoy dancing with such a handsome man? It's exciting to be admired by a good-looking stranger. Oh well, there will be other dances. Right now I just want to go to bed.

> An extensive campaign against predatory animals in the national forests reached almost extermination levels in 1919. During that year forest rangers, government officials, and private hunters killed 6,796 coyotes, 958 lynx or bobcats, and 42 wolves.

Cecil Smith stopped by the Harts one day in mid-November. It had been snowing for several days, and drifts were piling up against the house. Bess saw Cecil and Jim talking in the yard. Both looked pretty serious. Jim came into the house as Bess was taking rolls out of the oven.

"Why didn't Cecil come in for some coffee? It's been a long time since we saw him—he should have warmed up."

"He wanted to get home before the storm hits. He's been in town and brought you a letter from Aunt Myra. Damn, Bess, Cecil has lost several head of cattle to the blamed milkweed. That stuff is so hard to get out of the hayfields. Folks are saying the only way to get rid of it is to plow the field up early in the season before the seed-pods form, but we can't afford to lose the hay crop. It's too late to do anything to the stuff that's already stacked, but I'd better keep a close eye out for it next year. If I dig it up by the roots that should do it, but we got a helluva lot of acres to go over. In the meantime Dad and I will have to see if there's any sticking up out of the snow. The cattle won't eat it if they have a choice, but you never can tell."

"It's always something, isn't it?" Bess shook her head. "I wonder what town people do for worry."

"They have their own problems. Carl says Walt Kerlee's Pastime Saloon burned down while he was gone to Glenwood Springs a few days ago. Everybody has trouble from time to time. Don't fret Bess, it'll turn out okay. We'll manage."

Oil shale company incorporations in 1919:

Grand Valley Oil & Shale	Starkey Gulch on Parachute Creek, north of Grand Valley
Campbell Refining Corp.	Conn Creek, north of DeBeque
Continental Oil Shale Mining & Refinery	Upper Piceance Creek
Champion Oil Shale & Refining	720 acres at Rulison
Monarch Oil Shale Co	Conn Creek, north of DeBeque
Belvedere Oil Shale & Refining	Upper Dry Fork of Roan Creek, north of DeBeque

One week later Jim couldn't find any bare ground much less milkweed. On the day before Thanksgiving, one of Western Colorado's worst, and most prolonged, storms hit the area. Some places received twenty-four inches in twenty-four hours. The Meeker mail carrier was stuck in drifts twelve miles out of Rifle. Teams of horses were sent out from Rifle to break trail over the top of Morgan Divide, covered with over three feet of new snow. Railroad service was tied up and the cattle, which were being held in pens, couldn't be shipped. Ranchers had to buy expensive hay to feed them. Snow was over the fence tops on Battlement Mesa. People accustomed to extreme weather were stopped in their tracks by the white onslaught.

"Damn it, I guess I'd better go open up one of the haystacks," Jim grumbled as he looked out the window on Thanksgiving Day. "At the rate the snow is comin' down, the stock won't be able to find any feed by tomorrow. I don't recollect ever seeing it come down this fast. I'd better pick up Dad and get some water holes opened up in the slough. Do you still want to go over to the folks for dinner today?"

Bess looked out the window in the back door. She could barely make out her garden patch, which was only twenty-five feet from the door. "I'd rather keep the children here unless you think it would make your mother mad. She probably has a huge turkey roasting."

"Well, nothing says we can't have Thanksgiving dinner tomorrow or the next day, after the storm moves on. I'll talk to her when I get Dad. I doubt she'd want the kids to be out in this weather." Jim looked appreciatively at the three pies which Bess was removing from the oven. "Don't worry, we'll just eat our part of the dinner right here."

"Nothing but pies? I don't think so! I'll rustle something else up. How long do you think it will take to get the ice broken and the stack opened up?"

"May take a while. We'll first have to hitch up the team and tromp down a feed ground for the cattle. Tell you what…go ahead and feed the kids when they get hungry but leave me a piece or two of pie." Jim struggled into his heavy coat, muffler, and the overshoes he seldom wore over his work boots.

Bess knew she'd not see Jim for a while. "Be careful out there. Don't try to do this without your dad there to help you. Tell your mother I'm sorry about the dinner. I'll keep some food hot for you."

Much like animals hibernating from the cold, citizens of Western Colorado hunkered down to wait out the worst of the storm. Only the most essential tasks were done until December 12 when, having spent its fury on the West Slope, the storm moved on. Temperatures then plummeted, creating a white, frozen wasteland.

Infrequent reports from town indicated that four to five feet of snow had fallen in Glenwood Springs. Bob Green was unable to deliver the mail for the first time since taking over as the rural carrier for Battlement and Morrisania Mesas. He'd been forced to stay overnight with a ranch family until the morning came.

The rural schools closed for several weeks, which would have pleased the pupils more if they could have gotten outside to play. Kitty's unwelcome vacation was a trial for both her and her mother. Instead of helping Bess with Freddie she just stirred up discontent in both the boys. Bess was grateful to have Kitty go back to school the second week in December.

"Remember, Kitty, your grandpa's going to pick you up this afternoon because your father and I are riding into town to see Aunt Myra and Uncle

Elmer. I've been worried about them since this storm broke, and I've got to see if they're all right. We should be back by supper time, but your grandma will take care of you until we arrive."

Jim yelled for Kitty to hurry along. He wanted to get her to school and get back to pick up Bess. They'd leave Bob and Freddie with the elder Harts because it was bitter cold. Bess knew Aunt Myra would be disappointed, but she couldn't take the chance of them getting a chill.

There were times when a man couldn't do better than a good horse, especially when you didn't know what condition the roads were in. This was one of those times. Jim and Bess decided it would be much better to just ride the horses. There hadn't been enough traffic to beat down a path on their road, and they couldn't guarantee the main road would be better. If nothing else, the railroad grade would be cleared.

The main road was plowed to the width of one vehicle, so they made good time. They worried they might meet someone and have to get out of the track into the deep snow. The sun did little to dispel the bone-rattling cold as Jim and Bess huddled deeper into their coats. The seven-mile ride seemed much longer than on a summer's day. The couple was grateful when they pulled into her aunt and uncle's yard. Myra and Elmer, having heard their shouts, stood at the door, waiting to welcome them. As she'd grown older, Aunt Myra had lost some of her frenetic energy, but she still bobbed on one foot and then the other.

"Land's sake, I'm glad to see you. We've been worried sick, wondering how things were on the ranch."

"I can say the same for you, Aunt Myra. We needed to come in and see if you were getting along okay. Have you ever seen anything like that storm?"

"Gracious me, why are we standing around by this cold door? Come in where it's warm. I just finished making a new pot of coffee. Jim, I'll bet you'll eat a bowl of soup and a piece of apple pie."

"You bet right on that one, Aunt Myra. But first I'd better go put the horses' blankets on and get them a drink and some grain. I'll be right back."

Bess took a critical look at her aunt and uncle. Hard work must agree with the couple because they both were holding up well. Myra was fifty-nine and Elmer sixty-four, yet they were hardy enough to take care of themselves in spite of Uncle Elmer's heart problems.

"I was so worried about you!" Bess said. "I was afraid your hired hands wouldn't be able to get out here, and you'd have to tend all the stock by yourselves."

"Gus walked up the tracks and then waded through the deep snow," answered Uncle Elmer. "Between the two of us we've been able to get the cows milked and the stock fed, though we haven't done much else."

"How are the children, dear?" Aunt Myra ladled up the soup and cut the fresh-baked pie, while Bess poured coffee in the thick white mugs. "Did the school close down?"

Jim came in from the barn, having stopped outside to stomp the snow from his feet.

"How're your cattle holding up, Jim?"

"Well, Elmer, we're managing, but if this keeps up all winter, we're gonna be in a bind for hay."

"You never mind about hay. If you run short you're welcome to come get a load off me. My hay crop did well this year, and I'll have some left over."

Bess and Jim left the Carpenter place midafternoon, following a good visit. Bess saw they were secure, but she wished she lived closer so she could look in more often. She hoped, once spring came, she'd be able to see them more often.

1920

> The Spanish flu struck many families in Grand Valley and the surrounding area with resultant fatalities. None, however, were more devastated than the Hurlburt and Shehorn families. Joe Shehorn, his wife, Lottie Hurlburt Shehorn, and their year-old baby girl died within a two week period. Two older children, Daisy and Oscar, survived and were raised by Lottie's family.

A series of storms had gone through the area in the first days of 1920. While none left the amount of the one on Thanksgiving 1919, each contributed a few more inches of snow. It was a rolling white landscape dotted with little knobs of fence posts sticking out of the ground. Keeping the cattle inside their property would have been a problem, except the herd stayed on the feed ground waiting for the next minimal allotment of precious hay.

The Battlement Mesa road was icy with the layer of packed snow. It glistened in the chill afternoon sunshine. Bess wished that this road could be scraped down like the main highway, but there wasn't equipment to spare. Come spring it would be nearly impassable when the snow started melting, not that the main road would be much better.

REBUILDING THE COLORADO RIVER BRIDGE FROM GRAND VALLEY TO BATTLEMENT AND MORRISANIA MESAS. TAKEN 1920.

"Our Father who art in Heaven…" The minister's voiced intoned the final prayer at the Battlement Mesa Cemetery, and the mourners started to file past the family to offer condolences. An elderly man, Uncle Bob to most folks, passed on after a month-long illness. His family had gone back and forth by train to St. Mary's Hospital in Grand Junction.

Bess and Jim didn't stop to visit, but nodded to others while they hurried to the team and wagon. They needed to get to the Strong home before the mourners. The ranch ladies throughout Wallace Creek and Una had brought food, and Bess would help serve dinner. She didn't know how many family members would be there, but she could count twelve in just one family. Many neighbors would also stop in to pay their respects and visit for a while. The house would bulge, although the men would likely move out to the barn, despite the biting cold. They'd smoke a bit and perhaps sample any available liquor.

"Uncle Bob had a nice service, don't you think, Bess? I suppose Annie and Ray will now help her mother and Bob Jr. out with the work." Jim tucked the reins under his leg while he rolled a cigarette.

"Hmmm?" Bess was lost in thought. Every funeral reminded her of her own losses. Despite their present good health, she had to face the eventual loss of Aunt Myra and Uncle Elmer. "Yes, I suppose so, if you can call any funeral nice. Mercy, it's cold! I'm glad we're almost at the Strongs'. A cup of hot coffee will taste good. Will you haul some water so I can get it boiling? I hope they banked the fire so it hasn't gone out."

Later Bess poured steaming mugs of coffee and offered plates of food to the family and visitors. She thought of the many families represented at the funeral. It was a comfort to have a close-knit community around you in times of trouble.

I wonder who will be there when the time comes for me? Let it be a long time from now.

The unusually severe weather continued. Jim and his father were worn down by the daily grind of feeding, tromping down new feed grounds, and watering the cattle. A miserable calving season followed, and the men were up day and night. The Harts couldn't afford to lose many out of their small calf crop. The cows were brought to the pastures closest to the barns although it meant hauling hay a longer distance. If need be, shelter would be available in an emergency. The men carried burlap sacks to rub down the newborn calves to dry them off before moisture froze on their little bodies.

Sometimes a cow who dropped a dead calf could be fooled into taking an orphan. The dead calf would be skinned and the hide put on the orphan like a jacket with its little legs sticking through the other leg holes. The cow, smelling the scent of her calf, would occasionally let the new one suck. Just as often she'd try to drive it off.

If the cow couldn't, or wouldn't, care for her offspring, the men had to ride to one of their houses to deposit the calf behind the cook stove. Bess or Nellie would then try to get warm milk down its throat through a nipple. After they were on their feet, the calves were transferred to a pen in the barn. Kitty and Bob fed them by a bottle until they could be weaned to a bucket.

On the less frigid days Bess relieved the Hart men so they could get a few hours of blessed sleep. She left Bob and Freddie with Nellie Hart while she rode through the herd. Bundled up to her eyes in coats, scarves, and gloves, Bess didn't curse the long bulky riding skirt like she usually did. It added another valuable layer of warmth in the near zero weather. The weight of her outer wrappings, however, caused a dilemma when she almost needed help to mount her horse.

Despite the freezing cold Bess took pleasure from the moments of solitude away from the daily routine of housework and children. She moved through the herd, watching the cows and their calves or searching for ones that she knew were ready to calve. The icy winter sun did little to relieve the chill, but illuminated the landscape with shiny crystals which sparkled like rare white gems. Bess fantasized that she was inside a giant, shimmering globe.

The last cow finally calved. Normally the weather started warming up. The Harts held their breath, hoping the hay would hold out until the grass started growing. It was not to be. The unseasonable cold, with frequent storms, lasted well into May.

On April Fool's Day the temperature again dropped below zero while another six inches of snow fell upon the ground. The total snowfall was six feet for the winter season. Between storms the snow melted, making quagmires out of the roads. The only sure way to travel was by horseback, and then only early in the morning before the frost left the ground. Anyone foolish enough to take their car onto the roads could plan on stopping at least every mile to clean out the packed gumbo from the fender well and tire spokes. The Hart family was fortunate to live close to the road going to and from Battlement Mesa. Their house provided a break for people passing by. Otherwise they would have keenly felt the isolation others felt that winter and spring.

May 1920 brought some solutions to old problems as well as creating a few new ones. Railroad service was severely impacted by a railroad strike across the nation. The worst of the strike was over the last part of April, and farmers heaved a sigh of relief that their cream would again be picked up and regular spring shipments sent.

Just as the strike was coming to an end, the raging rivers of Western Colorado flowed over roads, bridges, and railroad tracks throughout the region. By June 4, the area was virtually isolated from the rest of the world. Train tracks and bridges were destroyed by floods in the Gunnison, Glenwood Canyon, Dominquez Canyon, and Paonia areas. Two New Castle ranchers drowned when the cable tower holding a swinging basket over the Grand River broke and dumped the men into the swirling torrent.

• • • • • • • • •

On a June morning Bess could see Jim coming up the field from the river. She could tell by the set of his shoulders something terrible had happened. He came into the house, hung up his hat and wiped his forehead with a bandanna.

"The bottom third of the alfalfa is under water, Bess." He sat at the table, his head hung down. He looked utterly worn out. "But, that's not the worst of it. The ditch is also gone."

He didn't have to spell it out. Bess knew what that meant for him and his father. Not only would they lose at least the first cutting of hay, but it would take the two men several weeks to get the mud and debris mucked out of the ditch. While they did that, all the other springtime chores would be neglected. They needed to take the cattle out on the mountain. The top field had to be irrigated with the run-off from Pete and Bill Creek. Bess laid her hand on his shoulder and stood there in silent sorrow. There were no words to comfort her husband.

Every time we think we are getting ahead, something happens to make us start over at square one. Is there some sort of divine plan to keep us humble? Why does life have to be so hard?

The Hart families needn't have worried. When word got out to their neighbors about the flooded ditch, people stopped by to offer their help. Wade Stuart said he'd send down his hired hand to help trail the cattle out on top the mountain. Several others offered their assistance with the ditch. One man said he had a small horse-drawn scoop, called a fresno, which would make the job of digging out the ditch much easier. He promised to bring it and his team to the Hart place as soon as the water level went down.

By midsummer the Harts were back to almost normal, thanks to the help of their good neighbors. The cattle had been moved up to the summer grazing. Bess received a late shipment of chicks, and they were growing fast. She sighed when she looked at her garden. The seeds were a good month late in popping through the ground because of the below-average temperatures. Bess was obsessed with restocking the cellar with canned goods, and she fervently hoped the garden would start producing before the first frost. Hard telling because the weather had behaved so strangely the past few years. Maybe she could get some produce from Uncle Elmer if her garden failed.

Newspapers, when they reached the Harts, carried many articles about the booming oil and oil shale industry throughout the summer of 1920. Grand Valley and DeBeque were overrun by speculators. One landowner said he'd been offered a hundred dollars per acre for land that was useless except for poor grazing. Numerous families were moving to the surrounding mountains where the husband would do the assessment work on the oil shale placer claims. Many owners were concerned they'd lose their claim if the assessment work wasn't done before the first of the year.

Jim agreed to join a crew doing assessment work for Jimmy Doyle on the LaPaz claims located behind Mount Callahan. The two-week hiatus in late August and early September would provide the Hart family with some ready cash in case the garden and the cattle shipment weren't enough for them to get through the winter.

Bess looked at Jim, really seeing him for the first time in a while. He was thin from the heavy winter work, which had run right into the summer. "Jim, are you sure you want to go up there? You need to take a break. I swear you don't have a spare ounce of fat. You've been going steadily since calving season. We don't need the money that bad. Why don't you just stay home?"

"I'm at a good sparring weight," Jim said with a lopsided grin. "Don't worry, Bess, I can handle it. Jimmy's kinda counting on me and the rest of the guys. He's had trouble gettin' men to do the work because all of the other companies are hiring, too. I hate to let him down. The work won't be any harder than here, and it will be a helluva lot cooler. The only things I dread are the damned gnats. They might not be as bad now as they are in the spring, but you never know. Do you have any spare cheesecloth I could take up there? Some of the men drape it over their hats and tie it under their chins. It doesn't keep all the little buggers out, but it will help. Oren Herwick says he takes the shale oil that's bein' produced in their little retort and smears it on his arms, head, and neck. Makes him smell to high heaven, but it sure keeps the pests away."

> On August 27, 1920, *The Rifle Telegram-Reveille* reported there would be a unique performance during Apple Pie Day, to be held the following week. Just before the noontime pie and coffee banquet, an aviator and a representative from the newspaper would go aloft to distribute one thousand copies of the "Aeroplane Edition" to the crowd below. There would be special coupons in some of the newspapers for cash, in-kind gifts, or discounts for goods.

While Jim was away, Bess and the boys took an afternoon off to go calling on Isabella Stuart. After a nice visit, with Zane Grey's newest book tucked in her bag, she started down the high mesa road. Looking over the panorama she saw numerous cars and wagons on the road across the river, going west to DeBeque. From Bess's vantage point they looked like little bugs crawling along the bare, dry, sagebrush-dotted landscape. There were seldom more than twenty or so travelers along this route each day, and Bess was curious what had happened to increase the traffic.

Just as she reached the bottom of the hill and started to turn east, Bess saw Abe Wooley riding toward her. Curiosity won out over her desire to get home, and she awaited his approach.

"Howdy, Bess. You on your way home?"

"Hello, Abe. Yes, I've been up to Mrs. Stuart's, and I noticed all the traffic on the road. What in the world is happening?"

"Oh my God, Bess, it's a mess down there! Early this morning the westbound train was hit by a big slide on the hill just outside DeBeque. The locomotive and tender were thrown over the bank toward the river. It's a miracle they stopped before they hit the water. The engineer, fireman, and two young brothers from Glenwood Springs were killed, and they think maybe a third brother is still trapped under the locomotive. Another young kid was pinned by his hand and leg. They went into DeBeque and got Dr. Graff to go cut off the kid's hand so they could get him out. Doc says he's afraid the kid will also lose his leg."

"Oh my goodness, what a tragedy! Wasn't that a passenger train? What happened to them? Were any of them hurt?"

"Nosiree, it's a wonder, but the passenger cars stayed on the track. They sent an engine from the east to pull those cars back to Grand Valley. I think the railroad took the passengers on to Grand Junction by autos.

Jim Hart arrived home from the assessment work that evening, and he'd already talked to some folks going down to view the wreckage. The Harts got in their Model T the next morning to join the other gawkers at the scene. As Bess gazed down the hill, she shuddered to think that it could easily have been hundreds instead of a handful of fatalities. They could see the temporary tracks that were laid over a portion of the gigantic slide. The railroad had to keep moving no matter what. Fifteen cars of peaches from Palisade were sitting on a siding waiting to be shipped out to the market.

Further down the bank the locomotive and coal tender lay on their sides, almost at the water's edge. A steam crane was being erected to pull them onto a spur track, which was also being built. Authorities admitted it might not be possible to move them until the earth dried out and the slide became more stable.

There was still no sign of the third brother. Another man's clothing had pinned him between the engine and second car. Rescuers cut off his clothing to free him whereupon he became hysterical and ran away from the wreck. Everyone wondered if this might be the third brother, and if he was injured more extensively than thought. People hoped he would eventually appear in DeBeque.

●   ●   ●   ●   ●   ●   ●   ●   ●

Most of Wallace Creek turned out for a picnic in the vicinity of Harve Creek's cabin, located on the trail to the mountain. The women decided to meet the men coming down with the cattle and have a picnic. The herd would be trailed on down to the Horse Mountain Ranch where each owner's cattle could be separated out. The busy summer months were behind them, and everyone was taking a short breather before the next work began. At an elevation of seven thousand feet, the day was a mixture of golden warmth blended with a cool, brisk breeze, which carried just a hint of the cold that was to come. The women were glad to see each other after a busy summer apart, and they chattered away while setting out the food. Soon everyone was filling a plate from bowls and platters of beans, potato salad, fried chicken, roast beef, and light rolls served with freshly churned butter.

Mrs. Black lowered her ample bottom down upon the blanket beside Bob to eat her plate of food. "Well, there, young man, I'll bet you're really glad to be in school now. Isn't it fun?"

"No ma'am," Bob stated in an emphatic six-year-old voice. "I hate it! Mama, kin I go over to the corral with Dad? I ain't hungry."

"I'm not hungry," Bess corrected her son absent-mindedly. "I suppose you can go. You've eaten most of your food. You stay back from the cattle, you hear? I apologize for Bob's rudeness, Mrs. Black, but that boy purely hates school. He reminds me of Wade Stuart Jr., who would also rather be on the ranch than in school."

"Don't give it a thought, Bess. These young folks are a lot sassier than we were at their age."

Bess turned in time to catch two-year-old Freddie by his shirt tail. He was speeding after his brother. "No, you don't young man! You are going down for a nap." His plans thwarted, the child set up a howl while Bess spread another blanket under one of the huge trees. Patting her son's bottom while he sucked vigorously on his thumb, Bess soon got him to sleep. She quietly arose to help the other women clean up the leftovers.

Bess spied a new face and walked over to a young blonde woman standing off to the side, looking lonely and out of place. Her brightly printed georgette dress was fancier than the serviceable dresses worn by the Wallace Creek women.

"Hello there, I'm Bess Hart. I don't believe I've met you."

"I'm Sissy," said the young woman in a small child-like voice. Her large brown eyes looked at Bess with gratitude for making the overture.

"I'm glad to know you, Sissy. Are you visiting someone on Wallace Creek?"

"Oh no," Sissy giggled. "I'm Al Taylor's wife. We just got married two months ago."

Bess realized with a shock that Sissy was talking about Alan Taylor, the man who occupied more of Bess's thoughts than he should.

"Well, my word," Bess stammered, "I haven't heard a thing about Alan getting married. We haven't made it to any dances this summer so this is news to me. Has Alan been courting you for a while?"

"No, we met when he was in Grand Junction a few months ago. I was working at the Beanery, and he came in to eat several times. He asked me to a picture show and then a dance. Before we knew it, we were going to dances all over town. He said he liked the way I danced. I guess you could say it was a whirlwind romance. We were married before he came back to the ranch." Sissy flashed her finger before Bess's face. "Just look at my pretty ring."

"It's lovely, Sissy. Are you living in the foreman's house? I'll bet it was a mess because I know it hasn't been lived in for a while. Hasn't Alan been staying in the bunkhouse?"

"It really wasn't too bad. Mrs. Stuart sent one of the hired girls over, and she did most of the work. I'm not too good at that sort of thing."

"I'll bet Alan is glad to be in his own house and eating his meals with you instead of a bunch of rowdy cowhands."

"Actually, he's still eating his noon meal at the big house. I'm not too good at cooking either," Sissy tittered. "Ma did all the cooking, and I never had to learn. Al gets his own breakfast before I wake up, but he's trying to teach me how to cook at supper time. So far I've learned how to fix steak and make some fried potatoes. I tried to bake a cake, but that awful old stove made it fall. Al says he doesn't mind. He says I'll figure it out in time."

Bess was shocked. She'd never met a woman who didn't know how to cook. "I'm sure Alan's right. You'll be a good cook in no time at all. Maybe Mrs. Stuart would let you work with Cook for a while until you learn some of the basics."

"I guess it would help pass the time," Sissy said with doubt in her voice. "There sure isn't much to do on this ranch. Al's gone from daylight to dark, and I'm about to go crazy 'cause there's no one I can visit with. I went to see Mrs. Stuart one day, but she was doing the ranch accounts and said she couldn't talk. Al told me not to go back again because she's really busy. We don't even get to a weekly dance. I never thought marriage would be like this."

"Oh dear! Excuse me, Sissy. I've got to go rescue Freddie. I thought he'd sleep longer than he did. We'll talk more later. Congratulations." Bess called over her shoulder as she hurried to grab her son who was headed to the creek a short distance away. Having retrieved Freddie, she wandered among the other women whom she hadn't seen for some time. Bess almost laughed out loud at the thought of Sissy and Isabella Stuart having a serious conversation.

Whatever possessed Alan Taylor to marry someone like this young woman? I'll bet I know the answer to that question!

• • • • • • • • •

There weren't enough railroad stock cars to ship all of Western Colorado's cattle. After a short wait, Wallace Creek ranchers finally loaded all their stock, and the season's work slowed down. Jim Hart looked at the check for $2,800 and shook his head.

"This is what we get for twelve months worth of work. By the time we pay the shipping costs, deduct the money for next year's pool herder and grazing fee, pay off the grocery bill and lay in a few more supplies there won't be a lot for us and the folks to split. I'm sorry it can't be more, Bess."

"Nonsense, Jim Hart! There isn't a man on Wallace Creek that works any harder than you. It isn't your fault that cattle prices are so low. We've managed before, and we'll manage again. Look on the bright side—we're shipping more cattle each year. When the prices rise to pre-war levels, we'll be getting a pretty penny."

Bess patted Jim's shoulder. Her optimism sounded hollow, even to her own ears. It was discouraging to work so hard for so little. These were the times when she felt sorry for herself, but she tried not to dwell on it. Self-pity was a waste of time.

"You forget you'll get a small check from the sale of your honey. Maybe there will be enough to buy some nice gifts for the kids' Christmas. We might not have much, but it's all ours and not the bank's."

As the November 1920 presidential election grew close, Bess saw another side of her husband. Jim Hart was the mildest of husbands, mostly concerned with the task at hand instead of the affairs of the nation. It was with some surprise that Bess realized Jim was taking more than a casual interest in the political system. He'd started scanning the newspapers, especially *The Daily Sentinel* from Grand Junction and *The Rifle Telegram-Reveille,* both with pro-Democratic leanings. Walter Walker, *The Daily Sentinel* editor, blatantly marked a sample ballot with all Democratic candidates and published it in the newspaper, urging everyone to vote for those people.

"By damn, Walker has the right idea! Someone has to stir up people and make them get off their duffs. We need to elect men who'll help the average citizen. Big corporations have tied up everything in this country. That's why our cattle prices are so low. Midwest farmers are having the same problem with their corn and wheat crops. It's time that we stood up and were counted. Too bad we don't have a union like the labor workers. Then we'd make the public sit up and take notice."

Unfortunately for the Democratic party, James Cox and Franklin Roosevelt, the presidential and vice-presidential nominees, were soundly defeated. Their defeat was due in large part to Woodrow Wilson's failure to bring about the League of Nations before his stroke the previous year. Garfield County, however, voted a few Democrats into office. Jim thought that was better than nothing.

• • • • • • • • •

It was Christmas Eve, and Bess was beginning to wonder what had happened to Jim. He'd gone to town early in the morning and it was now milking time. Bess heard the cows lowing restlessly in the corral, waiting for their ration of hay while they gave up their twice-a-day offering of milk. Jim had been secretive when he'd left that morning. Bess hadn't probed because she was sure he was planning a special surprise for the children. Finally, she saw him driving the team up the road, their pace slower than usual. As he drew near Bess saw a fairly large object, wrapped with a tarp, tied to the back of the wagon. Whatever it was, it must be breakable because Jim was taking every precaution. He pulled off the main road and saluted as he drew near. There was a big grin plastered on his face. He drove the team right up to the screened porch and ordered everyone inside while he unloaded the parcel, being careful to keep it covered.

Jim came in to get the milk buckets, and Kitty launched herself into his arms, while Bob circled his legs. "Daddy, what ya got? Tell us!" They squealed and clung to him while he pulled them around the kitchen. Freddie, not to be outdone, held up his arms to his father.

"Hey there, you're gonna pull me over! Don't you know what day it is? It happens I met a man in a red suit while I was comin' home, and he said that he had too much to carry in his sleigh. He asked me if I'd deliver this for him. There'll be other things under the tree tomorrow morning that Santa will bring during the night, but he said it would be okay if we saw this one now. We need to get the chores done first, though. Let me go tend to those old cows so they quit bawling."

After Jim returned with the milk, Bess strained it and took it to the cellar. The Hart family hurried through dinner and the dishes. The children were tense with anticipation and, for once, didn't lag at their chores. Finally it was time. Jim opened the door to the icy December air and started jockeying the large crate into the room. Bess and the children silently stood and watched him slide the mystery item over the floor to an empty spot along the wall. He pried off the boards until dark varnished wood appeared.

"Aw Pa, it's just a piece of furniture," cried Bob. "Looks like a plain old dresser to me."

"Well, it is a piece of furniture but it's a magic piece. Just wait and see."

The last few boards were removed, and Bess let out an excited squeal. "Oh my word, Jim, how wonderful! Come here, children. You're in for a big surprise!"

Bess helped Jim open a box within the crate and lifted out something shaped like a plate. Jim grabbed a crank on the side and turned it until he could crank it no more. Bess settled the plate onto a revolving round table in the top of the cabinet. She lifted a metal arm and carefully placed it down upon the rotating base. The children were startled to hear many voices coming from the machine.

"Silent night, Holy night; all is calm, all is bright…"

They stood transfixed by this amazing machine that could make music. All three began jumping up and down in their excitement. The song was interrupted by a series of terrible scratching sounds.

"Careful, careful," Bess said. "When you jump around like that you make the needle bounce and it scratches the record. Do you know what this is? It's called a Victrola. Isn't it wonderful? Let's see what songs we have here." She hugged her husband as she went by. Jim was still grinning like a kid.

"You never asked me about the honey shipment check so I just put it back, plannin' on gettin' us something nice—something everyone would enjoy."

Before the evening was over, all the twenty-some records had been played and replayed. After their initial awe, the children joined their parents in dancing around the kitchen and into the parlor, warmed by the recently installed heater. After they tired of dancing everyone settled down to listen to the wonderful old Christmas carols. The children snuggled down into their parents' arms. Soon Jim and Bess carried the limp, sleeping bodies to their beds. They started placing the presents under a fat pinon tree. Bess decorated it with ornaments, remembering to add the old tobacco can cutouts which had become a tradition.

Arm-in-arm, the Harts walked to their bedroom, filled with love for each other and their family. It was a good Christmas.

In addition to many forerunners, three new oil shale companies began operations in 1920:

Washington Shale Oil & Products	210 acres on Conn Creek, north of DeBeque
Union Oil Company of California	Parachute Creek, north of Grand Valley
Index Oil Shale Co.	640 acres at Rulison and 640 acres on Mount Blaine

"Ma, have you seen my dolly's dress, the one with all the ruffles that Grandma made for her? I want to take it with me when we go over there tonight."

Bess looked at her daughter who would soon be nine years old. Kitty, already tall, resembled Bess at that age, except her hair was even more red than Bess's auburn locks. She'd continued to be an excellent student in school. Bess was very proud of Kitty's studious side, about the only thing they held in common. Their strained mother-daughter bond had improved a little over nine years, but Bess still felt maternal shortcomings. She was stung to the core whenever Kitty ran to share some confidence with her grandmother rather than Bess. Nellie Hart was able to give Kitty the enthusiastic love and appreciation that Bess wished she could display. Try as she might, Bess simply could not convey her innermost feelings to the girl. Whenever she tried, it usually came out sounding brusque, something that Bess neither felt nor wanted to show.

The only child she felt lighthearted with was Freddie. She knew she indulged him far too much, but he had a way of melting her heart that neither Kitty nor Bob was able to do.

"If you'd keep those doll clothes in that little case, you wouldn't have to run around trying to find them all the time. I think I saw some clothes behind the heater in the parlor where you were playing this morning. Your father is waiting in the car so you'd better get your coat on. Bob, have you got everything you want to take to Grandpa and Grandma's? Freddie, please stand still so I can get your coat buttoned."

The Stuart family was again hosting a party on New Year's Eve. The weather was relatively calm, so most of the Wallace Creek families would probably be there. Bess squirmed, knowing she was perhaps looking forward to it for the wrong reason. Alan and his wife would surely be there, and while she didn't relish seeing one, she certainly did the other.

Automobiles competed for space with horses and wagons in the snow-packed yard. A scent of spruce greeted the couple as they stamped their feet just outside the back door. The scene within was familiar to them. "Remember that first New Year's Eve?" Jim squeezed Bess's shoulder as he removed her coat.

Bess scanned the room to see which friends were already there. Isabella Stuart was at the piano, and she waved with her right hand while continuing to play with her left. Wes Venere had replaced a broken string on his fiddle, and some man she'd never seen tuned up a guitar. The dancing would soon begin.

Jim joined Bess as they went around the big room greeting friends: Annie and Ray, Aunt Ila and Carl, the Karrs, the Wooleys, the Laidenhills, and other friends and neighbors. Bess causally glanced about the room, seeking another tall figure with blond hair. She was disappointed. Neither Alan nor Sissy Taylor was at the party.

After several hours Josephine Stuart replaced her mother at the piano when Mrs. Stuart went to the kitchen to supervise the preparation of the midnight supper. Bess excused herself to help. Mrs. Stuart was her usual efficient self, whooshing about with cake knives and pie cutters, issuing orders to the cook and her helper.

"Here, Mrs. Stuart, let me do that for you," said Bess.

"You can cut the pies, and I'll slice the cakes," Mrs. Stuart replied. "I think Cook has everything else well in hand. How have you been? Did you have a good Christmas?"

"Oh yes! Jim surprised us with a Victrola. We've almost worn out the records already! How about your family?"

As the two women chatted, Bess found the courage to mention the one thing she was dying to know. "I'm surprised that Alan and Sissy Taylor aren't here. She said she loves parties and dancing so much."

"Oh, Bess, you haven't heard? I assumed that everyone on the creek knew she ran off. I saw a strange car drive up to their place one day. I didn't think much about it and went on with my tasks. Alan came over that evening to ask if we'd seen her. A man friend came clear from Grand Junction to get her, and she left while Alan was in the upper fields feeding the cattle. She stole what little money he'd saved up and took everything they'd acquired since their marriage. Let me see, it must have been about Thanksgiving when she left. Alan, of course, doesn't say much but he's been moping around since then. Good riddance to trash, if you ask me."

Later that night Bess donned her coat to step outside for a breath of the cold night air and to use the outdoor privy. She lingered on the path as she viewed the faint light coming from Alan's quarters.

What would it be like to love someone so much that you'd grieve when they left? I grieved for Mother and Lin but they were blood-kin. How would I feel if Jim left me? I'd like to tell Alan how sorry I am. He'll find someone better, someone who'll really appreciate him. Of course, I can't. Married women can't do such things. Go back inside, you silly goose.

1921

The first week of January 1921 brought disquieting news to DeBeque. Prior to coming to the area, Dr. Graff, their physician, had been charged with a death in the Denver area. The case was finally dismissed by the Denver County Attorney. The Colorado Board of Health then hired Dr. Graff to treat influenza patients in the DeBeque area. The physician worked tirelessly during the epidemic, and his quick action later saved the pinned lad in the train wreck. It was a blow when the doctor was denied the reinstatement of his medical license, despite the testimony of a number of influential citizens. The DeBeque area would, once again, be without a medical doctor.

The second piece of news was the murder of a section hand by a fellow worker. The murderer, an Army deserter, knew the victim had saved over one hundred dollars during his summer work with the railroad. He was soon apprehended five miles east of DeBeque while trying to run away. They took him to jail in Grand Junction, with another man who was in custody as a possible accessory. When the news reached the Wallace Creek area, the women shivered to think that the murderer had come so close to their homes.

January's mild weather made the farmers and ranchers edgy because they were so dependent on irrigation. The year's snowpack spelled the differences between their family making a few dollars or going deeper in debt.

In spite of the warmer weather, the papers reported all the ice had been cut by January 20, and it was quality ice. Several men worked together to build a cottonwood log structure down by one of the river sloughs on the Hart ranch. It was a cooperative venture where all who helped fill it with ice would be able to draw upon its cool contents the following summer.

Senator Ed Taylor and many other influential people introduced legislation to change the name of the Grand River to the Colorado River, a name that was given by the early Spanish explorers.

In his resolution to the House of Representatives the esteemed Senator stated, *Historically and in compliance with the policy of the United States Geographic Board, the stream should have been named and known as the Colorado River throughout its entire length from its source in Grand County, Colorado, to its confluence with the*

Green River in Utah and thence to its mouth in the Gulf of California.

Many people thought this was a ploy the politicians dreamed up to get more newspaper coverage. It didn't really matter what it was called as long as it continued to flow, but it never hurt to remind those downstream folks whose water they were drinking.

It would be a number of years before the final approval was given for the name change.

Farmers and ranchers were greatly concerned about how they were going to send their livestock and produce to market if the freight charges kept spiraling upward. Six western stockmen's associations appealed to the Interstate Commission for a reduction of freight rates. Stock prices had decreased forty to fifty percent in recent months, and they were not able to make enough on the stock sales to pay the freight. A stopgap measure was ordered to suspend the freight increases from February 15 to June 15 in hopes stock prices would again climb. Everyone knew the suspension was just one more way of putting off the inevitable.

"By God, Bess, I don't know what we'll do if the stock prices don't come up before fall." Jim brought a new supply of papers home from town. He shook his head while reading. "Taylor doesn't seem to be looking into that. He's doing something to build schools and roads, never mind our ranch kids won't have a roof over their head." Senator Taylor was proposing legislation that would send back to the counties fifty percent of the royalties received from coal, oil, oil shale, gas, and sodium production on public domain lands located in each of those counties. "I guess we can always let the land and cattle go and work for the oil companies. In another year or two we'll be tripping over them, anyway."

"What do you expect from a politician, Jim? I keep telling you the Democrats are just like the Republicans; they sell out to the highest bidder. Not one of them cares how it affects the little guy."

Everyone gathered for a Valentine dance at the Wallace Creek school. Folks wondered if they'd see Bill Karr's new bride. His wife, Louise Fryer, was no stranger to some Wallace Creek families, having been born and raised in DeBeque. Bess hoped Louise's life would be easier than hers. The life of a ranch woman was hard at best.

Bess was serving sandwiches, cake, and coffee when she looked up to see those amazing blue eyes staring down at her. Her pulse quickened. "Hello, Alan. Would you like something to eat?"

"No thanks, Bess, but I would take a cup of coffee, if you don't mind." He seemed inclined to linger and talk.

Bess struggled to regain her composure and carry on the conversation. What should she say about Sissy? "How have you been Alan?"

"I've been better. I guess you've heard about me and Sissy splittin' up?"

"Yes, I have, and I'm so sorry. Maybe if she'd been closer to town she wouldn't have felt so isolated…"

"You don't have to make excuses for her. I guess we all know what kind of a girl Sissy is. I was a damned fool for gettin' mixed up with her. Sorry, I didn't mean to cuss in front of you."

"Well, it seems to me you've got a right to be angry. It isn't every day a wife deserts her husband." Bess scrutinized Alan's face. To the casual eye his handsome good looks were the same, but Bess thought she could see a narrowing of his eyes and his full sensual lips looked more tightly compressed. "Have you heard from her?"

"Yeah, I got a letter from a Grand Junction attorney telling me if I want to file for a divorce on the grounds of desertion Sissy won't contest it. It seems she's left with her new friend for California. I'm in no hurry to set her free. If she wants a divorce, she can pay for it. Well, I'll see you around." Alan put down his cup and walked rapidly away. Bess stared after the man wanting to touch and soothe him, not understanding the strong feelings she had for him. Alan disappeared out the door and wasn't seen again that night.

> High water in the Grand River destroyed the DeBeque pumping plant on June 17, 1921. Cost estimates suggested it would take several thousand dollars to repair the damage. In the meantime citizens of that community were forced to find alternate means for drinking water.

Glenwood Springs citizens were jumping with joy over the road work in the Glenwood Canyon. It was being done by about forty convicts from the prison at Cañon City. Business people touted the route as a part of the Pike's Peak Ocean-to-Ocean Highway. Jim told Bess he'd talked to Si Herwick, who said the road was the smoothest he'd ever ridden on. A person could drive an amazing speed on the gravel surface. Si was enthusiastic because the improved highway would cut travel time when he went up to see old cronies in Eagle County.

There was also proposed legislation that caused alarm for the citizens of DeBeque and Grand Valley. Senators Bannister of Mesa County and Callen of Garfield County were introducing petitions from citizens in their areas to "construct a highway from New Castle, Rifle, and Silt to connect with the Midland Trail to Grand Junction, avoiding the tedious trip via DeBeque. Tourists would enjoy a more pleasant, easier trip by way of Buzzard Creek and Plateau Valley than the dusty, uninteresting drive down the Grand Valley."

"That's gonna make the oil shale promoters mad," chuckled Jim. "I wonder where in hell these guys have been livin'. Sure it's a nice drive in the summertime, but what would they do in the wintertime when the snow is ass deep to a tall horse? Besides, the railroad isn't gonna move their tracks so our road will still be used the most. I'll bet DeBeque isn't happy that they might lose all the shipping trade. Remind me not to vote for Callen the next time around."

● ● ● ● ● ● ● ● ●

The snowpack hadn't been deep over the winter, and the hay crop from the upper field was sparse. Then the rains started in July, bringing some welcome moisture and greening up the parched landscape. Jim even thought he might get another cutting off the upper field if a few more storms came through, but he didn't reckon on a gully washer the last day of July.

Bess stood before the window, coffee cup in hand, watching the drizzling rain plopping gently into the sea of mud that was their front yard. Rivulets wended their way down the slope through the small gullies made by the recent watery onslaughts. When she grew tired of standing in front of the window, she paced back and forth. Concern was evident on her face. If not for the cloud cover, the sun would be coming over the hill about now.

Where could he be?

Visions of Jim lying in the barrow ditch between here and town had haunted her all night. She was literally sick with worry.

Jim went into Grand Valley the previous day for some supplies and should have been home by dark. The recent rains probably made auto travel slow, even over the newly constructed gravel road. Unfortunately, the rain started in late afternoon just about the time she estimated Jim would be starting home.

The downpour was relentless. It increased in force until it looked like the house might float off its foundation. Bess couldn't recall a worse storm since she'd lived in Colorado. The rain was accompanied by one bolt of lightning after another, some of them hitting so close she feared the house would be struck. Then the wind came like a force out of hell, rattling everything inside. The noise from the wind was exceeded only by great claps of thunder.

The children were terrified, not only from the storm but because their father was someplace between the ranch and Grand Valley. Bess put all three in her bed and soothed them throughout the long night. She knew she should check on the stock, but decided there wasn't a thing outside worth losing her life over. Although she was terrified for Jim, she tried to believe he would get to safety, wherever he was.

The lightning and wind abated around dawn, and the children dropped into an exhausted sleep. Bess quietly closed the door and started a fire in the cook stove to make coffee and cereal. It would have tasted good during the night, but she'd been afraid to build a fire in case the wind blew the stovepipe down.

When she next paused by the window, she saw a horse and rider slowly making their way up the road. Thank God! It looked like Jim. He must have been forced by the storm to leave the car and beg a horse to get him home. She met him at the screen door. He was covered from head to toe with mud, and he looked like he was on his last legs.

"I've been so worried about you. Where have you been? I kept seeing you lying in a ditch someplace."

"Bess, let me take the horse up to the barn and get him fed and watered. He's had a helluva time gettin' me home in this flood."

Jim soon returned from the barns and chicken coops. He'd stopped to survey the damage caused by the storm. Bess hoped the hogs and chickens survived the mini-flood, but it would be a miracle if they were alive.

Jim sloshed through the kitchen door having left slicker and boots on the front porch. His face and hands were mud-speckled, and he went to the wash basin to clean them. "By God, that was some toad strangler! We were damned lucky. The main current came down on both of sides of the house. We're just high enough to escape the worst of it. But, we now have two new ditches in the alfalfa field."

"Never mind about that! Where have you been?"

"I've been up all night helping in Wheeler Gulch. I'd just finished gettin' the supplies yesterday when a guy came tearing down Parachute Creek in his car, yelling that the tram broke and they needed help in recovering the bodies.

A few of us jumped in the guy's car. Others cranked up their own cars, and we all headed up the creek. My God, what a sight. Bess, you can't believe how bad it was. The tram cable apparently slipped from the swivel, and the tram car crashed right down the mountainside, all two thousand feet of it. There were bodies all over because the car was smashed to smithereens on the big rocks as it came down the hill.

"One poor guy's head was cut off when the cable snapped. Let me tell you there wasn't much left of some of 'em, but there were a few survivors. I think three of them were still alive when the rescuers got to them. They'd been taken out by the time we got there, and we started lookin' for more bodies. We picked up the pieces as long as we could see, and someone came from town with a lot of lanterns so we could go on lookin'. Then that damned storm hit, and we were forced to take cover for a while. The lightning was bouncing off those cables and the water was running down the hill like a river. We did the best we could in finding everyone, but I wouldn't be surprised if there weren't more body parts up there in the mud. Another crew spelled us this morning. I need to check out our place and tend the stock, then I'm goin' to bed."

"Don't worry about tending to the stock. Eat some oatmeal and go to bed. I'll get you a better breakfast after you've been able to get a few hours rest. The children will sleep for a while because they were up most of the night. They were so scared—we all were. I don't think I'll let you out of my sight for a while." Bess brushed back Jim's wet hair in a caress. "I was so afraid for you."

Shortly after noon the family was gathered around the kitchen table having a combination breakfast and lunch. Bess had worked outside a good share of the morning, tending to the poultry and animals. Jim looked only slightly rested, but Bess wasn't able to make him stay in bed.

"What about the hogs and the chickens? Did any survive?"

"Yes, they did. I guess the hogs huddled up in their shelter, and the chickens were in the coop. I doubt I'll get any eggs today cause they're pretty upset. I gave them feed because they won't be able to come out to scratch. The mud is a good six inches deep. My garden is a muddy mess but it missed the worst of the water. I think some of the plants survived."

Jim shook his head. "It wasn't doing all that well anyway. We need a couple weeks of sun to dry everything out. I wonder how the pool herder managed up on top the mountain. Those damned spooky cattle may be clear over to Collbran by now."

"Do they need more help up the gulch? Will you have to go back up there?"

"Nah, I think they'd have all the bodies brought down by the time I could get up there. I knew you'd be worried sick, else I would have stayed on a while longer. There were quite a few guys up there by this morning. Oren Herwick was up there all night with me. He heard the big bosses will be on the train today to start their investigation. The place will be crawling with 'em until after the inquest. You know the funny part of this? There wasn't one Grand Valley man killed. The dead had all recently come here to work from other places. One of the guys that was killed, Jim Botts, lived in DeBeque with his wife and kids. Damned shame."

Jim and Bess donned their slickers and boots and spent the rest of Sunday repairing the damage caused by the storm. Bess scowled at the beaten down plants in her garden but thought they'd revive in a week or so if allowed to dry out.

The hogs were slogging around in six inches of sticky mud, which almost ran over the top of their feed trough. Jim took a shovel and cut a trench to drain some of the water out under the pen. The shelter was on the uphill side and had escaped the worst of the mud, but Bess knew the animals couldn't stay there unless the water level was reduced. The chickens dozed on their perches, their heads beneath their wings. The day continued to be gloomy, and they apparently thought it was night. It was a tight chicken coop and they'd be safe for a while.

Bess felt electricity in the air as she and Jim dug the trenches around the hog pen. She fancied she could almost smell the sulfur, but knew it was her imagination. They needed to prepare for another possible long night, unless the storm moved on east.

Jim went to his parents' in late afternoon to make sure everything was all right at their place. Bess was relieved when he came home and reported all was well. "Ma and Dad are doing okay, but the livestock's in too much mud. It's a good thing there are ditches on both sides of the house. They kept most of the water out of the yard. I'll bet we lost some cattle up on the mountain, from lightning strikes if nothing else. Ma said it was a good thing that she didn't know I was out all night, 'cause she would have had a heart attack."

Jim and Bess decided there was still too much mud in the hog pens so they herded the animals into a makeshift pen in the corner of the barn. The pigs, instead of eating, just stood and squealed. It was a tight fit with the horses and cows, but at least they'd be safe through the night.

Thundering, torrential rains battered the area again that night, and into the next day. Jim slept from total exhaustion, but Bess couldn't relax enough to sleep. She watched from the windows as lightning illuminated the landscape. The ground was saturated, and there was no place for the water to go except down the hay field and into the river.

Earlier in the evening Bess expressed her concern to Jim. "I'm worried about Aunt Myra and Uncle Elmer living so close to the river. I don't know how much it's risen, but I'll bet anything it's up in the fields. It would have to get pretty high to get to the house, but all the same I think we need to check on them."

"Tell you what, I've got to get the horse back to the livery so I'll saddle both it and my horse and go in tomorrow. I don't know when I'll be able to bring the car home. That damned 'dobe mud will just ball up around the wheel spokes on the car."

Jim left the ranch early the next morning just as a watery sun peeked through leaden clouds. If the mud proved to be too deep he could always follow the railroad right-of-way that contained cinders. Bess didn't rouse the children. They'd had another restless night. She looked longingly at her bed and thought how wonderful it would be to curl back into its warmth. She thought of Jim out in the boggy mess and got busy on the household chores.

Jim returned in late afternoon, he and his horse looking very fatigued from fighting deep mud and slippery cinders all the way. "Well, the tram disaster isn't the only thing that happened in Grand Valley this week. The bank was robbed last night!"

"You must be joking! A bank robbery in Grand Valley?"

"No, by damn, I'm not. When Judd Sipprelle opened up this morning he found the vault cut into and everything ransacked. The front door was pried open, and they cut through the brick wall of the vault so someone could open the door from the inside. Then they wrapped the safe with wet blankets and set off a nitro charge. They're guessing all the thunder covered up the noise of the explosion. Pretty smart bunch of robbers, if you ask me. They figure around twenty thousand dollars in cash and bonds were taken. Man, between this and the tram accident, the town's crawling with all kinds of officials. I haven't seen that much activity in a long time."

"Well, I guess you got your money's worth by going into town today, but I want to know how Aunt Myra and Uncle Elmer are?"

"They're holding up okay. The barn's big enough to get most of the barnyard livestock inside. Gus White moved the dairy herd up in the field closest to the railroad tracks. A flash flood came down Hays Gulch and brought some more rocks over the road but the water is goin' on down to the river. You can't get a car or buggy under the train trestle right now, and Uncle Elmer is fussing about not gettin' the cream shipped. He won't starve to death if he misses sending it for a few days. Aunt Myra is making more cheese and feeding whole milk to the hogs. Don't worry Bess, Gus has managed to get there every day. If he has to, he can even walk up the railroad track to get to the place. He promised me he'd let us know if the folks need us. Don't worry, okay?"

Western Colorado continued to be deluged with heavy downpours the entire month of August 1921, bringing almost four inches of moisture to crops that couldn't be harvested, even if they were growing. September, however, dawned sunny, if cooler than normal, and the plants, having waited so long to grow, appeared to be in a frenzy to see how fast they could mature. Bess was kept busy from dawn to dusk preserving all the surviving produce from her garden. Jim was able to get his hay stacked and had gone to help his neighbors. The furrows in the field remained to remind them of the wettest August on record, but the winter prospects didn't look quite so grim.

All the ranchers gathered for the roundup. There were some cattle losses, but the remaining herd looked fat and sleek. If the prices were higher, it might have been a profitable year. Steers were selling for eight dollars per hundred pounds, calves going for a little higher, cows a little less. By the time Jim settled up his part with the pool herder and paid for shipping costs, there would be little cash for the next year.

"Maybe I should sell the damned cattle and go find a job. God knows it won't pay to winter and summer them only to go deeper in hock."

"I know we don't seem to make any progress," Bess replied, "but we, not the bank, own our land. That is something for you to remember, Jim."

The Harts took advantage of a clear but chilly November weekend to pay a visit to Uncle Elmer and Aunt Myra, do some shopping, and attend the movie and dance at the Oil Shale Theatre. The children went with Bess and Jim so they could go to the picture show, like they'd been promised. The children would go back to the Carpenters' place after the show, and then Jim and Bess would attend the dance. Big Jim would do the night and morning milking so the family could have an overnight visit.

Freddie, just past his third birthday, was pleased to have a new adoring audience. He charmed Uncle Elmer by crawling into his lap, something the other two had been too bashful to do. Bess gazed at the man and child and considered how much impact grief had upon the human soul. Before Lin's death she could never have imagined her uncle would change so much. He'd become this caring, nonjudgmental person who not only tolerated her and her children but actually looked forward to seeing them. It was sad that it hadn't happened sooner, but better late than never. The older Bess got, the more she realized it must have been hard to have two orphans foisted off on him.

Bess readied the children for the movies and left them to visit with Aunt Myra while she went to the bedroom to change for the evening. She held up her dress to admire the brilliant color of purple. She knew she wasn't supposed to wear anything that shade because of her red hair, but she'd spied the fabric in Doll Brothers Store and was enchanted by the vibrancy of the color. She'd used some of her egg money to purchase the material and, in her spare moments, worked on it all summer. The dress was a lightweight crepe, very straight with a lowered waist, which clung to the curves of her body. The hem fell just to her calf, the shortest length she'd ever worn. Her legs felt naked without the accustomed weight of fabric swishing around them.

Jim came into the bedroom to hurry her along and was struck by the classic beauty of his wife. "Man alive! I'll have to fight off all the dance hall romeos tonight!"

Bess blushed under his admiring gaze, not wanting to break the appreciative spell by speaking. Taking his arm, she guided him out the room to gather up the children.

The hall was blazing with lights, and Jim was forced to park a block away because of the many cars that had arrived before them. Bess ushered the excited children through the door, while Jim paid the twenty-five cent admission price for each family member. The children were squirming in their seats, barely able to contain their excitement. At last they were going to see a silent film!

That night's feature was *Peck's Bad Boy*, starring the child actor Jackie Coogan. Bess would have preferred seeing something a bit more uplifting, like the *Three Musketeers* or *The Last of the Mohicans*, but in Grand Valley you watched what was available. She knew the children would enjoy the movie's childish antics.

Bess was correct. Kitty, Bob, and even little Freddie were spellbound by the moving figures. Winnie Waterman played a perfect piano accompaniment for the printed dialogue at the bottom of the screen. There were laughs galore at the naughty antics of Henry Peck and his cohort. Their loudest laughter was when Henry let the man-eating lion out of the circus cage, and again when he loaded his father's lumbago pad with ants. The children were horrified when Henry's little dog, Buddy, was captured by the dogcatcher. They loudly clapped when Buddy was rescued along with all of the other captured dogs.

Henry Peck's mother doted on her son and thought he could do no wrong while his father was the butt of Henry's numerous pranks. Although Bess joined in the laughter, she thought a good spanking would have done the hero a world of good. She hoped Freddie wouldn't try to duplicate any of the pranks in the movie. Later Bess heard Kitty tell Bob that it must be nice to have a mother who wasn't so strict. Bess pretended she didn't hear, but she couldn't help feeling sad she and her daughter didn't see eye to eye.

When Jim and Bess returned to the hall, people were milling around outside the big double doors. Folks were waiting for men and boys to push the chairs to the side of the room and slicken the floor.

Bess was surprised how many women were now smoking cigarettes in public. The modern practice was becoming commonplace, but Bess still felt a small shock every time she saw a woman light up. It just didn't seem very respectable although she wondered how a cigarette might taste.

Jim paid the dollar admission, and guided Bess to a pile of coats on a row of chairs. People, who didn't have the advantage of leaving their children at home, brought them. The kids played until they were tired. When ready for sleep they'd climb upon the soft comfort of a pile of coats and go to sleep. Mothers brought nursing babies and retreated to a corner when the child got hungry. She'd lay it down in a pile of blankets or find another pile of coats. No one thought much about the custom. *Ma, he's making eyes at me…*

Bess and Jim circled around the room to the rhythm of the catchy new tune. Armand DeBeque's orchestra was playing that night. Everyone was having a good time and, thus far, there was no sign of rising tension between the fight-prone men. Bess was lost in the rhythm of the music when she saw the tall man across the floor. Alan Taylor lounged against the wall by the door, talking to Jake East. Jake was pointing to his hand which, Bess heard, had been severely burned in a gasoline fire. Alan glanced out at the crowd. Bess saw his blue eyes come to rest on her and lock. As Jim twirled her round and round, Bess imagined the eyes followed them across the floor, inviting, seductive.

The music ended, and Jim took her back to a group of wives sitting along the side. Alan Taylor was gone, and Bess couldn't account for the disappointment his leaving brought.

What it is about Alan that causes these thoughts? I love my husband, or at least I think I do. I barely know Alan, so why am I drawn to the man? Maybe it's just that he's different, and God knows I'm so tired of the same old thing day in, day out. He shouldn't look at me the way he does, but I feel so pretty when he does. What's the harm in letting him?

She pushed the daydream aside and eavesdropped on the latest gossip. "Did you hear Bert Robin was sentenced to four months for messing around with that hussy? It's about time some of these men were convicted of adultery. Maybe they'll think twice before they carry on like that."

"Well, if you ask me, I think the woman should have served the same sentence. Trying to take a man away from his wife. Too bad the judge was easy and sent her home. I wonder what the husband is going to do." A small shiver ran down Bess's spine as she listened to the comments about adultery.

I just enjoy being admired. I'd never do anything like that, at least I don't think I would.

To Bess's relief, the conversation then turned to a group of young people and who was dating whom. The young folk, oblivious to the sideline commentary, were having a delightful time. Bess felt a twinge of envy that she hadn't experienced such a lighthearted youth.

The dance was drawing to a close, and the music tempo changed to a waltz. The dancers were moving slowly to the rhythm when Bess felt a hand on her shoulder.

"Good evening, Jim, mind if I steal your lady for a waltz?"

"Well, hey there, Alan. No, I don't mind if Bess doesn't."

Having made the transition from one pair of arms to another Bess was unprepared for conversation. She said the first thing that came out of her mouth, " It smells like you've been sampling Gene Thomas's moonshine."

Alan whirled her around in a fancy dance step. "Yeah, I had to work up courage to come ask for a dance."

Bess was taken back. "Wh-why on earth would you have to have courage to ask me to dance. Do I look that cranky?"

"No, that beautiful! I'm afraid I'll make a fool of myself over another man's wife."

He tightened his embrace until Bess felt she was one with his warm body. She should have protested but she didn't want to. His masculine smell of alcohol, tobacco, and bay rum pleasantly attacked her senses. The couple savored the dance, not talking, just feeling each other's body move in time to the music, lost in a forbidden moment.

• • • • • • • • •

Bess insisted the elder Harts come to Christmas at her place. Nellie Hart resisted, but Bess firmly replied that they should take turns with celebrations, so Nellie wasn't always the one to do the most work. Her mother-in-law said it wasn't a problem, and she brought far more than requested. Bess sighed when she saw the older woman packing in all the food dishes but decided not to make a fuss. Nellie Hart may have mellowed through the years, but she was still accustomed to getting her own way.

The Christmas of 1921 was leaner than the previous year when Jim bought the Victrola. Bess sewed new clothes for the children. They supplemented a few store-bought gifts—a book for Kitty, toy soldiers for Freddie, and a penknife for Bob.

The family sat in the parlor after the bounteous meal, and Bess was struck by the worn look of her in-laws. She guiltily realized she had only been concerned about her own family and hadn't paid much attention to the elder Harts for some time. Big Jim's complexion was reddish-purple, and he had more difficulty moving these days. He regularly complained of his "rheumatiz." Nellie's bandy legs had became more bowed with the years, as she added a few more pounds. Bess realized that Big Jim and Nellie were sixty and fifty-eight-years, respectively. She and Jim needed to take on the harder work of the elder Hart's place. She'd also try to help Nellie although she could almost bet that her offers would be rebuffed. The two women had found a common, if uneasy, ground from which to communicate. Bess knew better than to push her luck.

• • • • • • • • •

Loretta "Rett" Underwood and Willard Eames were two of the most popular young people in the area. Bess read the year-end newspaper account of their wedding. She could picture Rett, in her gown of white crepe and lace, standing next to her handsome young groom while the Rev. Paul Baum performed the ceremony. The report said Loretta's sister, Ida, played the wedding march. Mrs. Baum sang several songs and was accompanied on the piano by Anna Rupp. The guest list included family names such as Sipprelle, Wasson, Clem, Duplice, Gardner, Studt, Vance, and Eaken as well as the immediate family. Bess wondered how fifty people could fit in the modest Underwood home.

Bess was sorry she and Jim decided not to go. The weather was stormy, which made the road from Wallace Creek to Battlement Mesa a quagmire. Jim said he'd hitch up the team and wagon because he knew they'd never make it to the top of Kearney Hill in the Model T. Bess decided it would be a mess to arrive mud-splattered from riding in the open wagon, so she declined. The article reported that some guests weren't able to get there, but a goodly number of people drove out from town for the evening wedding. Bess wished she'd made a greater effort to attend. She occasionally chided herself for not being more social.

1922

Jim attended a big Farmer's Union meeting in Rifle in February. Coming home late that night, he was fired up about the injustices being committed on the farmer and rancher. "Bess, we've got to unionize if we're gonna to survive. Prescott Eames was there. Did you know he and Alice are now livin' in Rifle? Anyway, he's the secretary/treasurer, and he introduced me to some of the other fellows. I think there were about a hundred folks there, including some women. You'll have to go with me one of these days. They were talkin' about the farmers bein' taxed more than their share. It wouldn't be so bad if we were still gettin' good prices for our crops. Our prices have decreased seventy percent since 1913 but the cost to purchase farm supplies has increased over one-hundred-fifty. We've got to stick together or we'll all go under!"

Bess listened with one ear, not giving a lot of attention to Jim's sudden interest in the Farmer's Union. She knew most of the cattlemen would jeer at him for joining an organization intended for "socialist dirt farmers,"and she figured Jim would change his mind once the market started up again.

Bess would soon have a far greater challenge that spring of 1922. She and the children took advantage of a sunny Saturday in March to go into town for a visit with Aunt Myra and Uncle Elmer. The Model T chugged up the partially dry road, pitted with large mud puddles. She tried to avoid the worst of them, which resulted in the little car bumping and swerving all over the road, causing the children to giggle. It was rumored that a contract would be signed in the fall for road construction to the Garfield-Mesa county line. Someday the gullies would have concrete bridges so the wagons and autos wouldn't have to drive down into the bottom where the gumbo mud made the crossing difficult. It couldn't be too soon for Bess. She'd heard of folks who had gotten stuck, and she didn't want to be stranded for hours while waiting for someone to come along and help pull the car out.

On the way home Bess and the children stopped at Doll Brothers Store to pick up chicken feed and other supplies. As they were leaving she met Wilma Driman and her two sons entering the store. Bess stopped to chat, and her children gathered around the boys to play. Bess noted both Wilma's boys seemed listless, not at all like their usual active selves. Freddie admired a boat one of the boys was holding in his hand. Before Bess could reprimand him,

Freddie grabbed the toy. At one time that may have been cause for outrage, but now the boy just whined for Wilma to take him home.

"It's getting late," Bess said. "I guess we'd better start home. Children, get in the car. Freddie, give back the boat."

"Let him keep it, Bess. They have more toy boats at home. Look at those boys—they're already in the car. They must be anxious to get home. I'll see you at the next dance."

That week Gretta Pottenger, the Garfield County school superintendent, was visiting all the schools in the west end of the county. An afternoon tea was planned for the lady at the Wallace Creek School. The mothers, and a few of the fathers, would come to meet Mrs. Pottenger, and proudly clap as their children sang, recited, spelled, and answered math questions. Bess was anxious to watch her children's exercises, but Freddie felt a little hot and was lethargic. He was content to just rest on the rug in front of the stove and play with his new boat. She mentioned this to Jim when he came in for lunch.

"Why don't I stay home with Freddie? You can go and see how the kids do in the program. I know you'd like to meet Mrs. Pottenger. I don't really care if I go, except to see Kitty and Bob. They can show me what they did tonight."

Bess gratefully accepted Jim's offer and hurriedly put Freddie down for his nap before changing her dress and getting into the Model T. The afternoon was pleasant. Bess liked Mrs. Pottenger who'd grown up in Garfield County and taught in rural as well as town schools. She was a widow, trying to raise three young children on her own, and that was cause for genuine sympathy from many. Bess noticed she was a no-nonsense kind of person who'd made some impressive changes, including the adoption of a uniform book code throughout the county. This policy helped the children who moved from town to town and got behind because of using different text books.

Bess was proud of her bright daughter, who excelled in the spelling bee and arithmetic exercise. She wished she could say the same for Bob, who hadn't really changed his mind about school. He went only because his parents made him go, not because he enjoyed it, unless you counted teasing the girls and pulling pranks. The second grade class was to perform a recitation in which each child memorized a part. When it was Bob's turn, he stammered and stuttered over the familiar words, which Bess had drilled into him every night for a week. Bess closed her eyes in exasperation.

When Bess and the children arrived home in the late afternoon, Freddie was still asleep. This was unheard of for the active child. Bess went to the bedroom to check on him and discovered he was burning up with fever! Picking him up in her arms, she carried him to the kitchen wash basin where she wet a cloth and sponged his face. The child groggily focused his dark eyes upon his mother.

"It hurts, Mama," Freddie huskily cried.

"Where does it hurt, darling? Show Mama where it hurts."

The child pointed to his throat and cried out when Bess probed the outside.

"Kitty, bring me a spoon. Freddie, Mama has to look down your throat. Let's go over by the lamp, and I want you to open your mouth as far as you can. Will you do that?"

The child cried out when Bess depressed his tongue but listlessly laid in her arms while she examined his swollen throat. His tongue and tonsils were covered with a white coating, which suggested a severe infection of some kind. His cheeks and forehead were flushed, but he had a pale area around his mouth. This was something Bess had never seen. She knew it was more severe than simply a childhood cold.

Throughout the night Bess sat by her child's bed or held him in her arms when he cried out. She sponged the hot little body, although it didn't seem to help, and trickled water down his throat, which he swallowed with great difficulty. She couldn't be sure if he was merely asleep or in a semi-conscious state. Jim sat with her for a share of the night until she told him to rest in case he needed to go for Dr. Miller.

As dawn approached Bess knew that none of her home remedies had been successful in bringing down Freddie's temperature. She laid him down, put coffee on to boil, sliced some potatoes in a pan of bacon grease, and then went in the bedroom to rouse Jim.

"Jim, I think you need to go get Dr. Miller. Freddie's no better, in fact his fever seems to be getting worse. I don't know what else to do."

Jim quickly donned his clothes, ate a few bites of food, and went to the shed to fill the car radiator with water. He cursed under his breath as he cranked on it for five minutes before the engine finally came to life. After feeling Freddie's burning forehead, Jim was on the road in just a few minutes. He and Bess knew how easily a high fever could become lethal for a child.

By mid-day Jim returned, with the doctor's auto following close behind. Dr. Miller was quickly ushered to the bedroom where the three-year-old rested. The anxious parents hovered about the bed, watching while he did the examination.

"Hmmm…Freddie, open your mouth wider." The child whimpered. The doctor ran his hands over the boy's naked body which displayed a growing red rash on the groin and under his neck. Bess was baffled by the dark spots in the creases of Freddie's body. They almost looked like bruises, but she knew they weren't.

"Yes…I think that's what it is," said the doctor. "You been around Wilma's boys lately?"

"Yes. Last week. Why?"

"Cause they also have scarlet fever. Had it for almost a week. When did you see them?"

"They were in front of the store last Saturday. The boys didn't look very perky, but they didn't look as sick as Freddie."

"They were just coming down with it. They're pretty sick now. The town school has been quarantined because several kids are down with it. It'll stay closed until we're sure there won't be any more cases.

"Jim, go get Kitty and Bob from school. They may not catch it from Freddie, but we can't take chances. Don't go inside and expose the other children. Holler for the teacher to come outside, and tell her to send notes home for all the parents. I need to be notified if anyone else gets sick. I'm sorry, but I have to place you under quarantine."

Jim left immediately for the school, and the doctor walked Bess into the next room. "Bess, there is not much we can do for scarlet fever except treat the symptoms. I'll leave some powder which might help Freddie's fever go down a little bit, but we'll have to wait it out. You're doing right to bathe him in cool water every hour or more often. Get water down him. I'll leave a dropper with you. Squirt a teaspoon in his mouth every fifteen minutes. If he spits it out, keep trying because he's very dehydrated. His fever may last as much as a week. You'll have your hands full taking care of him around the clock. Ordinarily I'd say Kitty and Bob could go over to Nellie and Big Jim's, but I think you should all be under one roof. If Kitty or Bob gets sick there's no sense in contaminating two places. You'll have to fumigate when Freddie's well. Send for me if he gets worse."

The following week was one long, sleep-deprived blur. The doctor prepared them for the progression of the illness and what to watch for. The red rash soon spread over most of Freddie's body. The small red bumps felt like sandpaper. His tongue was so swollen he had trouble talking. The white coating changed to the color of strawberries. Bess and Jim were diligent in feeding fluid through the eye dropper, even when Bess feared they would choke Freddie because of his swollen throat.

They kept Kitty and Bob from coming into the room and touching Freddie or the things that were used for him. The children silently ate the quick meals Bess put together. Kitty quietly played with her dolls, and Bob with his cowboy figures. They showed no sign of becoming ill for which Bess and Jim were very grateful. The parents took turns applying cold compresses and forcing fluids around the clock. Even when it was Jim's turn, Bess found she could do little more than take cat naps. She eventually let him sleep for longer periods.

The news circulated quickly around Wallace Creek, and food started to appear on the doorstep with, "We thought you could use this dish. We're praying for you," or similar sentiments. Neighbors stopped by on their way from town with mail or supplies for the Harts. Everything was left at the door. People didn't dare cross the quarantine line.

One clear dawn Bess groggily awakened from one of her infrequent naps and went to sponge Freddie. When she touched the little ravished body, it was cool…the fever was broken! She pulled the child to her and cuddled him. She wasn't going to lose her baby! Freddie would survive.

The symptoms disappeared as they'd come, one by one. Freddie's throat gradually returned to normal, then his tongue. The rash disappeared, but his skin started peeling. Bess had to watch Freddie otherwise he'd dig whole strips of it off his little body. Kitty and Bob were restive at being cooped up for more than a week. Kitty was anxious to get back to school although her homework was left at the door for her to do. Even Bob thought school was preferable over this forced exile. They had to wait until Dr. Miller lifted the quarantine, and the house was thoroughly cleaned.

Bess finally relented and let Kitty and Bob play in the afternoon sunshine. They were instructed to run into the house if they heard or saw someone approaching. She believed they wouldn't catch the germ because they hadn't touched the little boat which she tossed into the cook stove after Freddie got sick. Bess wondered how Wilma's boys and the other sick children were faring. She hadn't heard of more cases on Wallace Creek.

The harsh March winds finally gave in to the warm April sunshine, and the Hart family once more resumed a normal life. Freddie was recovering nicely, and Dr. Miller finally released them from quarantine. The house had been cleaned from top to bottom with fumigants, and the children were back in school. Bess looked at herself in the mirror and realized that Freddie wasn't the only one who'd lost weight. Her dress hung on her and the face staring back at her looked haggard. She'd try to make herself eat more.

Neighbors stopped to tell the Harts the quarantine was lifted in the Grand Valley school. Only a handful of children had been taken ill, but now a flu epidemic was threatening. Many women with nursing experience were moving into homes to take care of entire families. It wasn't as bad as 1919 and 1920, but Dr. Miller was kept busy running from one house to another. He'd just traded one illness for another.

> On June 9, 1922, the Stockmen's Association held their annual meeting in Rifle. One of the speakers was from the Department of Agriculture. He told the audience of a $25,000 appropriation for the control of hydrophobia in wild animals. He reported the prairie dog, kangaroo rat, prairie mice, ground squirrel, coyote, wolf, and mountain lion were being exterminated as fast as possible. A resolution was passed by the assembly to support the eradication of all predatory animals which threatened the livestock industry.

On the last Saturday of July both Hart families planned to escape the heat of the lower valley and travel up the canyon toward the peaks named Pete and Bill for a nice, cool picnic. Bess looked forward to resting under the tall mountain alder trees, which gave off such welcome shade. The children looked forward to wading in the clear, cold trickle that was still coming down the stream bed. Bess, Jim, and the children piled into the Model T and traveled the short distance to pick up Nellie and Big Jim. They spent some time trying to decide how four adults and three children would fit into the little car and still leave room for the fried chicken, potato salad, and fresh bread.

"Do you smell smoke?" Big Jim looked around for the origin of the scent.

"Yeah, I do," said Jim. "I wonder who'd be burning this time of year? I hope it isn't someone's place."

"Don't say such a thing," snapped Bess who was sniffing the air. "That would be about the worst thing that could happen to a family."

The family's attention was drawn to the northeast, where a plume of black smoke appeared over the low hills. "I'll be damned," said Jim. "That's got to be comin' from town. What do you say—should we go see what's happening?"

The children were glad for a chance at some excitement. "Yes, Daddy, let's go see the fire!"

The elder Harts nodded their heads, and Bess knew she'd be out numbered if she said no. She'd much rather be under the cool green trees up in the gulch than watching a hot, smelly fire. Then she realized there might be something both Hart men could do to help. It depended on the severity of the blaze, but it looked like a big one.

The Model T with its overload of passengers chugged into town to a scene of heat and confusion. The smoke was coming from the vicinity of the Oil Shale Theatre. Jim hurriedly parked in a vacant space by Doll Brothers Store so he and his father could go offer their help. The intersection of First Street and Parachute Avenue was clogged with wagons, horses, and autos. People milled around, visiting and gawking at the destruction. Bess, Nellie, and the children followed more slowly in spite of Kitty and Bob tugging at their mother and grandmother. Bess didn't trust Freddie to stay by her side so decided to carry him.

When they reached the bank corner, it was apparent why there was such a plume of smoke. The Odd Fellows Hall, its downstairs movie theater, and the Country Club Hotel with adjacent pool hall had burned to the ground. The house of Hugh O'Toole was also badly damaged. The blaze was under control, but men were still mopping up. It was more smoke than fire by that time. Bess overheard bits and pieces of conversation.

"People say the fire started in the movie theater."

"Nah, I heard some kids snuck in and were playing with matches."

"Those buildings could have been saved if the town had better water pressure."

Bess was drenched with perspiration from the suffocating heat. It was hot enough with just a typical August midmorning temperature. Freddie fussed to get down from her arms, and she wanted to scream with impatience. Her arms soon ached from trying to control the exuberant toddler.

"Mother Hart, I'm going to take Freddie for a walk down the street, so he can run around. Kitty and Bob, do you want to stay here with Grandma?" They were so intent on watching the activity she barely got an answer. Nellie took the children's hands and joined a circle of women who were making wild speculations about the cause of the fire. With a sigh Bess walked up Parachute Avenue to the school, where there was a bit of lawn and some shade trees.

Bess shivered at the sight of the devastation. Since a girl, she'd been fearful of her house burning after seeing large fires in St. Louis. She could hardly imagine anything much worse than losing all you owned and becoming homeless.

About a half-hour later Bess thought Freddie was tired enough to behave so she slowly made her way back to the crowd of people who were telling and re-telling the various details of the nighttime fire.

"I guess Hugh was the first one to spot the blaze. He was closin' up the pool hall and saw the flames comin' outta the pitcher show…"

"I hear kids were in there smokin'. What the hell are kids doin' runnin' around that time of night? Where were their folks?"

"Well, that's not what I heard. Someone told me there was a frayed cord on the movie projector, and it set fire to the celluloid film."

"We need a better fire alarm, that's for sure. If folks hadn't seen the flames, we'd never have gotten that blaze under control. Of course, Mrs. Clayton got on the switchboard and woke up everyone who owned a phone."

Bess walked to Jim and asked him what time it was. He pulled his pocket watch out of the top pocket of his bib overalls. "It's about 11:30 A.M. Are you gettin' tired? I suppose we should go," he said with a reluctant note in his voice.

"If you don't want to go, hold Freddie for a while—I'm tired." Bess handed over the squirming tyke and looked around for Kitty and Bob.

"Do you still want to go up to Pete and Bill for the picnic?" Jim asked.

"It's pretty late for that," Bess peevishly replied. "By the time we got clear up there everyone would be starved."

"Hey, I've got an idea! What do you think Uncle Elmer would say if we went out there and had a picnic by the river? It's nice under the cottonwoods, and maybe we can find a little slough for the kids to wade in."

Bess didn't give in graciously. She wanted to be cranky for a little longer, but she was pleased that Jim made the suggestion. They'd at least get to see Aunt Myra and Uncle Elmer.

The couple were pleased to join them for the picnic. Aunt Myra brought a whole basket of food in spite of Bess's insisting there was already plenty to eat. The afternoon was pleasantly spent eating, watching Kitty and Bob play in a muddy but shallow part of the slough, and visiting among the adults. Bess became tired of chasing Freddie and tethered him to a willow bush so he could run around without falling into the water. Myra and Nellie chatted nonstop, while the men discussed crops and cattle prices. Bess was content to recline against the trunk of a large cottonwood tree and observe her family. It was nice to have them together; all the people in her world. She studied the elders.

If only time would stop right here so they'd remain the same. It's wonderful to have a good relationship with Uncle Elmer after those first angry years. Aunt Myra couldn't be more dear to me. She's done a wonderful job of filling in for my mother. Then, there is Dad Hart. My Jim is so much like him—easy-going, friendly. Even Mother Hart has her good points. She loves my children as much as they love her. They're getting older, and I don't want to face the day I lose them.

• • • • • • • • •

"Joe Bellis! Come on in and sit awhile." Jim hailed Joe as he drove down the road, and Joe turned into the Hart's yard. "Glad to see ya! What brings ya down this way? You still chasing John O'Toole?" Jim chuckled as Joe climbed from the pickup.

"Hell no," Joe laughed. "I've come to spread the good word. You folks are gonna have a decent road before long. All my letters to the county commissioners paid off, and we finally got the contract signed for five miles of highway west of town. Hoffman, out of Clifton, has the dirt work, and I have all the gravel and concrete. That'll keep us busy for a while this coming winter, if the weather's so we can work on it."

Joe Bellis, entrepreneur and oil shale promoter, had been the burr under Garfield County's saddle for some months. It started when Joe offered to provide, free of charge, his expertise as road supervisor in the Grand Valley district. He'd suspected some double-dealing between one of the commissioners and a man named O'Toole who had been named supervisor over Joe. From then on Joe pursued the matter, sending in periodic letters to both the *Grand Valley News* and the *Rifle Telegram* about alleged inappropriate use of county funds. There were secret meetings between state highway officials and the Garfield County commissioners. That now appeared to be in the past.

"Yeah, I've got to get busy and find the gravel pits and get some agreements from the owners. I figured I'd take a look down here by the Johnson place. If I can use it I won't have to haul the rock from further up the river, and it'll help Walt Johnson's pocketbook. I wonder how much dirt is in it, 'cause Si Herwick will need good clean sand and gravel for the concrete work on the bridges. I've already ordered a screening plant. Damn, Jim, it's gonna take fifty-six thousand yards of gravel! That'll keep a crew busy for a while. Think you might be interested in some winter work?"

"Hell, yes, I would! With the cattle and hay prices the way they are, I should probably sell all the damned stock and just get a full time job. This ranching business is a losing proposition."

Bess was standing in the doorway, listening to the conversation. "Well, before you do that remind yourself you haven't been missing many meals lately. Hello there, Joe. Come in, and I'll heat up some biscuits and gravy."

"Thanks a lot, Bess, but I'd better get on over to Walt's before he takes off after dinner. Good to see you both. By the way, you might consider hiring out yourself and your team. We'll need about forty of 'em." Joe drove off in a cloud of swirling dust.

"By damn, Bess, this might be an answer to our problems. If the team and I could work a good share of the winter that would go a long way in helping out."

"A winter job would be a boost to our income, but it would mean I'd have to take over a lot of the outside chores. It all depends on how bad the weather is. If it's a mild winter, the stock can graze along the river for some time. But if snow piles up, we'll have to feed the cattle. I'm not sure Dad and I can do it alone. I don't think he should take on additional work."

As usual there was never an easy answer to their cash problems. Bess dreaded doing the outside work on top of her inside chores, but she felt guilty knowing Jim would also be working long, cold hours.

"Well," said Jim, "I guess we'll just have to wait and see what November and December brings. I can always quit if it gets too bad."

> A large Democratic rally was held in the Grand Valley school auditorium during the early part of October 1922. District Attorney Frank Delaney and the Honorable David Ahearn extolled the virtues of the Democratic candidates while comparing their records to those of the Republican opponents. Both men spoke at length about the record of Congressman Edward Taylor, who was an ardent supporter of oil shale development and the creation of the coast to coast highway.

Despite being tired from working a twelve-hour day Jim bounded into the house. "Look at this, Bess!" He shoved a newspaper into her hands. "It was a Democratic victory in Garfield County! Most of the candidates won except for the sheriff's race. It was too close to call between Winters and Baxter so the county will have to count the absentee ballots to declare the winner. And Dick McGuirk lost the assessor's job but, hey, this is a good percentage for a Republican county. I think Dinsmore and Wheatley's editorials turned the tide. We need more like them."

Bess listened to Jim with a detached interest. She did not particularly care who won because she thought the majority of politicians were self-serving. If she could meet even one who could prove he was really concerned about the average, dirt-poor farmer and rancher she might become more supportive. She tried not to dampen Jim's enthusiasm. What did it hurt for him to believe either political party would be the working man's savior? He worked so hard, and she was glad he held out some type of hope for their future. She wished she felt the same optimism.

Jim continued, "There's also an article in here from Dinsmore about the federal grazing lands. He says if we don't start using all our allotments with either sheep or cattle, someone else will. The big problem is the grazing applications will probably come from out of state.

"Dinsmore also says it makes no sense for us to continue to run cattle when we can make a better profit from sheep. Bess, maybe he's right. George Kerlee seems to be doin' pretty well. I understand he's increased his herd size this year and got a fair price on his shipment. It was sure better than we got from our cattle. We'd probably get a lot more mileage out of that bottom land if we were runnin' sheep on it. They can survive on forage that the cattle won't touch."

Bess bit her tongue to keep from exploding. She'd been trying to get Jim to run sheep for years, and he'd always been against it. Then some Democrat publisher wrote an editorial praising the practice, and Jim decided it was now acceptable.

Why won't he listen to me? How can he can turn a deaf ear to my ideas and accept those of a stranger?

Bess seethed with resentment. She brushed by Jim and went into the bedroom to help Freddie prepare for bedtime. She didn't dare tell Jim how she felt because she was afraid she'd say something she'd later regret.

Why do men assume that women know nothing about farming or ranching? Why do they think we're only smart enough to run our households and have babies?

Bess jerked on Freddie's long nightgown, catching his ear and making him yelp.

"Mama, are you mad at me?" His plaintive question brought Bess to the present.

"No dear, Mama's just tired. I'm sorry I caught your ear. I'll kiss it and make it better."

Bess swore she'd find a way to make Jim hear her. In the meantime she consoled herself with the knowledge they'd be getting some sheep next year.

I shouldn't look a gift horse in the mouth, no matter the circumstance.

● ● ● ● ● ● ● ● ●

The Battlement School was ablaze with lights as Jim drove into the already-crowded yard. The sounds of the musicians tuning up could be heard over the noise of the crowd filing into the building.

"It looks like the whole countryside is here tonight." Jim stopped to shake hands with some men, while Bess entered the kitchen to place sandwiches and a burnt sugar cake on the full table. Laura Herwick started water boiling in the big coffeepot on top the coal stove, while her sister-in-law, Mary Duplice, tied up ground coffee in a big square of cheesecloth. Irene Gertner and Martha Jacks were cutting some of the cakes and pies.

"Do you need some help?"

"No, Bess, I think we're about done. That's a fine-looking cake. Burnt sugar, is it?"

"Yes, I thought it would taste good for a change. The family prefers pie so I don't usually bake many cakes. I hope it tastes good."

Bess went into the main hall and placed her coat on a growing pile. She hoped the mothers would make sure their babies were well-diapered. She'd gone home last time in a damp coat.

The Wooley and Underhill girls were standing along the side of the room talking behind their hands. Bess followed their gaze and spied several young ranch hands who were returning their interested looks. Bess bet the girls would have plenty of dances that night. Bess couldn't help scanning the large room to see if she could see Alan Taylor. Not seeing him, she went over to sit with Addie Wilson and Carol Morton. They'd barely started visiting when the orchestra struck up a lively tune.

Well, Toot Toot Tootsie good-bye.
Toot Toot Tootsie, don't cry...

Bess couldn't resist tapping her toe to the beat. She wondered if Jim could hear the music from outside. As she glanced toward the doorway, he was standing there, looking to see where she was sitting. Others were already on the dance floor, and Jim wended his way to her side. She became caught up in the fast-paced rhythm of the song. After several dances they stood visiting with other couples while they cooled off. The hall heated up, thanks to the huge coal stove at the end of the room and the heat of the dancers.

Jim and Bess exchanged dance partners several times in the following hours. Jim made sure some of the older, single ladies took a turn around the floor. Bess was catching her breath on the sidelines when she sensed a presence. Whirling around, she found herself touching Alan's outstretched arms.

"Hullo, Bess, would you like to dance?" Without waiting for an answer, he swept her onto the floor. At first they didn't talk. It was enough to be in each other's arms. His scent was familiar and heady. Bess was sure their fascination with each other must be apparent, but, at that point, she didn't care. Alan tightened his hold on Bess until she melted into his body. She moved her feet in response to the command of his legs. She closed her eyes, giving in to the sensation.

"Umm, the old biddies are watching us, Bess." Alan pulled away and loosened his hold. "How have you been? I haven't seen you at any of the recent dances."

Bess, opened her eyes, resenting the fact that Alan had broken the silence. "Since Jim started to work on the road, the ranch work never gets done, and we're exhausted by the time Saturday night comes around. How have you been?"

"I'm okay…but I'm still lonesome." Alan whirled her around and around, cutting short the conversation just as the music ended. He thanked her and walked away, nodding to Jim who was coming across the floor. Bess stood breathless, more from the experience than from the dance.

"You want to sit this one out, Bess? You look a little flushed. Al was sure whirlin' you around."

"I think I'm just tired. Let's dance to this waltz, and I'll cool down."

I'm dancing close to my husband while I tingle from another man's touch. What is the matter with me? I'm playing with fire, but I can't stop.

She didn't see Alan again that night. She supposed he'd left after dancing with her. She was disappointed and relieved at the same time.

1923

The DeBeque grade school building burned in February 1923. The fire didn't spread to the nearby high school building because of firefighter persistence. Over one hundred children were in the school when the fire broke out, but they were evacuated in an orderly fashion. One man was hurt when he fell from the roof while trying to douse the blaze with water.

Bess finished her Friday chores and sat down to rest with a cup of tea. Kitty and Bob rushed through the door.

"Ma, guess what? Charlie Johnson shot a man last night and he's in the pokey!" Bob was dancing up and down in his excitement to tell the news before his sister could.

"Slow down, slow down. What are you talking about?"

"It's true, Ma," Kitty chimed in. "Charlie Johnson killed Orange Martin last night. Edna told me."

Bess shivered. The shock and surprise was too much to comprehend. "Orange Martin? Doesn't he work for Charlie?"

"He did, but Edna says they had a fight."

"What about Blanche? Did Edna say anything about her? What about Pearl and Freddie?"

"Well, Pearl wasn't at school. Edna says they are staying at her aunt and uncle's."

Bess went out into the early March twilight to shut the chickens in their coops and herd the cows into the barn. Jim would be home soon, and she usually did the chores before starting supper. Thoughts of the Johnson family consumed her while she went about the tasks. How could something like this happen in their little community? Murder happened in big towns like Grand Junction, not Wallace Creek. What could have provoked Charlie to do such a thing?

When Jim came home, he had already heard the news on the road crew. He was equally baffled about the murder. "I hear that Charlie called the sheriff in Glenwood Springs and then drove into town. Deputy Zediker and Doc Miller met him and his brother on the way in. Zediker sent Lee Parmenter with him to Glenwood Springs where Charlie turned himself in to the sheriff. Coroner

Clark arrived on the westbound train to examine the body. Charlie shot Orange four times so it damned sure wasn't an accident. He told the sheriff that family troubles were the reason he shot him, but most folks think it was over their bootlegging operation. Someone said Orange was grumblin' he hadn't gotten enough money from Charlie, and I heard they almost came to blows once before. Damn! This will sure tear up the Johnson family."

Wallace Creek and the surrounding area buzzed with news, both true and false. Rumors were rampant about the reason for the killing. The theory of bootlegging gone bad was further strengthened when Sheriff Winters and District Attorney Frank Delaney found a cache of booze buried under several feet of dirt on the Johnson property. They also found where a still had been set up but removed before the sheriff arrived.

Tragedy brought out the gossipmongers. Bess saw a group of women going by her place on their way to the Johnson ranch. She knew these women would proclaim their sorrow and support for Blanche while milking her for any tidbit of information. Before the shooting these same women would not have spoken to Blanche if they'd met her in the store. Bess thought Blanche would be wise to hide out for a while and let the busybodies get their information elsewhere.

The titillation died down after a few weeks, and most lives got back to normal. Bess would occasionally look across the river and wonder about the Johnson family. It went to show you never knew what a person might do when their back was against the wall.

> A family named Summers was sitting on a claim situated in "Horse Bottom" at the two forks of Parachute Creek. The father and eldest son came to Grand Valley one day in mid-March, 1923. The father left on a prolonged business trip to Glenwood Springs. The son retrieved their mail and started home. When the boy failed to arrive at the cabin the mother and two small children started down the trail, looking for him. They discovered his frozen body about one-half mile from the cabin and were able to drag him back to camp but couldn't notify anyone of his death. The father heard of the tragedy when he returned home several weeks later. Men on snowshoes came over the mountain from Piceance Creek to take the body to the mortuary.

For Jim and Bess the continuing debate of sheep versus cattle was emerging again only with less intensity. Jim conceded sheep might be a better choice for the ranch, but there were obstacles.

"I admit that I'm worried about what our neighbors will do if we start running sheep. Hell, Bess, I heard that a Greek was almost lynched over in Meeker this past year for driving a herd of sheep through town. Even the cattlemen's wives beat on the herd with brooms. What would we do if that happened to us? Besides, I don't know a damned thing about sheep."

"For pity sake, we aren't going to bring in two thousand head! We'll learn as we go along. Think of all the others who are running sheep now—the Werhonigs, Kerlees, Mahaffeys, Parkhursts. Granted they don't live on Wallace Creek, but there are plenty on Battlement and Parachute Creeks. We're financially ahead right now, thanks to your road work, and if we ever plan to do it I think this is the time to get started. Selling off more of the cattle last year was wise because the prices haven't gotten any better. If we get just a few sheep to start we could run them down on the river for most of the year. I've been talking to Mae Wooley. She's willing to let me have some bummer lambs to raise if I'll give her back the wethers, or castrated males, in the fall so she can ship them. That way I can keep the ewes and start building up the herd. The children can help me. I think it will be good for them."

Jim, in spite of his many misgivings, reluctantly agreed Bess could take on some lambs. "You know I'll have to continue workin' on the road crew if we're gonna do this? Are you sure you can do everything?"

"Of course I can! Kitty is good help in the house, and Bob would rather be outside working with the stock. Kitty can take care of Freddie, or I'll take him with me. This is our chance to get ahead, Jim! Let's not miss the opportunity. Your Dad can run a few head of cattle on his place, and we'll eventually concentrate on sheep. Just think, with the sale of the wool we'll get two crops instead of one."

DeBeque, Colorado *Oil Shale News* Friday, May 25, 1923:

"Mary Beth, the sixteen-month-old daughter of Mr. and Mrs. W.H. Kennon of Wallace Creek swallowed an open safety pin Tuesday morning. The pin lodged in the child's throat, and her mother was unable to remove it. The parents hurried to Grand Junction with the child. At the hospital x-ray pictures were taken and it was believed they showed the position of the pin. An operation was performed, but no pin could be found. The child is in serious condition as the result of the operation but reported to be doing as well as can be expected, with a favorable chance of recovery."

The lambing season began, and the bummers were being brought out to Bess on a regular basis until she was caring for twenty-five sheep. It was a lesson in patience and heartbreak for Bess while learning to raise the tiny animals. The saying, "A sick sheep is a dead sheep" proved to be true. She relied heavily on Mae Wooley for advice on how to feed them and how to nurse the sick ones back to health.

The space behind Bess's cook stove became a nursery. Some of the tiny creatures were nearly dead when brought to her. She found a baby lamb was a lot like a human baby. Food went in one end and came out the other. Bess boiled their milk when they got diarrhea, or scours, and she cleaned their bottoms. She rubbed their middles when they bleated with a stomach-ache. Sadly, there were those who couldn't be saved, but she tried her best.

Bess stayed one step ahead of her flock by reading every article on sheepraising she'd saved through the years. In the few minutes before bedtime she'd sleepily pore over the articles, digesting information available through the Colorado Extension Service and other sources.

Whenever a number of lambs needed to be fed on the bottle, Bess, Kitty, and Bob would each have to nurse one or two of them. When the animal was well enough to toddle around the kitchen and cry for its human mother, it was time to move them to a pen in the barn, with the other lambs.

Spring and early summer whizzed by. The children complained there was never time to do anything but work. It seemed each completed task only brought another. On weekends Jim helped his dad with the cattle, cleaned the irrigation ditches, or mended fences. It was a never-ending job, but Bess didn't waver in her aim of raising sheep on the Hart ranch.

● ● ● ● ● ● ● ● ●

Bess opened her eyes to blinding light. She struggled to focus her eyes and saw her son's little face peering down at her. "Ma, you okay? Wake up, Mama!" Freddie ran to the house to get his sister, and Bess again closed her eyes.

"Come on, Ma, swallow some of this water." Bess could feel the cool wetness of the tin dipper being held to her lips. She opened her mouth, allowing the welcome fluid to roll down her throat. Bess looked up to see Kitty kneeling above her. Looking around, she realized she was lying amongst the corn stalks. Their shade felt cool compared with the heat overhead.

"Wh-what happened?"

"I don't know. Freddie came running in the house, saying you'd fallen down in the garden and were asleep. Did you faint?"

"I guess so. The last thing I remember was how hot I felt. Maybe I just got too much sun. Can you help me up, Kitty? I'll go stretch out for a while. Don't cry, Freddie—Mama is all right."

After resting Bess reassured her children she was fine and asked them not to tell their father because he would worry. Bess might have known Freddie couldn't keep a secret for very long. Jim and Bob barely stepped in the door before Freddie spilled the beans.

Despite Bess's protests Jim thought several days of rest would help. When the children discovered they would be staying home to help their Grandfather Hart tend to the livestock they set up a howl, which was rapidly squelched by their father.

"Stop it! I know you're disappointed, but you kids are needed here right now. It's important for your mother to get away for a few days, and we can't all go. Your grandma can't do the household chores for both places. I promise I'll take you into town soon, but right now you have to stay with me. I don't want to hear more about it, you understand?"

"Yeah, Pa," they responded in unison, but Kitty, as usual, argued the point.

"I don't think it's fair. We've worked all summer just like Ma has. Why does she get to go to town and we don't?"

"I just told you, young lady! Your mother has worked ten times as hard as you kids. See how skinny she is? Now, I mean it; I don't want you goin' around with long faces or she won't go."

Bess reluctantly agreed to go into her aunt and uncle's after she heard Jim's persuasive argument. She'd looked in the mirror that morning and saw how haggard she looked.

I have to admit that taking care of twenty-five lambs, on top of everything else, has been harder than I thought it would be.

Aunt Myra greeted her at the door and ushered Bess inside from the heat. Bess was not the only one to show the ravages of the summer. She was shocked to see how old Uncle Elmer looked. He was having difficulty breathing, and Aunt Myra confided that Dr. Miller put him on medicine for his heart. It had, thankfully, eased his breathing and lessened the swelling in his feet.

"We're so glad you came up to see us," declared Aunt Myra, surprised but delighted to see her niece. "You're going to rest and eat so you gain some weight back. My goodness you are thin!"

"Jim worries too much, Aunt Myra. I don't have it any worse than you or other farm wives. If I could make myself eat it would help, but I feel like I have a big knot in my stomach most of the time."

"Well, for the next few days, that's your only job. We need to get you on your feet!"

Bess's appetite improved as soon as she got away from the stress of three children, the sheep, and a ranch household. The nights were cooler under the big old cottonwood trees in the Carpenters' yard. Bess loved to lie in her bed with the window wide open so she could listen to the rustling of the leaves. She slept very well.

On the third day Bess decided she must go home. "Aunt Myra, I'm sorry but I can't stay. I feel very guilty about leaving Kitty and Bob to do much of my work. They are just children and shouldn't have to do that. I feel so much better. Your food and a lot of sleep have restored me."

Her aunt and uncle reluctantly agreed. They understood why she had to leave. The last night they sat in the parlor and chatted about many things, content to just be with each other.

"Tell me, Uncle Elmer, what do you think about our new president? Do you think he'll do as good a job as Harding?" Bess, knowing Elmer's politics, sat back with a grin on her face.

"Well, that won't be hard to do now, will it? That Harding was quite a talker, but he was shy on keeping promises. Typical of a damned Republican."

"Now, Elmer, you shouldn't talk ill of the dead," interjected Aunt Myra.

"Why shouldn't I? It's the truth. And I don't know that Calvin Coolidge will be any better. Maybe if he gets rid of those Harding cronies something will get done."

President Harding had died the previous month from a heart condition. His White House tenure was marred by scandal of his dalliances and of his many friends who'd been put in high level administration positions.

"Have you heard that Bert Taylor, over on the Piceance, was found guilty of the murder of Slim Brunts?"

"And then we had a murder right at Una," Bess said. "Who would have thought?"

"Yeah," Uncle Elmer replied. "Bootlegging is a pretty big business these days. Hell, everyone knows who's making and who's selling. This damned prohibition is the stupidest thing the government ever did. They aren't collecting a penny of revenue from liquor sales, and the bootleggers are gettin' rich off of it. Hope the temperance people are mighty pleased with themselves."

Uncle Elmer squeezed Bess's arm and went to bed. She and Aunt Myra headed for the kitchen to finish the nighttime chores.

"My dear, I hope you take better care of yourself. Any time you need a rest just come on up."

"I'll sure try, Aunt Myra. I suppose I have been working too hard. It's been a difficult summer, but it will pay off in the long run. I'll have fifteen ewes to start next year. If Jim can work for just a while longer, I should be able to build the herd up. Mae Wooley has been wonderful to make this deal with me."

"You know, Bess, you and your uncle are very different, but you are alike when it comes to thinking of ways to make a living. Elmer always figured out how to make a dollar or two, and you do the same thing."

Bess lowered her voice. "Aunt Myra, Jim is a wonderful man, but he'd be content to keep plodding on for the rest of his life. He never thinks about doing different things to get ahead. When I suggest something he doesn't trust my judgement. Why are men unwilling to listen to their wives? The only reason I got the sheep was because the editor of the *Rifle Telegram* encouraged ranchers to switch from cattle to sheep. When Jim sees the results I think he'll be happy. Right now he's taking a terrible badgering about becoming a 'goat-herder.' When we get the wool check next spring, it will pay off. Of course, it will take some time to build the herd up."

"Bess, dear, I know it's important for you to get ahead but money isn't everything—especially if it harms you." Aunt Myra took Bess's hand and patted it.

• • • • • • • • •

The short respite from her daily grind refreshed Bess. She drove back to the ranch with a renewed sense of purpose, if not energy. The hot weather was at last abating, and she could once again relish the autumn's cool morning air. The cottonwood trees along the river bank were in their fullest golden glory. The oak brush, higher up on the hills, was a brilliant reddish hue mixed with the lemon yellow of the aspen trees. Even the air was colored by the minute golden dust particles floating about. It was a grand sight as Bess sat on a stump along the river and watched the lambs grazing nearby. Soon autumn would be over, and the cold would set in. She'd have to arrange her schedule to accommodate feeding and watering the stock. Just another thing to worry about but not today. Freddie was with his grandfather, and she was enjoying her solitude, thinking of nothing, planning nothing. She was content to be.

A Model T pickup chugged down the road. Bess didn't recognize the driver but waved as it drew near. To her surprise, it stopped. The driver got out and started walking toward her. At thirty yards she couldn't make out the man's features. As he came closer, a shock went through her; it was Alan Taylor!

He stood in front of her, his eyes scanning every inch of her body. Then he spoke, "You've lost weight." His eyes scrutinized her face, her body. "Have you been sick?"

"No," she answered, her voice cracking, "It's been a busy summer. I must look a fright." She nervously smoothed her cotton dress.

"You never look a fright," he replied. "Even when you're working too hard because of those damned goats you've got." Alan looked distastefully at the lambs.

"Oh, yes, Mr. Cowboy, I expected you to make some sort of nasty comment about my sheep. Just you wait, I'll have two crops to your one, and I won't have to feed them as much. We'll see who the smart one is. I suppose everyone is talking about crazy old Bess getting a bunch of sheep?"

"Not to me. Everyone knows it's been a struggle for you on this hard luck place, and I doubt they mind you finding a way to take in a few bucks. It's just too bad it has to be sheep."

Bess decided to change the subject. "Isn't this a wonderful day, Alan? It makes me want to play hooky."

"Why don't you? Come—get in the pickup, and I'll take you for a drive."

Bess was shocked, not by the proposal but her reaction to it. She couldn't remember ever wanting to do something as much as she wanted to do this. Just one look at the handsome man in front of her, and all reason left her mind. His blue eyes bore into her soul urging her to say yes, urging her to do things she'd never done before. She remembered how it felt to be held in his arms while they danced. She could feel herself slowly giving in to the invitation. Then a car drove by! Bess didn't recognize the vehicle, but she suddenly saw herself and Alan from the occupant's perspective. Did the driver know Alan's auto? What would they think—what would they say? She was jerked back into reality.

"You know I can't do that, Alan. I'm a married woman." There was no coyness about Bess. She'd never learned to play the flirting game. Her answer was direct and honest.

"I didn't expect you would, but you can't blame me for trying." Alan quickly looked around, and then he moved closer to Bess. He put his hands on each side of her face, holding it in a gentle but a firm grasp. "You've captured me, Bess Hart." He lowered his head and gently touched her lips with his. Then he pressed harder and more insistently. Bess felt her knees go weak while her lips met his with abandon. A familiar warmth was starting to spread throughout her body. And then it was over.

Alan released her face and stood looking down at her. "That was something to remember me by." He turned, walked back to his pickup, and drove away.

Bess sat down on the stump. She was stunned.

What happened? I must be dreaming!

She touched her lips, which still tingled from the intensity of the kiss.

No, it was real.

Scattered thoughts and feelings invaded Bess's mind, running rampant, holding her prisoner in their grip.

Now you've done it! See what your flirting has caused? My God, what if Jim finds out? It would kill him. I can't let this happen again. Of course, I didn't go to Alan, he came to me. He's so handsome. Why in the world would he want me? His kiss was everything I imagined it might be. I'm playing with fire, but I want more. I know I shouldn't…this is madness! All the same, it's exciting to be wanted by such a man. I feel like the princess who has been found by her prince!

> On October 4, 1923, several hitchhikers were injured, and a new Studebaker car was wrecked near Grand Valley. An unnamed driver was taken into custody by Sheriff Winters. The cause of the accident was reported to be caused by the occupants consuming a gallon jug of whiskey.

The subpoena was delivered to Jim by Deputy Zediker. "Can you beat that? I've been called for possible November jury duty. Zediker says W.B. Eames, Ed Gardner, Abe Kerlee, and Paul Lindauer have also been called from Grand Valley. I suppose it's the Johnson trial, and I tell you, Bess, I don't want to serve on that one. That'd be too close to home."

Jim was relieved his name wasn't on the list of the final twelve jurors when the trial convened in November. In fact, no one from Grand Valley was picked. One wag said it was because the district attorney didn't know for sure who might be one of Johnson's customers. The Hart family, indeed the whole area, listened for news of the trial testimony. Bess was glad Blanche and the children had moved to Glenwood Springs to be near Charlie. She hoped the residents of that city were kind to her.

Both the prosecuting and defense testimony made light of the actual bootlegging. They called Jake Easche to describe the actual operation. He testified the still was located at the head of Smith Gulch. He said it was a three-way partnership. Cliff Harris made the moonshine, Orange Martin carried the supplies in and the liquor out, and Johnson supplied the grain and sugar. Jake also stated he ran sheep up in the gulch, and they traveled back and forth, so he supposed they may have erased evidence of the operation. When folks heard about his statement, they laughed because it was a well-known fact Jake deliberately ran his sheep in close proximity to the stills in order to wipe out any signs.

By piecing together all the hearsay information, the Wallace Creek folk discovered that Martin and Johnson met in town the day of the killing. Some said they verbally fought over something, others said they didn't. Orange Martin did travel to Johnson's ranch at Una that evening. He was shot four times, the first one to the heart being fatal. Johnson maintained he shot Martin because of his attention to his wife, Blanche Johnson. District Attorney Delaney asserted Martin was shot because they fought over money owed from the bootleg operation.

Everyone was certain Johnson would be convicted and sent to prison. After all, he admitted to the killing, and they found the booze in the cache. The community was in a state of shock when they heard Charlie Johnson had been acquitted! The Old West code of conduct was alive and well; it was okay to protect your woman or your still.

That view wasn't shared by all of Grand Valley. Some folk plainly didn't want Johnson's kind in their town. A large delegation met the No. 3 train, when it arrived in Grand Valley the evening of the acquittal, to tell Mr. Johnson he'd better move on, if he was smart. They never got the chance to deliver the message. Charlie Johnson wasn't on the train. He and his family disappeared while in Glenwood Springs. If his relatives knew his whereabouts they certainly weren't talking.

The papers were full of bootlegging arrests every week. Clara Thornton from Glenwood Springs was arrested for the fourth time and found guilty. She faced a sentence at Cañon City.

"Can you believe that, Jim?" Bess shook her head. "I can't imagine a woman doing such a thing."

"Well, I guess if they need to feed their family a person will do about anything. It's risky, but the profits are mighty good. For every person who gets caught, there are three or four who don't. Prohibition's a crazy law, Bess, and no one is gonna pay much attention to it."

"I hope you don't get any ideas about doing such a thing, Jim Hart. You'd find me long gone when you got out of jail!"

Citizens of Western Colorado eagerly awaited the construction of a powerful Denver radio station, in November 1923, which should be able to transmit its programming to all areas west of the Mississippi River. Listeners would have the latest crop and market reports available on a daily basis, not to mention wonderful musical programs.

1924

The Glenwood Springs Land Office was besieged by over one hundred gas and oil filings in one week. A clerk from the Cheyenne Land Office was brought in to help out.

The wind-driven snow swirled around the eaves of the little house and settled to the ground at an alarming rate. Jim entered the porch door through a flurry of the large flakes and shook them onto the floor before entering the kitchen.

"Man alive, that stuff is really comin' down," said Jim. "If this keeps up we'll be snowed in by mornin'."

"How's the stock doing?" Bess asked.

"Well, they're all hunkered down, but they should be okay for now. I ran the sheep into the field where the old cedar shelter's located, and they'll be all right if they stay there. The cattle are fine unless it turns really cold, and then we'll have to make sure they get some extra feed."

A New Year's storm blanketed Colorado, bringing below zero temperatures in its wake. The moisture was a welcome sight, but the frigid cold was sure to bring some stock losses throughout the state.

"I guess it was good we made it home from the dance about the time the snow started. I wouldn't want to be driving the car in this kind of storm. If a fellow had a team of horses, he might have a chance of finding his way home, but I doubt the car could do that." Jim laughed at his own joke, choosing to ignore Bess's one-syllable responses. She seemed a million miles away.

In truth she was still reliving the dance. The Oil Shale Theatre had reopened with a fanfare following the disastrous fire in 1922. The Woodmen of the World had apparently provided the funding, or maybe they just insured the building. Whatever the case, the hall now sported the big initials "W.O.W." across the front marquee. Si Herwick's son, Oren, would be scheduling events for the building.

The entire countryside turned out for the dance. The large room was packed with people by the time Bess and Jim arrived. The usual single men lined the back of the hall, slyly eyeing the eligible women while making small talk among themselves. Bess helped Kitty off with her coat. Bess unsuccessfully searched the room for the person who towered above the rest—her Prince Charming.

Kitty was struck with excitement. She'd pleaded with her parents to let her come with them. She'd turn twelve years old in February, and she wanted to join her school chums and young people from Battlement Mesa. Kitty's campaign had gone on for days, until Bess was ready to say no just because she was so annoyed. Jim, however, intervened on his daughter's behalf, and Bess relented.

Bess explained the rules to Kitty: "Stay with your friends at all times. If you need to go outside to the privy I'll go with you. There is a lot of drinking, and fights happen all the time. I don't want you or your chums out there if one breaks out. And I want you to be careful with whom you dance. See all those young men over there? They're rowdies, and they may take liberties with you. If anyone bothers you, come on the dance floor and get me. Do you understand, Kitty?"

"Yes, Ma, I promise. Now can I go see the Wooley girls? Oh, there's Helen. Helen…Wait for me!"

"She'll be fine, Mother Hen," Jim said. "Come on, let's dance." A fast-tempo song started, and Jim led Bess onto the floor. Bess often caught people glancing at them as they glided around the floor. If only the rest of their lives were as good as it was on the dance floor, or in bed.

The supper intermission occurred at midnight. Many folks went across the street to the restaurant for a piece of pie or a sandwich. Jim was tired from dancing with both Bess and Kitty and needed some refreshments. The little café was crowded, and they had to wait for a small table to become vacant. While waiting, Bess looked up to see Alan Taylor guiding a young woman by the arm. The couple was heading in the direction of the Harts. A shock went pulsing through her. Bess couldn't stop staring at them.

What is he doing here with a woman?

"Well, look here, it's our friend, Al." Jim vigorously pumped Alan's hand. "How you doin'? I don't think we've seen you in months."

Alan nodded to Bess and Kitty. "I'm fine—how 'bout you? How are those smelly sheep doing?" He grinned and winked at Bess. "I'd like you to meet Lila Kane. She's from DeBeque. Well, I guess we'll see you back at the dance. We're gonna have a smoke, aren't we darlin'?"

Bess and Jim acknowledged the young slip of a woman who was a duplicate copy of Alan's former wife, Sissy. The same blond hair, the same wide-eyed gaze, except this time the eyes were baby blue.

Good grief, she's hardly out of school. Talk about Alan robbing the cradle!

Bess watched as Alan escorted the girl through the crowd at the door, placing his hands around her shoulder in a protective gesture. Anger bubbled up in Bess.

Well, Alan Taylor is a grown man. I guess he can date anyone he pleases, even if the woman is young enough to be his daughter! But, why did he kiss me when he has another woman? Just wait until he asks me to dance!

Bess sat in sulky silence while Kitty and Jim chatted about the dance.

After intermission the orchestra struck up a waltz. Bess was dancing with George Wooley when she spied Alan and Jim talking on the sidelines. Alan then stepped over to Kitty and asked her to dance. The look on Kitty's face was pure rapture. What adolescent girl doesn't want a handsome gentleman to notice her? Bess smiled slightly at the sight of the gangly young lady and the tall lanky man.

He'll soon ask me to dance and I don't know how to react. I want to dance with him, I always do, but I'm hurt and confused. How could he take liberties with me and then bring another woman to the dance?

George intercepted her look. "That daughter of yours is growin' up fast. It must be nice to have youngsters."

Bess squeezed his hand in reply. She thought it was simply a shame that George and his wife didn't have children, because George was good with young people. She knew one baby had died. Maybe the couple couldn't have more, but Bess hoped that wasn't true. George would make a fine father.

Despite Alan's attention to Kitty, he avoided Bess. Against her will, Bess's eyes were drawn to his tall figure no matter where he was in the hall.

When is he coming to ask me? It's getting late, and Jim will want the last dance with me. Alan had better hurry!

At 2:00 A.M. Alan still hadn't asked Bess to dance. It seemed he was making a deliberate attempt to distance himself as much as possible. Bess felt devastated by the rejection.

How could he do this to me? I don't understand. This is the man who kissed me and said I had captured his heart. Now he's treating like this—why?

On New Year's Day Bess alternated between anger and hurt. Was Alan Taylor just a flirt who liked to kiss and run? Bess, with shame, then realized she didn't have a right to be hurt, angry, or jealous of Alan Taylor.

What could I have been thinking? I'm acting like a silly school girl! I've been starry-eyed about another man, hoping for more of his exciting attention. Well,

Alan Taylor, I won't do that again! I can't believe how foolish I've been. Thank heaven I haven't shamed myself more. It could have been so much worse than a kiss.

Embarrassment engulfed her. In the days following the dance Bess strengthened her resolve. Her pride would not allow another opportunity to bring shame on herself, even when the resolve caused an aching emptiness. Despite flirting with danger, Bess had looked forward to their brief encounters. They had been the only brightness she'd felt in her drab life. Now that, too, was gone.

I'm almost thirty-six years old, and I should be satisfied with what I have—a good husband, three healthy children, and my little flock of sheep. It's time to concentrate of making a good living instead of mooning over some man I can't have, a man who was only toying with me.

> Western Colorado's newspapers reported the area was alive with prospectors and oil company officials. An oil company had brought in a large oil well at Hamilton Dome, near Craig. It was producing six thousand barrels daily. Midwest Oil planned to drill five more wells before April 1, 1924.
>
> Continental Oil was drilling west of DeBeque but had not been as successful with their wells. Although gas was found, the amount of oil at 2,000 feet was insufficient for commercial production. They estimated the drilling would have to go as deep as 6,500 feet in order to find enough volume.

The New Year's storm was the last severe one that winter. A weak sun came out, but it gave no warmth. The area was trapped in nature's icebox for many days, with the temperature hovering at zero or below. Bess and Jim were both out with the stock. Jim tended the cattle, and Bess took care of her sheep. According to their agreement, she had given back the castrated males to Mae Wooley in the fall so they could be shipped. That left her only fifteen ewes, but it may as well been double or triple the amount because they required the same effort. Every day the sheep were herded out of their pasture to the river slough to drink. Jim had already broken the ice for the cattle, but Bess carried a hatchet in case the holes were frozen over. It was a bitterly cold time for Bess, in both body and soul, but she was determined to be successful with the sheep. If she needed to baby them, she'd darned well do it. Bess felt she'd received far too much ribbing about the folly of raising sheep for her to quit. She'd prove to everyone that she was right!

The sheep needed to be moved every day or two to a new grazing spot then herded back to the shelter for the night. The old cedar shelter was too far away for her to hear any ruckus during the night, and she started inquiring about a dog that was trained to be with the sheep. A good sheepdog would alert her if he heard coyotes or other predators stirring up the flock. Unfortunately, no one who owned a sheepdog wanted to part with it. Bess finally heard about the death of an old man who'd run a few head of sheep. She stopped by his little place one day and found his son and daughter packing their father's possessions. They both lived out of town, and the acreage and livestock were already sold.

"I thought maybe your father had a sheepdog for his herd. If so, I'd be interested in buying it. I'm looking for one that is already trained."

"Well, there's old Laddie over there," the son replied. "He's a great dog and real good with the sheep, but he's a little long in the tooth. I'll bet he's close to ten years old."

Bess looked in the direction the man was pointing and saw a scruffy-looking dog of uncertain parentage. He had the wiry hair of a terrier, his face looked like a collie, and his legs were short and slim. Bess thought he was about the strangest looking dog she'd ever seen.

"Here, Laddie," Bess called to him. The dog loped over, sat in front of Bess and looked at her rather quizzically. A big, yellow tom cat followed and settled himself down by the dog. They both seemed to wait for her next move.

"There's only one problem about letting you have Laddie," said the daughter. "He and old Tom have been together for a long time. My dad spoiled both of them. I'm afraid neither one would be happy without the other. I'll tell you what, if you'll take Tom so we don't have to shoot him, we'll let you have Laddie."

Bess quickly agreed to the deal before either could change their mind. "That would be fine. We had a tomcat, but he left one day and never came home. I imagine the coyotes got him."

Bess was glad she wasn't far from home. The tomcat threatened to claw his way out of the box. Laddie alternated between sniffing the box and howling at the top of his lungs. "You've proven one thing, Laddie. Your howl should wake me up from a sound sleep."

The newest members of the Hart household were warmly greeted by Bess's children that afternoon. Bess brought the dog and cat inside so they would get used to her. She didn't want the cat to run away and go back home. Neither

Laddie nor Tom had ever been around children. They were less than enthusiastic about these little people, especially the youngest!

"Freddie quit chasing Tom!" Bess admonished her son as the cat slid under the bed. "He's not used to children, and you have to give him a chance to know you."

Laddie moved to Bess's side and looked up at her while he tolerated Kitty and Bob's petting. "They're okay, fellow. Smell their hands. See, it's okay." Laddie stiffly sat, accepting the strokes while continuing to watch Bess for permission. It was clear that Laddie already knew who his boss was.

Bess knew she'd found a gem in the ugly little dog that evening when she went to round up the sheep. Laddie knew exactly what she expected of him. He took after the young ewes, snapping at their hooves and bunching them up so they could be driven into the shelter. Bess was grateful to the old man for his excellent training of the dog. She could never have done as good a job.

There was finally a respite from the cold, and the sheep survived the winter. Bess was able to decrease the amount of time she spent with them. As tired as she was, Bess knew there was only one way to build up the herd with a minimum of expense. If they offered her the opportunity, she would continue taking more bummers from the ranchers with big herds, who didn't have time to tend to them. If she got another batch of lambs this spring it would help increase the flock, and she'd be able to breed her ewes in the fall for next spring's lamb crop.

Bess was tired from her double duties and admitted she hadn't realized how much physical cost there would be. She couldn't put on any weight despite forcing herself to eat. Bess squared her shoulders and shrugged off her poor health. She'd manage somehow.

> A federal grand jury indicted twelve men from Garfield County for bearing arms against sheep growers, Henry and Herb Jolley, who were trying to move their band of sheep across the Colorado River Bridge at New Castle. Two of the twelve men were sons of the county commissioner.

A box social was planned for February 16 at the W.O.W. Hall in Grand Valley. Jim asked Bess if she wanted to go. He thought Kitty, having proven to be trustworthy at her first dance, should be permitted to go with them. It would be an early celebration for her, because she'd be thirteen on February 22, 1924.

Bess couldn't think of a plausible reason to stay home. The weather had been unseasonably warm, so she had been able to catch up on her work. It was doubtful Mae Wooley would deliver many more bummers. The conditions were excellent for lambing, and the herders should be able to take care of the orphans. Still, Bess dragged her feet, desperately trying to think of a reasonable explanation for not going.

I don't want to risk seeing Alan. I can't be sure how I'll react if he asks me to dance. I'd like to be friendly but cool to him. That shouldn't be so difficult, but I'm afraid to trust myself. Despite my shame, I still catch myself thinking of him.

She and Kitty worked on their baskets, which were lined with her best napkins. They decorated the baskets with bits of ribbon and decorations, which were salvaged from the hand-me-down box. Mother and daughter giggled as they hid the baskets from Jim, because men were not supposed to know which basket belonged to whom. Despite Bess's misgivings, she had fun watching Kitty's excitement. She wanted her daughter to experience the good times she'd never had. Bess would make sure Jim or a family friend knew which was Kitty's basket, in case an unsavory character looked like he might bid on it.

Bess thought of the dance many times during the next week and dreaded its approach. It would be easy to hide, but that wasn't her way. She'd have to eventually face Alan Taylor and it might as well be sooner than later. Bess was, therefore, surprised when she woke up the day of the dance with the worst cold she could remember. She wrapped her throat with a cloth containing camphorated oil and made her way to the kitchen to build the fire. She put on a big kettle of water to boil so she could breathe the steam. Maybe that would clear her head by the evening.

When the children woke up to eat breakfast, Jim had already gone to milk. Bess was coughing and feeling very ill. "Kitty and Bob, please watch out for Freddie. I don't feel well, and I'm going back to bed for a while."

When Bess woke an hour later she was coughing with every breath. She called from the bedroom, "Jim, Kitty, I just don't think I can make it to the dance tonight."

Jim and Kitty came in to see her. "Don't worry about it, Bess. Lie down and get some rest. We don't have to go to the dance, do we Kitty?"

Kitty nodded, but Bess could see tears welling up in her eyes.

"No, I insist you both go on. I've already made the cherry pies and baked rolls yesterday. Kitty, you can fry some chicken can't you? Make some potato salad, too. You can fix enough for the boys to eat tonight. Do you want to do that?"

Kitty, grinning from ear to ear, shook her head up and down. " Of course, I can do it, Ma! Daddy will you kill me a chicken?"

Jim smiled at his little girl, acting so grown-up. "I suppose I can't disappoint you." His forehead furrowed as he looked at Bess. "Maybe your cold will force you to stay in bed and get some rest. Don't worry about the sheep. I've already taken them down to the river, and I'll take 'em again before we leave for town."

Bess was still awake with fever, a runny nose, and coughing when Jim and Kitty arrived home after midnight. Kitty sleepily nodded when Bess asked if she had a good time.

"Yeah, Ma, Clarence Reed bought my basket. He really liked my chicken and potato salad. I'll tell you about it tomorrow." Kitty tottered to her bedroom, bumping into the door as she made her way.

"There was big news in town tonight," Jim said. "You ought to see Parachute Avenue. Another fire happened on Wednesday. It burned businesses to the ground. This time it took out Riley's Pastime, the West Side Supply, Jenny's Mercantile, the Grand Valley Hotel, Maude Day's restaurant, and the old Enterprise telephone building."

"What about Thad Bailey's store?"

"No, by damn, it was saved by Milner's Pool Hall, which has the stone walls. Same with Morrow's Garage on the other end of the block. When the fire got to the stone walls, it finally died out. Everything is a mess. They say the damage may run as much as fifty thousand dollars. Fire's a terrible thing, Bess."

Bess shivered. "I know."

Sensational events during February 1924 shook the town of Meeker. The Sheriff of Rio Blanco County and the Meeker Town Marshal, among seventeen men at Cunningham's Pool Hall and the Meeker Hotel, were arrested by several state prohibition officers in a sting operation. The officers were joined by twenty-one town citizens who wanted the wide-open gambling and bootlegging to be abolished once and for all. During a series of raids the enforcement group discovered six stills which were confiscated. All men went to court and pled guilty of the crimes. Fines of up to $250 were assessed against the miscreants.

Two days later Rev. D.A. Gregg, pastor of the Meeker Methodist Church, reported someone threw a brick against his home. He said he fired upon the three or four men who ran away. When the undersheriff arrived he discovered the minister had previously positioned armed guards around the church property, as if expecting trouble. The official pushed open the church door and discovered a small fire that looked to be newly set. He was able to stamp it out.

District Attorney Frank Delaney telegraphed Colorado Springs for two of the best bloodhounds in the state. The dogs would try to track down the scent from the brick that had been thrown. The attempt was thwarted, however, because someone poured red pepper on the street from where the brick had been pulled. The pepper was finally removed. Each dog sniffed then headed for the front door of the minister's residence. They completed several tests, and each time the dogs targeted the door. A Grand Jury later indicted not only the sheriff with malfeasance of office, but the Reverend and his followers for setting the fire in the Methodist church. This ended the immediate problem for Meeker.

Spring 1924

Ranchers watched for signs of spring snowfall, hoping to make up the severe moisture deficit in the mountains. Apart from a few brief storms, Western Colorado remained dry. February turned into March, and everyone looked forward to the normal heavy storms of that month. They were disappointed. The clouds occasionally appeared, but they failed to produce the precious moisture. People were worried.

"Hell, Bess, I might as well sign on with the road crew for the summer, cause it damned sure doesn't look like I'm gonna get any hay off the top field. I may get only one cuttin' off the bottom ones. We'll either have to buy hay or sell off the stock. Otherwise I don't think we can make it."

Bess agreed the outlook was grim. "But, Jim, we've been worried before, and something always happens to pull us through. I guess we're just like Freddie's rubber ball. We seem to bounce back." She wished she could be as encouraging to herself as she was Jim.

Jim and the team started working on the road four days a week, while Bess and her father-in-law once again assumed the ranch chores. She and Big Jim worked together to feed and water the stock. She had only five orphan lambs, who were all doing well, so she wasn't up all hours of the night trying to keep them alive. She was grateful because she fell into bed at night so tired she could hardly think.

Bess was worried about Big Jim. His face was a deep beet red, and Bess knew that was not normal, even for a sixty-four-year-old man. She made sure Bob went with his grandfather whenever she was busy doing other chores. She gently asked Big Jim if he was feeling all right and suggested he should see Doc Miller. Big Jim vigorously denied any health problem and insisted it would be a waste of time to go see the "sawbones." Bess decided to let the matter rest for the time-being.

One morning they had finished moving the ewes. The pair started to the house for a cup of coffee and piece of pie that Bess had baked in the predawn hours. They spied a cloud of dust coming from the main road and both stood waiting for the car to draw closer. Now that the main highway was almost finished, most people used it instead of the old Wallace Creek road. They finally identified the car putt-putting up the road as Dr. Miller's. Bess and Big Jim waved as the car drew near. With a turn of the wheel it came to a halt in the dooryard.

"Hey there, Doc." said Big Jim. "What are you doing down this way? Someone sick?"

"No," replied the doctor, "I've been looking around for some property, and I came over to see the old Spencer place. I decided to make a loop by coming this way and then back over the new road."

"Why don't you get out and join us for a cup of coffee and a piece of pie?" Bess said.

"What kind?"

"Apple."

"Well, that's too good to pass up." The doctor climbed out of the car, automatically taking his medical bag. "I'm lost without it." He shrugged when he noticed Bess looking at it.

The two men visited, while Bess stoked up the fire and put on a fresh pot of coffee. While it boiled, she cut the pie and lifted it onto plates.

"Young lady, you're too thin."

"That's what we tell her, Doc. She works too hard, but we can't make her slow down."

"Well, if I did, who'd take care of this family? Jim has about all he can handle, working on the road four days and doing the rest of the ranch work on weekends."

"They tell me the part of the road to Una will be done by July."

"That's what Joe Bellis told the men. We hope he also gets the bid on the next stretch from Una to Nigger Hill." Big Jim automatically used the common name for the hill which marked the boundary between Garfield and Mesa Counties. It had been named for a respected African-American man by the name of John Barker, who operated a ferry on the Grand River in the very early days of settlement. Big Jim didn't intend it to be a racial slur, he'd never met the man. Even school superintendents and publishers of newspapers used the description in official documents.

As the men chatted over their pie and coffee Bess thought the doctor was paying close attention to Big Jim. Was he seeing the same symptoms she was concerned about?

"When was the last time you had an examination, Jim?"

"Oh hell, Doc, I can't remember. It's been quite a while, but there's nothing wrong with me that a little rest won't cure."

"All the same I might as well take a look at your blood pressure and pulse while I'm here. You must be past sixty. It won't cost you a thing. Bess's already paid me with her pie and coffee. Bess, would you give us a little privacy for a few minutes?"

"Of course Dr. Miller. I've got to take a look at my latest crop of bummers. I'll be back in ten or fifteen minutes." Bess hoped they couldn't see the grin on her face as she went out the door. Talk about good timing!

When Bess returned she immediately saw the tension on her father-in-law's face. The doctor took a vial of pills out of his case. "Jim, I want you to take this pill every day and no dragging your feet, you hear me? I imagine your family would like you to stick around for a while longer, don't you?"

Big Jim grumbled under his breath. "Yeah, I guess so," he finally said.

"Good. I want you to take these for a month, and then come see me so I can check your heart and blood pressure again. Will you do that?"

"I'll make sure he does, Dr. Miller. I've been concerned for a while, haven't I, Dad?"

"Yeah, she and the missus have both been nagging me a bit. Now are you satisfied, Daughter?"

"I surely am," said Bess smiling at him. "I surely am."

Big Jim grumbled the pills made him pee so much he hardly got any work done. Within a short time Bess could tell he was losing much of the red puffiness. He had more energy and didn't stop to rest for long periods. Bess, Jim, and Nellie all sighed with relief.

> On March 19, 1924, Mattie Gilman of Conn Creek, north of DeBeque, shot into the back of her husband, J.A. "Shake" Gilman. The *Rifle Telegram* reported that Mrs. Gilman was imbibing a concoction made of ether and sweet spirits of nitre when the shooting occurred. More likely it was the moonshine the couple were known to produce. Law enforcement officials transported Mr. and Mrs. Gilman to Glenwood Springs, where she was lodged in the jail, and they took him to the Glenwood Springs Sanitarium. Dr. Hopkins amputated his right arm. The second bullet entered the area of the tenth vertebrae and splintered both ribs and part of the backbone. The ultimate cause of death, however, was his severe blood loss, which occurred before medical help was able to reach Gilman at his Roan Creek ranch.
>
> This incident was the final one in a long line of fights between the Gilmans, who were well known in the DeBeque area for their public altercations. Mattie Gilman was subsequently tried and convicted of second degree murder and sentenced to not less than ten years in prison.

"Holy hell, what's this world comin' to when a wife kills her husband?"

"Well, I can think of a few husbands who deserve the same fate."

"You should have seen her at the trial. She looked so pitiful, but you should have heard her using filthy cuss words to the men taking her to jail."

The dance hall was abuzz with the latest news from the Glenwood Springs trial. During the course of it, many people discovered convenient reasons for business in Glenwood Springs, so they could watch a small part of the court proceedings. On April 18 the jury read the verdict, and a number of De Beque and Grand Valley citizens were there to hear Mrs. Gilman declared guilty. This was the first time a woman was tried for murder in Garfield County, and it was a juicy scandal that people would chew on for some time.

As titillating as the Gilman Trial may have been, the real excitement was about the industrial activity in not only DeBeque but Rifle. The town had recently received word that a vanadium mill would soon be built there to process the vanadium coming from the mine on Rifle Creek. It would provide temporary work in the construction phase and steady employment after operations started.

There was more. Continental Oil was reportedly investigating the feasibility of building a pipeline from the Moffat Dome, fifty-seven miles north, so they could transport the crude oil to a refinery in Rifle. The refined product would then be shipped out by rail. People were predicting Rifle would soon be bursting at the seams with all the new development.

This was good news for the farmers and ranchers in the area who might have to obtain employment outside of their land. They were watching the skies for any sign of moisture and hoping they wouldn't have to sell their livestock for cents on the dollar. The market was poor, at best. If it was flooded with thousands of animals being sold for pennies a pound, the prices would likely go further down. Both Hart families would have to decide how many animals to sell in order for the others to survive. They didn't know the condition of the summer range, but it couldn't last long into the summer unless there was heavy rainfall.

Jim knew his job on the road would only last until July. He was doubtful his team would be employed on the next portion of road construction from Una to the county line. Local gossip said that Winterburn & Lumsden of Grand Junction would be bidding on the seven and one-half mile project. The company owned steam equipment, plus their own teams of horses.

That Saturday night Jim talked to other men at the W.O.W. dance who were thinking of applying for work in the Rifle area, even though it would mean a longer work day. With enough fellows going, they could cut down travel costs by taking turns driving back and forth.

The April evening was unseasonably warm, and the women were dressed in lighter spring dresses. It was fun to wear garments that swished around their knees for a change. Bess had discovered, to her dismay, most of her dresses just hung on her frame. Searching the back of her wardrobe she found a straight-line, flapper dress, which formerly belonged to Bibby Stuart. When she'd received the box several years ago, Bess stored it away, thinking she'd alter some of the dresses for Kitty when the time came. The dress was made before hems climbed to the knees, so it was longer than the current dresses and a little more fancy. The electric blue crepe displayed a border of iridescent bugle beads around the neckline. A floral decoration made of the same beads was attached close to her right hip.

On a whim Bess donned it and discovered the dress fit her almost perfectly. She twirled in front of the wavy dresser mirror, feeling better about herself than she'd felt for some time. She'd just passed her thirty-sixth birthday, but she'd been feeling much older. The only redemption to working with sheep was the lanolin in their wool had helped her hands remain in decent shape. She also noticed her auburn hair was brighter from exposure to the sun. That helped to hide her few gray hairs, although she tried to pull them out as soon as they were discovered.

Now, Bess and Jim had finished a set and were visiting with some of their friends. Bess was searching the room for Kitty when she saw Alan. For a split second her resolve wavered, but Bess, trembling, forced her eyes away. She looked at any area in the room except where he was standing.

I will not be vulnerable this time, nosirree!

Bess was saved by the music starting up. A fellow rancher and Jim exchanged wives for the dance. Bess kept up a friendly conversation with Ed Maholley, finding a kindred spirit in the sheepman. Bess never lost an opportunity to pick the brains of area sheep growers. They became so interested in the topic, both were surprised when the music ended.

"Thanks for the dance, Bess. I'll be back, and we can continue our talk. You know you can always holler at me if you run into a problem with your sheep."

"That would be nice, Ed—thanks for the offer. I've got a lot to learn about being a sheep rancher."

Bess was still deep in thought about her conversation with Ed when she felt a hand on her back. Thinking it was Jim she turned to tell him about her conversation with Ed, but looked into Alan's face.

"Hello, Bess. May I have this dance?"

Bess struggled about what to do. She couldn't make a scene, but she didn't dare dance with this man. "I'm actually waiting for Jim to come," she stammered. "I have something I need to tell him." She knew the excuse was lame, but it was the best she could do under the circumstances.

Alan swept her into his arms and danced into the middle of the other couples. "Tell you what, why don't we just take a turn around the floor, and Jim can cut in when he gets back. I have something I need to say to you, Bess."

"I can't imagine what you need to say to me. We haven't seen each other for such a long time."

"That's the point. I don't like the way things ended with us, Bess, and I want to explain why I handled things so badly."

"What are you talking about, Alan? You don't have any reason to apologize to me."

"Don't pretend nothing's the matter, Bess. You aren't that kind of woman. You and I both know something happened out in the sheep pasture last fall. I was surprised how great that kiss felt. Until then you were just a pretty lady I could do a little flirtin' with. After that it changed, and I was scared.

"Look, Jim Hart is one of my friends and, no matter what kind a man I am, I've never believed it's okay to come between a husband and wife. That's why I brought that girl to the New Year's Dance, and why I stayed away from you. I thought if you got mad at me you'd soon forget and try to be happy with Jim. He's a great guy, but I don't think you're in love with him.

"Anyway, when I saw you tonight, I decided I couldn't let you go on thinkin' the worst of me. Bess, I care more for you than I should, and I think you also care for me, but we both know we can't ruin your marriage over this. Jim Hart is a fine family man, and I doubt he'd ever consider doin' the same thing to you. I envy him, I really do. I'd give anything if I had the kind of wife and kids he has, but I don't.

"I'm gonna stay my distance. Maybe we can have a dance once in a while, but I won't stop by your house when I know you're alone. It wasn't by accident that I just happened to see you that day, Bess. It was planned. I need to tell you one more thing. If there ever comes a time when you need me, all you have to do is snap your fingers. If I can't have you any other way, I can at least be your friend. That also includes your kids."

Bess felt elation and anguish. It was wonderful to hear Alan declare his love for her, but it was devastating to know it could never be consummated.

He really does love me! How can I let him go?

"What about me? Don't I have a say in the matter? Are you telling me you're making the decision for both of us?"

"'Fraid so, sweetheart. I can't allow Jim and the kids to be hurt. But I mean it…I'll be there when you need me. You know I will."

Alan tightened his hand on her back. Each finger subtly caressed her flesh, as if to memorize how she felt. "Oh Bess, you're so skinny. I wish I could kidnap you and put some flesh on those bones, but I can't. Promise me you'll take better care of yourself."

Bess silently nodded while she blinked away the threatening tears. She needed to be strong until she could go outside to the privy and compose herself.

"Good, now give me a big smile because Jim just came inside, and I don't want him to think I'm abusing his wife."

Bess was forced to smile and laugh softly at the absurdity of that last statement. "When will I see you again?"

"Don't know, sweetheart. I can't give you a definite time because then we'd both be doing nothing but living for that coming day. If we're gonna do that, why hell, I might as well kidnap you and ride off for the hills!"

Jim prevented them from further conversation by breaking in. "Hey there, buddy, mind if I have the last dance with my wife?"

"I don't know, Jim, she's a mighty good dancer. Maybe we should arm wrestle for the pleasure of her company." Alan was grinning, but Bess saw the glint of anguish in his eyes.

> Five hundred white-robed and hooded members of the Ku Klux Klan paraded through the streets of Grand Junction on the evening of August 24, 1924. The parade formed at the Rood Avenue Armory and silently marched to the beat of a single drum along Rood Avenue, then Main Street. A fiery cross and a huge American flag preceded the marchers. The parade climaxed an afternoon meeting to introduce the Grand Wizard, Dr. Locke, from Denver. It was rumored there were up to one thousand members of the Klan in the area. Although there had been previous demonstrations of burning crosses, this was the first major proof of Klan force on the Western Slope.

Bess wiped the moistness from her face and set the iron down on the hot stove top. She poured a stale cup of morning coffee and watched the rain come down. All the doors and windows were open to the cool, musty smell of wet earth. The moisture, which would have been so welcome in the spring, was finally falling. The puddles in the front yard grew larger and larger.

Except for one good rain in late May, the weather remained hot and dry. A bare trickle of water came down from Pete and Bill. It was barely enough to get the Hart cistern filled for the summer.

Bess looked out over the stubble of the alfalfa field closest to the river. Everyone had gotten their hay stacked just in time. Jim feared it might be infested with the army cutworms, which had ruined other hay crops that season. Parts of the area had been covered with hoards of adult moths in the springtime. They'd congregated on trees, houses, any place they could stick. The bugs soon flew on to the mountains, but ranchers feared they would return in the fall to lay their eggs. The only sure cure was to burn the fields, and kill as many as possible. Bess sighed as she reflected that, with ranching, one problem was always replaced by another.

Bess sipped her coffee while picking up the latest issue of the *Rifle Telegram*. There was a report about Admiral Rousseau, personal representative of President Calvin Coolidge, who'd recently inspected the various oil shale enterprises in the area from DeBeque to Rifle. He was scouting locations for the best possible naval oil shale plant, assuming Congress could be persuaded to part with $1 million during the next session. He'd convinced the secretary of the navy to also take a look at the potential for supplying oil for the nation's fleet.

The real reason Jim brought home the paper, however, was the announcement of the road contract award to Winterburn & Lumsden of Grand Junction. It wasn't exactly a surprise. Most folks had anticipated the firm would get it. The company offered many more resources than Joe Bellis. It wasn't known how much local help they'd hire, but Jim was certainly hoping he'd get hired on as a day laborer. If he couldn't find outside work, it would be slim pickins in the Hart household the coming winter. Bess reminded herself there was always plenty to eat, no matter what, but she couldn't stop the scared feeling in the pit of her stomach.

The sheep were doing well with the grazing along the river. Nevertheless, there wouldn't be enough feed to last the winter unless some good fall rains brought the grass up before the first frost. Bess had traded one of their calves for a young ram, and she planned to turn him in with the yearling ewes in the fall. She'd have her first lamb crop next spring. Now that her long-held dream was almost a reality, she could hardly believe she was actually on her way to becoming a sheep rancher. If her family was going to prosper, this was the way to do it, in spite of criticism. Even Isabella Stuart tried to convince Bess that it was folly. Something in her persevered despite the negative comments. Was it just a stubborn streak? Maybe so, but she'd watched Uncle Elmer take on different ventures, and she knew this was the safest bet for ranchers.

The region experienced one project after another. The state was letting highway contracts in all directions, the oil shale possibilities were emerging again, the new vanadium plant was being built east of Rifle, and petroleum drilling was continuing. Ranching was now seen as the most risky venture. Livestock prices were still relatively low. Bess thought it was funny—the best prices were going for hogs. No matter which animal you raised, another one brought the most.

It was growing near the noon hour on that July day, and Bess looked out to see if the children were coming up the field. She'd sent them out midmorning to check on the sheep, and they should be returning soon. They'd be wet and hungry when they arrived. She'd stirred the vegetable soup and pushed it to the front of the stove to get hot when Bess saw them coming. It looked like Bob was carrying something in his hand, but she couldn't tell just what it was.

The children rushed through the porch screen door all talking at the top of their lungs.

"Mama, sthee what Bob hasth," exclaimed Freddie with his pronounced lisp.

"Ma, it was really scary," said Kitty.

Bob was the last in the door. He stood at the threshold, holding something behind his back. Bess started toward him when he whipped out the object and extended it to her. "He's pretty good size, ain't he, Ma."

Bess, instinctively backed away toward the hot stove. "Bob Hart, get that snake outside." Then she saw the tail. "M-m-my God, it's a rattler!" The color drained from her face. Bess grabbed a tea towel off the table and walked toward Bob. Grabbing the snake from his hands she went to the screen door and flung it as far as possible. She then dropped the towel on the floor.

"Ahh, Ma, what did you do that for? It's dead." Three pairs of eyes looked at her accusingly. "We're gonna cut off the rattlers."

"You'll do no such thing! That snake is staying where it is until your father gets home. If he wants you to have them, he can cut them off. Oh, my word, how did you kill it?"

"Bobby hit it!" Kitty and Freddie were still excited. "It crawled out from a hole in the bank, and Bob hit it with some rocks. He saved us!" Bob stood off to the side, looking a little embarrassed by all the praise.

"That may well be," Bess replied, "but haven't I warned you to always be on the lookout for rattlesnakes and run if you see one? That thing could have coiled up and got you! You could have died, and there'd be nothing I could do!" Now the emergency was over, Bess was thinking of all the horrible things that might have happened.

All afternoon, as the rain came down, the children periodically went to the door to see if their prize was still there. Bess went as well, but she shuddered every time she looked at the long reptile lying in the mud. When Jim finally pulled into the driveway that evening all three dashed out in the rain to show their father the product of their adventure. Jim looked the snake over and counted five rattles on it. "That's pretty good," he said. "I've seen some with ten rattles, but none that were killed with a rock. Good work, son. I'll skin it out for you after dinner. Why don't we put it here on the step?"

On July 29, 1924, the Grand Valley post office was robbed. The robbers completely removed the safe then hauled it, in a truck stolen from the Alber Meat Market, to a spot down by the railroad tracks, where dynamite was used to blow it open. Railroad Agent Freeman said he'd heard the blast and had seen an auto roar down Front Street in the direction of DeBeque. The alarm wasn't sounded, however, until Postmaster Wasson opened the post office the next morning to a scene of destruction. He reported the enterprising thieves actually got very little money for their efforts because he banked the receipts every day.

Several days later the Palisade post office was also entered in the same manner. This time the thieves made off with $15,000 in stamps and about $500 cash. It was soon determined the robbers had taken refuge in a coal mine, possibly where some may have been employed at one time. For almost two weeks local and federal officers set traps in the mine and searched the foot prints in various tunnels. One set of prints suggested a woman was part of the gang. She was dubbed "The Bandit Queen" by newspapers. Officials believed the thieves had confederates on the outside who might be helping them to escape through part of the old mine workings. It was estimated the mine contained as many as two thousand rooms. There was talk about sealing the portals and air shafts so the air would soon be depleted in the mine. That was not done.

On August 12, 1924, federal guards were removed from the mine portals. Officials made exhaustive searches, and there didn't appear to be continuing signs of life. The case was closed without concrete evidence about what happened to the besieged occupants. They either died or were assisted, in some way, to gain their freedom.

The children were particularly noisy and quarrelsome. Bess reminded herself the chaos would be over once she got them out the door. First day of school was often hectic. Hopefully they'd not do too much damage to each other on the way to school. Bob, as usual, dragged his feet. If anyone was destined to stay on the ranch, it would be that boy. He resented doing anything not related to his primary interest. Kitty, on the other hand, could hardly wait to see her chums and get her nose in the books. Bess looked at Freddie, who fidgeted while she tried to comb his cowlick down. Freddie was an unknown. He would turn six on September 15, 1924, and would be in the first grade.

In spite of her favoritism of the boy, Bess acknowledged Freddie would likely be a handful for the teacher. She'd tried to do some preparation by teaching him the ABCs and his numbers. He could also print his name fairly well when he chose to. But Freddie much preferred to wiggle around, drumming his fingers on an imaginary drum, kicking the chair, generally ignoring her commands to pay attention. Nellie Hart insisted a smart swat on the backside would cure a lot of Freddie's inattentiveness. In Bess's more frazzled moments she wondered if her mother-in-law was right. Then she would look into those deep, brown eyes so like her brother Linn's and give in to him one more time.

Bess grew impatient, calculating how many chores she had to do today. "Freddie, I want you to mind your sister, do you hear me? And, Kitty, you make sure he gets to school in one piece. Don't let him scuff along in the dirt, or he'll be filthy before he gets there. Bob, do you have your supplies? Why don't you also carry Freddie's, so he won't lose his pencils and tablet? Here are your lunches." Bess handed a lard pail to each of the children. "Don't be peeking before lunch!"

She shooed them out the door and stoked up the fire under the large kettle of water simmering on the front of the stove. She'd have time to feed the chickens and gather eggs before starting the weekly wash. Jim was working for Winterburn & Lumsden several days a week. He'd milked the cows before taking off for work after sunrise. Thankfully, that was one less chore to worry about.

There weren't enough hours in the day to get everything done, but Bess didn't complain. Hard work was the perfect antidote for a distressed mind. If she was busy thinking about all the chores to be done, she was too busy to be thinking of things best left alone. She hadn't seen Alan since the April dance and now felt only a dull ache when she allowed herself the luxury of remembering. She knew it was for the best, because nothing good could have come of it. She was grateful Alan had the strength to end it, because she feared she didn't. Now her energy could be spent on being the best wife, mother, and rancher she knew how to be.

As Bess gazed around the ranch she felt pride at the way it looked now compared to fourteen years ago when she'd arrived.

The ewes are doing well on the riverside forage, and next month I'll turn the buck in with them. We got a good price for both calves. That fellow down at DeBeque didn't seem to mind paying top dollar. It'll soon be time to move the cattle off the mountain and get them ready to ship. We need to cut out one of the steers to butcher, as soon as it gets cold enough. With cattle prices so low, it didn't matter too much whether we eat it or sell it. I was lucky to sell eight of the pigs to Albers Meat Market. We can butcher the remaining two at the same time as the steer.

I must remember to get Thanksgiving and Christmas orders for some of the turkeys. I need to do it right away so Ray Eaken doesn't beat me to the stores. The chickens are producing well enough for me to sell eggs every week or so. That, combined with my cream checks, is almost enough to cover any groceries we need to buy.

Bess sighed with satisfaction and thought of the coffee jar up in the cupboard. She and Jim put away money whenever they could spare it. It was a relief to have something to fall back on in case of an emergency. For the first time Bess felt almost as self-sufficient as Uncle Elmer and Aunt Myra. It was a good feeling! She wasn't given to deep introspection, but Bess understood that the poverty-stricken early years with her mother had left a deep impression on her soul. Despite her early struggles with Uncle Elmer, she had admired him for the way he'd been able to carve out a prosperous and successful life for himself and Aunt Myra. Bess hoped that Jim and she could do as well for their family.

As she later scrubbed overalls against the metal washboard, Bess thought about her last visit with her aunt and uncle. Uncle Elmer was growing worn, although it would take more than advancing age to stop him. He managed to put in a day's work, but he'd sold off most of the dairy herd. He suffered greatly with his "rheumatiz." His large hands looked like gnarled tree trunks, with his fingers bent every direction. Aunt Myra, five years younger than Elmer, was also doing less. The garden was smaller, although Bess couldn't see that her aunt canned less food. Myra, still bright-eyed, was always delighted to see Bess and her family.

Bess hung up the last basket of clothes and sat down to have a welcome cup of coffee. Looking at the calendar she realized Grand Valley Days would be held the next weekend. She felt a conflict about going, but she knew that Jim and the children would be all set to go.

Maybe we can just go for the day and come home that night. I think my fascination with Alan Taylor is over, but I don't really want to see him again. No, that's not true. I'd love to see him, but I don't dare. Maybe we can take Mom and Dad Hart and have a picnic on the schoolhouse lawn. That way we'll definitely have to come home before milking time and not stay for the dance.

If anybody thought it strange Bess was proposing an outing with her mother-in-law no one mentioned it. The family was excited they'd be getting away for a day. Bess felt a little guilty when Nellie expressed such pleasure at being included.

Would I have thought to ask them along if not for my plan? I honestly don't know, but I doubt it. What difference does it make if everyone is happy?

The next few days were full of activity. Farmers and ranchers had to plan ahead so they could be gone an entire day. Bess had clean clothes for the family, and it wouldn't take long to prepare the picnic, but she still needed to preserve more of the garden produce. She had Kitty do the ironing, while she canned for the next several days. Although her cellar was already bulging, she wasn't about to let any food go to waste. No matter how much she put up each year, her growing children consumed it all.

When Saturday morning arrived everyone was bathed, hair trimmed, and attired in clean clothes. If Bess knew her boys, their shirts and pants would be soiled soon after they arrived in town, but at least they were clean at the top of the day.

Jim and Big Jim sat in the front with Freddie on his grandpa's lap. Nellie, Bess, Kitty, and Bob squeezed into the back seat. By the time they were loaded the car springs were sagging. They started for town, moving along at fifteen or twenty miles an hour. Bess felt she was suffocating from Nellie's considerable heft, and Bob's growing body, but appeared to be the only one suffering from the travel accommodations.

"I wonder who'll be in the parade this year," Bob said. "Pa, you remember that big black team of Frank's? I hope they're in it, again. Those animals are sure big!"

Kitty asked, "Grandma, what do you want to see? I'll bet you'll head straight to the quilt contest to see who has a chance of winning."

"You could be right, Kitty, but I also love the parade. It's nice to see everyone all decked out. I suppose you will be looking for your chums, won't you?"

The family was grateful for the new graveled road with its bridges. It made travel into town much quicker than just a few years back. It was particularly appreciated because there had been a region-wide gully washer the week before. They could see where the water washed over the road in places, but the heavy base of gravel held firm. The number of cars was increasing because of the better road. They met vehicles going west, and several young bucks, in faster cars, passed them by. Bess found it hard to believe there was so much traffic these days.

Jim chose a spot on First Street by the Keck & Hollenbaugh Dry Goods store, across from the drugstore. A scraggly tree grew along the sidewalk, so the women would have a bit of shade until the parade started. The men opened the car doors and stepped out.

"Bob, please get out. My legs feel like they're broken. You're getting to be a heavy boy."

"Yeah, Ma, you can sit on my lap goin' back!"

Bess climbed out and attempted to straighten her rumpled clothes. She'd worn a georgette dress for the day because it wrinkled less, but she hadn't counted on holding her son. Maybe the creases would ease out if she moistened a cloth and rubbed them. Jim's canvas water bag was hanging on the car. Bess wet her hanky and ran it over her dress front, but it didn't help much.

Nellie called out, "Help me, I don't think I can get out of this blasted thing!" She was unable to hoist herself upright.

"Jim, help your mother out of the car!" Bess didn't intend her voice to be so sharp, but the men often failed to pay attention to the needs of their wife and mother. "It's really hard to get out of these back seats," she added in a gentler tone.

The street was filling with spectators. Parade participants were mostly made up of horses, horse and buggies of various forms, and now the newest cars. There was no school band, but the glee club would ride on a farm wagon and entertain with a few songs.

The parade started from the corner of Railroad Avenue and First Street. Several veterans led the procession, carrying the U.S. and Colorado flags. Behind them marched more veterans of the Spanish-American War and World War I. The Harts could hear the glee club singing the *National Anthem*, followed by *America the Beautiful*. The sight and sounds were stirring to the observers.

Clean and shiny carriages were pulled by horses, the pride of the rancher's barn. This was a day to show off prized saddle and draft horses. Young women, in lovely summer dresses, rode in the carriages and waved to the crowd. People on horseback provided the bulk of the parade. Some were dressed in their western finery, some ladies were on sidesaddle. The more theatrical participants dressed as Indians. Others rode mules while playing concertinas. Bess allowed herself a few moments of sad reflection about the parade eight years ago when Lin had happily ridden down the street with Kitty.

New model cars were driven by the people trying to sell them. They made up the tail end of the parade. Bess saw Jim's face full of longing as they passed by. She knew he wanted a better car, but she didn't know how he intended to pay for it. She was sure he and most of the other men would be inspecting all of the vehicles after the parade.

Later, the foot races started, and Dr. Fred Miller was ready. He donned his running shoes and, when the gun started the race, left the other men in his dust. As usual, the crowd cheered him on, which they would have done even if he hadn't won. He was loved and respected by most who knew him.

Bob tugged at Bess's arm, "Ma, kin I enter the races?"

"I don't know, Son, can you run in those boots?"

"No ma'am, but I kin run in my bare feet!"

Bess turned to Jim. "What do you think, Daddy, should we let him?"

"Yeah, why not?" replied Jim. "You go show those town fellers how fast you are."

Bob came back a while later with a red ribbon in his hand. "Ma, look what I got! I won second place."

"That's wonderful, Son. Let me hold it, while you put your boots back on. There's glass all over these streets, and I don't want your feet to get cut."

"Mama, I want to run a race!" Freddie jumped up and down in his excitement.

"I don't think they have races for little boys, do they, Bob?"

"Yeah, they do. Want me to take him over to enter?"

"Ma, Juanita and Helen asked me to walk up the street with them. May I?" Kitty looked at Bess with imploring eyes.

"As long as you promise to stay on First Street. I don't want you wandering off!"

Jim and Big Jim edged over to the new cars, which were parked in the vacant lot by the post office. That left Bess alone with Nellie. Bess sighed, "Mother Hart, is there something you'd like to see or do?"

"Well, now that you mention it, I could use some headache powder at the drug store. Can we get done before the boys get back?"

"I'll tell you what," Bess replied, "I'll wait here for the children, and you go across to the store. Just take your time and look around. You don't get into town very often." As her mother-in-law waddled off Bess sank back in the front seat of the car and fanned herself with the damp handkerchief. The day was a warm one, and the tree gave little shade.

"Elmer, see who's here! Hello, Bess, dear, where is everyone at?"

Bess jumped out of the car to hug her aunt and uncle. "I was hoping you might come into town. We have a carload, and I didn't know whether we'd be able to go out to the ranch. I'm so glad you're here. Did you see the parade?"

"No, we just got here. What's that in your hand?"

"This ribbon? Bob won it in the foot race. He took Freddie over for the little boys' race. They should be back soon. Kitty walked up the street with two of her chums. Mother Hart is over at the drugstore, and the men are across the street drooling over the new cars. We've packed a picnic lunch and plan to eat it on the school lawn. Please say you'll join us."

When the Hart family piled into the car for the return trip that evening, they were tired from visiting with family, friends, and neighbors. Bess didn't care much for the boxing match between Art Johnson and a man from Glenwood Springs. She didn't think it was very civilized for two grown men to pummel each other into pulp. But she enjoyed the close baseball game between the Grand Valley and Rifle teams.

It had been a good day for everyone. Bess was glad Aunt Myra and Uncle Elmer had joined them. The closest she came to contentment was while surrounded by all of her family. She was also glad to be going home knowing she'd avoided an encounter with the man whom she thought about far too often.

· · · · · · · · ·

It was nearing election time, and the Hart household was rife with Jim's opinions on the slate of candidates and the state of the nation. Elmer Wheatley, editor of the *Grand Valley News,* declared himself a candidate for county judge on the Democratic ticket. That, of course, met with Jim's approval although he and others wondered what would happen to the newspaper if Elmer were elected. There were big debates about the Klu Klux Klan backing most of the Republican candidates at all levels. A shiver ran down Bess's back every time she heard the KKK mentioned. She remembered, as a young girl, seeing the crosses burn in front of the homes of black or Catholic families in St. Louis. They were bullies dressed up in sheets, preying on people who were different. Bess fervently hoped they wouldn't get such a stranglehold on people in Colorado, but the newspapers were full of stories about Klan rallies all over the West Slope. The papers predicted the general election victories would depend on who was in the Klan and who wasn't. Bess believed all politicians were self-serving, but Klan-backed politicians were downright dangerous.

Bess prevailed in her argument to ship more of the cattle and purchase additional yearling ewes. She argued that they already owned the buck, so they might as well get more lambs come next spring. She won out when she reminded Jim they didn't have enough hay from the meager summer harvest to feed all the cattle over the winter. On the other hand, the recent rains had helped the browse to spring up down by the river. The sheep would do well on it for some months before they'd have to be fed hay. Bess could supplement that with cottonseed cake, if need be.

The older cattle were shipped off to market. Prices remained about the same as they'd been the year before. Bess wondered if they'd even recouped their costs of raising the stock. An average heifer brought just a bit more than forty dollars. When they got their check Bess set out to do some searching. She bought ten decent-looking Columbia ewes from Harold Park. He swore the Columbia sheep were better mothers than the black-faced Suffolks, and the wool yield from each was almost double. That was good enough for Bess. She willingly paid $7.50 for each because they'd already been bred. Harold agreed to deliver them around Thanksgiving. Bess would soon have a total of thirty sheep.

Robert Dorman, of Grand Valley, was arrested on October 5, 1924, for indecent exposure and attempted rape. When Mr. Dorman, along with two other men, escaped from the Garfield County Jail a county-wide alert was sent out by Sheriff Winters from Glenwood Springs. Grand Valley Marshall James Ulrey paid visits to Dorman's old haunts around Grand Valley and again arrested him only two days after his escape. The fifty-six-year-old man wasn't through trying for his freedom, however. On October 30, 1924, he and another man kicked out a piece of wall and, once again, escaped. This time he got no farther than South Canyon where the undersheriff had stationed deputies. In November they sentenced him to nine years in the Colorado State Penitentiary.

The stormy weather of September turned into cold rain and snow during October. Bess welcomed the change because her garden finally quit producing. There wasn't one spare inch of empty shelf space in her cellar.

On the other hand, she fretted because there wasn't decent shelter for the sheep, especially if it continued to rain and snow. The ewes were bunched up under the cottonwoods, a poor cover from the elements. Bess needed something that would protect the sheep in case of a blizzard. The small cedar shelter was too small to hold thirty ewes.

"Jim, do you know anyone who has a fresno or other dirt-moving equipment we could borrow for a few days? Who was your friend who helped rebuild the ditch after the flood? Didn't he have a fresno?"

Jim was reading the official vote tally for Garfield County in the newspaper and grumbling or laughing according to whether a Democratic candidate got elected. Elmer Wheatley had lost by less than forty votes for the judgeship; that was a close one. Jim looked up from the newspaper, annoyance in his voice. "What do you want a fresno for?"

"We need to put up some kind of shelter for those ewes. If we had a fresno to dig out the hillside, we could line it with the rocks from the next field, put some posts on top, and cover it with brush and dirt. I think that would be the cheapest way to get a shelter and a lambing shed for them. If this weather is any indication, we might be in for a rough winter."

"Well, let me think on it and see what I can come up with," said Jim. "I'll check around with the guys at work." He went back to reading his newspaper. Bess hoped he'd remember the conversation.

A few days later Bess was herding the sheep down to the river field when she had a sudden whim to take them to the easternmost piece of their property. She needed to see what kind of feed might be there. She'd never visited this part of the ranch because they didn't cultivate it. This was the desert claim she'd filed on some years back. It was also where Jim kept the beehives. She opened the gate, and let Laddie run the ewes onto the property. It was three-quarters of a mile from the house, and she'd have to spend more time herding them there every day. It would be worth the extra time, however, if it offered enough feed to supplement the other fields.

She wandered along behind the ewes, who were nibbling on the brush and weeds. Bess climbed a small rise and, to her surprise, spied a tumble-down barn built into the hillside. It was hidden from the road and Bess hadn't realized such a structure existed. The old fellow who filed on the homestead had apparently built it. The logs and cedar posts, above ground level, looked like they were still sturdy. These would go a long way in the construction of a sheep shed.

That evening she eagerly waited for Jim so she could tell him about her find. "Well I'll be," he replied. "I'd forgotten all about that old barn. I reckon the posts could be used. I think I've also found a fresno so maybe, if the weather holds, Dad and I could work on it over the weekend."

Jim and his dad dug out the hillside in the sheep pasture, near the house. Ten-year-old Bob manned the horse and stone-boat filled with lava rocks, while Bess rolled on more. There was an abundance of rock, thanks to Battlement Mesa's ancient volcano, which had spewed its lava millenniums before. Bess hadn't thought it possible to run out of them, since they littered every field in the area, but she discovered that lining the walls of a shelter required many more than she'd anticipated.

Bess thought her back must surely be broken, but she tried to ignore the worsening pain. Only a few more loads, and they'd have enough to finish off the top layer. "Let's take this load in, Son, and see how many more we'll need. Your dad and grandpa should be back soon with the first load of posts."

They pushed the last rock into the moist hillside, which served as the back and side walls of the shed. It would be shallow and long. Once the framework was up, she and Bob could start cutting brush to lay upon the cedar posts before putting on a layer of dirt. The shelter would be a snug place for the sheep to bed down from the blowing snow, which generally came upriver, from the west. Bess stepped back to survey it with pleasure. In spite of the cold and her aching back, she hesitated to go home. She stood planning the next step of the construction until she heard her son's plaintive voice, "Ma, can we go home now?"

"Of course, Bob. You must be starved! You've been such a help to me this morning. Let's go see what Kitty's fixed for dinner."

The sheep shed was completed before the first storm of the season came roaring in just before Thanksgiving. Bess felt much better knowing the sheep were protected from the worst of the weather. They were also close enough so she'd hear Laddie barking if any predators bothered them. She sighed with relief, knowing most of the season's work was done. There would be enough hay to feed the few cattle and sheep, the larders of both Hart families were full, and it looked like it would be cold enough to butcher the next weekend. Taking a deep breath, Bess realized they had survived one more work-filled summer. It would be good to take a little rest.

On November 17, 1924, J.R. Latham of DeBeque won a civil judgement against J.C. Hardison for being shot by Mr. Hardison in the latter's store during December 1922. Mr. Hardison had previously been tried on a criminal charge and was acquitted on the grounds he was insane at the time of the shooting. Mr. Latham asked for $20,000 in damages and was awarded $5,000 by the jury. Both men were widely known in the DeBeque area, and the trial attracted a great amount of publicity.

The cement and road crews were laid off until the weather turned warmer so Jim was able to catch up on the maintenance chores he'd let go all summer. He was bringing the wood and coal in for the day when Bess stopped him. "Jim, do you realize we've never spent a Christmas with Aunt Myra and Uncle Elmer since we've been married? Your mother has always insisted we spend it with them, or we need to be home for some reason. This year I want to spend Christmas with my family."

"Ah, Bess, you know how Ma looks forward to spending Christmas with the kids. She'll be hell to live with if we go into town."

"I'm sorry she feels that way. She's been able to be with them for fourteen years. Just once, I'd like Aunt Myra and Uncle Elmer see the kids open their presents."

The conversation ended without resolution, each person hoping the other would come to their senses. No more was said, but in the coming days Bess made it clear she was preparing to be with Myra and Elmer. The children liked the novelty of spending the holiday in town, even Kitty who often seemed more like Nellie Hart's child than Bess's.

Eventually the children spilled the beans to their grandmother. She took it as poorly as Jim predicted. He came back one morning after helping his dad, and he looked very grim. Bess thought that it was good Nellie Hart knew. That would give her time to get the tantrum over with before they left on Christmas Eve. If there was any charity in Bess's heart for Nellie she squelched it.

I've lived under that woman's thumb all these years, and I'm not going to give in on this. I should get my way once in a while.

On the next trip to town Bess committed herself, by telling Aunt Myra to expect them on Christmas Eve. Her aunt was so excited she could barely speak, and she soundly hugged Bess. That was enough to seal it. In the meantime, Bess hadn't heard a word from her mother-in-law who was, undoubtedly, sulking.

Early one morning, several days before Christmas, Jim told Bess he needed to go into town for supplies. She was busy with her work and idly wondered what supplies they might need, because they were well stocked. She thought he was probably picking up a special Christmas present, so Bess didn't pry. There were many things to do before they left for town on Christmas Eve. She was soon too busy to wonder what Jim's mission might be.

The sun was setting when Bess saw the Model T coming up the road. Kitty was cutting out baking powder biscuits to stick in the oven to bake. Bess put the last of the potatoes into the bubbling kettle of stew and pulled it to the hottest part of the range. She felt the cold air as Jim opened the door. "Well, it's about time. I thought you'd gotten lost."

"Yeah, well, it's been a busy day, but I've got what I went for. Turn around."

Bess straightened up from the oven door and turned to his voice. "What do you have? Oh, my God! Aunt Myra, Uncle Elmer, why are you here?" Bess stepped over to embrace her aunt and uncle.

"Well, Jim talked us into coming to your place for Christmas. He wanted all of us to be together, and he says you have such nice holidays. I hope it's all right."

"It's more than all right! It's wonderful to have you here. But who's tending to the place? I've never seen you both spend a night away."

"Elmer talked Gus and Emmy White into coming out for a few days. They'll keep the fires burning and tend to the stock."

Bess hurried to get her aunt and uncle settled in. She instructed Kitty to change the sheets in Bob and Freddie's room. The boys could bed down in the parlor on a pallet of quilts. As she went by Jim she whispered quietly and coldly, "You might think you've outwitted me, but I'm telling you the problem about your mother isn't over."

1925

The intrepid automobile traveler of 1925 could expect to be on the road nine hours between Grand Junction and Glenwood Springs, if he experienced no breakdowns, flat tires, or road delays.

Something awakened her. Bess couldn't say why, but she was suddenly wide awake. She was bundled up to her neck in the heavy quilts, hesitating to move for fear of touching a chilly part of the flannel sheet. The brilliant full moon was high in the sky, casting its silvery light earthward. She could easily make out the shape of the sheep shed and other outbuildings. The latest snow reflected the moonlight, sparkling like it was covered with diamonds, each one more dazzling than the last. The chilly scene was one of considerable beauty. Bess yawned, fighting sleep to gaze out the window. Beside her Jim softly snored, and the rhythm of his in-and-out breathing began to lull her as well.

There! There it went again. She strained her ears to hear more accurately and then jumped out of bed, screaming. "Jim, wake up…wake up! The coyotes are in the sheep!"

Jim woke with a start, fumbling to pull on his pants and shirt, which were draped on the chair by the bed. He quickly stepped into his boots.

Bess had already thrown on a long coat and made a quick decision not to don her sturdy shoes because they required lacing. She and Jim reached the porch at the same time. Jim grabbed one of the heavy work coats hanging on the wall while reaching for the 30-30 rifle and box of shells. Bess stuck her feet into a pair of irrigation boots, which hadn't been put away in the fall before streaking through the screen door screaming like a banshee.

As they ran the thirty yards to the sheep shed, they could hear the sheep bleating. Laddie was barking and growling amidst the high-pitched yips of a coyote pack. Jim fired two shots into the air as he ran toward the shelter. He couldn't make out dog from coyote at that distance, but he hoped the shots would scare the marauders away from the sheep so he'd get a clear shot at them. "Bess, call your dog," he commanded as they ran to the rescue.

"Laddie, come boy," Bess gasped at she ran. "Laddie! Come!" She was vainly trying to identify the plucky little dog in the midst of the melee.

"Sombitch!" Jim singled out one of the coyotes and stopped running long enough to take an unsteady aim at the creature. The sound of the gunshot was followed by an instantaneous "thunk" as bullet hit flesh. The coyote let out one sharp cry, fell to the ground, and was still.

"Laddie, Laddie! Come boy, come here fellow." Bess could see the dog whirling around as the coyotes circled him, nipping at his heels and back. He looked like he was losing blood, but Bess couldn't be sure in the moonlight. The sheep had all pushed into the shelter where they huddled in a circle. Several of the coyotes were rushing in to nip at them. The young, less-experienced ewes were helpless against the predators. Picking up a hefty limb, Bess plowed into the group, swinging as she went, striking at the backs of the coyotes. She felt, rather than saw, when she connected with the body of one, making him yelp and back away. One by one they disappeared before her eyes, slinking into the sagebrush. Jim shot at the coyotes' backs and knew the bullet hit the mark when he heard an animal thrashing around.

Bess rushed first to the brave little dog who was panting hard but still on his legs. She ran her hand over his back and legs and felt the warm stickiness of blood. Laying him down, she and Jim ran to the thirty pregnant sheep who were still standing in a circle, bleating. She reached for an old lantern and box of matches, hanging from the wood beam, and succeeded in getting it lit with shaking hands. She and Jim knelt to examine the ewes on the perimeter of the circle, feeling for wounds along their face and legs. Bess discovered few places where wool had been pulled out, and a few superficial bite wounds, none seeming to be serious. But she also knew the sheep were in shock and could easily abort their lambs. Tears of anger and frustration welled up in her eyes.

"Damn, damn, damn!"

Jim scraped around, picking up some bunch grass and small twigs which he successfully set ablaze, quickly adding larger branches and tumbleweeds until there was a moderately good fire. Bess realized she was shaking almost uncontrollably and found the sudden warmth welcome. It had remained below zero for six weeks or more, and she doubted that it was very much warmer this night.

"Why don't you take Laddie up to the house and check his wounds? I'm gonna skin out these bastards for their pelts. Might as well make a little money on 'em. I doubt they'll come back tonight. If they're out there, they won't come near the fire."

Bess didn't argue. She didn't want to lose her good little sheepdog, of whom she'd grown so fond. "Come on fella, can you walk?" Laddie pulled himself up from the ground and slowly followed her. She could see that he was stiff with pain. Bending down, she folded his forty-pound body into her arms and struggled up the field toward the house. The brave little terrier softly whimpered in her ear.

Once Bess got a lamp lit and a fire started she was ready to examine Laddie. Kneeling in front of the kitchen range she probed his body, looking for puncture wounds. His long, ragamuffin coat perhaps saved him from some of the bites. He was sticky with blood, but she could tell from his bloody mouth that not all of the blood was his. Laddie had been successful in tearing a few chunks out of the coyotes.

Bess was relieved to see Laddie's wounds were mostly superficial and shouldn't get infected. To be on the safe side she poured warm water and lye soap into a basin and washed the cuts as best she could. Then she laid an old quilt behind the range and moved Laddie to it. "Lie still old boy...Just rest, buddy." Tom, the cat crawled in beside him, to lick Laddie's face and ears.

The eastern sky was starting to lighten when Jim came home, carrying the two pelts. He'd dragged the skinned bodies to the edge of the field where the magpies and the coyote pack would feast upon them. The next time he went to town he'd take the skins, which were each worth about fifteen dollars.

From that day forward Bess slept fitfully, listening even in sleep. She had to be vigilant for her little band of sheep. She also took to carrying the 30-30 rifle when she was out with the sheep. There would be no hesitation to shoot if she got a chance.

> The owners were recruiting one hundred men to start work the first part of April 1925, in the reopened Tennessee-Colorado Marble Quarry at Marble, Colorado. The quarry had been shut down for several years due to high freight costs, but recent large orders foretold continued operations. Alas, the successful venture was temporarily derailed. On the night of April 23, 1925, a disastrous fire swept through two shops as well as one mill. This resulted in a loss of at least a quarter million dollars. The owners immediately rebuilt the mill, and it resumed operations to complete its contracts.

"I'll be damned, Bess, you act like an old granny with those ewes. A person would think that these were the first lambs ever born."

"Well, they are to me, Jim Hart! Besides, for every lamb I save we'll be having two cash crops every year. And I can recall plenty of nights spent with your blamed cows."

"Yeah, but I didn't move in with them. You're beginning to smell more like a sheep every day."

Bess grudgingly admitted that might be true. Everything was on hold until each one of her thirty ewes lambed. So far Bess and the sheep had been blessed with good luck. The majority birthed only single lambs, but several brought forth twins. One ewe even produced a set of triplets.

From the backside of the stove soon came sounds of small bleating bodies. They were temporarily inside because their mamas couldn't or wouldn't feed them. The Hart children loved to pamper the wobbly little animals, but Bess acknowledged it was a smelly proposition. She planned to get them outside as soon as she thought they could survive in the barn.

The weather cooperated. Spring blizzards, which always struck terror in the hearts of ranchers, hadn't occurred. Bess, however, came in chilled to the bone after each nightly visit to the lambing shed. She kept the kitchen fire banked so she could quickly get warm. Several mornings Jim found Bess dozing with her feet propped on the oven door. She'd been too tired to undress and go back to bed. Jim offered to do some of the night visits, but Bess declined. She wanted him to get a good night's sleep because he was back working on the road crew twelve hours each day. She did finally agree that he could take the Saturday night shift, because he didn't have to be at work on Sunday.

The death of the first lamb was particularly hard on Bess. She was accustomed to the regular deaths which occurred on the ranch. This time, however, she took it as a personal affront that all her efforts, all her constant care, had been in vain for the stillborn animal. Jim said she should skin it out, and she recoiled as he offered his sharp knife. "No, I can't do that!"

"Well, then you'd better get the hell out of the sheep business, Bess, because this is part of it. That pelt will bring a couple dollars."

Bess angrily snatched the knife from Jim's hand. "Will you at least show me how to do it? I'll be damned if I'd want you to do anything with these sheep!" As soon as the words left her mouth Bess knew they were unfairly critical of Jim. He and his dad did all the rest of the cattle ranching and farming. The least she could do was learn how to tend to her flock. "I'm sorry. I'm just upset."

"I understand you have your heart set on saving them all, but I'm telling you this won't be the last one. Sometimes it just happens, and there's nothing you can do."

One late spring day Bess woke up and rejoiced that it was finally over. Her first successful lambing! Thirty ewes were grazing with forty healthy lambs, all docked and the bucks neutered. The traveling sheep-shearers had made short work of removing the wool. Bess looked at her first small wool check. There would be more pitfalls, but she felt like she'd passed a major milestone. She smiled.

> Congress appropriated $90,000 in March 1925 for the development of the oil shale industry. People began to, once again, gear up for the anticipated boom. This latest project was to ensure that the U.S. Navy fleet would always have adequate fuel to operate in the event of a world shortage.
>
> Naval planes arrived in July at the airfield east of Grand Junction. Their orders were to complete an aerial survey of sixty-seven-thousand acres of Naval Reserve land between Grand Valley and Rifle. The towns of DeBeque, Grand Valley, Rifle, and Glenwood Springs all competed to be the sites of the proposed shale plant. Each town tried to offer the most inducement to the selection committee. Joe Bellis, owner of a beautiful showplace home in Grand Valley, even offered to turn it over to the government employees for their use if they would pick his town.
>
> United Press stories predicted an additional one hundred and fifty thousand people in the Rifle, Grand Valley, and DeBeque areas. On February 15 they announced Pacific Oil was the latest company to take out options on thirty thousand acres in the DeBeque area.

The temperature in the W.O.W. hall was stifling from the heat of dancing bodies. Bess felt the moisture running down her back and between her breasts. Everyone mopped their faces when the music ended. People poured outside to breathe in whatever cool air they could find. The summer was brutally hot, with day after day of searing temperatures. In mid-July the thermometer at the grocery store reached a record one hundred and five degrees. The main topic of conversation was how much longer it would be before the rain came and the heat would be broken.

"Guess I'll take a break and go have a smoke," Jim said.

"Yes, I should also go out. I'll see if Kitty wants to go with me."

Kitty and Bess walked out west of the building to the outdoor privy. One guarded the door, while the other was inside. With all the young boys running around, a female could never tell what devilment might be under way. There were groups of men all around the building, smoking and nipping from their bottles. Bess wondered why the town marshall wasn't arresting those with bootleg liquor. He was nowhere to be seen. Even Bess agreed that Prohibition was a joke. There was now more booze available than before 1916, when Colorado went dry.

Kitty went back inside, but Bess lingered outside the door to the hall, fanning herself, reluctant to return to the stifling heat. She could overhear the conversations of several men.

"I hear you're done with your work up in the canyon. What you plan to do now?"

"I thought maybe I'd go down and talk to Stuart. I hear he's looking for a new foreman."

"A new foreman? What the hell happened to Taylor?"

"Someone told me he's left the country and gone to Montana or Idaho…somewhere north of here."

"You don't say! I wonder why he did that?"

"Hell if I know. Maybe he got itchy feet. It's not like he has a family or anything."

"Well, good luck. If you can't get on at the ranch there's always the assessment work."

"Yeah, but I'd just as soon punch cows as work with a pick and shovel."

Neither man paid attention to Bess standing white-faced and shaken at their backs. The news nearly brought her to tears. She stood there fighting them back, struggling to regain her composure.

Alan is gone! I can't believe he's not at the ranch. Even though it's been a year and a half since we last talked, I always knew he was just a few miles away. So many times I looked for him when I went to see Mrs. Stuart. And my daydreams…daydreams about running into him at the ranch or in town. He said he would always be there for me and the children. But now it's truly over.

In the coming weeks, as she went about her many chores, a lost and forlorn feeling would frequently wash over her. Alan had been the color in her otherwise drab life, the forbidden spice. It wasn't a question of grieving for him, for in truth, she'd never really had him. Rather, it was a longing for what she could never have. When she surveyed her own world, she saw nothing but shades of gray. Was that all there was to life? She feared it was so.

In the meantime life went on. The garden needed to be hoed, the sheep herded, the chickens fed, the washing hung, and the vegetables canned. The demands of life mercifully pushed against her sadness, thrusting it to the far, dark corners of night where fatigued sleep was the eventual victor. Her yearning was consigned to that spot where it could dwell undisturbed, but remembered. Thus the wound healed but was never quite erased.

● ● ● ● ● ● ● ● ●

The main highway jobs were completed so Jim hired on to do oil shale assessment work for several different claim holders, including Si Herwick and Joe Bellis. It meant long days for him. The pay wasn't as good as it had been on the road crew, but it would bring in some cash. That would be better than the predicted cattle and hay crop.

The heat and drought dried up the irrigation water early. Jim was grateful for his few shares of river water which usually produced enough hay to keep the reduced herd of cattle fed through the winter. However, this year he wasn't even sure about that.

There wasn't enough runoff to even fill the cistern, so Bess sent Bob and the horse to the river slough every day to bring back water for the garden. Ray and Annie Maylong offered to let Jim haul a few barrels of drinking water from their spring, but everything else was done with river water. Even after it settled, the water contained minute dirt particles. Bess hated to wash her clothes with the dingy liquid, but there was no choice. She used so much homemade lye soap the clothes developed holes. The weekly baths left a person feeling almost as dirty as when they crawled into the old galvanized tub. The Harts made do with what they had, but it was a long, miserable summer.

Upon later reflection Bess could never decide if she might have done more to avert the coming family crisis. It was easy to look back and say thus and such should have been done, but in the reality of life it was never that clear cut.

The drought finally broke, and several hard rains pelted the countryside in early fall. Jim went to help bring the cattle off the mountain. When the rain started, he discovered his rain slicker was tied on the spare saddle back in the barn. By the time Jim got home he was soaked to the skin and shaking with a chill. Bess put him to bed and piled on quilts. She instructed Bob to fetch the jug of bootleg booze out in the barn and she made a strong hot toddy for Jim to drink. The combination of the warmth and the alcohol quickly lulled him to sleep. When he awakened the next morning he said it was the best night's sleep he'd had in months. Bess was relieved he seemed no worse for the drenching, although she questioned him about his cough.

"Oh, hell, that's been with me for a while. Maybe it's too much dust from digging around the claims, maybe it's just a smoker's hack. Don't worry 'cause I don't feel bad."

The cough didn't go away, and in spite of Jim's protests to the contrary, Bess became increasingly concerned. By mid-October the assessment work was completed, and Jim came home to do all the chores left over from the summer. Bess would frequently see him immobilized by a coughing fit, which lasted longer and longer. One day she looked out to see him clinging to the fence rail, his handkerchief flecked with red spots. The sight terrified Bess. For a brief instant she was a little girl again, watching her mother cough up blood. Running to Jim, she put her arms around him and helped him into the house.

"Damn it, Jim, I knew you were sicker than you let on! Do you feel up to riding into town to see Dr. Miller or should I go in and bring him back?"

"I don't know, Bess. Why don't you just let me lay down for a little while? I think I've got a touch of a cold in my chest, but you can doctor me up for that."

"No, you don't, Mister! Not this time! I want Dr. Miller to listen to those lungs. There's more wrong than just a cold. I'm going to run over and get your mother so she can stay with you while I go to get Doc."

By the time Bess returned, with the doctor following her in his car, Jim was much worse. He was running a high fever, and the cough was occurring with alarming regularity.

The doctor thoroughly examined Jim. "I think he has what we call dust pneumonia. His lungs are almost half filled with fluid. I can't imagine how he kept going for so long. There isn't a lot we can do except let him rest, eat what he can, do some deep breathing of steam, and get rid of that tobacco. Other than that, it's just a waiting game for his body to fight off the infection and absorb the fluid. If he does all that he's got a chance of recovery, but it's going to take some time. Think you can handle the ranch and nurse him, too?"

"Of course I can," Bess replied. "The children will help me, and we'll handle it."

"Well, don't forget Nellie and Big Jim. They'll help, too, if you let them…and I want you to let them, do you understand?"

"Yes, Doctor," Bess meekly said. When Dr. Miller got stern he expected you to obey.

Jim's crisis lasted for days, his temperature climbing higher. Bess, true to her word, asked Nellie to help nurse him, and one or the other was with him at all times. They tried mustard plasters, onion poultices, and the infamous onion cough syrup. Anything they thought might help was used. For the first time in

Bess's fifteen-year marriage she and Nellie Hart were working with a single purpose...to save Jim's life.

Even when Bess wasn't tending to him she often found it impossible to sleep. She went to tend the stock in the early hours of the morning because she couldn't make herself stay in bed any longer. She'd stand at his bedside and listen to the rales and gurgling in his throat. Bess feared it would shut off his breath, and she'd roll him over so he could cough. He looked to be shrinking right before her eyes. No matter what Nellie or she fixed him to eat he'd clamp his mouth shut. He refused to take anything except small sips of water.

On the morning of the tenth day Bess left the house to milk the cows. Big Jim and Bob had been doing most of the outside chores. Bess knew it was too much for the old man so she went to help. Jim had thrashed around all night, but was finally sleeping, and Nellie would be with him until Bess spelled her.

Bess milked one cow and pulled the stool and the bucket over to start on the next. No matter what she was doing, Jim was on her mind.

I've never seen Jim so sick, so vulnerable, so near death. I'm terribly frightened. What can I do to make him better?

Then the tears came. She was consumed by gut-wrenching sobs which she'd contained for so many days. The emotions came tumbling out—fear, anger, grief, and desperation.

Pictures of Jim flew through her mind, vignettes of their life together, his loving kindness, his dedication to his family, his working hard to make a living for them. Jim was such a good man, and he didn't deserve this.

If anyone deserves to be punished, it would be me.

Resting her head against the gentle old cow's side, Bess spoke aloud an incoherent litany, "Please, please, please, don't let him die. You can do whatever you want with me, but please save him. I love him, Lord, I love him, and I don't know what I would do without him. You've taken my mother, my brother, my baby. Isn't that enough? Jim's never knowingly harmed another human being. I'm the one you should be wanting. I'm the sinner, not Jim."

Bess made her way to the house with a bucket of milk in each hand. Her chest felt sore from grief and anguish.

"Bess, come see! He's better!" Nellie rushed into the kitchen whispering so she wouldn't wake the children.

Bess ran to the bed and reached down to feel Jim's forehead. It was cool to the touch! His fever had broken. She plopped into the chair by the bedside and closed her eyes. "Thank you, Lord, thank you, thank you."

Jim's convalescence was long. It took weeks for him to regain his strength. At first Bess or Nellie had to coax each bite of food into his mouth. It was a great day of celebration when he finally admitted he was developing an appetite. Each woman cooked whatever she thought would taste the best to him. The rest of the family ate it without complaint. Right now Jim's needs and desires were the law. Bess knew the children were as affected by Jim's illness as she was. They had been silent, watchful participants throughout the crisis, and Bess took it as a good sign when they returned to their old selves. Freddie returned to being a noisy and rowdy little boy, Kitty resumed being bossy, and Bob teased Kitty at every opportunity.

As she ministered to Jim's needs throughout the coming days, Bess discovered a depth of love for her husband she'd never felt in her marriage. She looked at the pale, thin, quiet, man, and tenderness washed over her. This was the fellow who had always been there for her—when Lin was killed in the war, when the baby was born dead, when she insisted on getting her damned sheep. He'd been with her in every crisis, and Bess had been too blind to see. She was so hell-bent on mourning what she didn't have, she'd missed the biggest treasure of all. Someday, when he was stronger, she'd tell him all those things. Right now it was enough to just be there for him. Bess leaned over and kissed him lightly on the lips.

"What's that for?" Jim asked. Bess never showed any affection to him except when they were in bed.

"Oh, I don't know. Maybe it's because I love you." Having said the words, Bess knew them to be true. She'd spend the rest of her life trying to make it up to Jim. She stroked his forehead. "Yes, I do love you."

• • • • • • • • •

The whole family was assembled for Thanksgiving dinner. Aunt Myra, Uncle Elmer, Nellie, and Big Jim Hart were seated around the table with Jim and the children. Bess set the roasted turkey on the table to be carved. "Do you feel up to doing this Jim, or do you want someone else to do it?" She lovingly rested her hands on his shoulders, gently caressing the cloth of his shirt.

"I'm a little shaky. Maybe you'd better let Dad do it. I'd hate to drop that big old bird on the floor."

Bess smiled at him and slid the platter across the table to Big Jim. "Dad Hart, do the honors."

The Harts and Carpenters, not being church-going folk, never said prayers before a meal, but Bess felt this occasion warranted one. She asked if anyone objected. The elders looked surprised at the unaccustomed request but quickly gave their consent, "Of course—go ahead."

Bess cleared her throat. She'd never prayed aloud and didn't quite know how to do it, but was determined. She took a deep breath and said:

"Thank you for another year together, and for our Jim who has come through so much. Thank you for our family, for our health, and for the ability to care for ourselves. Please watch over each of us in the coming year, and we will continue to live the sort of life we think you'd have us live…Amen."

Bess understood, as the others did not, that the last sentence of the prayer was a personal commitment to her life and her marriage. She'd no longer search for the forbidden thrills because everything she needed was within these walls. Looking at the smiling faces around the table Bess knew at last…this was the family for which she'd always yearned.

The End

Book Two: Life Goes On

1926–1946

Bess and her family face many further challenges. The depression hits Western Colorado with a vengeance. The Hart family, like so many others, has to work hard to keep food on the table.

Death visits Bess's family circle. A natural disaster makes the family reel, especially Bess who feels she has lost much more than the others. She is forced to live in a manner that suffocates and angers her. The heat and the wind decimate the crops, and there are few jobs to supplement the little bit of ranch income. In the midst of this chaos Alan Taylor comes back to the area and once again creates doubts for Bess. The growing herd of sheep is her salvation, and she throws herself into the job of tending to them.

Just as the Depression seems to be on its way to recovery, World War II calls up a son. Bess spends four terrifying years while the young man fights far from his birthplace. The struggles at home seem mild compared with the devastating reports from the war front. Bess tries to cope with food stamps and gas rationing without complaining. Some children leave, some stay on the ranch.

Rural schools are seriously affected when many men and women leave the area to work in the war effort. Bess and other noncertified teachers are recruited to fill the gap. Bess realizes a dream to get some continuing education.

The Hart family saga concludes as World War II ends, and Western Colorado is bursting with energy development. Oil shale, uranium, oil, and gas exploration are predominant forces in the economy. Bess and Jim are now observers as their children start their own families.

Estimated completion, 2005–2006

Key to Locations
1. Train Depot
2. Packing Shed
3. Doll Brothers and Smith Store
4. Milner's Pool Hall
5. Keck and Hollengbaugh General Store
6. Country Club Hotel (burned in 1922)
7. Oil Shale Theatre/W.O.W. Hall
8. Drug Store
9. First Christian Church
10. Grand Valley School
11. Methodist Church
12. Post Office
13. Bank
14. Dr. Miller's Office
15. Grand Valley Lumber and Supply
16. Catholic Church
17. Hotel (also named Country Club Hotel)
18. Dr. Fred Miller's House

AERIAL VIEW OF GRAND VALLEY, COLORADO, CIRCA 1922
(COURTESY OF ZELDA HERWICK MONTOYA)

30100000105681

DATE DUE			